Paul Charles

was born and raised in the Northern Ireland countryside. He now lives with his wife Catherine in Camden Town, where he divides his time between writing and working in the music industry. He is currently working on the seventh Christy Kennedy Mystery, *The Justice Factory.*

First Published in Great Britain in 2002 by
The Do-Not Press Limited
16 The Woodlands
London SE13 6TY

Casebound edition: ISBN 1 904316 03 4
C-format paperback: ISBN 1 904316 02 6

British Library Cataloguing in Publication Data. A catalogue
record for this book is available from the British Library.

1 3 5 7 9 10 8 6 4 2

I'VE HEARD THE BANSHEE SING

The Sixth Detective Inspector Christy Kennedy Mystery

by

Paul Charles

Thanks are due to Jim, Daria, and Catherine for words on words, Andy for words on WWII, Cora for always being there for all of us, to Thomas and Regina for the room with a view (not to mention the tea and sandwiches too!). The mistakes are, as ever, my own. BIG thanks to Catherine for the words I love to hear.

This one is for my father, Andrew Charles, MM.

Prologue

THE GAGGLE OF Ulstermen were huddled in various corners amongst the ruins of the church. They were far away from home: Caen in Brittany. France, in fact. Their troop of the Regional Ulster Rifles had been reduced from twenty-one to nine after non-stop action over the previous seventy-two hours. Now, safe in the sanctuary of the church and guarded by one of their own, they were in varying stages of preparing for sleep.

Mostly, though, they were tired beyond sleep and every now and then one of them would crack a joke in a loud whisper to instant schoolroom sniggering. The eldest was twenty-two; the youngest a seventeen-year-old from Desertmartin. He had lied about his age in order to be with his mates on their great adventure. They had all lost a chum, a best friend or a neighbour over the course of this ten-day duty, so sleep didn't come easy for any of them. Eventually, however, mental and physical fatigue washed over their bodies, like a tide they were no longer able to resist.

The one left on guard duty found himself talking to himself. He felt he was the lucky one. He didn't want to succumb to the demons he knew were lurking just below his subconscious, ready to pull him down when he fell into a sleep. It was impossible to entirely blot out the horrific, gory scenes he had experienced over the last few days. He had seen one of his best friends, his schoolmate and neighbour for sixteen of his twenty years on this planet, literally cut in two by gunfire. The bullets physically cut through his midriff like a hot knife through butter. The guard would, for the rest of his life, be haunted by the look of horror in his mate's eyes as he realised that his legs were no longer attached to his body.

It went beyond disbelief, way beyond disbelief. This was the same mate he would have played football, Cowboys and Indians, or soldiers with during their childhood in what they now always referred to as The Beechland Days – so named after the tree-lined street of their youth. In those days you shot someone with your finger and when the game was over they got up again, you dusted yourselves off and went home to tea. Now, though, the guard remembered vividly the more recent scene where he was looking at his mate cut in two and the panic creeping across the face of his friend as he feigned a smile; a pathetic smile. Had he been secretly hoping that someone would shout that the game was over? Perhaps he was wishing to hear his mother call, 'Come in for your tea, Colin and Victor,' as she leaned precariously out of her front window. Before she closed the window she would shout, 'Come in now youse two, before your tea gets cold.'

'Come on, Colin, get up and come in for your tea,' he remembered shouting at his friend who was lying in the mud, his blood mixing with the brown of the mud, the stench heaving his stomach. The heaving was a waste of time though. "Heave away all you want," he had said to his stomach, now empty from continuous vomiting. 'Come on, Colin, get up and come in for your tea. Your Ma says your tea's going to get cold.'

'Shut up, Dugdale,' someone hissed at him from the shadows of the church.

He looked around but he couldn't see anyone who looked like they were still awake. He could only hear the rustle as someone struggled to get comfortable amongst the rubble. At least this distraction caused the images of his best friend to disappear. He could feel a cool breeze coming from somewhere. He crawled over in the direction of the breeze. It smelt new, it smelt fresh. All the air he had smelt over the previous few days was spoiled, soiled and already used. Most of the time you could even smell the previous user. But this cool breeze smelt new. Smelt invigorating. It was so pure it caused his stomach to heave again. There was nothing available to come up but a little phlegm. This viscid substance made his mouth taste dirty, part of it came through his nose and he had this weird agitation of smelling and tasting his phlegm simultaneously and not really being able to distinguish one sensation from the other.

Ah, the cool breeze was beautiful, spiritually and physically refreshing. He reached the hole in the wall and could now gulp in the fresh air selfishly, nourishing himself, not on protein but on freshness. The moon was shining, sparkling in the river down below him. It might have just been a trick of the moonlight but the water looked so clean and so pure, so cleansing, so refreshing. He wanted to immerse himself in the water. He wasn't religious or anything like that but he felt that if he could just put his entire body under water he could wash away all the images of death and destruction from his mind. He was sure he would come up pure and whole again, just like with a baptism.

He was on guard duty for the next three hours, though. Where were these stupid thoughts coming from? His enemy, their enemy and Colin's murderers, were in the world outside his window. He slapped his face, the sharp crack echoing loudly throughout the church. But still no one stirred.

Maybe he wanted someone to stir; maybe he wanted to be reassured that they weren't all dead. Maybe he wanted to be reassured that he wasn't the last person alive on this planet. He found himself slipping into a catnap. He was still conscious and aware of what was going on. He proved it to himself; look, there's the moonlight glistening on the river. How could he be dreaming? How could he sleep after what he and his friends had been through? Now he must be dreaming though, because he saw himself rest his rifle carefully against the wall close by and quietly raise his body up from its secure position. He definitely must be dreaming, he thought, because when he moved to get up, none of the millions of aches he knew plagued his body were there. Yes, that's why he knew he was dreaming. Hey, I'm in a dream, he thought. In my dream I'll go and enjoy a swim but because I'm only dreaming, the Germans won't be able to see me.

Twenty-five minutes later, as the moon was giving way to dawn, he was rudely awoken from his dreams by the sounds of vicious gunfire.

He felt wet.

He was wet.

He was in water.

He was in the river.

As the gunfire continued, he scurried out of the river and

hurriedly put his clothes back on, all the time looking back up to the church. He could see the flashes of light through the various holes in the church wall – some designed as windows over a hundred years ago and some war-made gashes from the previous few days' bombardment. The gunfire continued to rain down on his friends, neighbours and colleagues.

The same friends, neighbours and colleagues he'd meant to be guarding.

Chapter One

'...and he not busy being born is busy dying'

Bob Dylan, *Blowin' in the Wind*

THEY WERE CLOSE to finishing work on The Black Cat Building on Camden High Street when the body was discovered. Another week, at most, would have been sufficient for the civic opening. Now a police investigation would delay the grand reception for at least two more months.

The building had lain empty for several years now, possibly since Mrs Thatcher and her cronies had bullied 'Red' Ken and the Greater London Council into closing it down. Somewhere between those days and when it had opened a hundred or so years ago as a cigarette factory, the building, from the outside, had grown grey, boring and dirty, hiding from the world – well, certainly from those parading up and down the high street – its unique Art Deco features. Thankfully now, though, several marvellous columns had been painstakingly uncovered from years of plaster, paint and dirt. The final move in the celebrated refurbishment had been to seek out, from the darkened depths of some basement, the two tall, black cats and return them to their former glory with a lick of black gloss paint. Now they had been returned to their original plinths and were proudly guarding the building.

The black cat twins looked like they'd just recently, reluctantly, returned from sentry duty at an Egyptian pyramid. Had that, in fact, been the case they surely would not have witnessed anything as mystifying or horrific, on the sandy desert, as what must have taken place the previous evening a matter of several yards away from their post – close to the tarmac street of one of London busiest junctions.

Detective Inspector Christy Kennedy had never been to Egypt, he certainly had no wish or desire to do so and so he couldn't testify to the comings and goings over there. He had, however, been a police officer on the streets of London for close to twenty-five years and he had never witnessed a killing quite so grotesque. His stomach continuously wanted to exit his body via his throat. Not that he was particularly squeamish. No, hardly at all in fact. It was just when he witnessed some of the more extreme things humans did to each other that he felt a very sorry man, and he knew the dark clouds gathering around his shoulders would make him sick to the pit of his stomach and something would have to give. It has to be said that with all the rumblings and threats, his stomach rarely made good its threats; today it did.

Kennedy's usual remedy was to tune out, as quickly as he could, from the fact that it was the body of a fellow human, and concentrate instead on the fact that it was a piece of evidence in the murder investigation he was about to embark on. On that particular hot and sticky July morning he was finding this rather difficult.

The Black Cat Building had been buzzing away as electricians, carpenters, plumbers and a squad of odd-job men pottered away, rushing against time and towards a bonus. In their diligence none of them had recently found cause to visit the completed seventh floor. That was until the repulsive smell started to waft down the various stairwells and shafts and air ducts and what have you. Those with the keenest nostrils picked up the evil scent somewhere around 11am and then, one by one, they complained to their gaffers, who in turn complained to the site manager, a Mr Christopher Runciman – known to all in the building, and in his professional life, as the Archbishop. The Archbishop was an old campaigner; efficient, resourceful and above all, one hundred percent honest, which made him the perfect candidate for his chosen vocation. He had single-handedly turned site management into an art form. Another three days and he would have signed off on this project and stolen a much-needed three-week holiday in his beloved Cornwall.

From the waist down he fitted in perfectly with the workforce – blue denim jeans and light brown, steel-capped boots. From his US army belt upwards, however, was another case. A white shirt, school tie and snazzy waistcoat graced his slight frame. Even though all of his day was spent in and around and travelling through dirt and dust and freshly painted walls, he always managed to remain spic-and-span; always ready for an inspection from above.

His day, though, not to mention his clothes, was about to be ruined when he saw the contents of the large room on the seventh floor.

He'd joked with the various gaffers when they came to see him to complain about the smell. He gave them various excuses: dog-do; unofficial toilets; someone relieving themselves of last evening's intake of alcohol; burning rubber; Camden Council's weekly meeting. On and on he continued with his wisecracks and jokes until he ran out of excuses. Coincidentally, it was around about the time that he ran out of excuses that he first started to inhale whiffs of the vicious smells himself.

Everyone he spoke to seemed to agree that the smell was coming down from above ("Undivine intervention," as one of the Geordie carpenters put it (so the Archbishop set off on his search, starting on the completed third floor. The further he climbed, the stronger the smell. By the time he reached the sixth floor it was unbearable. By the time he reached the top of the stairwell to the seventh, he was forced to cover his nostrils and mouth with a laundry-fresh handkerchief.

Each floor was centred around the stairwell and the door from this access opened into a reception area – the idea being that visitors would announce themselves at the main mahogany reception desk on the ground floor. They would then be directed to the relevant floor where, once again, they would check in with a receptionist who would, in turn, show them through to their final destination. As you looked at the building from the street, the entire right-hand side of the seventh floor was being reserved for a boardroom. Probably the most important room in the building and the one whose refurbishment was the most lavish, not to mention the most expensive. The walls were lined with oakwood, reclaimed from a vicarage of the small parish church close to Ballyneagh, County Derry, in Northern Ireland. The designer had been trying to recreate the "old money" feel of a high-powered firm of American lawyers. He'd succeeded.

'I said, "Oh, God, not the vicarage",' the Archbishop blas-phemed for the second time that day when later recalling his search for the benefit of DS Irvine and WPC Anne Coles. 'You see, we've all taken to calling the boardroom "the vicarage", you know, because of where most of the contents were taken from.'

He had walked into the boardroom, taken one look at the remains, been sick over himself (no time had been available for a more careful aim) and on the floor, turned and walked out again and went immediately to ring Camden Town CID.

Now it was Kennedy's turn to view the scene.

The wooden shutters had all been left open and shafts of hot sunlight shone through the windows at forty-five degrees. The heat and the stench burnt their way into the very skin on the inside of his nostrils.

Hanging in the centre of the room were the remains of an elderly man.

He was suspended on a rope, fixed to a candelabrum. The other end of the rope appeared to be tied to the man, under the arms you would guess from the angle the body hung at, but closer examination revealed the rope was attached to a silver meat hook that was gouged into the back of the corpse. And still there was worse to come.

The old man had been stripped naked and his eyes had been removed from their sockets and placed on the large mahogany table below him. His stomach had been sliced open and his entrails and guts were hanging from the opening.

Chapter Two

DOCTOR LEONARD TAYLOR arrived about two minutes later, took one look at the corpse and immediately went to Kennedy and said, 'Are you okay, old chap? This is quite a gory one.'

Apart from that one statement, he showed no physical signs that this was anything more than another job. He had long since past the point of being upset at the state he (sometimes) found bodies in. He did, however, know what the scene would be doing to Kennedy's insides and that's where his concern lay – with the living rather than the dead.

The scene-of-crime photographer snapped away at the body from every available angle; he even stood up on the boardroom table (feet and table both protected, of course) to capture those vital extra angles. It was at this stage in the proceedings that the awkward job of cutting the body down commenced. Kennedy didn't want the body cut down, in fact. He wanted the rope and knot intact and so the frail, lean and lifeless limbs had to be raised to take the weight from the rope so that the rope could be marked and cut. The marks were achieved with a felt-tip pen; first, they drew two rings a half-inch apart, and then a single dot close to each ring on one side of the rope and two dots on the other. This way, the forensic team could later match the rope up exactly in their lab.

Kennedy preferred not to look at all of this and Taylor supervised it as best he could. Rope marked, it was then cut with ultra-sharp, curved scissors. Next they placed the body on a section of the floor covered with plastic. There were no rings, nor watches, nor jewellery of any kind upon the person. Taylor assessed the man was in his early seventies. He still had a full head of hair (snow white) but his skin hung around his bones like badly packed Christmas presents.

'I'd say, due to the lack of blood, he was killed elsewhere, method not apparent at this stage, brought here, had his eyes removed, his stomach slit open and was then hung up like a chunk of beef,' Taylor offered, uninvited, to Kennedy. Kennedy was busy at this stage circling the room, trying to see what, if any, evidence had been left behind. There was nothing immediately visible to the naked eye. The fingerprint men claimed the entire room had been wiped expertly and efficiently.

Kennedy left Taylor and the team to their work and returned to the ground floor, to the office Archbishop Runciman had commandeered as his own. He'd made it very cosy. The walls were packed with plans of the various floors, schedules, wall charts and a poster of someone or something called Principle Edwards' Magic Theatre. The concrete floor was carpeted, not with the latest from Allied Carpets but with cardboard boxes all unfolded and laid flat on the floor, edges silver-gaffer taped together. The floral arrangement was quite a bizarre pattern composed of a mishmash of Sony television, Kellogg's cornflakes, Ballygowan mineral water and Andrex Supersoft toilet rolls. The temporary office was furnished with a foldaway desk – which was packed to overflowing with documents, papers, notes, pencils, a penknife, a radio, a small portable TV – two sets of Ryman portafiles; three deckchairs (yes, deckchairs) with multi-coloured canvas covers on white, iron foldaway frames; and a swivel chair.

'Have you any idea who the old man is?' Kennedy asked as he gingerly lowered himself into the chair.

'Sorry, I haven't a clue. I must admit I didn't look at him for too long a period, what with the eyes and all that, I'm not entirely sure I would have recognised him even if I'd known him, if you know what I mean. But there was nothing familiar about him from the little I saw,' Runciman said, taking his seat behind the desk.

'So when's the last time anyone would have been in the boardroom?' Kennedy asked, finding the deckchair extremely comfortable.

'Well now, let's see,' Runciman replied rising from his chair and visiting one of his wall charts. He was confident in his manner, almost like he could have been the headmaster at some outpost of the British Empire. 'You see here,' he continued, pointing proudly to one of his schedules covered from top to bottom with Magic-Marker inks, 'The pink one is for work completed. This is floor by floor, of course, and we are looking at the one for the seventh floor. So according to my records, we finished the vicarage – sorry, I mean the board-room of course – on March 20th. That's right, we completed it on St Patrick's week. I was a bit worried we were not going to get that one done on schedule. Some of the chaps from across the pond like to celebrate St Patrick's Day. From my experience you can usually write off that entire week, St Patrick's week, with that particular section of the workforce. The day before they're always getting ready for the celebra-tions, and then they need at least the following couple of days to get over it. But you can't complain. They work very hard the rest of the time.'

The Archbishop looked like he was about to return to his desk but instead, before he sat down, he went over to another chart, a rather large one, containing all the electrics. He seemed to be pressing his finger against one part of the chart. Kennedy tried to see what he was pointing at but before he had a chance to focus on the small print, the chart sprang off the wall. It was attached to a door that was obviously acti-vated by some spring device. The door opened to reveal a large cupboard, obviously the Archbishop's private area. It contained a kettle, a teapot, milk, sugar, packets of biscuits, a little stove and various unmarked packs of health food of some kind.

'You never know when you going to need this, do you?' Christopher Runciman smiled. 'Fancy a brew-up?'

The Archbishop could not have asked Kennedy a better four-word question. The detective nodded positively, very positively in fact. He watched the tea-preparing ritual commence.

'So you're saying there would have been no one in the boardroom since March 20th?' Kennedy asked.

'Correct.'

'Don't you check the floor regularly?' Kennedy asked as the Archbishop delivered an excellent cup of tea and some exceedingly good cakes.

'I believe the night watchman checks all the floors every day before he locks up.'

'What time would that be at?' Kennedy said, very contented now that his stomach's heaving had dropped down the Richter scale.

'Difficult one that, you see it varies so much. Sometimes we've been open continuously for up to ten days at a time, twenty-four hours a day. It depends on the job. Let's see...' Runciman rose from behind his desk, taking his tea with him, and returned to the wall and yet another schedule. 'Yes, Rankie and the boys were working late last evening on floor two, fixtures and fittings. So, that being the case, the place wouldn't have been locked up until they left. You can double-check that with Rankie and Geordie, the night watchmen.'

'Would it be difficult to get in here illegally?'

'Nagh, it's a work site. The Black Cats don't scare anyone. We're forever chasing people away who knew the building when it was a factory producing Black Cat cigarettes. They just want to see what it's like these days. Mostly harmless stuff.'

'It wasn't harmless stuff going on yesterday evening,' Kennedy reminded the site manager before polishing off another cake and washing it down with a swig of tea.

'Aye, that's true, what's that all about?'

'Too early to tell.'

'A bit like all that black-magic stuff we used to read about in the '60s in the Dennis Wheatley books. What was the big one called, the Devil an... no, The Devil's Daughter? No, that's not it either. Ahm, let me see. Yes! That's it, *To the Devil a Daughter*. Did you ever read that one?' the Archbishop asked, excitement clearly visible now that he'd remembered the correct title to the book.

'Can't say that I did, but I think I get the picture. So you're saying it wouldn't be hard to get in here?' Kennedy said, noting Runciman's excitement and the large, lopsided grin now covering his face.

'Not really, no. The company spends most of the security budget ensuring nothing is stolen from the building,' Runciman smiled again, 'so you'd have no trouble getting a body into the building. Getting it out, now that would be a different ball of wax altogether.'

He thought for a few moments and then grew quite morose.

'I suppose you have to joke about it in a way. I'm not really being flippant, it's just that I've never really seen anything…' Runciman began and then froze in a cold shudder.

'I usually find hot tea with lots of sugar helps,' Kennedy offered.

'Did any of the rest of the workforce see the body?' Kennedy continued as Runciman crossed his small office in search of a second cup of well-sugared tea.

'No, not at all,' Runciman started, appearing hurt. 'I knew what to do. I sealed the room until your bods got here.'

'Good. Good,' Kennedy continued in his quiet voice. 'Tell me, do the lights on each floor work?'

'Yes, they're all working perfectly normally. Just flick a switch or two by the inside of each door.'

At that point there was a knock on the Archbishop's door.

'Enter,' Runciman called out in what Kennedy guessed would have been his usual response.

'Excuse me, sir,' Irvine said as he peeped his head around the door. 'Dr Taylor has done as much as he can on site, he wants to know if it's okay to remove the body.'

'Yes, yes, that's perfectly fine,' Kennedy responded as he turned awkwardly in his deckchair to face his detective sergeant. In his own way, Irvine was as eccentrically dressed as Runciman, with his well-worn tweeds; green waistcoat; green, white and brown checked shirt and blue bow tie. His outfit was completed with his brown-and-white full brogues; hardly the way to dress on a July day but Kennedy had never noticed a bead of sweat falling below his copper-coloured hairline.

In contrast, Kennedy was wearing a cream pair of chinos, a blue shirt (top button undone) and a black-and-green tie loosened a few inches away from his throat but always at the ready to be done up should he need to visit his superior, Superintendent Thomas Castle. He carried a lightweight black windbreaker, just in case of those summer showers. Winter or summer, sun or rain, he wore sensible shoes: classic, traditionally cut in brown leather, and shined to perfection with three years of daily spit-and-polish sessions. Kennedy liked the fact that you invested something of yourself in your shoes. He had several pairs in light brown, brown and black in various stages of development. The only pairs he didn't like to wear were the pairs he'd never worn. He would polish these daily for a few months to remove their newness before introducing them to the Camden Town beat.

Kennedy swiped his fingers through his jet-black hair; hair that was just a fraction shorter than what was acceptable for a police officer. As his fingers completed their journey, the hair fell back into its natural style; centre parting with an ebony shine and just about covering his ears.

'Yes, that's fine, DS Irvine. Tell Dr Taylor I'll speak to him later when he's had a chance to…' Kennedy began. He was about to use the force standard of "cut him open". Then he thought about Runciman and the fact that the body had already been cut open. He quickly concluded his sentence with: 'done his work'.

'That's unbelievable, just unbelievable,' Runciman began when his office door had been closed.

'Sorry?' Kennedy inquired.

'Your sergeant, his voice… I mean he sounds identical to Sean Connery,' Runciman replied, still staring at the door in disbelief.

'Yes, incredible isn't it?' Kennedy smiled. 'Tell me, have you had any other trouble in here since work started on the building?'

'No, not really. I mean, we've have someone trying to nick the Black Cats but I think that was just a bit of a prank. I mean they're hardly going to fit discreetly at the bottom of any of the gardens around here, are they?'

'So, what, people broke in but didn't manage to move them?' Kennedy prodded.

'No, not exactly,' Runciman explained. 'What happened was that they've been out the front for some time now. They're heavy bastards, Morecambe and Wise – that's what the boys call them – and we had to lower them into position by crane. Anyway, the night watchman caught these four or five blokes about two-thirty one morning and they'd been trying to slide Eric and Ernie from their position by the door, along planks onto the back of a lorry. I mean if Geordie, the night watch, hadn't caught them they'd have done themselves an injury trying to move the bastards and even if they'd been able to move them onto the trailer of the lorry, they'd have gone straight through the flat-back.'

'And that's been it?' Kennedy asked, rising awkwardly from his comfortable chair.

'Pretty much,' Runciman seemed to grow reticent as the interview wound to a close. 'The locals seem to have left us alone, not like some other sites, I can tell you. There was this one around the back of Buckingham Palace and everything used to do a Whitehouse, you know, "go for walkies". But anyway, I'm sure you're not interested in all of that. In Camden Town, though, they've been good as gold, I can tell you.'

'Thanks. We'll be talking again, no doubt. Someone will be along shortly to take a full statement.'

They shook hands for the first and final time.

Chapter Three

AND THAT WAS pretty much it for a couple of weeks. Nothing happened on this particular case. Dr Taylor's autopsy revealed that the old man had died from heart failure. What brought on the heart failure was not apparent. The other atrocities had been carried out after death. They'd taken his fingerprints; nothing on record. They'd circulated a description of the man to the media; nil response. They'd circulated his dental records; no response. They kept an eye on the ever-growing missing persons file; no suitable or likely matches.

They'd carried out door-to-door inquiries in all the streets around the Black Cat Building; no one could recall a single thing happening in the early hours of the night in question. Forensic and fingerprints hadn't turned up one single piece of evidence.

There were no leads left to follow.

That was the plain and simple fact.

Someone had committed the perfect murder.

But had it been a murder, Kennedy wondered? The only information Taylor had been able to give him about the death was the fact that the old man had died from heart failure. Doesn't everyone's heart fail when they die, Kennedy thought? And why would someone wait for you to die of natural causes and then perform this weird ritual with your corpse; removing your eyeballs, slitting open your stomach and hanging you up on a silver meat hook?

A case destined for the unsolved file: the file ann rea was always quizzing Kennedy about and the file she was always planning to do an article, or maybe even a series of articles, on?

'I'm so intrigued, Kennedy, about people who commit murders and then get away with it. What do they feel like?' local journalist, ann rea, friend, cohabitant and (sometimes) lover of Christy Kennedy inquired hypothetically.

'Ah, now, there's a question,' Kennedy began expansively. They were walking off a Queen's meal, a meal they'd enjoyed at the Queens' Restaurant & Pub at the foot of Primrose Hill. 'I suppose it would all depend on whether it was a premeditated murder or a murder that happened on the spur of the moment, you know, because circumstances got out of control. The murderer who plans everything dispassionately, works it all out to the very last detail, obviously lives with the possibilities a lot longer so you would think that they would be more able to cope with the consequences. Whereas, say with a crime of a passion, where you have someone who finds themselves, even unwillingly, taking someone else's life, I would imagine they would be more prone to nightmares and regret.'

'You might be over-simplifying things, Kennedy,' ann rea said, taking his hand and leading him up the hill as opposed to the Regents Park direction they'd been heading in. 'The person who meticulously plans everything may be using this process, of planning, to vent his anger or frustration and is so immersed in the planning that he is oblivious to the physiological consequences. Once he has carried out his plan and has nothing to occupy that part of his mind, or his day, the regret sets in.'

'Yeah, you could be right. I must admit I haven't really thought about it too much. I'm much more intrigued by how the murderer reaches that point; the point where he, or she,' Kennedy said, as he stole a sideways glance at ann rea, 'commits themselves to murder. You know, are we all capable of making such a choice? It's just that we've never been faced with the right or wrong – I suppose it's more accurate from my professional point of view – set of circumstances.'

'You really think that we're all capable of murder?'

'In principle, no. I think that we all have… we all have our set of values and we make our decisions based on them. In practice, I don't know. We all do some wrong though, don't we? It's all a matter of to what degree we are prepared to step over the line separating right from wrong. For instance, James Irvine is not a bad person. I don't think he would ever commit a crime for instance, even though he does fiddle his expenses. Now, do we say it's okay if he fiddles a couple of pounds a week? Is that okay, is that acceptable? When does it become unacceptable and a crime? When it's a hundred pounds a week? Is that unacceptable? And if a hundred pounds is unacceptable and a couple of pounds is acceptable then where is the line crossed from good to bad or right to wrong? You know? So, two pounds a week is okay but one hundred pounds a week isn't. So is ten pounds okay? Eleven pounds? And on and on upwards until you reach say seventy-six pounds. You see, seventy-six pounds a week is just a tad under four thousand pounds a year. That's a lot of money to embezzle your employer out of. But is seventy-five pounds okay? And seventy-six isn't? Or is it that seventy-five pounds isn't okay and seventy-four is? That's the thing, that is the intrigue for me; where is the line?'

'But that's over-simplifying things, Kennedy.' By this time they'd reached the crown of Primrose Hill and sat down on one of the two wooden benches with the best views in London. 'James knows that's what happens, people fiddle their expenses. I fiddle my expenses, for heaven's sake.'

'That's my point; you see, that's it, that's exactly it. Most people do. Most people believe it is their right to fiddle their expenses. I know you, I know James Irvine, neither of you are thieves. However, say you went into your office one day and there was four thousand pound lying around, would you take it?'

'No, of course not, Kennedy,' ann rea replied indignantly as she elbowed him playfully in the ribs.

'No, of course not,' Kennedy repeated her answer and added, 'Why?'

'Because it would be stealing,' ann rea replied.

'Say it was a hundred pounds?' Kennedy continued.

'No, definitely not.'

'No, of course not, not even a fiver, right?' Kennedy prompted.

'No, I wouldn't even steal a fiver. But I think we're discussing two points here at once, Kennedy. One, is fiddling your expenses stealing? Two, where do you cross the line where it's not permissible to steal, either by helping yourself to the four grand left sitting around or by massaging your expense figures?'

'Perhaps you're right. I always knew you'd keep me on the

right track. I suppose the point I'm making is that everyone believes it's okay to fiddle their expenses, but at what point does it become stealing? At what point does tax evasion become fraud? At what point does a gentle nudge,' Kennedy paused to rub his ribs, 'become GBH? At what point does one decide: "Right, that's it, I'm going to end your life"?'

'I didn't realise you were so fragile,' ann rea replied, moving towards his ribs. 'Here, I'll kiss it and make it better.'

'You'll scare the animals...' Kennedy started but he didn't get a chance to finish. ann rea had used the chance to tickle Kennedy on the sides and he was almost convulsing before he had a chance to fight her off.

'Are you thinking specifically about the body you found recently, down in the Black Cat Building?' ann rea continued once Kennedy had regained his composure.

'In a way, yes, I suppose I am; that and the recent Dr Ranjesus episode. You see, going back to your original question: how do murderers who get away with murders feel? He'd be the perfect person to ask. We know, we think, that Ranjesus murdered Rose Butler's friend, Sinead O'Sullivan, and now there's this new one where a nurse he was having an affair with has just literally disappeared from the face of the earth. So he'd be a good person for you to interview, and what a great opening question: "How does it feel to have gotten away with murder?" I bet you he never even spares a thought for poor Sinead. I bet you he has never had the slightest pang of conscience. Someone in his life was inconveniencing him and he removed her the way you remove dog-do from your feet. But we'll get him, we'll get him one day. Patience is a virtue.'

Kennedy paused to enjoy the view and it certainly was a wondrous sight. He and ann rea continued to sit in wonder, she with her head on his shoulder, he with his arm around her. The sun was going down and a fiery red sky was adding a perfect light to the distinctive London skyline, in its own way as breathtakingly beautiful as any of Woody Allen's Manhattan scenes. There was a power present, an indefinable power but a power nonetheless, which was probably at the root of what drove Kennedy.

'Now the Black Cats murderer,' Kennedy began, distracting himself with a thought. 'Did you know that they call the cats Morecambe and Wise?'

'Yes, Kennedy, everyone in Camden Town knows that.'

'Oh. Sorry. Ex-cuse me,' Kennedy replied feigning hurt, 'with that one. The victim was over seventy years old and there had to be at least two people involved in his murder, possibly more.'

'Why?'

'Physically, just getting the body into the building. Both James Irvine and Anne Coles have discovered, from their interviews with the workforce, that there might have been at least four or five people unaccounted for in the building on that particular evening. But no one can put a description on any of the strangers. You know, they caught them out of the corner of their eye, didn't recognise them but didn't really pay much attention to them as they were too busy at their own work. Everyone, without exception, is pretty vague about it, but it makes sense to me that several people were involved in this murder. Which meant it was planned. Why would a group of people conspire to murder a seventy-year-old man?'

'Maybe he was a child molester, perhaps; maybe even a paedophile?' ann rea offered. 'It would account for a group of people, i.e. a family, being involved.'

'Possibly, but we've checked and no one fitting the victim's description has been released from a home or a prison recently. But let's follow your thought for a minute. Say it was a child molester or a paedophile and a group of people was responsible. Did they all feel good about the murder? Did any of them have any doubts? Were any of them squeamish? Are any of them having nightmares? Do any of them have to threaten weaker members of the group or family to keep quiet? Are there members of the group being threatened now, petrified, you know, having seen what their fellow murderers are capable of? If a score was being settled why did they bring the corpse to that particular building? Why did they hang up the body? Why did…' Kennedy stopped mid-sentence.

He'd told ann rea how they'd found the body and he knew that she would keep it confidential. He also knew her ability to resist the sensational scoop had little to do with their relationship and a lot to do with her integrity as a writer and a journalist and, contrary to popular opinion, she was not a member of a minority group. He chose not to repeat the information that night on Primrose Hill because it seemed somewhat inappropriate, considering the beauty of the scene before them.

'This is more than vengeance,' he continued, drawing her closer. 'They could have just left the dead body somewhere to be found. In all probability the death would have been noted as heart failure. Taylor still hasn't finished all his tests, he's still working on it, but he's still not been able to add anything to the cause-of-death file, other than heart failure. So, our group of murderers wanted to make a point. They wanted to make a statement.'

'You mean they're not being as subtle as Dr Ranjesus?' ann rea said.

'Exactly. His victim, we believe we know who she is, disappears from the face of the earth. On the other hand, with the old man, we haven't a clue as to who he is or what he did but he's thrown right in our faces.'

'I can't believe that as we enter the last few months of the 1900s, with all your computers and the internet and Interpol and records and fingerprints and dental records, you can't find out the name of this man,' ann rea said in exasperation. 'I think I'll do another piece on him, maybe more from the unsolved-crime angle this time.'

'Mmmm,' Kennedy replied, as he pulled her closer still.

When Kennedy said "Mmmm" it usually meant that his mind was no longer on his work.

Chapter Four

LATER THAT VERY night, after some energetic "Mmmms" in fact, ann rea wrote her article. She wrote it late that night in order to make the following morning's deadline. The article appeared in that Thursday's issue of the *Camden News Journal*, only to be greeted by a tidal wave of indifference. However, various regional groups of newspapers picked up the story and it was syndicated in numerous local papers, including the *Mid Ulster Mail*.

The *Mid Ulster Mail* is circulated throughout parts of Northern Ireland and two weeks later – four weeks to the day, in fact, after the body of the seventy-year-old man was found – ann rea was sitting in her office when the phone rang.

'Hello, is this ann rea?' the girl at the other end began; she had a broad Ulster accent.

'Yes, this is ann rea?'

'Small "A", small "R"?'

'Yes.'

'Aye, and what have youse got against Belfast and Dublin?'

'Sorry?'

'Ye know, you obviously don't like capitals,' the voice at the other end replied, breaking into hearty laughter at her own joke.

'Oh, yes,' ann rea joined in the laughter. 'I'd never looked at it that way. Who am I speaking to?'

'Neena MacDoo.'

'And what can I do for you?' ann rea said, wishing she'd avoided the rhyme by saying something like: "And how can I help?" but she didn't, so she had to let it lie, as did Neena who made the sounds of someone lighting a cigarette. ann rea heard the whish of a matchstick, the deep drawing of breath followed shortly by the sigh of contentment.

Neena was now ready to talk:

'Well, it's about your article, you know, the one about the murder of the seventy-year-old man.'

'Yes?'

'Well, we ran it last Friday and we'd quite a few calls about it, two of which may be of interest to you. One, which might only be a joker, was someone from Ballyneagh who claimed the locals up there were upset because some former member of the vestry at a parish church had sold all the original wood from the parish vicarage to the developer doing up the Black Cat Building. Apparently, it caused quite a bit of a scandal up there when this chap sold the wood for lots of money. He then pretended he'd stripped the vicarage to refurbish the building and dumped all the wood as useless. Or so he claims. It turns out that he was paid five thousand pounds for the wood, original walls and floors, and the vicarage had now been done up to look like a holiday home, all white walls and grey carpet everywhere.'

'Interesting,' ann rea said, acknowledging her fellow journalist as she took some notes on the details of the caller, apparently an indignant parishioner. 'You said there were two calls.' 'Yes. The other bit of information I've already passed on to Detective Sergeant James Irvine. God, he'd a beautiful voice, just like James Bond. He sounded gorgeous.'

'Yes, he's quite nice,' ann rea said, smiling at the fact that the old Irvine charm even worked on the telephone.

'Could you put a word in for us?' Neena said, only half joking. 'Anyway, as I said, I've already spoken to him and told him that the other caller was from Portstewart, a little seaside village up on the coast, on the Derry and Antrim border.'

'Isn't that close to Portrush? ann rea offered, recalling Kennedy's stories about his birth town.

'Yes, it is indeed. I'm impressed,' Neena replied.

'Ah, don't be. I've got insider knowledge,' ann rea began, not giving too much away. 'You were about to tell me about the second caller?'

'Yes. She felt her father fitted the description of the old man. Apparently he's been living in London for quite some time. Your Irvine said he'd look into it and thanked me for the info. I just thought I'd pass it on to you in case you were involved in any follow-up story.'

'I've just become very interested in a follow-up story. Thanks for taking the trouble to ring me. Thanks very much.'

'Agh, no problem,' the thick Ulster accent came back in a flash, perhaps just a wee bit too quick. 'Perhaps you can return the favour some time.'ann rea knew, as she slowly returned the handset to its cradle, exactly what favour Neena had been thinking about.

'You're not his type,' she said to the quietened phone lying like a wounded cowboy, exhausted and lifeless, across the back of his horse. 'You're too available.'

Chapter Five

'PACK A BAG, we're off to the Port!'

'What?' ann rea replied in disbelief. It was three minutes later and she hadn't had a chance to contact Kennedy yet to check out the recent developments. Now here he was on the phone inviting her to some port.

'We're off to Portrush,' Kennedy replied, his voice noticeably edged with excitement.

'Does this mean the lady's father has panned out?' ann rea replied, adding what she knew so far.

'Yes, yes it does. She took a photograph of her father into the local nick and they faxed it over to us. I'd say it's a positive ID. I'm going over there to check it out.'

'You sound more like you're going to the seaside with your bucket and spade,' ann rea replied. 'Look, Kennedy, if I do manage to persuade my editor to let me go, how official can this be?'

'Oh, I'm sure we'll be able to cut you a bit of slack on this one. If it hadn't been for your story we'd never have discovered the identity of the victim,' Kennedy replied.

'What's his name? Is Irvine going? When do you leave? Where would we stay? Is it safe over there now?' ann rea gushed as a mountain of questions filled her head.

'Okay. In order: his name was Victor Dugdale; no, Irvine is not going; I'll connect with the RUC over there and they'll give me whatever assistance I need; the 18.30 British Midlands flight, which means we need to be in Paddington in about an hour and a half. We can stay with my parents, it's all fixed up; and yes, it is safe over there now. I think that covers all the questions, doesn't it?' Kennedy positively beamed down the phone.

'Good, I'll check and get back to you.'

Ninety-four minutes later they were on the Heathrow Express out of Paddington and thirty minutes after that they

were waiting in the relative tranquillity of British Midlands'
lounge, close to gate number ten. The new lounge was a far
cry from British Airways' 'cattle-market gate number forty-
nine', when one and all were made to feel like... well, to say
cattle would be an insult to the way some farmers treat their
stock.

At ten minutes past eight that same evening, they were
pulling out of Aldergrove Airport and heading towards
Antrim.

'Now it all makes sense,' ann rea began once they'd negotiated a couple of tricky roundabouts. 'You needed a driver
and it's muggins here who drew the short straw.'

'Oh, I'm sure we'll find other things for you to do as well,'
Kennedy replied playfully.

'Too darned right, Kennedy. Don't forget I'm here profes-
sionally. I'm the *Camden News Journal*'s first foreign corre-
spondent,' ann rea said, unable to keep a straight face. 'And
I'm only here because a lot of other papers picked up on the
'Unsolved Cases' feature and they're all looking for a follow-
up story. My editor is so excited about all of this, he couldn't
contain himself. He was a bit like Jason Robards in *All The
President's Men*; you know that scene where he, as Ben
Bradlee, feels he's got Nixon by the short and curlies. I think
Thomas, my editor, was busting a gut to find a legit excuse to
come over here himself.'

'Well, in that case, hopefully I'll make headway on the
murder investigation and you'll get your story,' Kennedy
replied, turning to enjoy the countryside views.

'And I'm sure we'll find other things to do as well,
Kennedy,' ann rea said playfully as she removed her left hand
from the steering wheel and used it to stroke the back of
Kennedy's neck. 'God, I can't believe how beautiful it is here.
How did you ever manage to leave here?' she gushed as they
saw Lough Neagh in the distance to their left. They were
among the rolling hills, driving on and on as though travelling
through a continuous set of Charles McAuley's soulful paintings.

'I didn't realise myself just how beautiful it is until I'd been
in London for about five or six years,' Kennedy said, still obviously Distracted. He turned to face ann rea and announced

proudly: 'If you think this is great though just wait until you see the Antrim coastline.'

Even this warning wasn't nearly enough to prepare ann rea for the vision of the Northeast coast of Northern Ireland, God's own country. The beaches were certainly the cleanest either Kennedy or ann rea had ever seen. The wind, though, now that the sun was well past its peak, was fresh and sharp enough to blow even the most stubborn of cobwebs from the brain. As they drove into Portrush, down the Coleraine Road, the sight of the bluest of oceans slightly to the right and the rugged Ramore Hill slightly to the left positively took their collective breaths away.

Kennedy allowed himself the luxury of nostalgia as he recalled the extremes of seeing the Harlem Globetrotters basketball team playing a demonstration match on the Ramore Hill Recreation Grounds to experiencing The Wheels (a pop R&B band) playing live on the East Strand Beach. He'd persuaded his father to take him to see the mesmerising Globetrotters work their magic when he was so much younger. On the other hand, Kennedy had been dragged along to the beach to see the free performance, courtesy of the *Belfast Telegraph*, by a mate who was a guitar fanatic and desperately wanted to form a group. He never did, form his group that was, choosing instead to become a civil engineer and was now married with three grown-up children and living in Portsmouth. Like the legions of friends, colleagues, mates and acquaintances who pass through your life, that particular friend was now relegated to his mother's updates – you know: 'Do you remember wee so-and-so who you used to run around with? Well, he's now off in Africa hunting elephants.' To which you'd look up from your newspaper just enough to reply: 'Really, mother, and what's for tea?''

It was hard to remember many exact details about either night just then, in the dying months of the millennium, excepting the excitement of a new experience when the newness was still nearly enough to make it better than any of the many repeat drinks from the same experience cup in your life. No two bottles of wine are ever the same no matter what their labels say; few are ever better second, third or one hundred and third time around. It was hard to remember much of that now as they drove into the hustle and bustle of Portrush. In the morning and afternoon it was the grandfather, grandmother, mother, father and children crowd who flocked to the streets, shops, beaches and Barry's Amusement Arcade. By the time Kennedy and ann rea arrived, this crowd had given way to the early evening crowd who were made up of teenagers on the razzle and the mothers and fathers out for a quiet meal, contented by the fact that their mothers and fathers were looking after *their* grandchildren. On holiday, everyone always accommodated everyone else to suit their own agenda.

Kennedy felt an overwhelming rush; he didn't know if it was from seeing the ocean again or from the buzz of enjoyment seekers on the streets. He felt compelled, beyond logic, to visit Barry's again.

'Pull in and park anywhere you can,' he announced as they were about halfway up Kerr Street, with the harbour just on their left.

'What about your parents? They'll be expecting us,' ann rea replied as she complied.

Kennedy couldn't explain, in words he thought ann rea would understand, the excitement he always experienced when driving, or catching a bus, into Portrush. They'd lived a bit outside the town while he was growing up, closer to Coleraine in fact. He knew that Portrush was the Blackpool of Northern Ireland and it was gimmicky but he'd always just loved it. Every time he arrived he'd be spoilt for choice about what to do with the money, which would be burning a rather large hole in his pocket. There were just so many things to do and all of them exciting. He could, and did, spend hours in Barry's, then there were the beaches, the swimming pools, the shops, the cafés, the record stores, donkey rides on the beach and, when he became too old for that, on the very same beach he could visit the Arcadia Ballroom for dances and bops. Kennedy never danced, though; he didn't feel he could dance so he'd just go dressed in his checked, flared hipsters and loud shirts, suck on a Coca-Cola, listen to the sounds and scout out the girls. And then, even later, there were the sand dunes to go and check out with the said same girls (hopefully). The same sand dunes where the friend who dragged him along to see

The Wheels had possibly started his family and definitely ended his career as a guitarist.

But whatever Kennedy did, he was always spoilt for choice and running around in a panic like the proverbial chicken with its head cut off.

'Ah, I think my parents know me well enough by now. I don't know what it is, ann rea, but I can never resist the attraction of this place, it's just still the experience,' Kennedy replied as he undid his seat belt and opened the car door. 'Just breathe in that air,' he announced.

'Aye, Kennedy, but the wind is strong enough to keep all but those with their own hair, or superglue, off the streets.'

'Spot the city girl. Come on, ye'll be okay.'

'Ye'll be okay, Kennedy? Steady on, we're only here to visit.'

They spent the next hour or so wandering around. Kennedy was surprised that that was all it took to check out all he wanted to. He couldn't work out if it had been memories through rose-tinted glasses or whatever, but Portrush seemed less crowded than before. It was cleaner. The Arcadia Ballroom was closed down. The ballroom section, in point of fact, had been demolished entirely leaving only the grand house that had served as the entrance to the ballroom. Barry's legion of Ulster 'Fonzes' were replaced with name-tagged students supplementing their grants: good news for the local councils footing the bills for their education; bad news, however, for the girls who came up to the Port to have their hearts broken only to find the Brylcreem boys had been replaced by polite, well-spoken mammies' boys with studs in their noses and every other imaginable place. Whereas Barry's once most exciting ride, the bumper cars, had been pretty much relegated to the kiddies corner, the new prime-time adventure was the roller coaster, a roller coaster that could have fitted into one of the coastal bungalows, as opposed to the skyscraper versions frequently spotted on the television. The helter-skelter by the entrance was still the same, still as charming and still a major attraction. The ghost train continued to extract shrieks of terror from its many passengers. The other major difference Kennedy noted was that it would have taken a fortnight's worth of pocket money from his youth to pay for one of today's cheapest rides.

He and ann rea, just to keep in the spirit of things you understand, took a ride on the 'Cyclone', and Kennedy noticed that on this ride, while whizzing around and around at ever-increasing speed, the buzz had gone! Was it age? Perhaps. Was it the fact that he'd travelled a bit since? Perhaps. Or was it just that Portrush had lost its edge? Become more of a Bournemouth than a Blackpool? The teenagers who had been crowding the beaches with Kennedy had all grown up and the current generation of teenagers had other priorities; priorities encouraged by a new world, a new system of communication. Virtual-reality video games made it possible for today's generation to enjoy a nightly trip to the moon or Mars, or bravely go where no one else had gone while remaining in front of their computer in the comfort of their bedroom, without having to wait for the annual summer holiday up to the Port. And if other trips were required, Kennedy was sure, from glancing around the streets, that there were many around to help with those as well.

The record shop was shut. The record shop owned by Paul Diveto's family. The one-armed Diveto had been the singer with the Interns, and what a singer he'd been. Kennedy used to go and see the band whenever he could and Diveto's voice was a joy, an absolute joy to listen to, and his on-stage histrionics, continuously bending double to catch his breath to sing the next line, made the Interns' Arcadia performances compulsive viewing. Kennedy wondered what Diveto and Nico and the other members of the Interns were doing now.

He knew what another of his teenage idols was up to now. The legendary guitarist, Henry McCullough, had started his career playing in the same Arcadia Ballroom with the Walter Lewis Showband; he'd then joined Dublin band The People, who changed their name to Eire Apparent when they moved to London. Henry then joined Joe Cocker's Greaseband, played the distinctive guitar intro on Cocker's classic cover of The Beatles' With A Little Help From My Friends, and toured America with Cocker, including a career-making appearance at the original Woodstock festival. The Greaseband then left Joe Cocker, the world's first air guitarist, and made a couple of records of their own, including acting as house band for the Jesus Christ Superstar soundtrack album. Henry then joined

Paul McCartney's Wings, toured with them for a time before returning, and settling, in Portrush and, Kennedy believed, he continued to play around Ireland with a cool band.

The bookshop was closed down as well. How could that have been allowed to happen? There were lots of new shops built with breeze block and pretty-board or refurbished units. But mostly they all sold the same souvenirs of your trip to the seaside and, for the traditionalists, even a stick of rock.

Ugly blocks of flats had sprung up as well. Kennedy whistled out loud in disbelief at some of the liberties that had been taken with the Portrush skyline. The theatre-cum-town hall on the corner of Kerr Street and Eglinton Street had closed down. The once bustling railway station just across the street from the empty town hall was now a pub with a go-cart track on the forecourt. The once-elegant Northern Counties Hotel had burned down and the charred remnants were allowed to remain as a testament to what had been.

Now, finally, after sixty years of dominance, Barry's Amusement Arcade was having to fight places like Fantasy Island for the dwindling crowds. A Postman Pat-type choo-choo train snaked its way around the streets, rarely distressing pedestrians.

And now Kennedy was back, back from London. Portrush, as a town, might have long since lost it, but at least Kennedy was back in this beautiful part of the world amongst its friendly people; people who had big hearts and ate even bigger breakfasts. He was here to investigate in the neighbouring sleepy little towns. Investigate the horrific, and apparently senseless, murder of a seventy-year-old man, Victor Dugdale.

He wondered aloud how there could be a connection. A connection between the sheer ugliness he had witnessed in the Black Cat Building in Camden Town and the natural beauty that now surrounded him.

Chapter Six

THE FOLLOWING MORNING, following one of the afore-mentioned legendary Ulster fries – two eggs, bacon, fadge (potato bread), fried soda and two friendly sausages – Kennedy and ann rea headed back out towards Coleraine, the deal being that they were going to split up. Interesting to note they'd split up during the night as well. Although Kennedy was in his early forties, his mum had made up separate rooms for himself and ann rea. Kennedy had warned his friend that this was a possibility. ann rea had reassured Kennedy that she was more amused by the innocence of the gesture than annoyed by it. They joked about it in the car before ann rea dropped Kennedy off at the local RUC (Royal Ulster Constabulary) station to make his local connections and interview Victor Dugdale's daughter. She then made her way to Ballyneagh to see what she could dig up from the vicarage people about their missing wood.

The desk sergeant from North Bridge House in Camden Town, Timothy Flynn, had already spoken to a mate of his in Portrush, DS McCusker, to ensure his boss would get full co-operation and not the usual static offered to those from the Big Smoke.

'God bless you, Tim Flynn,' Kennedy said under his breath as he shook hands with the Ulster detective sergeant. Kennedy was sure, from the firm handshake alone, that McCusker was a fine Ulsterman and would be an excellent host. He was always referred to just as McCusker. Flynn had advised Kennedy that no one knew McCusker's Christian name.

'Areye ritely?' McCusker said in strong Ulster-speak, keeping a vice-like grip on Kennedy's hand.

'Aye, I'm not too bad at all,' Kennedy replied.

'An Flynn, kaipinfit?'

'Oh yes, Tim's keeping very fit,' Kennedy replied. 'An yersel, formawrite?'

McCusker broke off the Ulster-speak with a laugh and offered: 'Aye, and I keep forgettin' yer from these parts.'

'Long time since though,' Kennedy replied.

'Aye, but ye know the lingo. We're nat going ta have any fun with you.'

The RUC station house was at the corner of Coleraine Road and Crocknamack Road. It was an old building with nothing but lapsed security arrangements and fences to show for the Troubles. It was certainly a bustle that morning. Being a holiday town meant that the local constabulary not only had to deal with crime and traffic but they also seemed to act as a Tourist Information Centre.

'Come on through,' McCusker began. 'We'll have a drop of tea and a chat and then we'll head off to see Doris Dugdale and she can tell you all about her father.'

'Sounds good to me,' Kennedy confirmed as he followed DS McCusker through.

Although McCusker was thinning on top he was already, at 9am, showing distinct signs of a healthy five o'clock shadow. Kennedy was continuously surprised by how people with so little on top still managed to have healthy (unwanted) beard growths; something cosmically wrong there, he felt. McCusker was about five-foot eight; slim build; clean, white shirt, opened at the neck; no tie; grey slacks, which were pressed so expertly you could have sharpened a pencil on the creases; and a pair of blue-and-green loafers.

He seemed a good chap but his tea was so strong Kennedy was convinced you could have walked across a lake of it, not that he ever wished to come across a lake of it. He drank half of the brown-coloured tar as a sign of good manners, and suggested they get started on their journey in order to avoid the other half. He wasn't sure exactly what he'd find in the murky bottom of his tea mug; he was sure, though, that he didn't want to find out.

'Ye never thought on coming home?' McCusker inquired ten minutes later. They were in an unmarked, dark-green Ford Granada, heading in the general direction of Derry and specifically Portstewart.

'Aye,' Kennedy replied, not implying to the positive but to acknowledge that he was considering the question. 'I've thought about it. Sometimes I feel I should want to come home a lot more than I do. But other times I think it's great that I've got somewhere like this in reserve to come back to eventually, you know, when I retire. But as that's not going to be for ages, I feel to come home now would somehow spoil it for when, and if, I do come home. When I lived here originally, like, I took it all for granted. I'd hate to do that again.'

'Aye,' McCusker began as he took a pack of Players from his pocket flicked them opened offered them to Kennedy (who declined), stuck one in his own mouth, closed the packet, replaced it in his pocket and pushed the car lighter into its nest. The entire operation took but a few seconds. 'As you say, you've been considering it.'

'And yourself, you here for good?' Kennedy asked as he found himself winding down the car window a bit in anticipation of the imminent nicotine fumes.

'Oh yes. Four and a half more years and then you'll find me on Kelly's golf links every day.'

Kennedy looked at McCusker and grinned self-consciously.

'Oh yeah,' McCusker began, 'I know what you're thinking. The poor bastard risks his life every day on the streets of Ulster, he puts up with the Troubles for thirty years just so he can go and play bleeding golf, half a mile from the police station, every day.'

'No, no, not at all,' Kennedy made a feeble attempt at a protest.

'It's okay. Perfectly okay and you're probably correct. It's just that I'm dammed if I'm going to sit at home every day waiting to die. I've spent thirty years avoiding that, every single day of my life. I'm not going to roll over and die. The old golf's a great social event. A brilliant life altogether.'

'Are you good at it?' Kennedy felt compelled to ask.

'Feckin' crap,' McCusker grunted as he took a deep drag on his cigarette, reducing the Player by twenty-five percent in one go. 'Now I know what you're thinking. You're thinking if that sad bastard doesn't give up on the fags, he'll be going straight to the twentieth tee.'

'Sorry?'

'You know, the nineteenth tee is the pub and the twentieth is the graveyard.'

'Oh, I see,' Kennedy replied, two degrees above morbid.

'Golf, you see, it's a social thing entirely. It's the perfect getaway from the wives' club. These golfing trips to Spain, Portugal and St Andrews, it's all an excuse for a lads' weekend away without the grandmothers of our children's children getting suspicious,' McCusker continued. He paused to finish the ciggy and stumped it out in the ashtray. Kennedy noted it was clean, very clean. He wondered what it would look like at the end of the day. He flashed a conspiratorial smile to Kennedy. 'Here, I'll let you into the worst-kept secret in Northern Ireland.'

'Which is?'

'Which is that the left-luggage section at Aldergrove is packed to overflowing on all these golfing weekends with golf clubs.'

'Sorry?' Kennedy laughed in disbelief.

'Well, they're heavy bastards to carry around with you if you're never going to use them, so why bother lugging them around with you? When the wife sees you go out of the house with a pink cashmere sweater, yellow shirt and red trousers she makes two assumptions – one correct, one incorrect.'

'The incorrect one obviously is that you're off to play a weekend of golf.'

'Yeah, and the other?'

'I haven't a clue,' Kennedy admitted.

'She knows that there is not a woman on this planet who is going to be interested in you dressed like that – dressed like a colour-blind Pringle mannequin,' McCusker replied breaking into a hearty laugh. 'Ah, we're here.'

If Portrush was Brighton with an architectural problem then Portstewart was Bournemouth discovering its second youth. Had the poor cousin blossomed into a shining light?

Doris Dugdale appeared to live in one of those houses in one of those streets that might as well have been a '70s housing estate somewhere, in the middle of anywhere, as opposed to being positioned about two miles from one of the most beautiful coastlines in the world.

'They call this the White City,' McCusker began as he turned the Granada (dangerously) off the main road out of Portstewart on the Coleraine side. 'So called because one day, in the long-distant past, all these...' and he raised both his forefingers (keeping a firm grip on the steering wheel) and pointed out either side of the car at the rows of uniform dwellings, 'used to have snow-white, pebble-dashed exteriors. Now look at them.'

Kennedy obeyed.

Some were painted blue, some pink, some lemon; some kept up the pretence of the white and some were just downright dirty. The kerbstones were all painted red, white and blue and a few withered Union Jacks flew from the street lamps. The further up the estate they drove, the more depressing it became and as they turned a corner Kennedy was expecting another row of the same but they came upon this little oasis, hidden amongst a grove of fir trees. As they drove through them, the road surface suddenly changed from uneven, with frequent potholes, to so smooth and even that you could have played snooker on it. The road twisted and turned a little, leaving the estate so far behind it could have been in Camden. They couldn't have gone but more than a few hundred yards when they came across a beautiful old cottage.

'This is us, we're here,' McCusker announced as he parked the car behind a white Morris Minor. It was in such beautiful condition that even Kennedy, not exactly a car man, stared at it in awe. McCusker smiled at the centre of Kennedy's attention.

'The difference between that model and most of the ones you see on the roads these days is that that one has not been restored, it's just been looked after properly. Doris' mother used that wee jam jar every single day of her life for over twenty years and then, when she took had her first wee stroke, it sat in yon garage collecting dust until Doris came home to look after her mother about two years ago. She dusted it down, had it serviced and hasn't had a bit-o-bother from it since.'

'It's magnificent,' Kennedy said as he let himself out of the car.

'Come on, let's see if she's got a cup of tea or two in the pot.'

Chapter Seven

'YOUSE TWO ARE an the go rite and early,' a voice from inside the door announced. 'Away with ye 'til I open the door, Blackie.'

There was the sound of kicking, yelping and scuffling inside the door until it was nearly fully open.

'Won't ye come on in. If she gets out I'll not see her until darkness,' the owner of the voice called out from her hunkered position, the door handle in one hand and the dog's collar in the other.

'Surely we will, Doris,' McCusker began. 'This is…'

'For heaven's sake won't you come on in, detective,' Doris interrupted.

A few seconds later two (police) men, one woman and a dog were all safely behind the closed front door.

'Sorry 'bout that but she's always looking to get out; she's on heat, you see,' Doris began. 'I'm Doris Dugdale. You must be the pol-iceman from London.'

'Detective Inspector Christy Kennedy,' McCusker said completing the introduction he'd started earlier.

'Good to meet you,' Kennedy said, accepting her recently apron-wiped hand.

'That's never a London accent,' Doris replied, breaking into a smile large enough to light up the entire Antrim coast-line.

'He's originally from these parts,' McCusker offered by way of explanation.

'Aye. And has the cat got his tongue then?' Doris said and smiled simply, a red flush rising to her colourless cheeks.

Doris Dugdale had a great smile. A smile, Kennedy figured, she rarely used. It transformed not only her face but also her entire body. It changed her from looking like a middle-aged, worn-out woman to a youthful woman. When she smiled she looked barely out of her thirties and her auburn, curly hair jingle-jangled in a girlie kind of way. She was dressed rather dourly, in a drab cardigan, full-length apron, shirt and calf-length skirt. She wore not a hint of make-up, where a hint would have worked wonders. She was slim but not thin, and about five-foot six, Kennedy reckoned.

'Goodness, would you look at me,' Doris began removing the apron and placing it on a hook behind the kitchen door as she led them into the pivotal room of the house. 'Would you like a cup of tea, the pair of ye?' she asked, as she stared at Kennedy.

'Aye, *we* would,' McCusker smiled.

'How about a bit of breakfast?' she added, continuing to hold Kennedy in her stare.

Kennedy was about to decline the offer of the breakfast but before he had a chance, McCusker jumped in there feet first.

'Aye, that would be right nice, Doris. Throw a few rashers in the pan then.'

There was already an appetising smell of freshly-baked bread in the kitchen and Doris Dugdale invited the two policemen to sit down at the table and immediately poured them both a cup of tea from a big teapot nestling on the Aga. Kennedy was surprised that the tea, which flowed from the spout of the white and flowery teapot, had already been milked.

'It's one way to keep it from stewing,' Doris announced by way of explanation.

Sugared up, Kennedy tentatively took a sip of the tea. He was shocked at how good it tasted. It more than made up for McCusker's earlier efforts.

'Rite great cup of tea you make, Doris Dugdale. Always have,' McCusker announced.

Doris took the compliment as though it was not the first time it had been offered and opened the oven door, took out a couple of freshly baked wheaten farls and gingerly placed them on a plate, saying: 'There, that's something to be going on with until I get you some real food. Be careful though, they're hot.'

Kennedy followed McCusker's lead and sliced through the middle of the farl and spread butter on the two inner sides. The butter immediately melted into the warm, rich bread and it tasted absolutely delicious. It reminded Kennedy of his mother's home-baked bread.

'So was it you who found Victor?' Doris said, as she limbered up the rasher wagon (frying pan), running a blob of butter around it until the butter was all but melted and the sizzling filled the kitchen.

'I didn't actually find him,' Kennedy started, recalling the horrific scene so many miles away in Camden Town. For a daughter who'd just lost her father she was incredibly cool about it all. Kennedy wondered why she kept referring to him as "Victor" and not "father" or "papa" or the "old man", or something else equally respectful and parental. 'He was found by a site foreman, actually.'

'Oh, I see,' she replied. She added six slices of bacon to the pan and the sizzle explosion drowned out her voice. She raised the pan a little from the heat until it settled down a bit. She then wiped her hands on a towel by the sink and joined them at the table. McCusker munched away on his farl. 'Was he dead when they found him?'

'Ahm, yes,' Kennedy began, sparing her the details. She was now closer to him that she'd been since they first met and he could see the blue of her eyes as she held his gaze. She smelt of soap and baked bread and a hint of coconut from her shampoo. 'Yes, he was dead when they found him.'

'How did he die?'

'Well, the medical reason is that he died of heart failure, but we've reason to believe there were suspicious circumstances,' Kennedy offered, choosing not to get into it further at this point. Not that there was, in fact, much further he could have gotten into it.

Doris let out a short laugh. She apologised and rose to turn the bacon over.

'Sorry. I was just thinking that he died of a failure of the heart, and my mum died of a broken heart.'

'Your father hasn't lived here for quite a while, Doris, has he?' McCusker added. Kennedy thought the observation was as much for his benefit as a question in need of an answer.

'Victor hadn't lived here since I was about ten. He came to visit occasionally and he'd sit here looking out at that...' Doris stopped talking and looked out the kitchen window.

Kennedy realised why, even when the local authorities had insensitively built the White City housing estate a few hundred yards from the Dugdales' front door, the family hadn't moved on. They'd planted a few trees to hide the eyesore and remained contentedly because, out of their kitchen window, they had the most amazing uninterrupted view of the coastline. To the right were the rolling hills of the neighbouring farmland. To the left were the fir trees hiding the White City but directly in front of them, in front of their fine manicured garden, were sand dunes and waves rolling up a sandy beach for as far as the eye could see.

'When was the last time you saw him?' Kennedy asked. It was a definite question but the way it was delivered made it sound more like someone trying to make conversation, which was exactly the way it was reacted to.

'That would have been my mother's funeral. September'll be two years since it happened. September 6th,' Doris said, adding four eggs and six pieces of fadge to the pan. Roddy Yates would have made light of that, Kennedy thought, and so would McCusker if his lip-licking was anything to go by. Kennedy had to admit that when breakfast (his second) was first mentioned the idea somewhat repulsed him – particularly after his mother's particularly healthy version: Alpen, OJ, tea and toasted wheaten bread – but now with the aromas tickling his nostril he couldn't wait to get stuck into the famous Ulster Fry.

'Have ye no heard from him since, like?' McCusker asked his final question before his nosebag was due to be fitted. If it wasn't fitted soon, Kennedy guessed, he'd be fit for tying.

'Nope. Card at Christmas, that's 'bout it,' Doris replied, matter of fact. She started to set two places at the table. She came rather close to Kennedy and pretty soon the smells from the rasher wagon were doomed to the dumper of life as the feminine scents displayed their stronger power. 'Sure, he means nothing to me. Hasn't done. Ever.'

'Do you know where he lived?' Kennedy asked, being forced to raise his voice slightly to compete with the sounds of the frying pan, Blackie scratching at the back door, plates being placed on the tin draining board beside the sink, knives and forks being thrown on the table, bottles of HP Sauce and tomato ketchup, and salt- and pepper-cellars being removed from the light-blue painted pine cupboard and in turn placed on the table.

'Blackie, would you ever give me a moment's peace?' Doris began as she shooed the dog away from the door with her foot. 'Sorry, where were we? Oh yes. Did I know where he lived? I've a London address there somewhere.' She cleaned her hands on the towel again and returned to the cupboard and hunted through a drawer.

McCusker kept glancing nervously at the frying pan.

'An don't you be worrying about yer baked necks, Inspector, I'll know by the whiff when they're ready,' Doris muttered into the cupboard as she continued her search. 'Ah. Here we are.' She closed the drawer, swung around, handed an envelope to Kennedy and made for the Aga, all in one beautifully co-ordinated movement. Doris Dugdale was a delight to watch in her own kitchen; everything was set for her convenience and she was the maestro working up her personal orchestra to a peak, but unlike any of the conductors who could only use sounds and melody, she had both of those plus smells and taste to help bring her work to a successful peak.

Kennedy checked the address before he sat down to his feast:

5c Regents Heights,
Regents Park,
London
NW1 7PC

'Jesus, Doris, that hit the quare mark,' McCusker said four minutes later as he washed down the last of the fry with a swig of tea. The detective positively loved his food and when he saw Kennedy was leaving a rasher and a couple of pieces of fadge he scoffed those as well, soaking up the yolk of the egg from around his plate.

'Clean plates,' Doris said smiling at Kennedy. 'That's all I want for compliments.'

McCusker became a little fidgety, sliding his feet back and forth on the red tiled floor and twitching this way and that in his chair. Kennedy would agree it wasn't the most comfortable of chairs; early pine-farmhouse style, they were a bit rickety and chipped and marked with the years, but Doris or her mother had made them quite funky by painting them two shades of blue – a dark-blue seat and light-blue legs and back. But they weren't so uncomfortable as to warrant McCusker's obvious uneasiness.

'Away with ye, Inspector,' Doris sighed. 'Yer not smokin' in here. If ye want a smoke, go on out to the garden and take Blackie with ye – a walk around the garden will do her the world of good. Here, take her lead as well, otherwise you won't see her for dust.'

It was McCusker you couldn't see for dust. He refilled his cup with tea and Kennedy was amused at how he disappeared into the garden, trying to balance the tea cup in one hand with Blackie pulling on the lead and trying to negotiate lighting up with the other. But succeed he did. Needs must.

'This address,' Kennedy began, sensing the new silence in the kitchen, 'how old is it?'

'Victor left it here when he came over for my mother's funeral,' Doris replied.

'What will happen to your father, will he be buried back here?' the detective asked, finishing off his own cup of tea.

'Don't know, don't care.'

'Ah now, he's…' Kennedy began.

'Look, Inspector, you should know that I only contacted that wee girl on the paper to help clear it up. I knew who he was. I would have done the same if it was old Scott,' Doris began.

Kennedy's eyebrows arched into a question mark.

'Sorry, but he means as much to me as the farmer who works the fields next to here. I know who he is but that's all. This is not one of those big moody trips, you know. Father deserts mother and child when the child is young. Child grows up bitter and twisted because she doesn't have a father's attention. Secretly wants the father's love again and sends out mixed, aggressive signals,' Doris said and then she stopped and smiled for a while.

'But he's family, he's your blood,' Kennedy said.

'Your problem is that you probably love your father and that's great, you know, for you. But because you love your father, my relationship with Victor seems strange to you. I didn't love my father; neither did I hate him. I just don't care about him. My mother brought me up and I wanted for nothing ever, and I mean love, comfort, clothes, food or even discipline for that matter. We were a complete family. We were a single-parent family but that doesn't mean something was missing. That's the mistake some people make. They say: "Oh, poor so and so, the father's run off with another woman, she couldn't keep her man and the wee wane's so pretty, it's a shame." Codswallop! A shame is where children are dying through lack of food because the governments of their countries are so corrupt that relief doesn't get through to them. Let me show you something, Inspector.'

Doris rose from the kitchen table and nodded for Kennedy to follow her. She took him through a hallway covered with paisley patterned wallpaper and through into the sitting room, also known in some houses as the good room or the courting room. Doris' good room was so good it looked like it could have been a show room in a furniture store. Nothing had been used and everything was so well polished the light shone off it and the smell of furniture and floor polish filled the room. She walked across the room to the other side, passing a fireplace on the left, across a polished wooden floor with red patterned rugs to an old oak sideboard with a wall unit resting above. The unit was filled with framed photographs of a girl of varying ages (the same girl) with a woman who was obviously the mother.

They were on the beach, they were running across fields, they were eating meals with friends, they were with Santa Claus, they were at Doris' graduation, they were outside the Strand Ballroom in Portstewart, they were at a wedding (Doris' wedding), they were on safari, they were in New York, they were in San Francisco, they were everywhere and they were smiling loudly in every photograph.

'Does that look like an unhappy wee girl?' Doris began as she took one of the photographs from the wall unit and polished it on her cardigan. 'Does that look like a wee girl who is missing anything? Does that look like a mother who is not capable of looking after her wee girl properly? It's all balderdash I tell you, Inspector, all this rubbish about a child needing a father and a mother to be normal, to have a good upbringing. You need to be loved, that's all. You need to be with someone who wants to be with you. That's worth so much more than being with someone who feels they have to be with you because you're blood. So I'm afraid if you're looking for someone to show remorse because a man who was positively a stranger in her life has died, then I'm not your woman. This is not a remorseful day.'

What's that all about, Kennedy thought as he appeared lost in the numerous photographs? He decided not to follow Doris up that particular avenue at this time.

'Who's this?' he inquired, pointing to a photograph in a silver frame. It was in full Kodak colour, seemed relatively recent – as in the last five years – and featured Doris, her mother and an elderly man. Perhaps, Kennedy thought, Victor had been replaced in at least Doris' mother's heart.

'Sure, that's only Uncle Norman,' Doris announced and then continued: 'And there's Blackie's mother.' She had led Kennedy away from the sideboard and continued along the wall of photographs to one of the larger shots. This one, right enough, had a black King Charles spaniel being cuddled by both Doris and her mum, both smiling away as contentedly as ever. Kennedy wondered had the dog died of pamperisation and if not, was there in fact such a word as "pamperisation"? Could you, in fact, smother a dog to death without the use of a pillow? Pumpernickel indeed! He found these strange thoughts to be filling his head when he was meant to be absorbing Doris' laughing gallery.

'And what's Blackie's mother's name?' Kennedy inquired because he felt he should.

'Why, Blackie of course. When they were both around they were Blackie and Little Blackie. I'll tell you it took me a long time to drop "Little" from Blackie's name after her mother died.'

'Oh!' was all Kennedy could find to say. He considered asking her had her mother also been called Doris but thought better of it.

'Mum was also called Doris, you know,' Doris began uncannily. 'Of course, there was no confusion because every-one, even my friends, used to call her 'Mum'.'

'I see,' said Kennedy, hoping he wasn't looking guilty. He

decided to change tack. 'Tell me, Doris, was your mother from around these parts?'

'No. Not too far away, though. She was from Maghera originally. Her family, my grandparents, used to have a farm just outside of Maghera. I used to go there a lot when I was growing up.'

'It'd have been a lot different when your mother was a wee girl.'

'Aye, that's true,' Doris replied, visibly relaxing a little. She sat down on the arm of a sofa and her ocean-blue eyes stared out of the window in the general direction of the blue ocean. 'I'd have liked to have grown up on a farm too, you know. I mean it was hard work and all that but it would have been satisfying hard work, if you know what I mean. I think being around animals all the time was where her love of them started.'

'Did she every consider continuing the farm, you know, when she and your father married?' Kennedy asked.

'Naugh, naugh, nothing like that,' Doris replied, laughing a laugh of disbelief. 'There were three brothers ahead of her in the queue. In those days the boys got the land and the girls got husbands.'

'What did your father do?' Kennedy asked, exercising some severe butt-clenching and hoping the question would fly.

'Oh, he went off to play soldiers,' Doris began with a sigh. 'Listen, we'd better go and rescue your friend or Blackie will have his breakfast run off him.'

At that she turned and left the room, shooting Kennedy's subtle probing down in flames.

'Sorry,' Kennedy began. 'I've got to ask you this, you know, for our inquiries and all that.'

Doris paused and looked around, not directly at Kennedy but at one of the photos on the wall. She threw Kennedy a "Well?" shrug of the shoulders.

'Would you know anything else about your father, his work, his friends, did he marry again, would you have any photographs?'

Doris interrupted Kennedy with a 'tut' and a click of her tongue. Kennedy felt he was going to receive a negative reply, or even worse a non-reply, so he cut off her chance of a reply.

'Look, I know a little of what you feel about him, but he's

dead. He died in mysterious circumstances and my job is to try and find out what happened to him and why it happened, and that hopefully leads us to who did this to him. The obvious starting point is to build up a picture of him and his life. At this point you are our only lead, so I have to push you.'

'Detective, if I'm your only lead I feel very sorry for you,' Doris began, still not looking Kennedy in the eye. 'Literally, I know nothing about Victor. That might be because I chose not to have anything to do with him, but the end result is pretty much the same. I know nothing about him other than what I've told you. There might be another old photograph somewhere around here but that's the height of it. Now, let's rescue Blackie.'

'Yeah, you're right, let's rescue McCusker,' Kennedy replied, drawing a warm smile from Doris. Kennedy continued in the more conversational tone: 'Tell me, do you ever go across to London?'

'Why on earth did you ask that? Did you want to meet me for a drink or something then?' Doris replied coyly.

'No, no. I meant... ah... more...' Kennedy stuttered.

'I know exactly what you meant, Inspector Kennedy.'

Chapter Eight

TEN MINUTES LATER, Kennedy – photograph of Victor Dugdale safe in his inside pocket – was *en route* to Portrush, wondering if Doris Dugdale had been telling the absolute truth when she said she hadn't been off the island (Ireland) since she'd come back home to look after her mother. ann rea, on the other hand, was having great difficulty interviewing Reverend Houston. He wasn't being awkward or anything like that. It was just that, well, ann rea felt a translator would not have been out of the question. Although both interviewer and interviewee spoke the same language (English), the Ulster interpretation was somewhat more personalised than ann rea had come across on the mainland. She tried to concentrate on Kennedy's advice: "When in doubt, repeat the word in your own mind. The majority of times you'll find that your pronunciation will also be your interpretation."

The journey to Ballyneagh had been easy enough. She'd found a radio station that was playing '60s classics: records like World Without Love by Peter & Gordon; Lazy Sunday Afternoon by The Small Faces; Prince of Heaven by local band Fruupp; Waterloo Sunset by The Kinks; and Here Comes the Sun by The Beatles. All fine music and in fact, ann rea was so immersed in the power of pop that she failed to take her exit off the main Derry road. A quick trio of left-hand turns and she was back *en route* again. But that's when the trouble began.

She knew she was in trouble when she stopped to ask directions of a particular gentleman, a farmer she guessed by his dress, and he said:

'Aye, ach it's a ferr wee dander, sa quare distance. Sprout thee mints 'til ye reach vision chops shop, turn rit, go to the roundabout, take the tenpastoo exit, second left, turn rit agin and it's the bigin, a red breek 'ouse on the rit. Mind ye dump the jam jar and walk. If ye walk fast yer'll be there in half the time.'

'Right.' What on earth was your man on about, ann rea wondered as she started the car up again. Luckily enough she spotted a member of the RUC who not only friendly but also spoke a decipherable version of the Queen's English.

The Reverend Steven Houston was out, supposedly chasing church mice that sang. Or at least that was what ann rea thought his cleaner said. She left her car at the rectory and went off in search of the only other address she had; that of the concerned parishioner who had rung up the journalist Neena McDoo from the *Mid Ulster Mail* in the first place. Miss Porter, a fifty-five-year-old spinster was apparently braver on the phone than she was in a face-to-face situation and the exchange was conducted through a seven-inch opening of the door. ann rea couldn't be sure but she was convinced that Miss Porter had her knee against the door to offer resistance to the foreign journalist, should resistance be needed. Miss Porter repeated that she "for one, and there are many others about here who agree with me but are too feeble to come forward" felt that it was a scandal that the common assets of the parish, "the finest wooden walls in the north", should have been sold just so that Judas (the caretaker, a Mr Terence Best) could have his "thirty pieces of silver". Five thousand pounds as near as dammit in real money, ann rea figured.

The only other information ann rea managed to extract from behind the green door was that the same Terry Best lived just around the corner from the rectory in a "wee white-washed thatched cottage that we, the church, also pay for, so there!" ann rea wandered off in that general direction, bemused and saddened. Saddened at how some people channel their energy into something so negative, especially when at the heart of it all (the church) was meant to be something so positive. Not a discussion she wanted to get into in these parts, she thought as she walked on. The other thing that saddened her was the fact that the beautiful blue sky of the morning had disappeared behind grey clouds and it was mizzling. Kennedy had often explained to her the phenomenon of mizzling and his explanation had been exactly on the button. Mizzle was a very gentle rainfall, very small raindrops that were velvety soft and floated down from the clouds rather than fell. It was actually pleasant, not to mention very refreshing, and she'd been thinking all this time that Kennedy had been having her on.

Terence Best was about fifty years old, ann rea guessed from his receding hairline, the crow's-feet around his eyes and that he appeared, in his movements, to be dealing with the fact that his body was slowing down and was not as responsive or as agile as it had once been. He was very prim and proper, lived by himself, had no sense of humour, and was dressed for his work in a pair of blue dungarees (which he'd definitely got his money's worth from). Partially hiding behind the bib of the dungarees was a starched white shirt and a tie. ann rea could make out the multi-repeated emblem on the tie but it was obviously some club or other, she thought. He wore a black pair of badly shined hobnail boots and was topped off with a brown-checked cloth cap.

He was, ann rea felt, unusual for an Ulsterman in that, although he answered each and every one of her questions, he said nothing beyond that nor instigated any conversation of his own. Thankfully, for ann rea, he was easy to understand.

Yes, he had stripped the oak wood from the rectory walls.

Yes, Rev Houston was aware he had done so.

Yes, Rev Houston had approved him doing so.

Yes, five grand had been paid for the wood.

Yes, he did think it was a lot of money.

No, he did not think he was selling off a parish asset.

No, he did not think the money should have gone to the church.

No, he hadn't pocketed all the money. Some had gone towards the shipping cost of sending the timber to London.

No, he hadn't pocketed the balance. The balance had gone towards a field trip for several members of the parish.

No, he did not feel it was appropriate to tell ann rea who was on the trip and where it was too.

Why? Because it was none of her business and she and her like and Miss Porter would hound everyone else the way they'd been hounding him.

Yes, he'd worked for the church since he left school.

No, there hadn't been many ministers during that time.

Yes, Rev Houston had been the minister a long time.

Yes, the Rev Houston had been the minister all the time he was there.

Yes, his cottage was the property of the church.

Yes, it had always been the caretaker's cottage.

No, he'd never sold anything else of the church's.

Yes, he did think the walls looked better painted.

No, he wasn't shocked that the wood was worth that much money.

No, there were no plans to sell other parts of the rectory.

No, there were no plans to sell any parts of the church.

No, he didn't dislike Miss Porter.

No, he and Miss Porter had never fought about anything else.

No, he and Miss Porter had never had a major falling out.

No, he was not aware of any other members of Miss Porter's family.

No, he didn't know where the minister was.

No, he didn't know when the minister would be back.

Just as ann rea felt like she was running out of questions, Terence Best offered up his first and only question of the one-way conversation.

'If that's all, do you mind if I go? I've a grave to dig.'ann rea looked at him, leaning against his red front door as he had during the entire exchange, hands either folded or clasped behind the bib of his dungarees. Occasionally he would take one of the hands out and use it to remove his cloth cap, which he would rub his forehead with before replacing the cap to its original position and the hand back into the comfort and safety of the bib.

'Yes, that'll be fine,' ann rea replied. 'Thanks for all your info.' She couldn't be sure but she thought he was breathing a sigh of relief. And was that just possibly a hint of a smile she spotted? It was hard to tell, though, through his few days' growth of a reddish-grey beard.

Next on her list to visit was the Reverend Steven Houston. ann rea decided that a return to the rectory was a waste of time; well, at least for the time being. Neither the housekeeper nor the caretaker was aware of the leader of the congregation's movements. However, Mr Best had said that he was off to dig a grave, as one does, ann rea supposed, when one is the church caretaker. Now did one dig a grave just before the funeral, as in hours, or did one dig it the day before? If it was the former then at least she knew where the Reverend Houston would be in a couple of hours' time.

She was amused at herself for putting a Kennedy-type logic onto the situation. She wondered what he would do at this point. Agh, that's it, she thought, Kennedy would start at the church. So off she sauntered in the general direction of the church. She assumed, correctly as it happens, that the spire she'd spied at the other end of the village – and the only spire in view from her side of town – was in fact Houston's house of praise.

The mizzle had ceased and she enjoyed window-shopping along the route, mostly in dinky antique shops, as she held her thoughts on Kennedy. She was so happy that they had got beyond the big "where are we going and are we going to go there together?" hurdle in their relationship. These days they just got on with being together. No, it may not be for happy ever after but yes, they were happy. She didn't know whether she really loved him or not but she felt great about the fact that neither of them was preoccupied with that one little point any more. Kennedy was a good man to be with. He was kind, considerate, clean, handsome –(not stunning but pleasing to the eye), dressed well (but wasn't preoccupied with clothes), amusing (but rarely conscious of the fact), and if he had his darker moments he'd either learnt to live with them or kept them completely to himself so successfully that she wasn't aware of any. He was also a caring, loving partner who pulled his weight; this could have been a by-product of living by himself all those years.

He wasn't perfect, though; not by any means. He'd his little quirks and foibles, for which ann rea was eternally grateful. She couldn't bear to live (not to mention sleep) with anyone who was either perfect or thought they were perfect. Talking about things spiritual, the amazing powder-blue sky above ann rea was now blocked out by the steeple of St Gabrielle's. The notice board at the gates of the church advised the flock of the times of the various services, all conducted, ann rea was happy to note, by the very Reverend Steven John Houston.

The church was an old church, a very old church covered in ivy, but from the look of the windows and roof, in a good state of repairs. It was small and the path from the front gate to the door of the church was lined with a grove of trees. There was also a pathway to the side that led, ann rea assumed, to the graveyard. She tried the handle on one of the grand double oak doors and it gave way and she pushed hard on the door until eventually it creaked open. This door opened into a small hallway with a notice board on the left and two large, black-marble stones mounted on the wall to the right. The one at eye-level was headed 1918-1919 and a list of sixty names had been masterly carved out of the stone. ann rea figured they were all casualties of the First World War. From the perfect position on the wall, the locals had apparently reckoned that it was to be the only war. But high above this stone was another one bearing the legend 1939-1945 and that listed about eighty names.

Eighty families in the small community who grieved over lost ones. A few families like the Savages and the Kanes had lost more that one member ann rea noted as she found herself involuntarily going through the list reading the names, not taking them in just marking their presence as a sign of respect. She thought of the poor stonemason who had spent his life mastering his art only to have to spend hours carving each of these names. How long did it take him to carve each letter, let alone a name? He probably knew each and every one of the people whose names he was cutting into the marble. ann rea suddenly had this vision of the master craftsman leaning over the stone, chisel in one hand, wooden mallet in the other, chip-chipping away, the chisel's cuts eased by the stonemason's teardrops. He would have known his work was to be the only outward, lasting sign of the soldiers on this planet. Obviously their families' love counted as well but in a hundred years' time, these two plaques would be all that was left to show that these people had died for their country.

She found herself wondering where they would find a wall big enough to house the names of those poor souls lost in the 1968-1999 battle.

A voice from behind her said: 'Ar youse in playin close?' ann rea turned quickly, startled and shaken from her solemn thoughts.

'Sorry?' she found herself saying to a clergyman.

'Are yew, you know, the pol-ice, you know, in plain clothes?' he repeated, this time laughing a little.

'Oh, sorry no, no, not at all.'

'Are yew wunna them?'

'Sorry?' ann rea said again not really amused at this farce; an English person and an Ulster person separated by the one common language.

'Ahm, what religion are you?' the minister began adding by way of explanation. 'You see, none of ours would ever spend time reading those plaques.'

Either her ears were getting used to his dialect or he was smoothing it out for her but now she was at least able to pick up on the majority of his words.

'Well, I'm not one of them as a matter of a fact, but neither am I one of…'

He cut her off with a laugh and then said, 'Oh, yew wanna those with a sore bum.'ann rea took an instant dislike to this man of the cloth; it wasn't just his lack of charm or graciousness, or his falseness, which she guessed came from the "The secret of success is sincerity, once you can fake that you have it made" school. No it wasn't any of the above. It was the way she was convinced he was a lech; undressing her with his eyes. She was aware of all the mixed signals women are supposed to give off; if you looked great, took care and pride in your turnout, clothes, hair, make-up, etc., were you really going to all that trouble for the benefit of the likes of Houston to get his rocks off? She knew that, for herself, she liked to feel good and taking care of her appearance make her feel great. She also knew, because she could see it in Kennedy, that when a man and a woman are in a healthy mental, spiritual and physical relationship they wear a sexual confidence. To the outsider, possibly, this may come across as flirting, but the reality was she was wearing a mini-skirt because it was warm and she knew her legs looked good; she had her black hair in a Beatles bob because that's the way she liked to wear it; her eyes looked the way they did probably because there was some oriental blood in her heritage; she wore a crisp, white T-shirt not because it was tight and showed off her breasts but because it was clean. The overall package was not meant as a sexy presentation but as a pride flag showing someone totally at peace with themselves, their life and their look.

But what was it about men (and before that, boys) and the way they look at women (and girls) and what exactly was the gratification they received from that? What was it about a bum that made some men catch their breath? ann rea had even noticed Kennedy's head being turned by a well-packaged behind. That, after all, was all that it was – packaging. How well the jeans or slacks fitted. Tailored to pull this bit up and let that bit drop. But that was all it took, a pair of well-chosen jeans. And the multitude of sins they could hide. Men were so naive when it came right down to it, you know. They'd be turned on by the swagger of a rump, that's all it took; little did they know that under the denim there were a potential mine-field of disasters waiting to be revealed. To fill the jeans well they had to have a full enough figure to squeeze in in the first place. That usually meant there was a spare pound or two of flab around. There were also the possibilities of thin ankles, fat ankles, farm-girl's knees, varicose veins and cellulite. Hell, if you wanted to go further than that, all that really was under the jeans was skin, fat, bones, blood and the human waste-disposal system. What was so sensual about that?

Why did men want, so badly, to see up a lady's skirt, down her blouse? Seemingly otherwise intelligent men would hold back while climbing stairs for that glimpse of something no more shocking than a little bit of stocking. What was that all about? They'd glance in the most unusual of shop windows just to catch a glimpse of a reflection of a woman with a revealing blouse. Why? What good did it do them? Breasts were certainly overrated, ann rea thought, not particularly pretty really, when you think of it. Functional, yes, when it came to succouring the offspring but why did men and boys react so? Did they do it because they were told from the begin-ning that that was what they had to do, because that was what being a man was all about? ann rea knew Kennedy preferred the mystery of it all, for their intimacy to be private, for their moments to be special, and that he would never cheat on her. But that didn't stop him looking and she knew he wasn't look-ing to cop a cheap thrill. He, like all men, just couldn't help themselves looking.

Maybe she just found it particularly rude and upsetting when the man looking at you did it in your presence and didn't care that you'd caught him doing it; in fact, even continued to do it – undress you with his eyes – after you'd caught him. That was just leching and surely ministers were meant to spiritually be beyond all of that. Weren't they meant to be in love with God or something?

She felt like saying to this particular minister: "If your right eye offends thee, pluck it out mate 'cause if you don't I'll poke it out for you."

Instead she retained her cool and politely asked: 'Would you know the whereabouts of Reverend Houston?'

The look of the lech disappeared as if the chap had benefited from divine intervention.

'Actually, I am he,' Houston offered. 'And what can I do for you?'

Now that he'd stopped leching after her she actually looked at the man for the first time. He'd a whiskey-red nose. That was the first thing she noticed about him. The bottle had done similar damage to his cheeks. He'd thinning, longish brown hair, all combed back. His hands were perfectly manicured and his clothes were all black, excepting for the dog collar. It was a classic black, not the cheap grey-black or shiny black – no, it was an expensive black. He was tall, less than an inch short of six foot, and slim but with the outward signs of his good living evident in his potbelly. ann rea thought he looked like someone who was about four months' pregnant. She smiled at this thought; a divine intervention of a different kind. ann rea introduced herself and told him about Miss Porter's call.

The reverend smiled and then said: 'Ah yes, Miss Porter, a particularly diligent member of Our Lord's flock. Why don't we go through to the back to the vestry and have Mrs McGonigle bring us some refreshments and you can conduct your interview there.'

'It's a storm in a tea cup,' Houston started up again five minutes later. They were sitting down in the vestry, which was immediately behind the pulpit. Lots of ornate wood still proudly on view in this small room; perhaps that's why he had brought her here to this private room, so that she could see for

herself that it wasn't all-out exploitation. They were enjoying
an inky tasting cup of tea and ann rea was trying to figure out
how much of it she would have to drink in order to be able to
still claim to have good manners. It was going to be difficult,
very difficult.

Reverend Houston cleared his throat and continued: 'You
see, the problem with do-gooders, with people that subscribe
to you with their fifty pence in the plate every Sunday morning, is that they think they own you. They think they are
shareholders in the company. They think that fifty-pence
piece and their misguided belief in the Saviour gives them the
right to have a say in something that really doesn't concern
them.'ann rea felt she couldn't let this go. 'Does she not have
a point though? The wood from the walls at the rectory was
sold for a staggering five thousand pounds. Doesn't someone
have to account for that?'

'As far as I can see, the main difference, perhaps the only
difference, between yourself and Miss Porter is that Miss
Porter at least gives us fifty pence a week.'

'Pardon?' ann rea replied in total disbelief.

'Now,' Houston continued ignoring ann rea, 'if we were
taking things out of the church – gold vessels, the eagle bible
stand, some of our antique bits and pieces – then that would
be a different thing altogether. But the rectory is my personal,
private residence and how I choose to decorate it concerns no
one but myself.'

'Sorry, does that mean you actually own the rectory?'

'Why no, of course not,' Houston shot back, unperturbed.
'Obviously the church owns the deeds to the rectory, as it does
to the caretaker's cottage and some of the alms houses around
the village, but that doesn't mean to say the church goes into
each of these premises and dictates how they should be deco-
rated. It's the 1990s, Miss rea, we've been in the dark ages too
long. I decided that I didn't want to live in dark, oppressive
surroundings. I decided that I wanted to live in an enlightened
environment. So out went the dark walls. It's as simple as
that.'

'Well it wasn't quite as simple as that, was it, Reverend?
The discarded wood realised a grand total of five thousand
pounds when it was sold in London.'

'Shows we have quite an enterprising caretaker, doesn't it?'

'Well some, like Miss Porter, may level a charge of exploitation at him rather than praising him for being enterprising,' ann rea continued, voice calm, showing signs of neither anger nor accusatory undertones.

Houston said nothing. ann rea consulted her notes. She needn't have but she wanted Houston to know that she already had the piece of information she was about to refer to.

'Mr Terence Best, I see, organised a trip with these funds?'

'Yes. Yes he did, actually,' Houston replied, getting back his steam again.

'Could you possibly tell me if this was a church-endorsed trip?'

'Why of course.'

'Good,' ann rea returned quickly. 'Could you give me the details of where it was to, when it was and who went on it, and could I also see some costings and official paperwork for the trip, please?'

'I think you'll find that over here,' Houston began, replacing his cup on its saucer. ann rea noticed he'd drunk as little of the liquid as she had. 'Over here, what with our special circumstances and all, church business is private business and I'm not at liberty to disclose such information.'

'But you have to. You said it was church-endorsed.'

Houston shone her one of his most insincere (Hughie Green-type) smiles, displaying well-worn and badly kept molars, yellow both in tone and smell. 'I don't have to do anything. Anything other than bid you good-day, Miss rea.'

He walked over to the corner of the room without changing his smile – even by the slightest fraction – opened the door, and with a flamboyant gesture of his free hand, invited ann rea to be on her way.

Chapter Nine

KENNEDY AND MCCUSKER were back in Portrush by the time ann rea had been shown the door by the Reverend Houston.

In fact, that (fact) is not one hundred percent accurate. If the truth be told here and, in this, it is important that the truth be told, at the exact moment ann rea was walking the plank, so to speak, Kennedy was not only back in the police barracks in Portrush but he'd also been shown to a temporary office and been on the phone to North Bridge House to advise DS Irvine of Victor Dugdale's London address.

Consequently, as one door on the case was closing (the Rev Houston's church), another (Victor Dugdale's last known address) was opening.

Opened, in fact, by the concierge at Regents Heights, the mansion block on Prince Albert Road, overlooking Regents Park.

'Aye,' the concierge agreed as he held the door open for DS James Irvine and WPC Anne Coles. 'I haven't seen Mr Dugdale around for quite some time since.'

'Did he have a habit of disappearing?' Coles inquired as she gave the hallway a quick once-over.

'When people have the kind of money it takes to buy one of these here apartments,' the concierge began – he was fifty(ish), friendly (ish), tidy(ish) and bland(ish) – 'then they're also buying a certain amount of privacy.' He immediately estimated the amount of privacy by announcing: 'His cleaner comes in every Tuesday and Thursday for an hour or two. She might be able to help you more.'

The concierge paused for a moment. He was dressed in a quiet grey uniform. The only reason either Coles or Irvine was aware that he was, in fact, wearing a uniform at all was because it was identical to the uniform worn by his colleague. Both men had greeted the police at the reception area on the ground floor. Mr Billings had obviously been the senior of the two, for it had been he who had volunteered that his colleague, Mr Bagley, would let them into the apartment while he remained at the helm of the block: the teak reception desk complete with several television monitors, telephones, notepads, microphones, red buttons and clocks, everything bar the captain's wheel in fact.

'You just said: "Had he a habit of disappearing?" Does that mean he's dead?' Mr Bagley asked.

'We're not entirely sure,' Coles replied, very matter of fact and keen not to give too much away. 'We're currently trying to trace him as part of our investigation.'

Mr Bagley seemed reluctant to leave Irvine and Coles to carry on with their work and search the apartment.

'Okay, I'll just stay here by the door until you've concluded your search,' he said, giving a fair impression of someone kicking their heels.

Coles was about to respond but didn't bother. She wondered was Mr Bagley just doing his job by making sure nothing "walked" from Victor Dugdale's premises under his shift, or could he possibly be saving some of the valuables for himself?

Irvine was obviously sharing her thoughts because he radioed to North Bridge House and requested a couple of constables to be sent over to Regents Heights immediately to secure the premises.

Meanwhile Coles started the search. Well, she didn't really start the search; she walked down the hall, opened the door at the end and crossed the room. At first glance the room looked like a living room or a lounge. Then the view out of the window caught her eye and the scene transfixed her.

It was the most amazing panoramic view of Regents Park she'd ever seen; particularly on such a day with the sunlight highlighting the thousands of greens. Yes, thousands of greens. Kennedy was forever telling them that he could work out how Johnny Cash had been to Ireland, not once but several times, and had seen only forty shades of green. Anyway, Regents Park's thousands of greens were being back-lit with the numerous rays of sunshine, which frequently broke the clouds in shafts of sacred light that looked, well, spiritual summed it up best for Coles.

'Well, if there is a God, He's surely not unhappy with us to-day,' Irvine announced from behind her. 'In the meantime, if we're to avoid the wrath of our leader we'd better get on with this search.'

So, methodically, they went about the rooms of the apartment together, both wearing gloves in order to protect what, if anything, might be there. After forty-five minutes they came to the conclusion (a point they discussed) that the room looked like a hotel room after the guest(s) had checked out and gone about their business.

There were no traces whatsoever of Victor Dugdale. No pictures, or letters, or mementoes. There were no traces of the man, no passports, no bills, no clothes, no toothbrush, no shaving gear, no shoes, no nothing in fact.

Irvine went back out to the hallway and found Mr Bagley still loitering with intent.

'Tell me, how long has Victor Dugdale lived here?'

'Well, let's see now. Mr Billings could give you the exact length of time but I'd have to say at least thirteen years. Yes. I've been working here about nine years now and I think I can remember Mr Billings saying that Number Five had been here about four years at that point.'

'Have you ever been in here before?' Coles asked as she walked down the hallway to join them.

'No,' Mr Bagley replied in the general direction of her chest.

'Never?' she said. She hunkered down slightly to catch his stare.

Mr Bagley shook his head violently as though he was snapping out of something. He looked embarrassed, only a little, and replied:

'No, never.' He'd regained his confidence and composure. 'I've brought people up to the door of Number Five before but this…' he paused to look around the hallway, 'is as far as I've ever been. We're not encouraged to go into the apartments unless, of course, we're invited and in those rare instances, Mr Billings, with his seniority, is always the one who goes in.'

'Did you know him well?' Irvine asked.

'As I say, our clients pay for their privacy and we're not encouraged to become familiar with the tenants,' Mr Bagley replied as he smiled to himself before continuing. 'We're not like taxi drivers, you know.'

'Tell me,' Irvine continued, choosing to ignore Mr Bagley's attempt at humour. 'Would there be a safe, or any similar security facility you offer to your tenants?'

Mr Bagley seemed unsure as to how he should reply, betraying how he'd gotten to be fifty-something and still continued to be someone's junior.

'Ah, you'll have to check that with Mr Billings. We're not encouraged to discuss our security arrangements with outside parties.'

'Don't you find it peculiar, though,' Irvine continued, appearing to lose a little of his patience with the man, 'that someone, one of your tenants for instance, would be here for something like thirteen years and not leave one little bit of themselves or their personality about the place?'

'Perhaps they'd something to hi…' Mr Bagley started but then he appeared to think better of it and he stopped short, calling on the Three Monkeys he was encouraged by his employers to impersonate: "Hear nothing, see nothing, say nothing".

'Agh, come on,' Irvine laughed, directing his sentence to Mr Bagley. He then appeared to think better of it, just like Mr Bagley had done, and turned to Coles and added: 'Let's go down and have a chat with Mr Billings.'

Ten minutes later, Coles and Irvine were in their unmarked car and making their way back to North Bridge House.

'That's got to be the strangest thing I've ever seen. Someone living in a place for thirteen years and not a trace of him in sight,' Irvine began.

'Unless someone had come in and cleared the place out,' Coles offered.

'Mr Billings says not,' Irvine said, reminding her of the brief conversation they had had with the senior concierge.

'But that could simply be because if someone did, it would prove that he wasn't doing his job properly,' Coles replied, somewhat bemused by Irvine's current state. She couldn't quite work out if it was due to the fact that as Kennedy was in Ireland, Irvine took it upon himself to take charge of the case, or at least the UK part of the investigation. Or perhaps his state of apparent anxiety was due entirely to the lack of personality around Victor Dugdale's apartment.

'Perhaps we'll find out a lot more when we get into the safe-deposit box,' she offered, trying to calm the troubled waters.'

'Well, if we're to believe Mr Billings that his firm are not like Harrods and they don't have the other keys to the boxes, we're going to have to get a court order to break into the box to solve this particular puzzle,' Irvine replied with a sigh. 'I'd better get onto Kennedy and bring him up to date. Not that that's going to take very long, mind you.'

'Ah, but don't forget that as Kennedy would often say: " When you find nothing it can say as much as a roomful of clues."'

'Aye and that's exactly what I'm worried about; it's saying absolutely nothing at all to me.'

Coles felt it was time to change the line of conversation:

'So, ann rea is over there with him?'

'It would appear so.'

'What's that all about? Why didn't he take one of us over with him if he's working on this case?' Coles said, searching for a bit of evidence in a mystery that was intriguing her much more than Dugdale's apartment.

'That's not a little bit of personal interest I'm detecting there is it, DS Coles?' Irvine began with a smirk and added as an apparent afterthought, before she had a chance to respond: 'You know, of course, that in the CID we don't encourage personal interest in fellow officers.'

It was Coles' turn to impersonate Mr Bagley as she sank deep into her car seat and said absolutely nothing.

Chapter Ten

'WE'RE ON THE right track,' Kennedy announced into the mouthpiece of a cumbersome-shaped cream handset.

'But it's an empty track,' a brittle Scottish voice replied through the earpiece.

'Just because a road doesn't have a signpost, doesn't mean it doesn't go anywhere.'

'Yes, quite, ahm…' Irvine was clearly struggling.

'Don't you see?' Kennedy said, interrupting Irvine. He always found it easier to do, interrupt that was, in a telephone conversation than in, say, a face-to-face conversation. 'We're trying to put flesh on the bones of Victor Dugdale. The more we find out about him and his family, his friends, even his enemies – maybe even particularly his enemies – then the more chance we have of finding out what happened to him.'

'Yes… but…' Irvine started.

'So,' Kennedy continued as though Irvine had remained silent, 'someone is trying to hide his past from us, which of course means that there is something to hide. So the sooner we can find that out, or at least a hint or a clue as to what it might be, the sooner we can get to the bottom of this.'

'You mean the safe-deposit box?'

'The safe-deposit box,' Kennedy confirmed.

'Well, the good news is the Super is on to that even as we speak. He thinks it will take until tomorrow afternoon to secure the necessary permission and court order to allow us to open it.'

'Good,' Kennedy announced and before he had time to offer any praise Irvine continued:

'We're going back to Regents Heights at seven o'clock this evening to speak to the neighbours. According to Mr Billings, most of the tenants are home by that time. I'm hoping that someone will be able to give us some more information on Dugdale.'

'Of course you're going to interview the cleaner?' Kennedy said as an afterthought.

'Of course,' Irvine replied, breaking at least two of the Commandments.

'Good, good. Keep me posted won't you?' Kennedy said and this time, before Irvine had a chance to reply, Kennedy had disconnected the telephone line, leaving him with nothing but an earful of electronic crackle, a reddening face and thoughts of the very mysterious Victor Dugdale.

DS Irvine tried to imagine a scenario whereby someone could alienate his wife, his daughter, have no visible friends or colleagues and be disliked enough that someone would want to murder him. Either that or scare him to death, like the way Victor Dugdale had suffered a fatal heart attack. Mind you, with what happened to his body afterwards Irvine wasn't so sure that Dugdale was better off dying when he did.

Now there was a point. What if Dugdale had died before his captors had wanted him to? Before they'd a chance to wreak havoc on his poor, weary limbs? And if so, how had that affected things. Irvine wondered had Kennedy considered that point?

Irvine also wondered how Dugdale had lived to be so old in the first place if he'd such vehement enemies. Such thoughts were still bothering him in North Bridge House as he returned the handset to the cradle of his phone.

No sooner had Kennedy replaced his handset, which in fact resembled the Hunchback of Notre Dame more than it did a telephone, than it rang again, springing into life before he'd had a chance to remove his hand from the objectionable design. The ringing sounded more like a cat purring than the good old coin-box telephone rings. But then again, the originals had needed to be able to wake up an entire village whereas the new one needed only to disturb a policeman from his slumber.

It was the desk sergeant.

'Aye, there's a wee girl here who's askin' for ye,' the Ulster-speak spoke.

Kennedy immediately assumed it was ann rea and said he'd be right out. He fancied getting out of the station for a bit and there was no better an excuse. He found it difficult just to sit around and think, particularly in a strange office.

He felt compelled to be working at something, anything, on someone else's turf. Was that just because he didn't want to be found appearing to being idle? Was that part of his inbred Ulster work ethic? ann rea would know for sure. But then again, he thought as he grabbed his jacket, it wasn't really a question he could ask her. Was it?

There were a few things you (he) just couldn't discuss with ann rea, and some things she couldn't discuss with him, he felt. He didn't feel that this was a flaw, however, on either side. At one time in his life he would have thought that it was; a flaw not to be able to discuss everything. You know, when you met the lady of your dreams, that was one of the ways that you would know it was she, because you could discuss absolutely everything with her.

Not so. Or at least that's how he now felt. He felt that the little bits that you keep to yourself made you yourself.

Either way, on this occasion at least, it didn't matter: he wasn't going to ask ann rea the question about the end result of his Ulster work ethic because it wasn't ann rea waiting for him in the reception of the Portrush Police Barracks – it was Doris Dugdale.

Chapter Eleven

'OH, HELLO,' DORIS Dugdale said, rising from her chair and putting out her hand and then withdrawing it.

'Hello again,' Kennedy replied, diffusing the situation by leaning across to her, putting his hand on her shoulder and giving her a quick peck on the cheek. He hoped that his disappointment wasn't his predominant air. 'So you're the wee girl?'

'Well, it's the first time in years that I've been called a wee girl. But I didn't want to correct the handsome young boy here. I thought it just might get you out in double-quick time.'

'Would you like to come through?' Kennedy asked as he used his right hand to show her back from whence he came.

Miss Doris Dugdale started to move in that general direction but then Stopped, mid-step.

'No, I'll tell you what. It's such a beautiful day outside, let's go for a walk on the Strand and I'll stand you a candy floss or maybe even some Daulse or Yellowman if you're very lucky.'

'Make it a lollipop and you've got a deal,' Kennedy said, only half in jest and then turned to advise the desk sergeant: 'Could you please tell Inspector McCusker that I'm out for a while with Miss Dugdale and I'll see him when I get back.'

Kennedy was about to leave a further message, one for ann rea. But he didn't and what's more, he didn't know why he didn't leave a message for her.

Like all Ulster women, Doris Dugdale was a quick walker and in no time at all they had walked back into town leaving Barry's behind them as they took a right down towards the remainder of the Arcadia Ballroom, on further down and eventually onto the sandy beach.

Kennedy felt somewhat cheated initially but said nothing, and luckily he didn't. About five minutes' walk on the beach and they came across their first ice-cream vendor.

'Right, what'll it be?' she announced, proving that she intended to keep her promise.

Kennedy, no longer familiar with any of the names on display and with no 99s in sight, pointed to a picture of his chosen lollipop. It was a rocket-shaped affair, which appeared to be made of ice cream streaked with strawberry flavouring and covered in a light chocolate. It was called a 'Strawberry Apollo' and the second he bit into the fumeless rocket he realised he had made the correct choice.

It was also the exact same second he realised that Doris Dugdale had changed her clothing since their earlier meeting.

She was now wearing a flimsy blue dress with white polka dots, which the wind had a (good) habit of drawing about her contours, showing them off to best advantage. She was neither brazen nor shy about the wind's flattering assistance. She probably never even gave it a second thought, and why would she?

Her sandals where probably the least flattering of all her clothes in that they revealed that she wasn't quite as young as she'd like to be. Kennedy thought that feet and ankles tend to age (and show their age) quicker than the rest of the body because whereas Doris' feet betrayed her late thirties/early forties, the rest of her would surely pass for someone in their late twenties, at worst.

A nice little pair of white ankle socks would have completed the illusion and no one, including Kennedy, would have been any the wiser. But then again he considered that illusions are rarely appreciated unless there is just one little flaw present with which to betray them.

The noise of the waves lapping twenty yards from them was like a continuous roar, which was all but drowning out the sounds of a day at the seaside; dogs barking; someone screaming with pleasure from possibly somewhere as far away as Barry's, maybe even a customer on their Little Big Dipper; an ice-cream van with its jingle playing loudly, travelling about the streets of Portrush; a transistor radio turned up so loud the speakers were distorting; several children shrieking with delight as the waves continuously chased them up the beach, always catching them and managing to wash the sand from their toes.

Kennedy and Doris Dugdale followed the tracks left by horses' hooves and Kennedy was amused by the fact that the hooves created not the double track that he would have supposed but (very) nearly a constant single line; like one you'd expect a two-legged horse to make.

They walked on and on in silence for what appeared to be ages. Kennedy turned back around to see how far the ice-cream vendor was behind them; that was the last time they had spoken. Now they had both, within seconds of each other, finished their lollipops.

He was shocked to see that the vendor was but a small dot on the horizon and the only sound he now heard was the sound of the waves desperate to come further and further inland, constantly driven on by some unstoppable force intent on reclaiming what was originally theirs.

Kennedy was enjoying himself. Enjoying the walk. Surprised at how much he was enjoying the walk.

'I find it great out here for clearing the head,' Doris said at last.

'Aye, it's grand all right,' Kennedy replied, turning to look at her for a moment. She was staring at the sand, picking her way. Her curly hair was all over the place but for some reason it didn't look a mess. That little hint of make-up that Kennedy thought would have worked wonders for her when they met earlier in her house had now been applied; a coat of lipstick – more pink than red – a little colouring to the cheeks, and even less eyeliner. Kennedy's earlier assessment had been correct; she was transformed and if she smiled as she had done in her cottage, well then, every man on the beach had better watch out.

'I can never work out, though, what it is that draws us to the sea, draws us to water,' she said, the wind catching her breath when she opened her mouth to speak.

Kennedy thought for a few seconds, tuning in to the sounds of his shoes crunching through the fine, soft sand.

'Perhaps it's the sound, the continuous thrashing, that makes you feel that no matter how alone you may be there's always something there. That can be very comforting,' Kennedy ventured, not entirely sure he could agree with himself. Sometimes you just have to spit the words out there into the universe to see what their shape looks like and how their tones sound.

'Perhaps,' she replied, taking a little skip, 'but I feel, with myself anyway, that I know it has a power, the sea that is, a power that can destroy and, by walking along so close to it, we have the ultimate control over its danger by being able to make the decision to avoid it.'

'Some of the time,' Kennedy felt compelled to add.

'Pardon?'

'You know,' Kennedy again turned to look at her but she was still staring at her sandals, 'sometimes we put ourselves in a position, on a boat, a ship, out swimming, where we can get into dangers we can't get out of.'

'Yes, of course, but even then we have the ultimate power over whether or not we go for a swim or venture into the boat or ship, or even an aeroplane.'

Again the sound of the waves was the only sound between them.

'Then of course,' she added at least a minute later, 'you have the ultimate power to surrender and walk into the waves.'

Something of a romantic view, Kennedy thought, but he felt he didn't know her well enough to contradict her.

They'd been in each other's company now for twenty-five minutes and Kennedy was still wondering why she'd come to see him. As if reading his mind she said:

'After you left the house I started to think of Victor. I started to think about him and about my mother.'

She stopped speaking and looked up from the beach, turned her head towards Kennedy and then looked beyond him to the wildness of the sea. In their reality the waves were as dangerous as a puppy dog but there were seven or eight youths trying to surf them. All were decked out in the required designer wet suits. A few bikini-clad girls would follow them out part of the way towards the waves, then they'd turn back towards the beach when the water reached their midriff thereby ensuring the water reached neither their hair nor their non-waterproof make-up.

'You're not really like a pol-iceman,' she began after a few minutes.

'Oh?'

'Well, you haven't asked me a question since we came on the beach.'

'Oh, you know, I figured you came to see me and if you'd
something to tell me then you will, in your own good time.'

'Neat. The thing is, though, I'm not so sure I came to tell
you something.'

'Oh?' Kennedy replied, unable to hide his disappointment.

'Agh good, you're a pol-iceman after all.'

They both laughed.

'It's just,' she began seemingly unsure of her words, 'when
you left I felt that I should have been feeling something, you
know, for Victor. My father. I hated myself for not caring that
he was dead. But it's just that some families get it so right. A
man meets a woman. A woman meets a man, the same man.
Something clicks and they fall in love, decide to marry and
start a family. They start to enjoy a family life. Now at that
point there is already a history. You know, both their parents
and the families their parents came from and the mixing up of
all of this stock.'

'Yes?' Kennedy prompted Doris Dugdale. He wasn't
exactly sure where this conversation was going, and a fight
three seagulls were having over an old leather boot that had
been washed up on the beach distracted him a little.

'So this man and this woman, they go off and start their
own family and try to make that work. I mean, I think they try
and make it work. But that's the thing about families you see,
it's all about working together to make it work. You have to
be totally unselfish. You have to... no... sorry that's wrong. I
was about to say that you have to make your plans for the
good of the family but that, in a way, implies a bit of selfish-
ness. But it's more that you plan rather than you have to plan.
Do you know what I mean?'

'I think I do. I think I see what you're getting at,' Kennedy
replied but as soon as he did he realised, from that blank look
on her face, that it had been a rhetorical question.

'Yes. So if the family plans are, in fact, family plans then the
family starts off from a position of strength. The father works
hard, not for himself but for the family. The wife works just as
hard but not as much to support her husband, it's more like it's
to support this third party that is the family unit. Then a child is
born and if the child is born into a *family*, a real family, then the
child at least has a chance. On the other hand, if the child is

born to two individuals who are more interested in themselves than in the family, then it's going to be a lot more difficult for that child. Don't you see? That child in turn, I'm sure, will have trouble starting a family of his or her own when the time comes.'

She frowned and turned and looked at Kennedy. He felt she was staring deep into his eyes, longing for his understanding. This time, however, he didn't respond to her rhetorical question.

Part of him was aware of what she was saying and part of him was thinking that this was rather a deep conversation for two people who hadn't known each other twenty-four hours ago to be having.

At the same time he was watching a motorboat speed up and down, close to the coast, and circling a small island about half a mile offshore. Every time the boat got close to the island, the noise of the high-powered engine drove scores of seagulls from their roost. Kennedy hadn't realised how big seagulls were. He was now convinced that they were big enough and strong enough to swoop down and pick up one of the babies, or even one of the small children, in the distance behind them.

'It's something I've been thinking a bit about recently and it's something that members of proper families never even think about because they have the power and comfort of the family life around them. I didn't. My mother brought me up. She and my father obviously got together for the wrong reasons and something happened. I don't know what it was that drove them apart, whose fault it was. Probably both. But one or both had dreams other than family dreams.'

'Do you think, though, that it was a conscious decision?'

'What, to split?'

'No...not to...' Kennedy faltered before finding the correct words to finish his question, 'pursue family values?'

'No. No. I think it's much more basic than that. I don't think that they actually had a choice. I think that my father was probably a selfish man and made some selfish decisions. I'm not entirely sure that makes him a bad person. I think a lot of us make hundreds of selfish decisions in the course of our day. But whatever decision he made, they were not family-orientated decisions.'

'What about the decision he made in choosing your
mother? What about the decision she made in accepting his
offer of marriage?' Kennedy asked. He wasn't entirely sure
but he felt there just might be something lurking beneath the
surface that might, just might, help him find out more about
Victor Dugdale. She mightn't even be sure what it was herself
and she might even be eager to help him find it.

'Well now, perhaps he wanted her because she looked
beautiful, perhaps he wanted her as a prize or trophy. Perhaps
he lusted after her and in those not-so-liberal times he had to
marry her before he could bed her. Perhaps she wanted him as
a way to escape her family. Hey, who knows, perhaps she
loved him. Whatever the reason, though, they weren't right
for each other and it didn't happen. That's the thing about
families I started to say at the beginning; some people have it
right and it's natural and it works. Of course that doesn't
mean it's always soft hay and green pastures because even in
families, even tight families, problems will come along. But
therein lies the main difference. Families will deal with the
problem as a family and the entire family will put their collective shoulder to the wheel and make their way out through the
most difficult of problems. Couples, non-families, whatever
you want to call them – I don't really know what to call the
unit that isn't a family, other than people like me and my
mother – people like us tend to deal with our problems selfishly, by ourselves, and that is where we really run into trouble.'

'But I'm sure you would have been there for your mother,
or your father for that matter if he'd have needed you?'

'My mother, yes, definitely. My father, no, never, and that's
the main point, you see, because I never, ever considered him
to be my father, because he wasn't… a father, you see, a real
father. You know, the foundation of the family. So our family
had no foundation and so it couldn't possibly survive. Now,
maybe because I grew up with my mother, I'm always going to
be of that opinion but the thing is, maybe he just didn't have a
choice in the matter. Maybe my mother decided that she had
made a mistake and maybe she dumped my dad. He never
married again, you know, so there could be something in that.
I've often wondered about that, was that some kind of sign?'

'What, you mean you think he may not have married again because he was still in love with your mother?'

Doris sighed, scrunching up her mouth so that her eyes were nearly closed and all the lines around her eyes were very noticeable. 'Oh, I doubt it. I'm sure if he had he could have made it work out somehow. Everyone loves a romantic.'

'What about… I mean, I don't even know if you're interested in finding out this stuff, but what about friends and neighbours who were around when you were growing up – did they ever make any reference to your dad, to your missing father?'

'No. There's never been any talk about him at all. It was like he never existed. In a way it was as though he'd been totally written out of our lives. And now that he's dead and my mother is dead I want… I need to move on. I want to stop being a daughter. I've been nothing but a daughter all my life and I know that I'll never, ever be part of a family.'

'Nagh, surely…'

'It's too late, Christy.'

'Nagh.'

'Yes. Don't you see, that's an important point for me? I know and accept that I don't have what it takes to be part of a successful family. Yes, there still is time for me to get married, and yes I still could possibly have children. But I don't have what it takes to be part of a successful family. And the real sad thing is that it's not even my fault. I don't think I could ever have done anything to change that eventuality.'

Kennedy thought it wiser not to say anything. He considered his own family and their structure. Was he stock from whom a successful family could spring? Did he have what it takes?

Doris Dugdale opened her purse again. She hoaked around in it for a time and, eventually, she produced a well-thumbed and aged piece of paper.

'After you and McCusker left the house I thought of the one piece of paper that still existed in the house and had some evidence of my father. I found it when my mother had died and I was going through her things. I was surprised she hadn't destroyed it,' Doris said as she continued to unfold the long, brown-coloured piece of paper. 'A marriage certificate,' Kennedy announced.

'The marriage certificate,' Doris agreed as she passed it over to the detective. 'I thought you might be able to trace their best man. I mean, the best man would have to have been his best friend, wouldn't he?'

'Well, yes,' Kennedy agreed as he read the name of the male witness who would also be the best man. 'It would appear to be a Mr Derek Shaw.'

'Yes, it would appear so.'

'Does the name mean anything to you?'

'Nope, sorry, not a thing,' she replied and then added: 'I suppose I could have given this to you at the barracks and saved you all this time. But I felt I wanted to chat with you. I didn't know exactly what I wanted to talk to you about. I just had this overpowering feeling earlier that you would be a good listener and you are, and I needed… Well, let's just say I feel a lot better after our walk and our chat. Maybe I have now stopped being a daughter. But as I say, I could have given this to you earlier.'

'What, and cheated me out of my Strawberry Apollo? No way!'

She laughed aloud and turned to face him.

'Look, I'm going to walk on for a while,' she began.

'I'll happily…'

'No, I think I'd like to be by myself for a time now.'

'Oh.'

'And you've a long way to walk back, it's a ferr wee distance,' she reminded him, slipping back into Ulster-speak.

He turned to see that Portrush was like a toy town on the horizon.

'But don't worry,' she added with a smile, 'if ye walk fast ye'll be there in half the time.'

They laughed again.

'Thank you,' she said as she took his hand to shake it. At the last moment she appeared to change her mind and she put her arm around his neck instead. She kissed him on the cheek and whispered directly into his ear: 'Thank you, Christy, I appreciate this more than you will ever know.'

And with that she turned and walked away by herself.

Doris Dugdale looked so sad as she walked along the beach. Her hair was blowing so violently about her head it looked like it was trying to lift her from the beach off into the air. Her dress, wind-assisted, had ballooned out behind her. She had to bend forward into the wind to move forward. She'd folded her arms about her chest the way solitary women do when they are outside, outside the protective arms of a family.

Kennedy carefully folded the marriage certificate and turned and headed back towards the centre of Portrush. The roar of the waves was now filling his ears and his thoughts.

Chapter Twelve

'MR DEREK SHAW!' McCusker said. It was twenty minutes later and Kennedy was back in the police barracks. 'No, I've never heard of him. Give me a couple of minutes though and I'll check with a few of my mates and run the name through the computer as well to see what we can come up with.'

'Good, thanks for that. Any news from ann rea?' Kennedy responded immediately. He was back in his makeshift office. His space was eight-foot square, it had no windows and was furnished with two grey-metal desks shoved together, two uncomfortable chairs and three filing cabinets. The decor was standard breeze blocks painted white. The Portrush Police Barracks, inhabited by McCusker (permanently) and Kennedy (for the duration of the case) was similar to the majority of the official buildings in Northern Ireland. A unique style of architecture known as 'Ulster Ephemeral'; not quite as classic as the Greek, or as grandiose as the English, nor even as regal as the Romans but, for all of that, very inexpensive to replace.

'Yes, actually, she rang when you were out on the beach for your walk with your woman. She's on the way back here now but apparently she had one more person to interview on her return journey. She said she should see you at about five o'clock,' McCusker said as he sauntered off, Kennedy assumed, in the direction of his mates with the computer.

Kennedy had hoped that ann rea would have been back by the time he'd returned from the beach. Now that he was left with time to kill it meant he had time to reflect on just how badly the case was going.

Yes, the following day at three in the afternoon he would have access to the contents of Victor Dugdale's safe-deposit box. And he now had the name Mr Derek Shaw. Fifty years ago, Shaw had been Dugdale's best man and, if he were still alive, he must certainly have some information on Dugdale.

But based on Kennedy's current lack of progress, he felt he was going to be very lucky to find Derek Shaw still alive.

The Camden Town detective had hardly enough information to keep his superintendent, Thomas Castle, happy. Luckily enough this was never an issue with Castle, who always seemed happy to let Kennedy "get on with it" and "follow his nose with the investigation". In spite of this however, he always encouraged his favourite detective inspector with: "Don't let it get too complicated, never be scared of the simple solution."

Kennedy would welcome any solution at this point, simple or otherwise. He couldn't remember a case where he had had so little to go on in terms of leads. Truth be told, if it hadn't been for ann rea he'd have absolutely nothing whatsoever to go on. This was certainly one instance where Kennedy felt that if Castle knew exactly what he had, his superior wouldn't be quite so confident about letting him follow his nose, successful and all as such an approach had been in the past.

Added to the above, Kennedy felt more than a little uncomfortable not being on his own patch. He was starting to appreciate all the little things he usually took for granted, like the efficient team back in North Bridge House, like the *Evening Standard*, BBC London 94.9 radio, Radio 4 and the *Camden News Journal*, all throwing up non-stop information, most of it not needed, or even wanted, but there was just something comforting about having it spat at you by these incessant, insomniac monsters.

Chapter Thirteen

ANN REA WAS also a long way from her patch (the exact same distance as Kennedy, in point of fact) and was in all probability seeking fodder for those selfsame aforementioned monsters. She, however, was enjoying a little more success than her detective lover at this point.

Her bone – again, not one with a lot of meat on it, she'd be the first to agree – was the excursion that had been paid for, seemingly, by the sale of the vicarage wood to the Black Cat Building in Camden Town.

She realised, she hoped, that the key to her mystery would be finding out the truth about this trip. Had the rare wood been sold to pay for this trip or, having already sold the wood, had Reverend Houston then proceeded to find suitable use for the funds?

On being shown the door by Houston, ann rea decided that the best thing would be to try and retrace her steps to see if she could pick up some more information about the excursion. At the end of the day she still had a story to write and this was still her only lead and, equally important, it was independent of what Kennedy was working on.

The caretaker, Terence Best, opened his door and was as friendly as apple pie to the Camden Town journalist.

'How did you get on with the Reverend Houston then?' he asked as he opened his door wider thereby, she assumed, inviting her in.

'Oh, very sociable he was. We'd a nice chat and then he gave me a personal tour of the church,' ann rea replied, crossing her fingers behind her back. As a journalist, she felt it was important never to tell a lie; well, *technically* never tell a lie would be closer to the truth. Stretching reality, well now, that was a totally different matter altogether, wasn't it.'

'We discussed the excursion,' ann rea continued, fingers

still firmly crossed.' Of course, Reverend Houston didn't have all the details as he wasn't, in fact, present on the junket. So I just thought I'd come back and talk to you again and see if you could fill in any of the missing details.'

Best stared at ann rea, looking more like someone who was expecting an answer than someone who was about to give it. She'd made two assumptions on the grounds that it would make it appear that she already had the inside track on this matter and thereby, by association, Reverend Houston's endorsement. At least that's what she wanted Best to think. The other assumption she had made was that Best himself had knowledge of the trip if, in fact, he hadn't been one of the actual day-trippers himself.

'I'm not exactly sure myself, to be honest. It was somewhere in the south of England and about two dozen or so went on it,' Best replied, beating ann rea at her own game.

'So which of the church's societies was behind the trip then?' ann rea pushed.

'Good question,' Best began. 'Now let's see if I can remember which of them it was. The problem nowadays is that we have so many societies the memberships crisscross quite a lot. So I'd have to think of a few of the names to pinpoint... Now let's see... the bridge club... yes, it might have been the bridge club because Paul and Robin were there. I'm sure... Yes...'

The caretaker's doorbell rang.

'Boys-a-dear,' Best announced as he rose from the chair beside the dead fire. 'It's busier here than Barry's of the Port today. I won't be a tick.' ann rea felt her fingers uncross as she heard the unmistakable tones of the Reverend Houston at the door. 'That scribe from the English papers is asking way too many questions.'

Houston stormed past Best into the living room and stopped dead in his tracks when he spotted ann rea.

'You've been very kind, Mr Best, but unfortunately I don't have time to take you up on your kind offer of tea. Perhaps another time,' ann rea gushed as she rose from her chair. 'Good day again, Reverend Houston,' were her last words as she charged past the two of them leaving them standing, jaws dangling on the chessboard-tiled floor, a floor clean enough for jaws to dangle on.

'God, that was close,' ann rea hissed as she moved past the gate. By now she was not exactly running, more gliding at high speed.

She felt a strange sensation in the pit of her stomach. Perhaps she'd been close to God but somehow she doubted that. She couldn't help feeling that she'd be better to get out of town immediately. She began to feel that the signs on the edge of the town should have read: "Ballyneagh. Twinned with Tombstone, Arizona."

There was one little errand ann rea needed to run before she left the village and it required a quick stop either at a newsagent or a book store.

Ten minutes later she was heading back in the general direction of Portrush. So spooked had she been by the Reverend Houston that she hadn't even bothered to check through the pages of her recent purchase, now lying on the back seat of her car in a plain white paper bag. The entire contents of that same paper bag were the latest edition of Red, a magazine favoured by ann rea; a bar of Cadbury's Crunchy Nut; and finally, and most valuable of her three purchases she hoped, the most recent edition of the *Ballyneagh Parish Gazette*.

Eventually, twelve and one half miles later to be exact, ann rea's curiosity got the better of her and she pulled into a lay-by. Suitably nourished by four squares of the Cadbury's Whole Nut, she started to read the report. Three minutes later she found exactly what she was looking for; the full membership list of the Ballyneagh Bridge Club. The third name on the list was Paul McCann and the fourteenth name was Robin Kane. ann rea was so engrossed in the mesmerising combination of her chocolate and the diocese magazine that she didn't notice a black Morris Minor van pull into the lay-by behind her. The van carried two middle-aged men, neither of whom was anywhere near as well preserved as their 1960s vehicle.

Chapter Fourteen

COINCIDENTALLY, JUST AS ann rea was making her discovery, Inspector McCusker was bursting into Kennedy's office a few miles back along the North Antrim coast, in Portrush.

McCusker was holding a piece of white paper, which he was unconsciously crumpling up as he gushed:

'Bit of a break for you, Kennedy.'

Kennedy's eyebrows arched into an "And?"

'*And*,' McCusker continued, 'we just managed to trace Derek Shaw, Dugdale's best man, for you.'

Kennedy's eyebrows repeated the "And?"

'*And* he's still alive and living along the coast, not too far from here in fact. He's got a little farm about halfway between the rope bridge and the Giant's Causeway.'

'Great!' Kennedy said. He left his mouth to do the talking this time.

'Yes. You're welcome. Well, let's get on up there sharpish. He's an old man and if he's anything like my old man he'll go to bed early and sleep so soundly a band full of Ballywappers wouldn't wake him,' McCusker announced and then broke into a grin as he concluded with: 'Besides, if he's that old we wouldn't want him dying on us before we've had a chance to talk to him, now would we?'

'Aye,' Kennedy smiled. 'It's just that ann rea should have been back by now. Perhaps we should wait for her?'

McCusker shot Kennedy one of those "but she's only a woman!" looks of disdain.

Kennedy's own curiosity got the better of him and he said: 'Yeah, you're right. Let's get over there right away before anything happens. I'll leave a message for ann rea with the desk sergeant telling her to meet me at my parents house later.'

'Good,' McCusker announced, seemingly satisfied with the arrangements. 'And who knows, we might even be in time for a bit of a late lunch.' He glanced at his watch and didn't try to hide the disappointment. 'Perhaps not. Let's hope it's near his supper time!'

The drive over to Derek Shaw's house was uneventful; uneventful as in lacking incident but certainly not uneventful as in lacking stunning scenery. Not only was this part of the world beautiful, it was also the cleanest part of countryside Kennedy ever had the pleasure to drive through. All the more incredible, Kennedy thought, when you considered the number of tourists who continued to enjoy the local treasures and pleasures each and every day.

As they knocked on the door of the thatched cottage, Kennedy noticed that McCusker's nostrils were working overtime.

'I'd say not only are we in time for a wee bit of supper but I bet you tonight's treat is going to be a wee bit of champ,' McCusker stage-whispered to Kennedy. 'I think…'

McCusker was silenced by the rusty creaking that signalled the door was opening.

'Mr Shaw? Mr Derek Shaw?' Kennedy inquired.

'And who'd be looking for him?' a raspy voice crackled from behind the door. Well, the voice actually came from behind half of the door because at that stage it was half opened. Or would that have been half shut?

McCusker shuffled around on his haunches a bit. He seemed to feel obliged to make the introductions. 'I'm Detective Inspector McCusker from the Portrush Barracks and he's Detective Inspector Kennedy from Camden Town CID.'

'Sure I know you, lad,' the man in the doorway replied to McCusker. 'Well at least I knew your Da. But what's a Londoner doing over in these parts?'

'Can we come in, sir?' McCusker asked.

'Aye. Surely. Go on through to the kitchen.'

The members of the police force did as they were bid and the old man closed the door.

The cottage owner looked old in the way Paul Newman looks old. But also like Paul Newman, there was still something handsome about him and, considering how old he was, Shaw, again like Newman, was very agile.

He appeared to be living by himself, yet he was clean shaven and wore a clean, white shirt; a RUR tie; green-cord trousers supported by green braces; spit-and-polished brown leather shoes; all topped off with a grey-checked cloth cap.

'So you are Derek Shaw?' McCusker asked once again in order to conclude the formalities.

'Aye, that's my name so it must be me!' Shaw smiled, acknowledging his name for this first time. Like the afore-mentioned Paul Newman he had ice-blue eyes that still sparkled with devilment.

Kennedy also smiled as he was invited to take a seat by the table. He spoke next.

'Did you know a Victor Dugdale?'

'Sure I did, aye,' came the short but friendly reply.

'He was found dead in London a couple of weeks back,' Kennedy continued.

'And I'd guess by the fact youse two peelers are here that he was found in mysterious circumstances?' Shaw guessed, betraying absolutely no emotion.

'Yes, that's correct.' He was about to add something when Shaw said:

'Sorry, look, forgive me my manners. Would you like a cup of tea or something?'

McCusker looked longingly over at the pot on the Aga cooker.

'I was about to make myself some supper – would youse two like to join me. I can throw in a few more spuds and it'll be ready before they hit the bottom of the pot.'

'Aye, like, that would be handy enough, you know,' McCusker replied, looking like he was barely able to contain his excitement.

'Just before that,' Kennedy announced, noting the imme-diate look of disappointment on McCusker's face, 'I'd like you to ID a photograph for us.'

'No problem,' Shaw replied as he went over to the dressing table and collected his glasses case.

Kennedy produced the photograph; Shaw raised the glasses to his eyes without actually putting them on.

'That's Dugdale,' he announced as he took the glasses back down from his eyes and replaced them in the case, which he shut with a snap. Then, without batting an eyelid, he took the kettle to the sink by the window and filled it from the cold-water tap. Kennedy replaced the photograph in a black leather-covered notebook, which he, in turn, replaced in his inside coat pocket. The whole procedure had barely taken ten seconds.

'You and Dugdale were friends?' Kennedy asked.

'Oh aye. But that would have been a long time ago,' Shaw replied as he took the full kettle back to the Aga. He raised one of the two lids and placed the kettle on the uncovered circle of heat. With the lids down the Aga tended to remind Kennedy of the early bicycle ice-cream carts.

'So you wouldn't have been friends in recent years then?' McCusker asked.

'Ah well, you see, after the war and all that we kind of separated. He stayed in England and I came back home. We've just drifted apart, like.'

'So he married before the war?' Kennedy continued. He was feeling slightly uncomfortable making Shaw answer all these questions. The war vet's voice sounded so raspy it seemed to Kennedy as though it might be quite painful to talk. Apparently not for pretty soon the words were spilling from his tongue like water over a waterfall.

'*During* the war, the more's the like,' Shaw laughed, 'he'd always be talking about Elsie and how beautiful she was and I swear to you he was continuously scared that while he was away at war someone was going to come along and whisk her away behind his back.'

'So you were both home on leave and he got married?' McCusker added impatiently, filling in a lot of the story.

'Not quite as simple as that. You see, he and I tried to join the Enniskillen Fusiliers and they wouldn't have us because we were too young. We were sixteen, nearly seventeen mind you, but not quite… enough. But the Regional Ulster Rifles, now they took us on. I'd been in the Home Guard, you see. Aye, me and my Da were in the Home Guard; he was a bit older, like, but they wanted everyone they could find. You see, the government was scared of the Germans dropping a pile of their boys behind our line by parachute, so the Home Guard was meant to stop them.

'Mind you, having said that I'm not sure why the Germans would have wanted to drop in here anyway – apart from the girls up here, of course. In my day the girls up around here were all gorgeous, aye, real beauties. Anyways, I liked being in the Home Guard. They taught you how to shoot and the war was on and all that and I was young and I wanted to see the world and so I joined the Regional Ulster Rifles. We were called Riflemen, aye. So Victor and I, we decided to join up together. I'd never been away from home before. Victor had. He'd relatives in Watford and sometimes he'd go over there for the summer. He'd go by ferry. But I'd never been away from home. My father was a carpenter and I was an apprentice and there was always lots to do. Aye, you could make a fair living with your hands in those days.

'So we joined the RUR up in Omagh. We went up there to the barracks, joined up and did our training and then we were taken over to England to a wee place outside of Portsmouth, and we did some more training and field craft and shooting and bike riding. Aye, that's right, they even trained you to ride your bike. Of course, I knew how to ride a bike and all of that. Victor wasn't too good away from home and we were training for the D-Day landing – with our bikes, folding them away and taking them onto the Liberty Ships.

'Would ye like a wee glass of port? All this talkin' makes me throat powerfully dry like.'

'Not for me, thanks,' Kennedy replied.

'Agh, go on then, fair play to ye. I'll join you in one,' McCusker started. When Shaw went about his business, McCusker winked at Kennedy and added: 'Aye and Inspector Kennedy will have a wee one as well. I mean, we'll need something to wet our whistle with until the champ is ready.'

Kennedy knew they were in for a long session, not that there was ever a choice of a short session in an Ulster house. His only form of entertainment growing up would have been a bit of *craic* and, as they say in those parts, 'the *craic* would be ninety'.

Kennedy was warming to Derek Shaw. He had a very friendly air about him and was pretty sharp for a man who must have been in his mid-seventies. On top of which he was the only living, unrelated person they had met so far who had known Victor Dugdale and seemed to be prepared to talk about him.

Kennedy had also remembered his father's advice about never turning down a man's hospitality, particularly when it was coming in the shape of a drink. You didn't even have to drink it, just accept it.

Soon Shaw returned from another room with a three-quarters-full bottle of port and he took three glasses from the dresser in the middle of the kitchen.

'So, you and Victor went off to war?' Kennedy asked, trying to get the conversation back on the rails again.

'What? Aye. Oh yeah. Boys-a-dear, but you're an impatient one,' Shaw replied, openly winking at McCusker. 'Now I'd see through it if you were my age and you needed to have an inch to your step to be sure of getting to the end of the story.'

Shaw took a generous gulp of port. 'Ah now. That's what I needed.'

'Tell you what,' McCusker volunteered, following his thirst-quenching visit to his port glass. 'You sit yourself there and tell your man all about you and Victor and I'll finish off making the champ.'

'Aye, that'll be right handy then,' Shaw replied with a smile on his face, not noticing that McCusker switched his own empty port glass for Kennedy's untouched glass.

Kennedy squirmed around in his seat a bit, hoping that his red cheeks were taken to be a result of the heat from the Aga and not his embarrassment.

'So anyways, where were we?' the World War Two vet continued. 'Aye, right, that's it, we'd just finished our training on the Liberty Ships and we thought we were off to Belgium to the battle but Victor and I were given a weekend pass and a chance of a lift to Aldergrove Airfield. Victor was so glad to get home. But he didn't go home, of Course, he went straight around to Elsie's. He was dressed to the nines, all kitted out in his uniform. He pulled me around there with him and there, in front of me and the whole family, he got down on one knee and proposed to her.'

'God, if he'd done that in our house to one of my sisters he'd have been thrown out on his ear,' McCusker muttered from the corner as he added a few more potatoes to the pot and then started to dice some scallions and their shoots.

'Now there's a thing,' Shaw replied. 'I've a feeling that Elsie wished that her father had done that as well; chuck him out with a red ear. Would have saved us all a lot of heartbreak.'

The end of Shaw's sentence was hard to hear because his lips Were simultaneously making themselves ready for the glass of port.

'But anyway, the mother and the sisters all went "Agh" and before you could say Bushmills it was the next morning and we were all off to the church for a speedily arranged marriage. I've always said that the church has a lot to answer for. If they hadn't been so accommodating for some of the last-minute weddings, there wouldn't have been so many war widows, not to mention fatherless children. I always said if the love match was real it would have kept 'til later, 'til after the war. But that's that, aye.'

This time Kennedy didn't make the mistake of saying: "So they got married, and…?"

This tack was obviously working in his favour because five seconds later Shaw said, 'So they got married and, twenty-four hours and a tearful, rosy-cheeked wife later, we were back at Aldergrove and then a quick flight over to Brize Norton and a quick trip back down to our camp, just outside Portsmouth. There's a bit more, like the tale about me and one of the bridesmaids but that's for when I get to know you better.'

Shaw laughed heartily. The laugh was so raspy you'd swear his Adam's apple was being tickled from the inside by rough-grade sandpaper.

Kennedy heard the kettle start to boil. Shaw went over to the Aga, lifted the kettle and returned to the sink area to wet the teapot he'd already prepared. Meanwhile, McCusker continued hovering around the potato pot like an expectant father.

Chapter Fifteen

'CAN YE IMAGINE what it was like travelling back to England, and the army, and the war, with someone who'd just married and discovered a new toy? Someone who'd just realised it wasn't just for watering the daisies with?' Shaw winked at Kennedy and McCusker even though at that moment McCusker had his back turned to them, concentrating on his potatoes.

'I mean, he'd always been a home-bird when we joined the army and that'd been bad enough, but now he was just skundering me with 'Elsie this' and 'Elsie that'. I was happy to get back to the normality of the camp, I can tell you.

'Then they bundled us up, folded bicycles and all, into the Liberty Ships and off we headed across the English Channel to France. We got absolutely hammered when we hit the beach, I can tell you. Aye, and we were dug down there, literally still on the beach, for about 36 hours. We lost a lot of boys.

'The following morning our tanks came along to give us some back-up but sure, didn't they go and run over most of our bicycles. At least we were able to move inland. You have to realise that most of us were seeing action for the first time. In my case it was for the first time since we had been training up in Omagh. Aye, up there this idiot had shot me through the helmet. I mean, with boys like him on our side – I seem to remember he was from Tobermore – the Germans were going to be able to stay at home and we'd lose the war all by ourselves. Anyway, at least they gave me a shilling for that and a new helmet of course,' Derek Shaw broke from his narrative to enjoy another of his raspy little chuckles. He stared at the floor as he spoke. He probably wasn't actually staring at the floor; more's the like way past it, back into his fifty-year-old war memories.

He stopped chuckling and paused for a second before continuing.

'We set up camp, I think it was in Caen Woods, and then Victor started to go all quiet on me. This was probably a fraction better than him bending my ear all the time about Elsie and what he was going to do with her when he got home. He'd changed. But then I suppose you had to take into account that he'd just married and he was seeing action for the first time. Not only was he was seeing action, he was right in the middle of it.

'I didn't know exactly what was going on in his head because none of us ever discussed it, but, for me it was like… well, here I was, I'd been taught all my life by my family, by teachers, by the clergy that: "Thou shalt not kill!". I remember thinking, on those long sleepless nights in the trenches, that the command did not say: "Thou shalt not kill except in times of war". I always took it that it was an unconditional "no" to taking someone's life, *full stop*! But here we were, guns stuck in our hands, a Bren gun in my case, and we were taken to a foreign country to kill people. No discussion. Just do it. More simply, either kill or be killed.

'Even now, when I think back on it all these years later, it still seems totally unreal. I mean, it was literally like living in the middle of a nightmare. People were getting killed left, right and centre all around you. And I'm talking about their boys as well as our boys. There was no difference to the carnage. They were in exactly the same position as we were. No one had asked their permission. You have to admit it was pretty surreal. I kept thinking that they'd never get away with it today; people would never go for it. But then you look around and they are getting away with it. And we did it all for the King's Shilling the day we signed up and a measly fifteen shillings a week. That's just 75 pence today, you know. Aye.

'I remember a time, probably about seven months after the wedding; our battalion was on the second front and we were trying to take Caen Woods. This day these old bombers flew over - there were about 500 of them and we were all watching them like school kids at a matinee as they dropped millions of bits of silver paper. A shower of silver paper poured down. It was nearly Christmas and it was totally bizarre. Apparently that was their method of cutting off radio contact so that our bombers could get through and do their work undetected.

'Then we saw them drop their bombs over Caen and it was all smoke and plumes of flames reaching up into the sky. Then we saw German guns fire on our aircraft. That obviously heated things up a bit because we saw some of these planes, which were now making for home, turn around and fly in closer. They were Lancaster Bombers. A few of them flew in so close they were shot down. We saw the crews bail out. You felt really sorry for them as they parachuted out. It seemed to take an eternity for them to get down and all the time they were dangling, they were sitting targets.

'We didn't know what happened to them. I hope they got out safely. I doubt if they would have been taken prisoner, but it did Victor's head in seeing them just drop to their apparent deaths before our eyes. He was nearly crying. He kept saying that we should be doing something more to help them.

'But we ourselves were also helpless. We were pinned down on Hill Sixty, just outside Caen. We waited until night-fall and then we were ordered to advance down into Caen itself. Boys-a-dear, Caen had been bombed to bits. All the houses were in ruins and the smell in the air was something rotten. With all the bombing, Caen was now all over the place; everywhere was so filled with rubble it was hard to know where we were going because there was no clear outline of the streets any more.

'We came upon this German patrol. They had dug them-selves into a key position and we really had to try and take that position because the next morning our troops were going to come into the city. At that point we were few in numbers but we were still ordered to take their position. We were getting hammered on by German gunfire. I found myself about fifty yards away from their guns. I kept up steady fire on them and Victor and some of the other Riflemen circled them and came in from the rear and eventually we managed to take out their main gun post but just as we did so, another German opened fire on us from a position over on my left. They obvi-ously hadn't seen me but I was very close to them.

'Our section commander was wounded at that point so I turned my Bren gun on them and I kept up heavy fire on them until Victor and the others had a chance to find some cover for themselves. My position was exposed as well but I had been able to use the element of surprise to my advantage. When the boys got behind some cover – a stack of rubble – my platoon commander ordered me to withdraw.

'That was the first time I'd shot someone. Well, of course, I'd been shooting at people in the distance before that time. You know, keeping up heavy fire with my Bren gun to try to keep the enemy down so your own boys could either advance or escape. But you never knew if you had actually hit anyone. And I was happy to think that perhaps I hadn't. However, when it's either them or you, it's a different matter altogether.

'They were so close and the 75mm guns they had had to be taken out or they would have taken out a pile of us and you know, when it gets down to it, that's what it was all about, either them or us. Hitler didn't come into it. Churchill didn't come into it. Even Monty didn't come into it and he was a decent enough chap. No, it was you and your mates or it was the Germans. And it wasn't like in the movies: "ping" and someone's shot as if they'd been stung by a wasp.

'You could see the fecking bullets fly through the air, particularly the ones from 75mms, little balls of fire and if they hit someone, then believe me it wasn't: "Oh, I've been shot, old chap, my war's over. See you back in the bar",' Shaw said, breaking into a Richard Burton voice. He continued, using his own familiar, hoarse Ulster Tones: 'Nagh, that wasn't what it was like. You got to see half of their heads blown off, and blood and brain tissue and grunge rain down all over you. Sometimes you'd be covered in so much gunk you'd think you'd been wounded yourself but then it would turn out to be your mates' blood you'd be covered in and in a split second you'd realise you'd have to get out of there or you'd be next.

'I'll tell you something else for nothing; there were few heroes on the battlefield. Wounded men and officers one and all would wail for Jerusalem when they were lying in ditches, watching their lifeblood flow away. And they were the lucky ones. Sometimes I'd find myself thinking that it was worse to see someone hit by a bullet and see pinky-red jets of blood fly out from the wounds than to be the one hit. The shock could kill you. And the stench of it all, sure wasn't that in itself enough to make you want to surrender the contents of your

stomach? Of course, that's assuming you'd been lucky enough
to eat something more substantial than the bully-beef rations
you carried with you. But through all of this you had to try to
keep some sense of clarity.

'Talking about food, how's the champ coming on, young
McCusker? Nagh, nagh,' Shaw continued, distracted from his
story by his apparent concern over his supper, 'don't worry
about peeling the skins off. The skins are the best part. Yeah,
that's it, just mix them all up together in the pot. Add a few
dollops of butter, champ it up a bit more and then, when it's a
bit mushy, add all your scallions and green shoots. Some
people add cabbage but I can't abide it, never could.

'That's it. Grand, man. Just bring it over here and dollop it
out onto our plates. God, I just love champ. I never tire of it.
You see, if you do this, make it into a kind of sand castle –
well, potato castle really – nice solid walls, and throw a chunk
of butter in here in the centre. Nagh, much bigger chunk than
that, McCusker. Here, let me show you. Yes, that's much
better. Now you see, when the butter melts it will stay on as a
pool in the middle of the castle and then what you do is scoop
it from around the walls – the sides, detectives – with your
spoon and then dip it in the melted butter in the middle like
this and there…'

Shaw's words trailed off as he sampled the first of the
champ.

'Isn't that just brilliant?' he said, licking his lips. 'I bet they
don't make this in any of those trendy wee cafés around
Camden Town, Inspector Kennedy. Now, don't you see, if
only Monty had supplied this for his troops on the battlefield
then we'd have been invincible. The Germans and their silly
sausages would have been no match for our chaps with a feed
of champ in them.

'I met Monty, you know. He was a decent enough man –
very approachable, very friendly. He'd give these talks to his
troops; try to tell them as much as possible about what was
going on. They awarded me a Military Medal you know, for
that incident I was telling you about, taking out the German
post and all of that. That's how I got to meet Monty in person.
He presented me with my MM up at a place in Holland called
St Anthonis. I'd my photograph taken with him. We got our

tea and all with him. He shook my hand and all of that. He was very nice, aye.

'Then I got wounded shortly after that and that was the end of me and *my* war. I got shot in the leg. It's bothered me ever since. I was in hospital down in Belfast. I enjoyed two Christmas dinners down there and then came back home and finished off serving my apprenticeship as a carpenter. Victor and me, you see, that had been our master plan; we were going to start up in business together. It was a great time back then, after the war, loads of opportunities; every corner you turned there was a new opportunity waiting, eager to shake your hand.

But I kind of lost contact with Victor after I was wounded; we just really fell out of contact. I mean, we'd changed; the war had changed us. In the beginning, when we were in the Home Guard, it was like we were all set for a great adventure, just like we were going off to a strange town up in Donegal or somewhere to play a football match. We all planned to come back after the adventure and take up our lives.

But we didn't, of course, pick up things where we left them. Things had changed. And that was that. It was never going to be the same again.'

Chapter Sixteen

KENNEDY WAS THOROUGHLY enjoying his champ. Of course, he'd had it earlier in his life while he was growing up in Portrush. He'd just lost the taste for it over the years, he supposed. Then again, surely his own 'psychedelic potatoes' were a variation on a similar theme with the colours of the title giving a wee bit of an extra kick in the taste department.

He was intrigued by the wartime memories of this veteran whom he was fast growing to like. Kennedy wasn't sure how much, if any, of the story was relevant to Victor Dugdale and he hadn't found out much apart from the fact that Doris Dugdale's mother, Elsie, had been a wartime bride. Doris however at just under forty wouldn't have been a wartime child.

'When we've finished our supper I'll take you next door and show you all my bits and pieces from the war,' Derek Shaw began. His castle wall had sprung a leak in a couple of places, adding more flavour to the potatoes.

'So you didn't see Victor after you were wounded?' McCusker said, cleaning his plate so thoroughly Kennedy doubted it would need washing.

'Well, I'd see him around, aye, and all of that. But he'd a wife and he went onto her father's farm and then, sure he moved to England and he disappeared for ages, like,' Shaw replied.

'Ages? What like, in terms of weeks or months?' Kennedy asked.

'Nagh. More like years.'

'A few years?' Kennedy again.

'Aye, a good few years.'

'Like as in how many years?' Kennedy pushed.

'Oh, about thirty,' Dugdale's best man replied.

'Had you fallen out or anything like that?' This time it was McCusker speaking.

'No, not really, we'd been through a lot. As I said, the war changed things and we'd both different lives to lead.'

'When would you last have heard from him?' Kennedy asked, the last to clean his plate.

'Oh, about forty years ago…'

'Forty years!' McCusker laughed in disbelief. 'What, not even Christmas cards?'

'Nope. He moved to England – never heard from him again.'

'What about his wife?'

'Aye, well I've seen her around over the years. Well I would, wouldn't I? Living so close and all of that,' Shaw said with a smile.

Kennedy was about to ask another question when Shaw said:

'Aye, I'm just about pooped. Let me show you these things and then I'll let you get on your way.' He stared at McCusker for a few seconds, smiled and added: 'Nagh, don't you bother with cleaning the dishes, I'll do them.'

McCusker laughed as well. Kennedy felt the laugh was more from relief than from the humour of the situation.

They walked through into the sitting room. It was more like a war Museum, in fact. It was decked out, floor to ceiling, with various war memorabilia and mementoes. Pride of place, just above the fireplace, was Shaw's medal case, complete with five medals, a citation from King George and a photograph. Kennedy recognised Field Marshal Montgomery seated in the centre of group and then, in the back row, three men to the left of Monty, one of them Rifleman Derek Shaw. He was but a youngster, no more than a boy truth be told, but the giveaway was the Paul Newman ice-blue eyes.

'Is Victor Dugdale in the photograph?' Kennedy asked after a few minutes studying in vain.

'No. No. Don't you see that's only for those of us who won medals? There,' Shaw said proudly, 'that's my Military Medal.'

Shaw pointed to the distinctive blue, white, red, white, red, white and blue-coloured ribbon, which was middle of the five medals.

Kennedy glanced briefly around the rest of the room, quickly checking the photographs and newspaper cuttings.

'Tell me, Derek, is Victor in any of these photographs?'

'Nope. We never seemed to have been in front of a camera at the same time,' Shaw said breaking into a laugh. 'Anyway lads, that's going to have to be it for now. You're welcome to come back any time you want. I'm not going anywhere, well apart from bed that is.'

'God, that was a great feed altogether, wasn't it?' McCusker said a few minutes later as they were driving along the coast road, this time in the direction of Portrush, leaving the mystery of the Giant's Causeway to the tourists. There were certainly many – tourists that is, not mysteries.

Chapter Seventeen

BY THE TIME Kennedy and McCusker returned to Portrush, it was just after 6pm and the town was quite quiet. It was the lull between the end of the day on the beach and the beginning of the evening's entertainment.

Kennedy ran into the station and was disappointed to find no messages from ann rea. He ran back out again and bummed a lift to his parents' house from McCusker. They bid each other goodbye, accepting that nothing further could be achieved until the following morning. ann rea wasn't at Kennedy's parents' house either.

Unusual, thought Kennedy, no message, no nothing.

He realised he hadn't seen her for eight hours. Yes, there had been a couple of messages but nothing since mid afternoon. Where could she be?

Two hours passed, still no sign of ann rea and Kennedy was considering ringing McCusker's home number. But he was at that awkward stage where, although he felt something was wrong, he didn't want to appear to be overreacting.

He realised he hadn't a single clue as to her whereabouts.

His parents were less than concerned. But that could have been down to the fact that he was (perhaps) playing down his reaction in front of them just so that they wouldn't be concerned.

If he have been in London, particularly Camden Town, Kennedy would have felt a bit more comfortable, what with all his connections and resources. However, he had to admit to himself that he didn't have a clue about how to tackle a missing-person problem in Ulster. Apart, that was, from contacting his new acquaintance, Inspector McCusker.

Should he ring the friendly Ulster detective?

He decided that he should.

But still he didn't!

When someone is missing it's only afterwards that you can

define the period of a "long time". At this stage ann rea had only been missing for, say, five hours. But, by this time tomorrow, would he be looking back and wishing he'd done something more positive about trying to find her by eleven minutes past eight when she'd been missing for just over five hours?

The thing troubling Kennedy, perhaps the most important point if he'd care to admit it, was that ann rea was an independent young lady and as such, was going to feel really upset (which meant, of course, that she was going to make Kennedy feel even worse) if Kennedy got the cavalry out to search for her.

Kennedy continued to allow his mind to play silly games with him. Like, at one point, he felt she was dead. He really did. He felt she was dead. But worse still, he felt better about the situation because now that she was dead he could deal with her case without the fear of her being embarrassed by his actions. Yes. It would all be fine now that she was dead and he could detach himself (and her) from the case and start the investigation.

The thing that troubled him most was the fact that now, even though he accepted the fact that she was dead, he hadn't started to grieve for her.

His mother and father must have thought he was mad, he thought, because he was acting with them like nothing had happened and yet here, underneath the surface, he was having all these bizarre thoughts about ann rea's death.

Then he started to think about what kind of trouble she'd fallen into by accident, or otherwise, which had led to her death. Had she, in fact, stumbled upon something to do with the death of Victor Dugdale – some piece of evidence perhaps, some vital piece of evidence that someone, perhaps even the murderer of Victor Dugdale, couldn't afford to let her escape with? Consequently, she too had had to be murdered.

He laughed out loud.

His parents both stopped looking at the telly and looked over at him, looked at each other, looked back at Kennedy one more time before averting their gaze back to the telly.

"Stop laughing!" he screamed at himself under his breath. "It's not funny. Someone has murdered ann rea." He tried to recall which lead she'd been working on.

All of a sudden, a chill ran down his spine and he got the

shivers. Kennedy could not recall a time he'd ever experienced a similar sensation.

"Oh God," he said, again under his breath. He'd suddenly realised he was the one responsible for getting her into this trouble. He was solely responsible for her death.

That's it, he thought, the wood. The wood, which had been taken from the rectory in Ulster and sold to the owner of the Black Cat Building in Camden Town, was vital in all of this. ann rea had gone off to try and find what that was all about. Namely, was there any connection whatsoever between that transaction and Victor Dugdale's death. And if so, what? What exactly had she found out?

He wished, no, he prayed, he prayed that one of his parents would turn around and say: "Where's that young lady of yours?" Maybe even a: "Isn't she a bit late?" Then and only then could she, ann rea, officially be late. Then, if and when he tracked down ann rea and she turned out to be safe, he could always say: "I wasn't bothered. I knew you'd be all right, of course. It's just that my parents were very worried about you and so I had to launch the search just for their peace of mind."

But what was he on about? She was dead. He'd already decided that, hadn't he? So there were going to be no embarrassing scenes. ann rea was dead and that was that.

He should have known better, shouldn't he? Now come on, really, he thought. What were you thinking of? Bringing an English journalist over to Ulster. Yes, the Troubles were meant to be over but no one ever really knew exactly what was still going on behind the scenes. A mate of his had told Kennedy that the definitive Peace Deal had been concluded a good few years ago and all the current comings and goings and throwing of shapes was all window-dressing to make it all, the peace and the dealing with the other side, palatable.

But with all the double-dealings going on, you never really knew which side you were on and which side to be wary of.

Had ann rea inadvertently gotten caught up in all of that? Had Victor Dugdale been caught up in all of that? Kennedy supposed that if Dugdale had been yet another victim of the Troubles, that would in some way account for his age. It was very unusual, but not unknown, for a septuagenarian to be murdered.

Kennedy was amazed that he was actually dealing with the death of his girlfriend – possibly the only person he'd ever really loved – and his mind was still off trying to solve a mystery. Was that going to be his way of dealing with ann rea's death? How could he, in fact, deal with her death? He was surprised, as in shocked, about how remarkably calm and collected he was about the whole affair.

Was that because there had been insufficient time since they had last seen each other, i.e. breakfast, for him to feel any sense of loss?

The telephone rang.

His mother beat him to the phone.

'It's for you, Christopher,' she announced. She was the only one on this earth who called him by that name.

'Hi, Kennedy,' ann rea's familiar tones beamed over the phone lines. 'Look, I'm in...' Kennedy could hear ann rea say to a third party: "Where exactly am I?" Kennedy could then hear McCusker's dulcet tones cut through the background racket: "Tell him we're up in Kelly's Barn – he'll know where that is."

'We're in Kelly's Barn,' ann rea said, passing on the message.

'I know. I heard,' Kennedy replied.

'I'm sorry I'm late, Kennedy. I've been having a great day. I bumped into McCusker just after he dropped you off. I'd been trying to track down a local journalist and he said she'd probably be here. Anyway, enough of me rabbiting on, why don't you come over and we'll have a drink and a bite? McCusker said he's famished and he's invited us both to a slap-up meal.'

'God, the legendary bottomless pit in living colour,' Kennedy said, remembering McCusker's intake for the day.

'You're not annoyed are you, Kennedy?' ann rea shouted above the racket of the pub.

'Goodness no, anything but. You can't begin to believe how great it is for me to hear your voice... it's just... McCusker and his food. Oh, I'll tell you later.'

'Hurry over, Christy. I've been dying to see you.'

'Hang on, I'll be right there and if McCusker gets a wee bit frisky just buy him a packet of Tayto Crisps. That'll keep him at bay until I get there.'

'See you,' ann rea said. It sounded as though she was already returning the phone to the rest as she said it.

Kelly's Barn – well, it had long since stopped being a barn – was packed to the rafters. Still, it didn't take Kennedy long to find ann rea. Well, he found McCusker first off. He'd been holding court at one end of the bar and Kennedy made his way through the hyper crowds. McCusker acknowledged Kennedy with a wink and gave a nod to the far end of the bar without a break in telling his joke. Kennedy turned to look towards the other end of the bar and there by the jukebox was ann rea, apparently deep in conversation with two girls Kennedy didn't recognise. ann rea was so animated in her conversation that Kennedy just froze in his tracks. It was just such a joy to stand and watch her, particularly after what he'd been thinking a few minutes ago in his home. He also found it fascinating to watch her without her knowing he was doing so. In that fraction of a second he realised that one of the main reasons her was so in love with her, and the reason he'd been attracted to her in the first place, was simply that she was breathtakingly beautiful. The more he got to know her, the more he feared he was taking this beauty for granted.

He could remember clearly the first time he had set eyes on her. It had been in the bookshop at Heathrow Airport, Terminal One, and he was as guilty then as he was now of spying on her. It had been a much easier exercise at the airport because, at that point, they'd never met and so he was just another stranger amongst the thousands of passengers.

Just like a lot of the strangers in the crowd in Kelly's. Some were discreetly eyeballing her. Others were not quite so discreet, with their pints in hand, blatantly flashing a glance in her direction every few minutes. They were probably checking out who she was with, who she was waiting for, if anyone. Perhaps some of them were even hoping to pluck up enough courage to go over to her and chat her up.

Two others, however, seemed to be completely ignoring her, even though they were positioned but a few feet away from the same jukebox. They were observing her in a way so discreet that no one, not even Kennedy, could, if requested, recall any details about them. The most anyone could possibly have observed about them was that they were dressed in smart, dark clothes and had no distinguishing features.

Unsighted by most, if not all, one of them swung a key ring around the forefinger of his left hand. The other hand was occupied with a bottle of Beck's. The key ring had two car keys and a Jordan racing emblem. The ignition key would never start any of Eddie Jordan's fabulous vehicles, though. It would, however, ignite the pristine engine of the black Morris Minor van parked outside Kelly's highly lucrative Barn.

Kennedy could keep his hands off ann rea no longer. He rushed over to her and surprised her from behind. Waterloo Sunset by the Kinks was on the jukebox and it might have been that wondrous song, or it might even have been his earlier fears for her safety, or it might have been down to the fact that she'd already had a few glasses of wine by that stage, but whatever it was they embraced and kissed like they'd never done before in public.

A few minutes passed in embrace.

'Could someone please get me a crowbar so that I can prise these two apart,' McCusker laughed, barely audible above the din. In the background, Ray Davies was singing about Terry and Julie and Waterloo Bridge; a bridge too far away, Kennedy thought.

'Kennedy, what was that all about?' ann rea asked in amusement. She then turned to McCusker and said, 'Give me a second or two to rearrange myself into a respectable human.'

'Hmmm,' McCusker grunted. 'Well, maybe youse should just wait until you're in the privacy of your home. We're a very religious country over here, as I'm sure you'd noticed.'

'Yes,' ann rea said and smiled demurely. 'Now, what was that you said you were earlier? Famished? Yes, that was it, famished,' she grinned, answering her own question and then grabbing Kennedy's hand she continued: 'Well, whatever famished is, I am!'

'In that case, let's away out of here and track down some food,' McCusker said.

Kennedy, still somewhat shell-shocked, followed them as they left.

A few seconds later two half-empty bottles of Beck's stood all alone on the window ledge by the jukebox.

Chapter Eighteen

ANN REA MIGHT have had a few drinks at that stage but her mind was still clear and sharp when it came to recalling the events of her day.

They were all seated in the restaurant at the White Cliff Hotel, a few miles out of Portrush on the coast road. They were sampling wholesome food – Kennedy expected no less from McCusker – while enjoying an amazing panoramic view of Portrush: a view made all the more spectacular by the way the falling dusk was back-lighting the skyline.

City lights, even town lights, are as unique and as reliable as fingerprints as a form of identification. Portrush's highlights were the harbour lights, Barry's lights, street lights and the strand lights picking out the line of the beach, the reflections of which were continually being distorted by the circles of the waves.

'So, I wanted to see if I could find out anything more about the members of the bridge club and see which of them went on the excursion,' ann rea began, 'so that wee girl, who our new friend introduced us to, is from the *Coleraine Chronicle* and she's going to check out what info she has on these boys tomorrow.'

'Give me those two names again,' McCusker began as he removed his notebook from his breast pocket. 'I'll run them through our computer as well.'

'Perhaps we should also see if the wee girl from the *Coleraine Chronicle* has got any info on Victor Dugdale as well?' Kennedy added hopefully.

'Good point,' McCusker replied. 'We'll see if he got up to anything apart from marrying his childhood sweetheart. "Child War-Bride Weds Local War Hero!" You can just see the headlines, can't you?'ann rea laughed and made a few tut-tutting noises. She then looked out over the view again.

'God, this is a beautiful place. A great place to have a hotel and a restaurant as well!'

'There's a nice wee story attached to this place too, I must tell it to you before I'm off. The hotel came up for sale a few years back and a mystery bid was put in for it. When the deal eventually went through it transpired that the best bid, and the one that eventually went through, was one from a wee girl from around these parts. She'd started off her career as a chambermaid in this very hotel and worked her way up through the ranks, working in every part of the hotel until she eventually became the hotel manager. So when the hotel came up for sale she knew exactly what it was worth and how best to run it. She was able to persuade a bank to finance her. And now she's doing really well with it.'

With that McCusker rose.

'Aren't you going to join us in a dessert?' ann rea asked. Kennedy just hoped his body language didn't betray his reluctance to such a suggestion.

'Nagh. I don't want to spoil my appetite for my supper, which will be waiting for me on the table when I get home. I'll leave youse two to enjoy your dessert, then you can walk along the beach back into the Port. It's a nice walk, it'll take you about twenty minutes,' McCusker began. He turned to face ann rea: 'Perhaps you can persuade your man here to show you around some of the sand hills.'

He winked at both of them but it was lost on ann rea.

Twenty minutes later, deciding to forgo the dessert, they ordered the bill only to find that McCusker had already taken care of it and soon they were out in the cool night air, winding their way down a narrow path in the general direction of the beach.

'This is good, Kennedy.'

'Yes, it is beautiful, isn't it?'

'No, I mean us being here on our little adventure and getting on with it... without...'

'Aye, you're right,' Kennedy interrupted. He didn't have anything particular that he wanted to say. No, it was more that he just wanted to avoid talking, yet again, about their relationship.

'Sorry. I just realised what you were thinking about.'

'Sorry? What?'

'You know, walking along here,' ann rea said literally the second their feet left the tarmac path and hit the sandy beach.

'Sorry?'

'You know, Kennedy,' she nudged him playfully in the ribs. 'Reminiscing about all the other girls you've had down here on the beach. What was it McCusker said about showing me the sand hills on the way home?'

'Yeah, yeah, yeah,' Kennedy mock-laughed. 'You've both got a great imagination, haven't ye?'

'So you're telling me you've never been down here before on the beach with a girl?'

'No. I mean, yes. Yes, of course I have,' Kennedy hesitated.

'And you're telling me you've never been down here, that you've never... you know... here on the beach with the tide rolling in and wetting your ankles?'

'Sorry?' Kennedy feigned ignorance; he didn't like where this was going.

'You know, doing the wild thing?'

'ann rea! Exactly how much wine had you had in Kelly's before I arrived?'

'Oh, you know. Enough,' she replied playfully.

Kennedy wasn't sure if it was his imagination but he felt proceedings seemed to be heading in one particular direction. ann rea was wearing a red dress, which fell down to just above her knees. She wore Kennedy's black blazer draped about her shoulders. As was the usual case he was overdressed, she was underdressed. Her cheeks were flushed from the wine and as long as they kept moving the cool sea breeze was refreshing.

'Agh, come on Christy. Tell me some of your secrets. What happened down here on the beach?'

'On this beach, nothing actually.'

'Oh bor-ing,' she replied dejectedly.

'Now the other strand, the one beyond Barry's, that's much more secluded. More hiding places, particularly up on Ramore Hill. It's more exposed up there but frequently used.'

'Kennedy, you old devil.'

'It was all harmless good fun,' Kennedy replied. He thought he saw a butterfly somewhere off in the distance. In this light he could have been mistaken though. ann rea did look stunning however, and such visions tended to bring out the odd butterfly.

'Good fun as in you never actually... you know?'

Kennedy stuttered around for a few seconds. Words were proving to be as elusive as the butterfly.

'Well not actually... you know,' he eventually admitted.

'What? Never?'

'No!'

'What never ever?' ann rea persisted with her line of interrogation.

'Actually, no.' ann rea turned to face him. She took his face in her hands and pulled Kennedy gently towards her. She kissed him fully on the lips. Kennedy found her tongue searching, exploring vigorously for his. She hugged him tightly, his jacket falling to the sand, she leant closer until her lips were right by his ear and she whispered.

'What, you mean I'm going to be the first?'

Kennedy opened his eyes a little and looked out over her Beatles-bob hair towards the sea. He heard the waves gently lapping upon the beach. He was convinced he saw the butterfly this time. He knew it was time to go chasing it.

'Yes,' he whispered back into her ear.

Then the search began for a place. That wasn't quite so romantic. They looked at a few secluded places but for varying reasons they ruled them out. Kennedy kept hoping the butterfly wouldn't disappear. ann rea's enthusiasm seemed undiminished and they had a few kisses along the way. Sometimes just walking along the beach was more awkward than others for Kennedy.

Eventually they came upon a little natural sand cove, which was about chest-high and enjoyed the luxury of a soft, grass floor. Neither of them actually said: "This will do nicely." That would have been just a wee bit too functional, not to mention unromantic, perhaps even a little crude. They lay down together. There was no fumbling with undergarments. No none of that, nor none of the, "Move your leg over more, back a bit, yeah that's it, oh, no, now your elbow is in my ear." No. There was no awkwardness. It was just beautiful and truly natural and, maybe because of the exquisite location, Kennedy found it difficult to keep the butterfly in sight.

His famous and much-used 'butterfly technique' did not include special instructions for love on the beach, and for first-time love on the beach at that. That, combined with the fact that Kennedy was with the most attractive person in his universe, a person who was not scared of giving, in fact a person who just loved to give; yes, that unique combination ensured that the butterfly disappeared a lot quicker than usual.

But, according to ann rea, that was okay as well. It provided them with a good enough reason to try again.

Next time the butterfly wasn't quite so elusive.

Chapter Nineteen

ANN REA BEAT Kennedy to the bathroom the following morning and so, bid by his mother, he went straight down to breakfast. They enjoyed a hearty breakfast, more like a feast, with Kennedy's parents.

'Someone's gone and brought the whole of the West Strand beach back with them yesterday,' Kennedy's father said, mid-bite, to no one in particular.

'Must had been me,' Kennedy admitted. 'I was down for a walk on the beach yesterday with someone I was questioning.'

'Aye, that'll be in then,' Kennedy's father said dryly, appearing to let the matter drop.

Kennedy tucked into his fadge, inwardly breathing a sigh of relief.

'It's just,' Kennedy's father started up again, 'I can't quite work out how you managed to question someone and have your head buried in the sand at the same time.'

'What?' was all Kennedy could find to say as ann rea looked like she was about to burst a gut trying to contain her laughter.

'Your hair, man, it's full of sand,' his father announced, 'so I figured you must have had your head in the sand. That might be the way the London Constabulary question their witnesses but over here we take the more orthodox approach.' Kennedy's father winked at ann rea as he took a loud sup of his tea.

Just then the phone rang. Kennedy wasn't completely sure but he was pretty convinced that even his mother was sniggering as she went to answer it.

'Christo…' she began from out in the hall.

Kennedy failed in his attempt to cut her off because she repeated the little-known Christian name. 'Christopher darling, it's for you. It's that nice man, James Irvine.'

Kennedy had his notebook opened at a clean page and pen at the ready by the time he took the phone from his mother, who Kennedy was sure still had a little smirk on her face.

'James,' Kennedy said, refusing eye contact with his mother.

'We got our court order and opened the safe-deposit box,' DS Irvine began.

'Good,' Kennedy replied.

'I'm afraid there wasn't a lot in there, sir.'

'Oh,' Kennedy replied in obvious disappointment.

'A couple of medals; a life assurance policy; three building society passbooks with a total of three hundred and seventy-four pounds on deposit; a couple of wartime photographs; an old shilling; and a small, leather-bound version of the New Testament. The New Testament has a bookplate on the front page saying it was presented to Victor David Dugdale on June 6th 1937 for good attendance at Sunday School in Ballyneagh.'

From the noises in his earpiece Kennedy guessed that Irvine was cradling his phone between his shoulder and his cheek, enabling him to read the inscription in the book.

'And that's your lot, sir,' Irvine announced.

'Right,' Kennedy said making it sound like an "Oh".

'Making any progress over there?' Irvine inquired.

Kennedy filled Irvine in on the investigation so far.

'Not a lot,' Kennedy conceded, 'but I feel like we're getting somewhere. Tell you what, could you fax me over a copy of the photographs you found in the safe-deposit box? You never know, they might trigger someone's memory.'

'Done.'

'Much else going on over there?' Kennedy asked absent-mindedly as he looked over the list of the contents of the box one more time.

'Nagh, not a lot. Superintendent Castle has had me chasing this clown who keeps shoving plaster of Paris into the parking-ticket machines. The whole of Camden is in chaos. Oh, and by the way, that nurse showed up. Remember the one that Rose feared Ranjesus was up to his old tricks with?'

'Oh!' Kennedy said, sounding half relieved and half annoyed, possibly by the fact that they weren't going to have an excuse to investigate the doctor. 'Where has she been?'

'She'd gone back home to Ireland and hadn't bothered to tell a soul, so Rose had feared the worst.'

They bid their goodbyes and Kennedy's eyes were still on the list as he returned the handset to its cradle.

Twenty minutes later he was in a similar reflective mood as he studied the faxed copies of the photographs Irvine had sent to Portrush Police Barracks. One by one he passed them across the desk to McCusker to see did they mean anything to him.

The first one was of a very young-looking Dugdale on his wedding day. Kennedy recognised the Paul Newman eyes of the best man, Derek Shaw. One of the bridesmaids was obviously more interested in Shaw than she was in the cameraman. The second photograph was a troop of fresh-faced (maybe with a little stretch of the imagination, even baby-faced) soldiers, including Victor Dugdale, Derek Shaw and seven others. The third and final photograph was again of Dugdale and Shaw and this time, they were much younger, possibly even in their early teens. They were dressed in their Sunday best, sitting at a kitchen table and looked like they were laughing their socks off. It was a photograph that even sixty years later showed what grand mates they'd been.

Irvine had also faxed the back of the photographs, which had a little writing. The photo of the troop bore the legend: "Caen (April 1944)"; the wedding-day one merely read: "12.3.43".

The one with the two swanks read: "Derek's b'day '37".

That was it.

McCusker didn't recognise any of the other members of the troop, 'But,' he said as he sprang up from behind his desk, 'I know someone who does!'

And that is how twenty-seven minutes later they came to be standing on Derek Shaw's doorstep.

Derek Shaw was as friendly as he had been on the previous day and invited them straight into the kitchen. When Kennedy passed the photograph over to him across the dining table, all of a sudden Shaw looked like he'd seen a ghost; maybe even eight ghosts. For the first time in their two meetings he certainly looked each and every one of his seventy-five years on this planet.

He stared at the photograph for at least a couple of minutes before saying a word.

'Goodness, this takes me back a bit.'

'Do you know the names of the other members of the troop?' Kennedy asked.

Shaw rose from the table and went over to the drawer of his pine dresser and took out a pair of wire-framed glasses that he fixed behind his ears.

'Let's see now, it's over fifty years ago and they all look so young. There's David Kennedy standing there at the back. He always pulled on his nose when he was nervous. And that's Alan Savage I think, over on the right; yes, that's him. Never wanted to get his hair cut properly. He always had the back and sides cut to regulations but on top he'd grow it as long as he could get away with and then hide it under his cap. Who else have we there? Oh yes, smart Alex, that's Alex McCelland between me and Dugdale. He knew everything about everything, even way back then,' Shaw advised the policemen with a sad smile on his face. He stopped talking but continued to stare at the photograph.

'And the others?' McCusker prompted.

'You know I can't, for the life of me, remember the other four Riflemen. Isn't that sad?'

'Well, maybe if you've time to think about it for a while it might come back to you,' Kennedy said, trying to encourage the veteran.

'Aye, it just might come back indeed, along with a lot of other nightmares,' Shaw offered regretfully.

Kennedy checked his notes before continuing, 'Ahm, Riflemen Alan Savage, Alex McCelland and David Kennedy, have you any idea where we'd find them today?' and then as an afterthought he added: 'Are they still alive?'

'No, sir, they all died in action,' Shaw said as he took off his cloth cap and turned it around in his hand, keeping the brim between his thumb and forefinger and turning it around with the other hand, all the time not taking his eyes off the photograph, even for a second.'

'All of them?' McCusker replied in disbelief.

'Yes indeed,' Shaw replied.

Kennedy was sure Shaw's trademark ice-blue eyes were filling with tears so the detective stood up.

'Look, sir, thanks for your time. We'll leave the photo with you and if you should remember any of the other names please give us a shout.'

As Kennedy and McCusker were leaving the kitchen, Shaw looked up from the photograph for the first time. 'Tell me, where did you come across this photograph?' he asked and then added: 'It's just that I'd like a copy, for myself like.'

'I'm sure that can be arranged,' Kennedy offered. 'We found the original photograph in Victor Dugdale's safe-deposit box in London.'

'Oh,' was all Shaw said as he returned his gaze to the photograph.

When Kennedy and McCusker were back in the car and heading once more in the direction of Portrush, McCusker was the first one to speak.

'Bit upsetting to see the old timer like that, wasn't it? I mean, all he's got now are his memories and we've just gone and helped him dig up some of the not-so-pleasant ones.'

'Aye,' Kennedy replied.

'What's on your mind, Kennedy?' McCusker prodded.

'Well, I was just thinking that it was strange that he'd be in a troop in the war and, apart from Dugdale, only be able to remember three of their names.'

'Perhaps that's because they were the three who died,' McCusker offered.

'Perhaps,' Kennedy replied as he sank deeper into his seat and into his thoughts.

Chapter Twenty

ANN REA HAD been amused by the way Kennedy's father had wound him up over breakfast. The thing she found most amusing was the fact that here was a detective inspector, a successful detective inspector in London Town, yet here he was still only someone's son and so still qualified for a bit of unmerciful winding-up from his father.

Kennedy had taken it all in good humour and even played along with it a bit; perhaps he'd been happy of the excuse to recall their previous evening's escapades on the beach. She'd certainly been happy of the opportunity to relive them. But that was then and this is now, she thought, I've work to do. And pretty soon, she was making her way towards Coleraine to visit her new friends on the *Coleraine Chronicle*.

The newsroom looked like nothing had changed since the last world war, except for the intrusion of computers, that was. There were monitors everywhere, pulsating an electric-blue beat throughout the room. Anita McCann, the friendly, efficient, resourceful and glamorous journalist ann rea had met the previous evening, was already at her desk slaving over a hot terminal.

Morning greetings over, she said: 'I've been checking through our files already this morning and I'm afraid, so far, I haven't managed to pull up anything on Kennedy's war-bride story. It'll take a time, though. The *Chronicle* started back in 1844, we've got back copies here in the building and there's back-up on microfilm over at the Irish Room in County Hall.'

'Oh well, I'm sure he'll manage okay on his own. I'd like to see if I can find out any more information about the excursion of the Ballyneagh Bridge Club to London?'

'Okey dokey,' Anita smiled, smoothing down her blue skirt. She was by far, ann rea assessed, the best-dressed person in the newsroom, so much so that all the other members of staff seemed somewhat underdressed. 'Pull up that chair then and let's see what we've got for you.'ann rea did as she was bid and Anita continued:

'So, what are the names you already have?'

'I think it's Paul McCann, no relation I hope?' ann rea began.

The Ulster journalist shook her head in the negative.

'And Robin Kane.'

'Okay. Are you sure these are two of the people who were on the excursion?'

'Well, I'm making something of an assumption. Terry Best, the caretaker, mentioned both of their Christian names and said he thought it must have been the bridge club.'

'Would it not be quicker just to get a list of the bridge club members?'

'I thought of that,' ann rea admitted, 'but I thought I might be in danger of making too many assumptions. I thought I'd leave that to crosscheck them at the end.'

'Okey dokey, I agree. Let's play safe. Let me make a quick call here to a mate of mine at a travel agents,' Anita said as she removed an earring and replaced it with the earpiece of a telephone headset. ann rea listened to one end of the conversation.

'Hello, Eamon it's…'

Pause followed by laughter.

'That's quick, you're getting better.'

Pause followed by more laughter.

'No, Eamon, it's information I want.'

Short pause.

'If I wanted to take a group of people from Northern Ireland over to London on an excursion, how would I go about it?'

Short pause.

'No, we don't think they flew.'

Pause.

'I'd say a maximum of a dozen.'

Longer pause.

'Yes, you're probably right, too small a group to take a tour bus.'

Pause.

'An Espace People Carrier, how many would that take?'

Pause.

'Ten, that might work. Would that be self-drive?'

A heartbeat.

'So ten including the driver? Okey dokey, and then where would I hire one from?'

Pause.

'McCausland's. Fine. Now how would we get it over to London?'

A beat.

'Which ferry?'

A pause.

'Somewhere around the Ballyneagh area.'

Pause.

'Which would be the quicker route to London, and please include in your timing the drive at the other end: Larne-Stranraer or Belfast- Liverpool?'

'Larne. Okey dokey. Now how would I go about finding out about the trip?'

Pause.

'Hang on a minute,' Anita said into the phone and then turned to ann rea. 'When would you say this trip was made?'

'I'd say about a month ago or a little over,' ann rea guessed.

'Say four weeks ago,' Anita spoke back into the phone.

Pause.

'Yes, we have two names actually.' Anita stopped to look down at her note pad, which was a large sheet of paper that covered the majority of her desk. The paper was covered with various doodles and scribbles and notes, all in different coloured pens and pencils, and each doodle or note seemed to be ringed with several circles. 'Paul McCann. No, Eamon, he's not a relation, nor even a long-lost husband. Eamon, can we get on with this please? Yes. The other name is Robin Kane.'

Another pause.

'If you tap into the company computer, will you get found out? Will you get in trouble? Eamon of course I'm concerned about your welfare. I'll still need you to find me cheap holidays in the sun.'

Long pause.

'We'll have to see about that, Eamon,' Anita said. ann rea

thought she saw the beginning of a blush form on her colleague's cheeks.

'In the meantime if you're sure you're not going to get into trouble, certainly have a check on their computer.'

Very long pause.

'Excellent, Eamon.' Anita, who'd been doodling for a couple of minutes, started to write furiously. ann rea tried to read over Anita's shoulder but couldn't see most of the page. After a couple of minutes' scribbling she said: 'Is that usual?'ann rea's interest picked up.

'But how would it have happened?'

Pause.

'But when they saw there were only nine passengers would they not have crossed off the names of those who didn't show?' Anita said as she turned to ann rea and gave her one of those "this is weird" kind of looks.

'Okey dokey, Eamon, that's brilliant. Thanks a million. I owe you one. Too-da-loo.'

Brief pause.

'No, Eamon,' Anita started back up, her voice increased in volume and irritation and just a hint patronising. 'That's certainly not what I meant.'

Pause.

'Well, yes, of course you can make up for it by buying me a drink; I'll see you in Kelly's tonight. Okey dokey. Must go. Tudaloo,' Anita said as she disconnected her phone, put the headset back on her desk and replaced her earring. She gave ann rea a nod.

'God, some men...' Anita started. 'They are all fine to be your very best friend until they see you start to date someone else and then all of a sudden they're on the trail of some other poor wee girl. Ah well, not to worry, he has his uses, particularly when I need my tan topping up.'

'So what was that wee bit of information you seemed confused about?' ann rea said avoiding, and not even sure it was being offered, the girlie talk.

'Well,' Anita began in a stage-loud breath and a "you're not going to believe it" look. 'They did hire an Espace People Carrier, and McCann and Kane were passengers. There were nine other names on the passenger list, a total of eleven pas-

sengers, but only eight showed up for the journey. Here...'
She handed ann rea the piece of paper. Anita's handwriting
was terrible, but ann rea saw that it contained the eleven
names:

1. D. Shaw
2. P. McCann
3. M. Derby
4. R. Kane
5. E. McKay
6. M. McIvor
7. T. Best
8. A. Greer
9. F. MacCool
10. A. Smart
11. M. Carr

'They caught the 10.30 ferry from Larne on Thursday 5th
July,' Anita continued. 'They were scheduled to arrive at
13.45 and they returned on Sunday 8th July on the 19.35,
scheduled to arrive back in Stranraer at 21.05. A much
quicker crossing – it must be all downhill on the way back,'
Anita said and enjoyed a wee giggle before continuing, 'so
they'd have been back home in Ballyneagh in time for supper.'
    'Does the ferry company not have the names of the no-
shows?' ann rea asked.
    'Apparently not. Highly irregular, don't you think? What
would have happened, heaven forbid, if the ferry had gone
down? Think of the confusion that would have caused,' Anita
said. ann rea got the feeling Anita was already thinking of a
possible news story. ann rea figured that the story would never
be written because Anita would want to protect her friend,
Eamon. ann rea rewrote the list in her notebook in her very
neat handwriting, along with the ferry details.
    She studied the list. The caretaker was listed, as was
Dugdale's best man whom ann rea knew Kennedy had
already visited. None of the other names meant anything to
her. But why had three of them not shown up for the trip? Not
entirely unusual, although still quite a high percentage of no-
shows. What was unusual, though, was the fact that the

names of the eight people who actually travelled were
unknown.

'Okay, I know how to get hold of Mr Derek Shaw and Mr
Terry Best, but how do I track down the rest of the people on
the list?'

'Well, normally I'd go to the church if I were you, but
you've already tried that route,' Anita said and then appeared
to be lost in thought. 'Okey dokey, here's what we'll do. A
mate of mine, Jim in advertising, he owes me a few favours.
He's originally from Ballyneagh, his parents still live there in
fact. You go to the canteen – that's the shoe box you passed to
your right on the way in – and have a wee cup of coffee; I'll
pay Jim a little visit and meet you down there in five or ten
minutes.'

Ten minutes later, as good as her word Anita showed up
with a new blush and a smile on her face.

'I wonder have Jim and Eamon ever met before?' she asked
as she helped herself to a cup of tea.

'You haven't invited Jim along to Kelly's tonight as well?'
ann rea giggled in mock shock.

'Variety, my dear girl, is the spice of… something or other.
Anyway, Jim knew two of the names on my list: M Derby,
who is in fact a girl called Margaret Derby, and Malachy
McIvor. Jim already had Miss Derby's telephone number.
She's a very serious girl, according to Jim, and he found out
Malachy's number for me. Here they are,' Anita said as she
copied the two names and numbers on a bit of paper and
passed them to ann rea.

'The other names?' ann rea ventured, not wishing to
appear greedy.

'Oh yes,' Anita answered, appearing startled as though
she'd forgotten all about them. 'Jim rang his mother but she
wasn't in. He says he'll speak to her before the end of day for
sure, and he's equally convinced that she'll find us contact
numbers for the remaining names on the travel list. Not a bad
wee morning's work, was it?'

'Amazing,' ann rea said. 'If there's ever anything I can do.'

'Oh, don't you worry. Next time I'm over in London I'll be
giving you a call. In the meantime if you're in Kelly's tonight,
mine's a gin and tonic.'

Yes, ann rea thought, and you'll be getting a few of them tonight if your morning's work is anything to go by.

Chapter Twenty-One

ANN REA WAS so excited at the information she had gained than she didn't notice the black Morris Minor van, with its two passengers, slip into the traffic two cars behind her as she headed back to Portrush. Nor had she noticed the vehicle as it had followed her on her outward journey. No, she was too busy thinking about something else entirely.

She was preoccupied with finding someone on the excursion list who would be willing to tell her what the excursion was all about. Had it just been 'jobs for the boys' and a way to spend the five grand proceeds from the sale of the rare wood? Was Houston involved in something illegal? Unethical? When Shaw had been racking his brains trying to remember the names of the people on the excursion list, he'd omitted his own. Perhaps he'd have offered his own name naturally if the Reverend Houston hadn't come barging into Shaw's cottage.

Hand on heart, she still wasn't convinced that there was a real story at the bottom of all this. You know, some geezers get together down at the pub one night for a drink. They'd met up with an antique dealer who was desperate to find some mature wood for a rich client in London. Perhaps there'd even been talks by that point about redecorating the vicarage and so one of them, say Terry Best, put two and two together, ran it past the Reverend who, perhaps, didn't really care what he did as long as he redecorated the place.

Then, to keep it in the family as it were, they used the money to fund a trip to London for the bridge club or some other church-related society. Surely there was nothing really outrageously criminal, or even unethical, about any of that? But why then were Shaw and Houston behaving so mysteriously? That was the only thing that kept ann rea on this trail. She didn't really care about the wood, or about them spending the money on the trip, but she felt that either Shaw or

Houston must have been trying to hide something or cover something up. What could it possibly be?

She'd already picked her next interview. She decided she would stick to her current run of luck with the sisterhood and go for the only female on the excursion list; well, at least the only female she had details of on the list, a Margaret Derby. Coincidentally, Margaret Derby worked in Portrush as a PA for a firm of accountants. ann rea still didn't know if Margaret was a Ms, a Miss or even a Mrs. All would soon be revealed as ann rea had arranged to meet her for a coffee in the lounge of the Embassy Hotel at noon. ann rea arrived first and, leaving her details with the receptionist, she went off and sat in the lounge, which had an amazing view of the West Strand, and enjoyed a few minutes' peace and quiet. She'd just resolved to bring Kennedy here for an evening drink (she was quite proud of having found a place off his well-worn path) when the receptionist brought through and introduced a young lady, Margaret Derby. ann rea noted immediately that Miss Derby was a Miss; she was about twenty and wore no wedding ring. Margaret preferred to be called Maggie, smiled a little and had very long, jet-black hair parted in the middle. She was slim but not thin, and was dressed in a blue miniskirt and a red T-shirt. Her bare arms and legs were (sun) burnt a deep tan. Maggie wore no make-up but the first thing she did when she sat down was to take a brush out of a small, black backpack and brush the August wind out of her hair.

'I'm afraid I haven't got long,' Maggie began slightly nervously. 'I've got to get a few messages for me mother in me break.'

'Oh, we shouldn't be too long,' ann rea said as she milked and sugared Maggie's coffee as directed. 'I wanted to talk to you about the excursion to London.'

'I thought you might,' Maggie offered, before ann rea had a chance to elaborate. She looked around the empty lounge once before continuing. 'Look, talk about making a mountain out of a molehill. The bridge club took a trip to London as the guests of West Hampstead Bridge Club. They were over here last year for a round-robin competition and they invited us back over to their patch. It's as simple as that and the Reverend Houston and Terry have been getting their knickers in a twist about you running around asking all your questions.'

Mystery apparently solved, ann rea sank back into her chair a little disappointed.

'How long were you there for?' ann rea asked after a sip of her coffee.

'Three days and two nights in London and another day for travel in total.'

'Did you all pay your own expenses?' ann rea prodded at the remaining one little potential bit of scandal.

Maggie Derby smiled for the first time; it was one of those "you're going to be disappointed" type of smiles.

'No. I believe that's how all this started, isn't it, some old busybody complaining about wood being sold? It's only a load of wood, for heaven's sake. Terry was told he had to decorate the vicarage. It was old and dingy and he was instructed to brighten things up. To be quite honest, I can't abide these old biddies who have obviously read too much Agatha Christie and want the vicarage to still look like it looked over a hundred years ago. The church's future is through its youth and I can tell you that they're not going to get many of the youth of Ballyneagh into wood-panelled, dark, depressing rooms. Give it a bit of lilac, a vibrant blue, green, red; we like a little bit of welly in our colours, if you know what I mean. Anyway, Terry, being the enterprising chap he is, saw a way of modernising the vicarage and putting a few bob in the fund. Has anyone bothered to tell you that as well as financing the bridge club's excursion, the funds also paid for the decorating of the vicarage?'

'Ah, no,' ann rea smiled, feeling about ten inches tall and wondering why no one had bothered to mention that one to her before.

'No, I thought not. It's always the same, isn't it? Instead of Terry and Reverend Houston feeling guilty and running around like a pair of eejits, someone should be thanking them for all their hard work.'

'Could you tell me the names of the other people on the excursion?' ann rea asked, trying to find a way to move on.

'I could,' Maggie began as ann rea poised her pen over her note pad, 'but I'm not going to.'

'Oh! How about the number of people who actually went on the trip?' ann rea pushed.

'No! There's been enough made about this so far. The bridge club went on an excursion to London. It was paid for out of the proceeds of the sale of the wood from the vicarage. End of story except, of course the most important part of the story…' Maggie paused as she picked up her backpack and took out her hairbrush for a second time.

'Oh?' ann rea replied, hooked.

'The most important news of the trip is that we won. We beat the West Hampstead Bridge Club by five rubbers to three. I'm sure you'll need that for your write-up, Miss Rea,' Maggie's well-worn smirk emphasising the capital. She gave her hair a quick few strokes with the brush, replaced the brush in her backpack, stood up, hunkered down for a final quick sip of coffee, stood up again and walked out of the lounge without another word except: 'Ta-ra'.

'Well,' ann rea said to her own half-empty cup of coffee, 'that's me told off well and truly. So ends my assignment.'

She hoped Kennedy was faring better. As it happens, he wasn't faring much better at all. When they eventually managed to get together and compare notes… well now, that would be a different matter altogether.

Kennedy was stuck in Portrush Police Barracks on a hot August morning. Mind you, with the office he was in it didn't really matter where he was, nor what time of the year it was for that matter. He and McCusker were chatting away about the case.

'There's something obvious that we're missing here,' McCusker said.

'Yeah, you're right, but we won't know what's missing until we have a few more facts.'

'I know what you mean, but there's something still niggling away at me, something I think I already know that's relevant but I'm having trouble,' McCusker replied, lighting his third Player of the morning. 'Tell me about the way Dugdale was found again?'

Kennedy repeated the information about Victor Dugdale and The Black Cat Building.

'Okay, what does all that tell you?' McCusker croaked between serious bouts of ciggy-influenced coughing.

'Well, first off, Dugdale lived in London about a twenty-minute walk away from the Black Cat Building. Second, the owners of the Black Cat Building had recently bought wood from somewhere close to Dugdale's birthplace. Third, someone wanted to make a point with this murder. You know? Dugdale could have been stabbed or shot and thrown in Regents Canal; we've certainly had more than enough of those over the years. So, someone wanted to make a point with all of this; and make their point very flamboyantly at that.'

'All the circumstances, you know, with the way the body was left hanging up and all of that, could it have anything to do with the Masons?' McCusker asked, squinting up his eyes from the smoke as he stubbed his cigarette out.

'No, we checked and when we told them how Dugdale was found they told us: "You're looking for a butcher more than a Mason."' Kennedy replied, already off on his next thought. 'Say, for argument's sake, he was murdered by someone from around here or Ballyneagh, they'd have to be fools.'

'Why do you say "they" and why are they fools?'

'Well, it would have been impossible for one person to have taken Dugdale into the Black Cat Building. There'd have to have been two, possibly even three of them. And fools because of all the fuss with the wood. The trail was bound to lead back here,' Kennedy said.

'Well now, let's think about this, that's not strictly true. What are the chances of someone writing a story on an unsolved murder for a local paper in Camden Town? And what are the chances of a local paper around here picking up the story? And then, what are the chances of an old biddy reading the story and knowing that some local wood had been sold to the very same Black Cat Building and ringing the local paper? They in turn ringing ann rea? And then the estranged daughter also sees the story and rings the paper, possibly identifying the body? I mean, at any one of those points it could have all come to a standstill. And then there is this additional smoke screen with the ritualistic murder. So they could have felt pretty secure. Really now, Kennedy, you'd have to agree.'

'Yeah,' Kennedy said reluctantly, 'but then when we got access to Dugdale's safe-deposit box we would have found the wartime picture and we would have traced some of the people in the photos eventually.'

'But that would only have been as a result of Doris Dugdale getting in touch with us.'

Kennedy was about to say something but he stopped and started to laugh.

'What?' McCusker asked. 'What on earth are ye laughin' at?'

'Well, here we are going on in a self-congratulatory state about how we've done this and how we've done that and how the article led us to the murderer, but we haven't the slightest clue as to the identity of the murderer or murderers. We haven't even got any more leads to go chasing at this moment...'

At that point ann rea entered the office, stopping Kennedy mid-sentence.

'So how are you? Sorry, I forgot what part of the world I was in. Of course, what I meant to say was how are youse boys getting on with solving the crime?'

'Ask us one on hurling,' McCusker smiled as ann rea pulled up a spare chair. 'We were just studying th' big pitcher.'ann rea's eyebrows rose as she stared at Kennedy.

'The big picture, ann rea, we were looking at the big picture. And yourself, how's your morning been?'ann rea recalled the scene in the Embassy Hotel.

'So the reality is, at this point I've not got a story.'

'Apart from the fact that the Ballyneagh Bridge Club thrashed the West Hampstead Bridge Club. God, woman, what are you on about, won't that keep your editor happy?' McCusker chuckled.

'Yeah and pigs will fly,' ann rea replied.

'Must remember to take an umbrella out with me then,' McCusker said as he poured ann rea another cup of the famous Portrush Police Barracks' stewed tea.

'Oh, and how did you get on with Anita?' Kennedy asked.

'Oh, okey dokey,' ann rea replied.

'Did she have anything in the files on Victor Dugdale?' Kennedy asked hopefully.

'She was going to check for us. She said the *Coleraine Chronicle* started in 1844. They do have a lot of back issues in their building but it's also copied on microfilm, which is kept over at the Irish Room at County Hall in Coleraine. She was going to get one of the office juniors to check it out for her as a research project. She said it would do them a lot of good. It may take some time though.'

'Oh,' Kennedy said dejectedly.

'She managed to find me a wee bit of information for my story though, sorry, make that non-story. She found the route the bridge club excursion took to London and the list of the party,' ann rea said as she took out a notebook and handed it across the desk to Kennedy.

1. D Shaw
2. P McCann
3. M Derby
4. R Kane
5. E McKay
6. M McIvor
7. T Best
8. A Greer
9. F MacCool
10. A Smart
11. M Carr

'God!' Kennedy blasphemed and, after thirty seconds study-ing the list, whistled as he passed it over to McCusker with: 'See who's top of the passenger list?'

'Why, our good friend, and even better cook, Derek Shaw!'

Chapter Twenty-Two

'SURE, YOU DIDN'T ask me that question,' was Derek Shaw's simple answer to McCusker's: 'You didn't tell us you were in London with the Ballyneagh Bridge Club.'

Kennedy and McCusker had to concede that neither had, in fact, asked that particular question.

'It's just that, you know, Derek, with you being Victor Dugdale's best man and all that, and then you being in London around the time of his death, I'm sure you can see we're a little surprised,' McCusker continued. It was creeping around to lunch time and they were, for the third time in twenty-four hours, sitting in the company of the old man with the young eyes.

'Aye, I'd say surprised and probably add excited,' Shaw returned with a sparkle in his eye, voice hoarse as ever. 'But I'm afraid I'm going to have to disappoint you. It was purely a coincidence. Now, you have to realise that's why they have that word, you know, "coincidence" in the dictionary because sometimes coincidences happen and this just happens to be one of those times.'

Kennedy, who'd said nothing in the exchange so far, studied Shaw closely. Shaw looked like a favourite grandfather who was up for a bit of devilment. The Camden Town detective wasn't sure he was going for the "coincidence" angle but, at the same time, Shaw seemed to be doing a fair job convincing everyone, including himself, that it was just that.

'I'd say it was much more of an extraordinary coincidence,' Kennedy said after some thought.

'Again I'd have to say that the reason there is that word "extraordinary" in the dictionary is because sometimes, rarely I admit, exceptional things happen and so someone had the bright idea of coming up with a word to describe it,' Shaw replied nonchalantly.

'Accepting that it was just that, "an extraordinary coinci-

dence", don't you think it would have been worthwhile
mentioning it to us?'

'Ah now come on, lads, I don't mind cooking your food for
you, but I'm not about to do your job for you as well. Talking
about which, would you like a cup of tea and a scrambled-egg
sandwich?'

Kennedy didn't want this distraction to his questioning but
with the rumblings in McCusker's stomach he figured there
wasn't much he could do about it.

'So,' he began, as Shaw went about melting butter into a
saucepan, 'tell us about the bridge club outing.'

'There's really nothing much to tell, lads. They were over
here last year, we beat them and they invited us over to West
Hampstead for a return match. We went over there, thrashed
them again and came back.'

'Could you tell us the name of everyone who went on the
trip?' Kennedy pushed as Shaw cracked five eggs into the pan.

'Make yourself useful there, young lad,' Shaw said,
addressing McCusker. 'Butter us some bread. Use that sliced
pan, it sure makes a great wee sandwich. Names of people on
the list, agh, let me see. I couldn't be sure, but Terry Best was
there. He's the caretaker over at the church; he'll know. I'm
not being evasive… I know people like Maggie Derby were
there but I'm getting old don't you see, my memory is not as
sharp as it was. Terry'll tell you, though.'

'How many were on the trip?' Kennedy asked, not exactly
sure what to make of Shaw's previous answer.

'Oh, I'd say about a dozen,' Shaw smiled. He appeared to
be letting the eggs fry. Kennedy could hear them sizzling at the
bottom of the saucepan and Shaw was leaving them alone.

'I mean, you were in a van with these people for the guts of
a day and a half solid if you count the return journey, so you
must…'

'One thing you learn, Mr Kennedy, as you get older is to
discipline your mind so that when you're doing something as
mundane as, say, travelling, you use the time to enjoy yourself
by daydreaming. Well, it's a kind of daydreaming; it's a semi-
conscious state and is an extremely enjoyable state to be in.
Consequently, you don't really pay attention to your immedi-
ate surroundings,' Shaw replied.

At that moment he used a wooden spoon to mix the eggs. Holding the saucepan away from the Aga he turned the spoon around, gently mixing the eggs without battering them or even scrambling them. In about a minute the eggs were prepared and ready for McCusker's buttered bread. Shaw scooped the eggs out onto the bread and washed the saucepan out under the tap. Unlike Kennedy's attempt at scrambling eggs, Shaw didn't have a lot of egg matter sticking to the bottom of the saucepan.

When Shaw turned back to the table in the kitchen he looked at Kennedy who was still staring at the clean saucepan in open disbelief.

'Cooking eggs is a bit like living our lives,' Shaw began expansively as he folded over his buttered bread around his eggs and took a large first bite, which he seemed to savour for a few moments before washing it down with a swig of tea and continuing: 'With the eggs the secret is to take them from the stove at the correct moment. There is a point before the eggs are cooked but when there is enough inherent heat in the saucepan to complete the cooking. If you pick the correct moment then you find the eggs don't bake themselves onto the base of the pan and you get your perfect sandwich. In life you have to be careful that you don't leave things on the fire too long. It's equally important that you let the energy you have already built up do the final bit of work for you. By doing so you find that (a) you use less energy and (b) you've less of a mess to clear up after you.'

'Are you telling us that we know all we need to know?' McCusker asked, his mouth full of delicious egg sandwich.

Shaw's ice-blue eyes twinkled as he smiled.

'No,' he began as he looked at Kennedy, still smiling, 'but I suppose I'd have to say perhaps you already do. I'm not sure there's much else to know. The funny thing about coincidences is that we tend to be too attracted to them, just because they are unusual. But perhaps we shouldn't be. But no, I was just looking at Inspector Kennedy here, marvelling at how clean my saucepan was when I finished and I remembered sitting at a similar dinner table watching my Uncle Matt produce similar results. He taught me how to cook the eggs that way. He also told me the story about how you can use the simile of cooking eggs to help live your life more efficiently. It stood me in good stead over the years, I can tell you.'

'So,' Kennedy began. He could see that McCusker was still focusing on the egg concept. 'You're telling us that you don't remember the numbers or the members of the trip.'

'You're burning your eggs again, Inspector,' Shaw smiled. 'What I was saying was that there are others, Terry Shaw for instance, who can surely give you more accurate information, my memory being what it is.'

'We'd better bring a bunch of groceries next time we visit him,' Kennedy began. It was thirty minutes later and they were on the outskirts of Ballyneagh on the way to interview the very same Terence Best. 'We're in danger of eating the poor man out of house and home.'

'A good one about the eggs, though,' McCusker replied as he negotiated the tricky roads in their unmarked car. 'I'd never heard that one before.'

'Do you think it could be some kind of clue?' Kennedy asked, voicing his thoughts.

'Only if you're the Naked Chef or Delia,' McCusker replied as he pulled up outside the gate to Terence Best's house. 'I wonder has your man indoors got anything in the pan for us.'

'I'd settle for a good cup of tea,' Kennedy said as he rang the doorbell on the blue door, which was in imminent danger of being overgrown by ivy.

Kennedy's first thought, when the caretaker opened his door, was that he'd seen him before somewhere. He couldn't place exactly where it was or when it had been but there was just something strangely familiar about this man's face.

'I wish all the bridge club's trips got as much attention,' Best replied when McCusker told him what they'd come to talk about.

'So, can you tell me who was on the trip?' Kennedy asked simply after a few minutes of niceties and when it didn't appear as though a cup of tea was forthcoming.

'Of course, I can get you the list,' Shaw replied.

'Don't you remember the names of the people who went with you, man?' McCusker said, either frustrated at the inability of all involved in this farce to name one another or at the fact that there was nothing in the pot for him.

'Yes, of course I do, but it's obviously very important. What, first with the English press yesterday and now today the local press and then youse two, the London police and the local police, I thought I'd better get it 100 percent accurate.'

'Oh go on, Terry, humour me. We're not going to throw you in the nick for getting one name wrong. Tell me all the names you can remember,' McCusker said showing his irritation.

'Fine. Let's see, there was old Derek Shaw, young Maggie Derby, they were both there, and myself of course…'

'And?' McCusker pushed.

'And Paul McCann and Robin Kane.'

'Okay, you're doing good, you're up to five,' McCusker kept up the attack.

Kennedy was slightly taken aback with McCusker's apparent overdrive. It wasn't a new gear; just one he hadn't used before in front of Kennedy. It was, apparently, having the required effect on Terence Best because he was thinking only of coming up with the list of names to satisfy McCusker's thirst for knowledge. Best wavered for a few seconds before continuing,

'And Eamon, yes, Eamon was there; that'd be Eamon McKay.'

'Good, good, Terry, Eamon McKay, that's another one. Come on now, you're doing well,' McCusker said, unconsciously, Kennedy was sure, doing a fair impression of Bruce Forsyth.

'And then there was Malachy McIvor and Audrey Greer,' Best finally offered with a sigh strong enough to have blown out a cake covered with the sixty-five candles required to commemorate his last birthday.

'Didn't he do well, Inspector Kennedy?' McCusker announced, convincing Kennedy that he had been dipping into old Brucie's repertoire after all in order to push Best to produce the results.

But he still hadn't finished.

'I make that a total of eyate people, Terry,' McCusker replied, slipping back into Ulster-speak for the number.

'Aye, reckon you're right, eyate av us.'

'Yes, that's correct, you gave us the eight names. Could you tell me then...' McCusker paused, adding the slightest of dramatics to the proceedings, 'why the passenger list had three additional names on it?'

'Sorry?' Best replied appearing confused and looking towards Kennedy to see if he was going to intervene.

Kennedy was enjoying McCusker's performance. So far on the case, it had been nothing more than plodding around in the dark and now both he and McCusker had a bone to chew on. Kennedy was happy to let McCusker get on with it; he knew exactly how fond the Ulster detective was of his food.

'On the passenger list we have, we've got an extra three names. A Mr F McCool, a Mr M Carr and a Mr A Smart.'

'Really?'

McCusker and Kennedy both nodded in the positive.

'I don't know what all that is about, that's for sure. Mind you, I didn't make the bookings. Perhaps that's three other people who were travelling separately, something to do with the travel agency or the shipping line, or a mistake or something.'

'Or something,' McCusker repeated. 'So, as far as you are concerned, there were only eight members of your bridge club on the trip?'

Best laughed. He then appeared to grow a little self-conscious. 'You see, there are only eight members in our club.'

'Tell me, Mr Best,' Kennedy began, preparing to ask his first question of the session, 'do you know a Mr Victor Dudgale?

'Aye, I've heard of him alright,' Best replied.

'When was the last time you saw him?' Kennedy asked, jumping up his list of questions a bit to try and introduce an element of surprise.

'Nagh, you misunderstood me. I don't actually know him, I've just heard about him.'

'Heard what about him?' Kennedy asked.

'Heard that he died recently,' Best replied.

'Oh, and how did you come to hear that?'

'Oh, you know, just around, you know the way you pick things up.'

'Tell me,' Kennedy continued, following a few seconds'
consideration, 'do you know if the Reverend Houston is
around?'

'In fact I do know, I know he's over at the rectory this very
minute. I'm due to go over and see him the minute youse two
leave.'

'Maybe we'll accompany you over then,' Kennedy replied
as he and McCusker rose to their feet indicating, quite firmly,
that it was not a debatable issue.

Chapter Twenty-Three

McCUSKER AND KENNEDY left it to Best to knock on the door. He was surprised that Best used the brass knocker instead of the doorbell. Could his action perhaps be a warning to those within?

The Reverend Houston proved to be more hospitable than at their previous stop and offered everyone, including Best, tea and sandwiches. McCusker accepted immediately but stated, firmly, that the detectives wanted to interview the Reverend. Best declined the offer, saying he'd other things he needed to attend to.

'Oh, it's to be a full-blown official interview then, is it?' Houston asked with a smile as sincere as any of Hughie Green's best. 'In that case, we should conduct it in the drawing room. If youse two pop up to the first floor and through the door directly across the landing, I'll order up the refreshments and be right with you.'

'Aye, and have your wee chat with Best as you show him to the door,' McCusker whispered to Kennedy as they walked up the staircase two abreast, examining the portraits of previous occupants on an oak-lined wall.

They entered the room as bid and Kennedy, from the beautiful staircase and wood-panelled walls, had been expecting a totally different kind of room. Instead of wood panelling, chip paper painted a dark green covered the walls. Again, the walls to this double-aspect room were covered with paintings, all portraits and mostly of people from the last century, Kennedy assessed. The floor looked resplendent, a varnished pine, well-trodden and marked with two centuries' worth of furniture movement. The ceiling had all its original cornicing, the extremely complicated design serving the central crystal chandelier.

There was definitely something wrong with the room.

As Kennedy was having this thought he realised exactly

what it was. The chip paper just didn't work and it didn't work because it was replacing the famous wood-panelled walls, which had been sold to Camden Town. This is what all the fuss had been about and rightly so, Kennedy thought, with the dark-green painted chip paper trying to hide the multitude of marks or, should that be, sins. Underneath, they'd gone for the cheap method of recreating what had originally been there. What they should have done was to re-plaster the walls, cover it with a lining paper and then paint it with one of the National Trust's lighter colours. This way they would have added a new outlook to the grand room and maybe even, at least in some people's book, improve the look of the room.

The Reverend Houston took his time coming to the room. In fact the tea and sandwiches arrived before him, all beautifully laid out on a silver tray. Tea was delivered and served by two similarly dressed young women. No part of this house, or the church or staff (four Kennedy had spotted so far – five if you count Best) seemed in need of money. Kennedy was sure the coffers could easily have stood the five-grand bounty the rare wood had realised.

Houston burst into the drawing room just as the two tea ladies had finished serving Kennedy and McCusker tea, finger sandwiches (McCusker had several) and shortbread (Kennedy had several). They had left the Reverend a cup of tea by his chair, the one by the fireplace, which afforded him a panoramic view, via a floor-to-ceiling window, of the magnificent, well-manicured gardens.

'Beautiful room, Reverend,' McCusker began as another finger sandwich disappeared in less than a bite. Just as the Reverend was accepting the compliment he continued: 'Shame about the walls though, it must have looked really brilliant before. You know, before all the farce about selling off the wood that used to cover these walls. What's that bit in the Bible about Jesus coming back and finding out what they were doing in His church, throwing a bit of a wobbler, overturning all the stalls and everything? I was just wondering what He would have done about this.'

Houston finished milking and sugaring his tea, raised the cup and saucer to his lips and took a sip before replying.

'Well firstly, Inspector, "brilliant" as in "looked really brilliant" implies a whiteness if you will, a bright or effulgent effect, and I have to tell you that dark, wooden walls, having lived with them in this room over the last fifty-odd years, were anything but bright or brilliant.'

'Oh,' was all that McCusker could find to say.

'And with regards to your other little parable, I'm afraid you got that one slightly wrong as well. I think you were referring to the one where Jesus came back to His church and found money lenders and traders set up all around His Father's house and yes, He did indeed cast them out as we'd expect Him to do and as we'd do today.'

'Yes, very interesting,' Kennedy began. 'We need to talk to you about your bridge club's excursion to London.'

'You sound like someone who's come to remonstrate with a father over a misbehaving son or daughter,' Houston said with a little laugh, not enough of a laugh to be genuine. Definitely one for effect, and so short and insincere that no one could, or did, mistake it for a laugh. 'I suppose in a way I am responsible for my congregation. Okay, which one of my flock has strayed from the path while in London?'

'Why only one?' Kennedy felt compelled to ask.

'Yes, you have a good point, Inspector. Entire flocks do tend to get laid astray by one bad sheep.'

'It doesn't mean that their sin is any the less a sin,' Kennedy didn't know where all of this was coming from; the words were just being drawn out of him by the situation.

Houston looked a little taken aback.

'That's an interesting point, Inspector, a very interesting point. So you obviously believe that the leaders sin no more than those who follow.'

'Yes, I think I do,' Kennedy replied hesitantly. 'I think everyone knows right from wrong and they make their own choices whether or not to cross that line.'

'Interesting point, Inspector Kennedy,' Houston replied, appearing totally enthused; either that or he was happy to delay what he thought they'd come to talk to him about. 'Now, in your right and wrong, do you mean a universal right and wrong or the individual's right and wrong?'

'Is there a difference?' Kennedy asked.

Houston was positively beaming from ear to ear.

"Is there a difference?' Excellent question. Excellent question indeed,' the Reverend Houston replied. 'Yes, I think there is. For instance, say someone breaks into a bank and helps themselves to some funds, that's stealing and it is wrong; they know it is wrong and they know that they are breaking your law. Now on the other hand, take a mother who has, say for argument's sake, four children at home, all hungry and waiting to be fed, and she goes to the local grocer and when no one is watching she helps herself to a few potatoes, a few apples, bananas, maybe even a couple of packs of burgers out of the freezer and she goes off to feed her family. Do you think she's like the bank robber and considers herself a thief and that she is breaking the law?'

'I'd say, without exception, she feels a lot worse and (even) more guilty than the bank robber for her sin,' Kennedy replied simply and quickly.

'You really believe that a mother who steals to feed her children is committing a crime? Where's your compassion, man?'

'Compassion, now isn't that one of the church's qualities. Surely if that same mother comes to the church and tells you about her plight, the church will look after her and help her back onto the straight and narrow again, thereby preventing her from having to steal,' Kennedy said.

'Yes, and we probably would, but what if everyone who was hungry or down on their luck came to us with their hands open, what would we do then?'

'Good point, Reverend. But equally, what about the poor grocer? What does he do when everyone in the neighbourhood comes and steals from him and then his suppliers stop supplying him because he can't afford to pay their bills? He, unlike the church, is not in the compassion business. What do he and his family do then?' Kennedy replied and before the Reverend had a chance to reply he continued: 'I know that this is all incredibly simplistic but if people steal they have to know that they are breaking the law so they don't continue to break the law. Otherwise the end result, in the extreme, is anarchy.'

'As you say, incredibly simplistic, but going back to your original point for a second, what if, say, someone is ordered to break the law. Where they have no choice, short of a court martial, but to break the law?'

'In that case, society obviously has to rely on the law makers, those giving the orders, to be responsible...'

Houston cut him off: 'But isn't this obviously where your theory falls down, because if you have two armies in battle, then the soldiers on one side must be in the wrong and therefore sinning?'

McCusker, who'd been silent so far in the exchange, said:'Sounds to me a little like Dylan's With God On Our Side.' He paused for a couple of heartbeats as Kennedy and Houston considered the song and then he continued: 'I don't think he resolved anything either.'

Kennedy smiled, happy that McCusker had completed that particular Circle. He said: 'Tell me, Reverend, do you feel that you ought to be remonstrated with for your flock's behaviour while they were in London?'

'Well, so far I haven't been made aware of any bad behaviour,' Houston smiled and put his cup and saucer down on the table beside him. The table also bore a Tiffany lamp and a soft, leather-bound copy of the Bible. Kennedy and McCusker were sitting in high-backed leather chairs, which formed a triangle around the hearth of the fireplace.

'How involved were you with the organisation of the London trip?' Kennedy asked.

'Hardly at all, Inspector. I'm sure you'll appreciate that I can't personally be involved in all the clubs and societies this church is involved with, there just wouldn't be the time.'

'Quite,' Kennedy replied, now distracted by the large painting above the fireplace. For the second time in recent memory he was looking at a face and he had the premonition he knew the face but again, for the second time, he couldn't put a name to the face. 'Tell me, who's the gentleman in the painting.'

'I thought I saw hints of recognition in your eyes. You think you know him, don't you?' Houston replied.

'I'm sure I've seen him before somewhere,' Kennedy replied, studying the fullness of the eyebrows.

'Terence Best, now there's a wee clue for you.'

'Terry Best, your caretaker, dressed up like a dog's dinner and someone painted him? Nagh,' McCusker grunted.

'Actually, it's my predecessor and Terry's father, the Reverend David Anthony Best,' Houston replied, completely ignoring McCusker. 'He was the rector here until just after the Second World War. He was a truly great man. He served this parish loyally for forty-six years.'

'I can see it now,' Kennedy replied as he searched through his mind for the other flash of recognition he had had recently, but he couldn't recall it; no, not even if his life had depended on it. 'So you weren't involved in the trip?'

'No, not at all.'

'Did you know about the funding?'

'Inspector Kennedy,' Houston said bursting into his mock laugh again, 'is that what this is all about, the sale of the wood? Look, I'm well aware that Terence sold the wood and used the proceeds to redecorate this room and pay for the trip to England. Actually, if you ask me I think he was quite enter-prising. It'd be great if some of our other clubs showed the same initiative instead of continuously coming to me with their hands out. There was nothing wrong with what he did, everything was perfectly legitimate. And not another word would have been heard about it if Mrs What'shername hadn't complained to the papers.'

'Do you know where the wood ended up?' Kennedy asked. McCusker seemed content to let the Camden Town detective get on with it at this stage. Kennedy felt it was as though they'd been partners for years.

'Inspector,' Houston barked as though it was a Sunday morning and he was up in his pulpit, 'everyone, but everyone, knows where that flaming wood ended up!'

'What about Victor Dugdale? Did you know him?'

'Mr Dugdale left these parts so long ago, left a wife and a wee daughter to fend for themselves by the way, no one around here knows very much about him.'

'Are you originally from these parts, reverend?'

'Yes, myself and the last four generations of Houstons,' the Reverend Houston beamed proudly. 'My great, great grand-father came over to the providence from Edinburgh as a minister.'

'So would you have known Victor Dugdale back in the '40s when you were both teenagers?'

'He's never the kind of person I would have mixed with, believe me,' Houston said firmly, with a great sense of finality about his sentence.

'Just one more little point, and nothing really to do with this case,' Kennedy began as the three rose to their feet, signalling the end of the interview. 'I was just wondering how the little book store, and the souvenir shop and the café at the back of the church were doing; they seemed incredibly busy as we walked in.'

'Oh, very well, thank you, Inspector. Yes, very well indeed,' Houston replied.

'Yeah,' McCusker added, dusting imaginary crumbs from his blue shirt, 'all's you need now is a wee branch of the Alliance and Leicester and you'd be all set.'

Houston's cheeks and whiskey nose went through all the shades of red to beetroot in the space of five seconds.

Chapter Twenty-Four

MEANWHILE BACK IN Camden Town, DS James Irvine and DC (the "W" having recently been removed to show, once and for all, that the police force had finally arrived at its liberated state of equality) Anne Coles were sitting in a traffic jam in West End Lane on the outskirts of West Hampstead.

They'd passed the Abbey Road Recording Studios easily enough. The studios were famous for being the home where so much of The Beatles' music had been recorded. Coles had wanted to take the longer route in order to bypass Abbey Road. She was totally bewildered at the throngs of people from all over the world still gathering outside the studio to pay homage, in an orderly fashion of course, to a group who had split up just over thirty years ago. She also knew, because she made a similar journey every day, that Swiss Cottage would be chock-a-block with home-bound traffic.

They needn't have bothered trying to avoid the traffic because they then became stuck in the build-up of traffic also wishing to avoid the bottleneck of cars trying to get on to Finchley Road.

'It would have been easier if we'd come earlier,' she said as she turned left into Dynham Road, trying to take a few back-streets.

'What, and missed this?' Irvine replied, holding onto the sides of his seat as they roared down the steep incline. 'Never!'

He made an attempt to imitate the sound of people on a roller coaster as he said: 'Weeeeee. Besides which, they don't open 'til five o'clock anyway.'

'Right,' Coles said as she hung a quick right at the end of Dynham Road, cutting up a large Mercedes van. 'If I got stuck behind that in these little streets we'd never get there.'

'Right,' Irvine replied, gripping onto his seat even tighter. 'I have this worry, Detective Constable Coles, that we're never going to get there anyway. I think you have this idea, you know, when you're driving a car, that you're still on your moped. I'm here to tell you that a motor car just won't fit through the same gaps as a moped.'

His pronunciation of "moped" was pure James Bond, as in Sean Connery's James Bond. In fact, if one closed their eyes, as Coles appeared to be doing now every time she took a corner, one would be forgiven for thinking that the great JB was right beside them.

'It's no' a moped,' she replied, trying a take off his accent. It didn't really come off, so she reverted to her own normal Queen's English to conclude her sentence: 'It's a Vespa 125 scooter.'

'Aye, I know, a broomstick with two pram wheels and a motor you nicked from one of the fans in the office,' Irvine jested as he relaxed a bit more. They had rejoined the traffic on West End Lane and their speed had been reduced to a walk.

Ten minutes, and two hundred and eighty yards later, they pulled into the front of the West End Lane Bridge School.

Now that Coles no longer had to wear the pillbox hat, or any of the rest of her uniform for that matter, she was letting her bottle-blonde hair down to flow where it wanted, instead of the elaborate contraption she stuffed it up into in order to get her hat on. If anything, it made her look younger and her smart, black, midi-skirted suit contrasted agreeably with Irvine's tweeds.

The bridge club was close to a parade of shops that led to West Hampstead Tube Station and therefore didn't benefit from the dense foliage of trees further down West End Lane. Around the corner to the right were the West Hampstead Studios where some famous '60s pop groups recorded. These studios used to be owned by Decca records and if they hadn't turned down the opportunity to sign The Beatles, with the infamous "guitar bands are finished" put-down, the Fab Four would have had to travel a little less distance from their native Liverpool for their recording sessions. As it was, the Rolling Stones and Them did a lot of their early work at the West Hampstead Studios.

Irvine imagined that the bridge club still looked like it had in the '60s but that, equally, it was a place never frequented by the likes of The Beatles or the Stones, or even Them for that matter. He waited until Coles locked the car door and joined him on the steps of the house before he rang the doorbell.

Bang went Irvine's theory immediately. The man who answered the door with his bell-bottom trousers, hairstyle and wrinkled face looked a dead ringer for Bill Wyman. Perhaps young girls did play bridge after all, Irvine thought as he introduced Coles and himself.

'Yes, I've been expecting you, like. I'm Wright Butler. Thankfully I didn't have a brother,' he paused. 'You know... so that me father would have had to call him Wrong.'

Great, Irvine thought, the man's at least fifty years old and he still feels compelled to apologise for his name.

'My friends call me Wrightie, and you can too. Come on in.'

Irvine got straight down to it. 'You know we're here to check out the details of the Ballyneagh Bridge Club visit.'

'Yes, indeed I do,' Wrightie replied. 'Very successful little venture it was too. They're good players but we gave them a run for their money, I can tell you.'

'Yes, we heard,' Coles said. 'When did they arrive with you?'

'Let's see now, that would have been on the Wednesday, no, sorry, Thursday evening. Which would make it Thursday July 5th.'

'How many of them actually travelled?' Irvine asked. They were in the cold reception room, 'cold' as in the decor. It looked more like a doctor's surgery than a club with its yellow, painted walls; brown, well-worn carpet; and a few coffee tables scattered around, all stacked high with magazines and newspapers.

'We'd eight of them. Apparently that's their whole membership. We've got a lot more members to call on... yes, you're correct, and they still managed to beat us. I personally think our lot take it all a teeny bit too seriously. The Ballyneagh crowd were having fun, a lot of fun, and they still managed to beat us.'

'Where did they stay?' Irvine asked.

'Well, usually we'd put them up, you know, between the members, but they insisted on staying in a hotel.'

'Which hotel would that have been?' Irvine continued, refusing the offer of mineral water or orange juice. Coles accepted the mineral water.

'The Holiday Inn over at Swiss Cottage. No, sorry, it's changed its name, hasn't it? It's now called the Marriott, I believe,' Wrightie replied, helping himself to a second glass of orange juice.

'That'd be quite expensive, wouldn't it?' Irvine asked, thinking they'd have stayed in a little guesthouse at best.

'Aye, it wouldn't have been cheap,' Wright Butler replied.

'Did you give them any money towards their expenses?' Coles asked.

'No. That would never happen. Excepting, of course, if it were to be an official competition. But on invitations, everyone covers their own expenses. Like when we went to see them first off, we covered our own expenses.'

'Tell me, did they put you guys up when you went to Northern Ireland?' Coles again

'Yes, not with the members who were over here though, but with other parishioners. Quite frankly we'd never have been able to afford to go over otherwise.'

'Would that be unusual, you know, not actually staying with the members of the bridge club?' Irvine's question this time. He felt they were getting nowhere fast and he'd been desperate to come up with some valuable information for Kennedy, but it didn't look like old Wrightie was going to give him anything valuable.

'There's no hard-and-fast rule. Hmmm,' Wrightie hesitated, 'how should I put this? Usually one of the opposing members would be involved in the accommodation and then there'd be a bit of a social get-together at their house. But when we were over there it was more everyone for themselves and no socialising. Which was fine. We thought it might have something to do with the politics. But don't get me wrong; we had a great time over there. Sure, isn't it a beautiful part of the world altogether? How could you not enjoy yourself over there?'

Coles studied Wrightie as he answered. He continuously sipped at his orange juice. He acted like a PR person, warm immediately, a bit personal without reason to be, but nothing very deep. 'Can we go back to their visit over here?'

'Certainly. What else would you like to know?'

'What would their day have been like?'

'They arrived on the Thursday, checked straight into the hotel. I believe they made telephone contact with our secretary. You see he, Jools Belgium, he'd have been their contact. That would have been the early evening. Jools invited them all over for a drink but they shied off. They were all pooped and wanted a rest before the first rubber the next day. Jools was quite surprised. He'd never known an Ulsterma... sorry, an Ulster person to turn down a drink before.

Anyway, the next day, the Friday, I was here when they arrived at five o'clock sharp. We'd a bit of a meet and greet and went straight into the match. They left here about ten o'clock. Again, we invited them for a drink. It was still relatively early and The Railway was still open. They wanted to get back to the hotel as soon as possible so they didn't bother.

'Saturday was a full day and they were here at noon. Ahm... how shall I put it? They looked... well, some of them looked like they'd been on the pi... well some of them, the older ones I'm talking about now, looked like they'd had a hard night the night before. That was much more like how we thought Ulster folk would behave. They played here on and off on the Saturday until nine o'clock. Then we'd a bit of a champers reception for them. You know, to the victors the spoils and all of that. Again, no big drinkers, but they were quite sociable and great storytellers. They came back to see us on Sunday morning for tea and coffee and goodbyes and they left us about noon, heading straight for the ferry.'

'Thanks,' said Coles, and she appeared to be putting together a question.

Irvine beat her to the draw.

'Tell me, Wrightie, how did they seem to you? I mean, were any of them acting strangely or anything?'

'No, not really. I mean the oldest, the one who looks a little like Paul Newman, he seemed to be keeping pretty much to himself. He could have been psyching himself up for the matches. Some people behave differently to others. As I say, by and large, they all seemed to be having fun, happy with their own company, very tight as I say, except for the old chap.

The other thing about him, you know maybe he was having a hard time due to the ferry trip and the long drive.'

'How about day to day, did they seem the same to you each day?' Irvine continued, once again beating Coles to a question.

'What's this all about? Has something happened to one of them? The old chap? Did he not make it back or something? Did anything happen we should know about? I mean, we have our reputation and all to protect, is there anything I should be aware of?'

'No, no, nothing untoward happened. The old chap, Derek Shaw, he's fine. A colleague of ours had breakfast with him only this morning. No, it's just a general line of questioning, there's nothing for you to worry about,' Irvine replied, looking at Wrightie's flares. 'It's just background information we're after.'

'What about the day-to-day thing, did you notice anything strange?' Coles repeated Irvine's question.

'Well no, I didn't, not really. The first day they were tired, we didn't see them. They next day they were fine. We played a bit. The next day some of them were wrecked, we played a bit more, and the last day they looked like they were getting ready for a long journey. That was it really.'

'You've been very helpful,' Irvine said, standing.

'I have?' Wrightie replied in open shock.

'Yes. We won't take up any more of your time,' Irvine replied smiling and making his way to the door.

'Not a lot to report to Kennedy,' Coles said, breaking the silence. They were in their car and heading back down West End Lane, only this time she took a left along Broadhurst Gardens in the direction of Swiss Cottage. It was just creeping up to seven on a fine August evening.

'Ah, you know Kennedy, he just loves to amass as much information as possible before he attempts to even look at the puzzle.'

'Do you think he thinks there's some connection between the Bridge School and the Black Cat Building murder?'

'From the little I know about Kennedy, I'd say he hasn't even looked at that yet for fear of jumping to conclusions. Anyway, we've done our work for the day. What do you say

to a wee drink at the Queens in Primrose Hill on the way back
to North Bridge House?'

'What? With me, DS Irvine? But you're forgetting, I know
all about your reputation,' Coles said, not sure how to assess
the offer.

'Ah, I was inviting you for a drink. A drink. Nothing
more.'

'I'm game then. A drink it is,' Coles agreed.

'Good.'

'I'm buying though,' Coles added.

'I'm Scottish, you're welcome.'

'Don't tell Kennedy though,' Coles added as an afterthought.

'What, that I'm Scottish? Sorry, too late, he already
knows.'

'No, idiot, that we're going for a drink.'

Irvine smiled and didn't say another word.

Chapter Twenty-Five

WHILE TWO OF Kennedy's colleagues were talking about him (indirectly), his friend and lover was thinking about him as she drove along the North Antrim Coast. She'd only been in the area for three days and yet it was beginning to seem remarkably familiar to her. She'd been happy to have her own business to go about. She'd positively hated to have been hanging on to Kennedy's coat-tails.

Her own problem now, though, was that unless she managed to pick up a new lead and soon, her story was going to run out of steam naturally and she might be recalled to London. God bless Anita McCann, ann rea thought. The journalist had delivered two more addresses of those on the excursion, just like she promised she would.

The "A Greer" on the list turned out to be Mrs Audrey Greer of Highfield Road, Coleraine and ann rea was heading in her direction without a care in the world. Well, truth be told, she'd one little niggle but she didn't want to make anything of it just in case it was her imagination; she thought she kept seeing a Morris Minor, a black Morris Minor van, following her. Either that, or there were a few similar vans in the area. She dismissed the owners as the members of some club or other. They seemed to have clubs for everything in Ulster. She certainly wasn't going to mention it to Kennedy; he'd think she was crazy. Mind you, ann rea thought, he probably was of that opinion already.

Mrs Audrey Greer was a gregarious lady whom ann rea pegged as being in her early fifties. She welcomed ann rea into her bungalow with a:

'Oh, hello, I've been expecting you.'

The outside of the bungalow was painted light blue, the garden unkempt and overgrown. There was a naturalness to it, however, that worked, for ann rea at least. Inside was spic-and-span with not a speck of dust to be found anywhere.

'Now you'll have a wee cup of tea with me won't you, and maybe even something a wee bit more dangerous than that?'ann rea wondered what Audrey Greer's interpretation of dangerous might be. Spirits? Pills? Surely not. She was soon to find out.

'I've got a piece of Black Forest gateau that will make your mouth water, literally. And sure, look at you. You're only a wee slip of a girl. You could do with a bit of fattening up. You should get that policeman friend of yours to take you out for a slap-up meal or two. In the meantime I can look after you. Wait until you taste this. Believe me, you're not going to believe it. Come on through with me to the kitchen and we can have a wee chat as I'm making the tea.'

The kitchen, like the living room, was neat and tidy but more functional and lived in. The hissing of the cold-water tap filling the kettle snapped ann rea out of a little daydream she was having about the wonderful Mrs Audrey Greer solving the whole mystery for her. She was very friendly, so far, to the journalist so the signs were good. She wore a grey skirt, a red twinset with a mauve brooch and matching earrings. Her hair was baby-fine and ann rea guessed it gave her a lot of trouble and consequently needed a lot of her attention. It was strawberry blonde and ann rea reckoned it was held in place very cleverly using John Frieda thickening lotion and hair combs, which held the height, sides and front. She wore glasses. ann rea further surmised, by the thickness of the lenses and by how much part of her features she'd allowed them to become, that she'd been wearing them most of her life. Her glasses were a lively red, pretty much like Denis Taylor's but not worn as high. She had a great set of teeth, perhaps even so great they were false, and her make-up would have probably been okay on younger skin – it was just that it appeared uneven and was breaking up due to her wrinkles.

'Now then, what's with all this attention our wee bridge club has been getting? You'd think we'd just won the Olympics or an Oscar with all the fuss we've been causing,' Mrs Greer said as she poured the tea, holding the lid on with one hand. She was obviously up for getting straight into it.

Good game, ann rea thought, good game.

'Well no, I mean I wouldn't go that far,' ann rea started

biting into the cake. 'Hmmm, you're right, this is delicious. Did you make it yourself?'

'Sadly yes, even sadder, though, when I end up eating it myself. Oh well, I always say you've got to indulge yourself in something and my weakness has always been my sweet tooth. What's yours?'

'Oh,' ann rea began, thinking that she didn't really know this woman well enough to tell her about chasing the butterfly with Kennedy. 'I'd have to say cappuccinos. I positively just swoon over them, particularly when there's no one else around and I can swoosh out the remains on my finger and lick it. Oh, delicious!'

'Oh, away with ye, yer having me on. Ah sure, I was young once myself you know,' she said winking at ann rea.

Really, ann rea thought. It was always strange when people said that. It was as though there was the possibility that there were some people on this earth who hadn't actually had a youth. They'd just appeared as a thirty-three year old. "I was young once myself, indeed," she thought as she said: 'Getting back to the trip, it's just that it was conducted in such unusual circumstances, you know, them selling the wood from the vicarage just to pay for it.'

'Well, I couldn't agree with you more. I mean, I can sympathise with Miss Porter. She's a true blue, a traditionalist, and she wanted the vicarage to be left as it was. Her point, and it's a very valid point, was that although the Reverend Houston now occupies the vicarage, as he has done for the last forty or so years, it's not actually his property to do with as he wishes; it belongs to the church and, as such, when he wants to make any changes he should go to the church and the Church Council to seek permission for these changes. Miss Porter feels it was all done behind our backs before we had a chance to even discuss it.

'I think another of her fears is that if he can do that without our permission, what else can he do without our permission? Personally speaking, I think it was all handled incorrectly. But am I to blame? No, certainly not. I'm a member of the bridge club; we were invited across to West Hampstead and instead of having to organise jumble sales and garden fetes and what have you, Terence Best said it was being paid for with church funds.'

'You mean you didn't know that it was being paid for by the sale of the vicarage wood?' ann rea asked, sensing a little of her story rising again.

'Certainly not, and I'd say that the Reverend Houston has to answer to somebody on this one. Between you and me, he's a bit of a maverick,' Mrs Greer replied, giving ann rea a quick wink as she made short work of the rest of her cake.

Now, ann rea thought, was that wink to do with Houston or the cake? Either way it looked like they were going to get down to a bit of good old gossip.

'Oh yes?' ann rea said enthusiastically. 'How so?'

'How so?'

'Yes, what else has he been up to?'

'Well,' Mrs Greer sighed and leaned in closer to ann rea. They were sitting on a floral-patterned red-and-white sofa in front of a dead fireplace. 'I know for a fact that he likes a tipple now and then.'

'A tipple?' ann rea replied with obvious frustration.

'Yes, but tell me who pays for his wee tipple?'ann rea frowned.

'Why, we do of course. I mean I don't mean "we" as in you and me – you're not a member of this parish, are you – but we, the parishioners of Ballyneagh, we're paying for it.'

'Yes, but surely he gets an allowance for entertaining?'

'Think what you like, young lady, but he didn't get that red nose in a joke shop.'

Hardly Woodward and Bernstein kind of revelations, ann rea thought. She tried a different tack.

'Tell me, Audrey, does the Reverend Houston ever go on any of your trips?'

'But he doesn't play bridge, does he?'

'Right,' ann rea replied, 'how silly of me, of course he doesn't.'

Another pause, another regrouping of ann rea's troops. 'Did you get to do much sightseeing when you were in London?'

'I haven't the heart for it, to tell you the truth, since Stuart passed away, God bless his soul.' Mrs Greer rose and went over to the mantelpiece and took a wedding photograph from the right-hand side. 'That's my Stuart. We were childhood sweethearts; we never spent a day apart in married life. I lost my father when I was quite young,' she said as she took a picture of a young soldier from the other side of the mantelpiece. She tried to hand it to ann rea who already had a cup in one hand and the wedding photo in the other. ann rea set the tea down so that she had a matching silver-framed photo in either hand. 'Yes, Daddy died in the war and Stuart and I married shortly after. He was as healthy as an ox. Worked outdoors all his life. One morning I woke up and found he'd not been to bed. I came down here and found him slumped on the sofa, just where you're sitting.'ann rea visibly twitched. Mrs Audrey Greer continued:

'He'd a tumour in his head that burst. The doctor thinks he would have died peacefully. He might even have been dozing when it happened. But anyway, as I was saying,' Audrey took the two photos from ann rea, dusted each in turn on her sleeve, and replaced them in their position above the fireplace before continuing. 'He... me and him used to go everywhere together, toured everywhere and so now, when I go places like with the bridge club, I just stay in my room and read or watch television when we're not playing.'

'I'm sorry. I mean about your husband.'

'Oh, it's all right dear, don't be. We had a great life together. Never an angry word between us, we lived a much fuller life than most couples who are together a lot longer.'

'Did he play bridge?'

'Absolutely not, he couldn't abide it. He loved the outdoors too much to be sat in, playing cards. Would you like a wee bit more cake?'

'Goodness no, it's time I was going anyway, I've got another member of the bridge club to see this evening.'

'Who's that?'

'Eamon McKay.'

'Aren't we privileged? A journalist over all the way from London talking to the members of a bridge club from the backwaters.'

And getting nowhere fast, ann rea thought but didn't say.

She was relieved, as she started back into Portrush, that there were no signs of the black Morris Minor van. She thanked heaven she hadn't made a fuss about it. How embar-

rassing it would have been for her, not to mention Kennedy.
Especially Kennedy, she thought.

Chapter Twenty-Six

'OKEY DOKEY, I think Anita McCann would definitely do that for you and, as a matter of fact, I know exactly where she is tonight,' ann rea said, doing her best impression so far of Ulster-speak.

They were back at Kennedy's parents' house, sitting down to tea. McCusker was also present. It was a wee bit too early for his own supper and he had a hunger he thought might be satisfied at the Kennedy dinner table. Kennedy had said he wanted to try to get the wartime photograph that Irvine had found in Dugdale's apartment into the *Coleraine Chronicle* to see if anyone recognised any of the other members of the squad.

'Grand, let's all head over there for a drink or two after we've finished tea,' McCusker announced as he got stuck into his meal. Actually, "snack" was the word he used to describe the Kennedy clan's evening meal.

'You think it's got something to do with that photograph, don't you?' ann rea said, reverting to her native tongue.

'Well, we've seen how few possessions he had, so the photograph must have been special to him for him to keep it,' Kennedy replied. For his mother's sake, he wished he could find something else to talk about. He knew how much she detested people talking about their work around the dinner table. But every question he could ask or anything he could find to say would invariably lead back to the case. Maybe he'd try to shift the emphasis onto ann rea. 'How's your story coming on?'

So, ann rea then recalled the guts of the interview she'd had with Audrey Greer.

'On reflection it all seemed a little controlled, you know, even her little titbits of gossip, none of it was really earth-shattering.'

'It sounds to me, young lady, like you were being fed a line,'

Kennedy's father said in his very slow Ulster drawl.

'Yes, I know what you mean, and I've just realised she knew all about me before I got there."

'How so?' Kennedy asked.

'Well, I've just remembered something she said: "You should get that policeman friend of yours to take you out for a few slap-up meals." Basically, she was saying that I needed fattening up a bit and that you should do it, Christy.'

Kennedy's mother shot ann rea a brief look of disdain over her version of a Christian name for her son.

'So you're saying,' McCusker said between munches, 'she knew all about you before you got there.'

'Exactly.'

'And what conclusion do you draw from that?' McCusker started. 'By the way, Mrs Kennedy, this is delicious. Nathin bates a vison chops supper.'ann rea turned to Kennedy, her frown said: "What on earth's he on about?"

'He's saying,' Kennedy whispered to ann rea 'that nothing beats a fish-and-chips supper.'

'Tell me, Mrs Kennedy, any more city spuds in the pot?' McCusker continued as he cleaned his plate.

Again ann rea turned to Kennedy and mouthed the word: "What?"

'City spuds are chips. He's asking for some more chips.'

'Oh,' ann rea replied aloud, and then remembered McCusker's original question. 'Oh, someone had talked to her about me before my visit, so perhaps it had been agreed what information to give me. You know, by slipping me the wee bits about the Reverend's fondness for a little tipple they'd throw me off the real path.'

'And what's the real path?' McCusker asked, a beam on his face stretching from one ear to the other as Mrs Kennedy served him another helping of city spuds. He proceeded to make himself a mouth-watering, delicious-looking chip buttie, allowing ann rea to continue.

'Well, I think it's all to do with the bridge club's trip to London. There must be something to hide if they're all trying so hard to hide it.'

'Fair point,' Kennedy offered refusing his mother's offer of more chips. 'But what is it they're trying so hard to hide?'

No one answered so Kennedy continued: 'Okay, let's look at what we know about our bridge club.

'Daddy and I will leave you to your business,' Kennedy's mother suggested as she rose and started to clear the dishes. 'We'll get on with the washing-up.'

'Oh, I'll help with that,' ann rea volunteered, jumping up.

'You sit yourself back down there. It seems to me that you've been making more progress on this than these two simple serpents,' Kennedy's mother said, looking first at her son then at McCusker and then offering ann rea a mischievous wee grin.

When the grinning was finished, Kennedy was about to say something but ann rea cut him off with: 'It's okay, I got that one; simple serpents are civil servants.'

'Okay,' Kennedy began, choosing to ignore his mother and seeing a look on his father's face that suggested he'd have preferred to stay on and hear the summary. Kennedy would have liked for him to stay too but, in another way, that would have forced ann rea to go and help his mum with the dishes so, without further ado, he continued:

'One: Derek Shaw, old soldier, Dugdale's best man, ice-blue eyes and good cook,' Kennedy paused.

McCusker laughed and Kennedy continued.

'Two: Terence Best, caretaker with bushy eyebrows and the son of Reverend Houston's predecessor. Three: Audrey Greer...' Kennedy stopped talking and looked at ann rea, giving her a visual prompt. ann rea picked up her cue immediately: 'Ulster's answer to Dame Edna, wannabe glamorous granny, probably in her mid-fifties, bit of a gossip and not scared of dropping Houston in it.'

'Four: Margaret Derby...' Kennedy started ann rea off again.

'Young, twenty(ish) authoritative, no-nonsense girl who wasn't giving anything away and certainly put me in my place. And number five,' ann rea continued, only this time without Kennedy's prompting, 'Robin Kane: young. I've only spoken to him on the phone but Anita says he's nearly twenty and looks a bit like the Milky Bar Kid. I've tracked him down to the garage he works at. Basically he told me it was none of my business and I felt he was about to tell me to eff off so I got off the phone pretty sharpish.

'And number six would be Paul McCann: he's a butcher and older. Basically he spent all the time on the phone chatting me up and calling me a wee girl. I'm due to see him at the Bates Hotel this evening at 9.30.'

'I'll go with you,' Kennedy said automatically.

'*No you won't!*' ann rea replied a tad too forcefully.

Kennedy glared at ann rea across the dinner table. ann rea glared a very definite "NO!" back again.

'Number seven,' McCusker began diplomatically breaking the stalemate, 'would be Malachy McIvor. Nothing known at this stage, and number eight would be Eamon McKay, again nothing known. You and I should tackle those two tomorrow morning and see if they can shed any light on matters.'

'Which all leaves us with the wartime photograph of Victor Dugdale and his troop,' Kennedy said solemnly. 'We know only five of the soldiers in that photograph. The very same Terence Best and Derek Shaw from our bridge club, plus Victor Dugdale of course, and the three people Shaw named: Alan Savage, Alex McCelland and David Kennedy. Which leaves us with three people we don't know.

Let's get Anita to put the photo in the *Coleraine Chronicle* and see do any of the relatives, or any members of the general public recognise our remaining four. Maybe they can even fill us in with some more background on the names we already have,' Kennedy suggested. He hoped he didn't sound as desperate as he felt. He thought they were still going nowhere but they had no option but to chase what was being presented to them. Apart from which, he was a little concerned about the run-in he'd had with ann rea. He was sure there wasn't really much McCusker could pick up on but, as an old friend of Kennedy's, a hippie called KP (who sadly had been murdered) would have said: "There definitely was a case of bad vibes."

'Okey dokey,' ann rea replied with a smile.

'And our chaps are also still trying to dig up some information on Riflemen Savage, McCelland and Kennedy. No relation, I assume,' McCusker said with a grin. 'But in the meantime my belly thinks me throat's been cut, let's get out of here and get a drink.'

'Okay, let's go see how Anita's doing with all her hot dates at Kelly's and we can give her the photo,' ann rea said, rising from the table.

Kennedy felt that she was definitely avoiding eye contact with him.

Chapter Twenty-Seven

ANITA McCANN **WAS** very "okey dokey" that evening, surrounded by her fan club. The scene reminded Kennedy of the girl who could open doors with her smile in the Eagles' song, Lyin' Eyes.

Did Kennedy think that Anita had 'lyin eyes'? Probably not; but when ann rea introduced the two of them she held onto his hand for an incredibly long time, leaving her fan club gawking in envy. All McCusker could do was laugh himself and say: 'Put him down, woman, for goodness' sake. He's already spoken for.'

'No?' Anita said, smiling at Kennedy. She turned to look at ann rea by which time Anita's furrowed brow was saying: 'You're not, are you?'

She turned back to Kennedy by which time the adoring smile once more graced her perfectly made-up face. She looked back to ann rea once more and her look changed to: "Oh, please!" then back again to Kennedy with her smitten smile and then – and only then – did she (gradually) let his hand go. During this exchange McCusker continuously stared at Anita's fan club whose collected faces presented a united front of "What's wrong with us?" Well, maybe not quite so politely as that.

Kennedy felt, as all this was going down, that ann rea was showing an inordinate amount of interest in the two well-dressed youths standing by the jukebox. It was unusual for ann rea to sulk like this; if indeed she was sulking.

Either way, he decided that he wasn't going to waste his evening worrying about what ann rea was thinking. He was in Kelly's to do a bit of business and have a drink or two.

'Kennedy's got a favour to ask,' ann rea announced out of the blue as McCusker made his way to the packed bar to get the first round in.

'Really?' Anita replied, smile back on her face and her well-polished tones standing out from the Ulster accents audible, very audible, all around them. 'Okey dokey, whatever you need,' she continued, using her signature words with Kennedy for the first time and looking deep into his eyes.

Kennedy produced a manila envelope from inside his dark-blue jacket. He removed a photograph from the envelope, all the time having to stand with his feet apart and steady himself from the thirsty drinkers. He presented the photograph to Anita.

'I was wondering if you could print this for us as soon as possible with a wee paragraph, you know, something along the lines of: "If anyone knows any of the men in this photograph, please come forward as soon as possible to help with our inquiries."'

'Okey dokey,' Anita replied, upbeat. 'We won't bother to say it's for the pol-ice or we'll have no replies. People will probably think it's something for Cilla Black and we'll get tons of replies. I'll try and get it in tonight for you.'

She studied the photograph for a few seconds before continuing with: 'God, sure they're only a bunch of wains, barely out of their nappies. And they're the ones that went off and fought the war for us. God bless them.'

Anita McCann seemed genuinely moved by the fresh-faced bunch. ann rea pointed out the members of the photograph they already knew.

'Best not mention that though,' Kennedy said, taking the photograph back again and replacing it in the envelope. 'Let's see what information we can gather on all of them.' ann rea kept looking at her watch and the two lads over by the juke-box.

The bar was growing fuller and noisier by the second, but Kennedy felt he seemed to be the only one growing more uncomfortable as the *TFI Friday*-type crowd grew. He did enjoy the odd glass of wine, did Kennedy, but not the nail-varnish remover circling around his glass and certainly not drinking it in the middle of the scrimmage where you had to fight continuously just to keep your spot on the floor. Fight to keep your balance, your wine in your glass and to hear what your friends were saying.

No, Kennedy much preferred to be with a few friends; say

ann rea and another couple and out in a restaurant for some fine wine, food and chat and not necessarily in that order.

In short, his idea of fun wasn't to be stuck in the middle of a stampede in Kelly's Barn.

However, McCusker, Anita and her cronies seemed to be actually thriving in the atmosphere. McCusker and Anita were knocking back shorts head to head and the more Anita drank the more her fan club closed in around her, all obviously hoping to be the one to catch her when she fell.

Once Kennedy saw that she'd put the envelope in the multi-coloured backpack lying faithfully by her feet, he thought that his job for the evening was done and he'd have loved to have gotten outta there.

The only problem was ann rea – she seemed to be genuinely enjoying herself, although she was restrained in her intake of alcohol, probably due to her assignment later on that evening. Kennedy felt he had to convince her that she let him accompany her on this interview. He felt that she didn't know what she could potentially be letting herself in for. Equally he knew that she wouldn't want her independence interfered with.

Where did you draw the line though? If, say, he genuinely felt that her life could be in danger, didn't he owe it to her to protect her? He realised the extent of his dilemma. He realised it was probably the same dilemma that worried fathers felt. They knew what was out there but equally they knew that they couldn't keep their beautiful daughters under wraps forever.

Perhaps he should just follow her and not tell her he was doing so. Wouldn't that be deceitful though? Yes, it might be deceitful, he thought, but at least she'd be safe. Again there it was; that line you had to tread, the line between right and wrong; between interference and protection. What was a man to do?

'I know exactly what you're thinking, Kennedy,' ann rea said, her mouth so close to his ear he could feel her breath. It was an intimate way for her to avoid having to shout. 'And part of me loves you for it, yet another part of me positively hates you for it.'

Kennedy was looking away from ann rea during this

exchange so he could hear her better. In doing so he was looking straight at the two youths by the jukebox; yet he didn't see them. He turned his head so that he could look into her eyes; then he put his mouth to her ear.

'Perhaps I could just follow you from a distance,' he said.

'NO!' she replied firmly, not taking the time required to put her mouth to his ear. Unfortunately though, at this exact point there was a lull in the conversation around them, so her 'NO!' sounded like a shout and everyone in their group heard it.

Everyone stared at Kennedy and ann rea for a few seconds and then Anita broke the awkward silence by engaging her fan club in conversation.

'No, Kennedy,' ann rea said, this time quieter, when they were (apparently) being ignored again. She took his hand and led him outside.

The once-rolling fields outside Kelly's were now manicured with mobile homes and caravans. The overall effect was one of a bizarre rockery. Some of the homes were still in use and some were braced up in preparation for all that the winter winds might throw at them. Kennedy felt a little chill as the cool August air hit them.

'Kennedy, I'm not a kid.'

'And this isn't Primrose Hill, or even Camden Town for that matter.'

'Kennedy, please stop this. I can look after myself. I don't want to be having this row with you.'

'That doesn't mean you're not being stupid.'

This last statement obviously hurt ann rea because she stopped dead in her tracks.

'Kennedy, how many times do I have to tell you that I don't need men around me all the time?' She paused for a beat. 'I don't need you around all the time fussing over me.'

'I don't fuss over you.'

'Agreed, you don't normally fuss over me but you are now and it's not pleasant. I have to tell you that I find it offensive. What makes you think that you could protect me anyway? We both know you'd be hopeless in a fight. Come to that, physically I could probably take you on myself. This leaves guile and cunning, and what makes you suppose that you're better than me in those areas?'

'It's not about being better or weaker and stronger. It's about men and women. It's not about strength and weaknesses, not about being macho. No, it's not about anything other than the fact that I care, so please don't penalise me over that. We all know you're a big girl and can look after yourself, but please just think of this as being safety in numbers.'

'If you're there, Kennedy, Paul McCann may not offer up as much information. He was hinting he had stuff to tell me,' ann rea said. They were now walking through the car park and she seemed a little distracted.

'What exactly did he say?' the detective in Kennedy slipped out again without him even noticing.

'He said... he said...' and ann rea stopped in her tracks. 'I keep seeing that black Morris Minor van everywhere I go.'

'He said that? That sounds weird.'

'No, no, he didn't say that,' ann rea continued, her moment of concern seemingly passed. 'He said he might have some useful information for me.'

'Oh really?' Kennedy said, his disbelief glaringly obvious in each and every one of his syllables. 'Oh, that's okay then. Your story is obviously safe.'

'What?' ann rea replied, now looking confused as though she was half listening to Kennedy and half preoccupied by the Morris van.

'Come on! Wake up in there, for heaven's sake. It's the middle of the night. It's dark. You don't know this guy from Adam, and even if he's on the level and if he is legit, why didn't he suggest meeting during daylight hours?'

'What, you never questioned anyone after the sun goes down?'

'That's different!'

'Of course it's different. You're a man. I'll listen to anything you want to say to me, Kennedy. That is until you start spouting shit like that. Tell you what, Kennedy, just leave me alone. Go away and leave me alone, I can look after myself.'

He nearly missed her last few words because she was off and running down the lane, away from Kennedy, and out of Kelly's gate.

He was tempted to run after her but resisted, knowing it

would be wrong and would probably make her even madder - if that was possible. He wasn't sure he'd ever seen her quite so mad before.

Kennedy walked back through Portrush to his parents' house. Many were the times, back in London, he'd wished for such a stroll; dreamed of the pleasures of such a walk. Now he was on his wee dander but ann rea might be in danger so his mind was elsewhere and he was not allowing himself to enjoy it. Back on the broken record of his relationship with ann rea.

Now with the streets of Portrush as a backdrop he would re-run various scenes in his mind's eye; all featuring, no sorry, make that all staring ann rea. Had she been right? Did he crowd her? Was he over-protective? Where did caring stop and over-protection start?

And why is one day (yesterday) great in a relationship – with the walk (and stop) along the beach – but the next (today), what with the row, a terrible one? Are there troubled waters simmering below the surface all the time, waiting only for an excuse to rear their ugly head? Are these problems symptomatic of a more fatal, cancerous growth? Or are they always lurking in a relationship, waiting to be kicked back into touch?

He walked down to the remains of the Arcadia Ballroom and stood there by the side of the once elegant entrance hall watching the moonlight glistening on the rolling waves, ever so slowly eating their way into the shoreline. Was this continuous erosion similar to what happened in a relationship, he wondered? Did you just chip away, day after day, wearing someone down as they wore you down? And if so, did this action and reaction go on forever? Or did you reach the point where it was okay, everything was fine and you lived happily ever after?

Was it possible that the happily ever after would be spoiled by the fact that both of you had the history of all the wearing down in the first place?

Where was ann rea now, Kennedy wondered, and what was she thinking? Had she gone beyond this, to concentrate on her interview with McCann? He knew she was eager for her information. Was she going to come rolling back home tonight having cracked her story and would the sort of buzz that such news would generate make them both forget about the row and their niggles?

Yes, the niggles would probably disappear back under the surface again where they'd remain; remain until the next time, that is.

Back at his parents' house forty minutes later he flicked through the television channels trying to find something to watch; something that would occupy and distract him until ann rea returned home. Once more he wondered was he behaving like a worried parent and not an equal in a relationship. He couldn't find anything on the television to distract him. He started to fall back into the "something's happened to ann rea" anxieties from the previous evening.

This time he immediately dismissed such thoughts as stupid and fell asleep on the sofa with the television gently purring in the background.

Four hours later, at 2.20am to be exact, Kennedy woke with a crick in his neck and, on coming to his senses, he was really annoyed. Annoyed with ann rea. She'd obviously come in, seen him asleep on the sofa and, as she was obviously still upset with him or the fact that she hadn't gotten the exclusive interview she'd been expecting, had gone straight to bed without bothering to wake him.

Okay, two could play at that game, Kennedy thought. He'd go to bed too. His own room, of course, and ignore her. He agreed with himself that she mustn't have got her interview or she'd have woken him gloating.

Her bedroom door was shut. Kennedy was sure his mother left all the bedroom and bathroom doors upstairs open unless someone was in there. He stood as quietly as he knew how on the landing outside her door and tried to figure out what to do. He didn't think about what to do for too long; his hand rose to his mouth level and he tapped on the stripped-pine door a couple of times.

He knew what his parents would be thinking if, in fact, they were awake and if, in fact, they could hear him. Wasn't it a fact that as you got older you slept more lightly, but this was counterbalanced by the fact that your hearing got worse? He hoped so. There was no response from within ann rea's room. He was about to tap again but this time his hand automatically went to the door handle. He opened the door slowly. It creaked as indiscreetly as someone trying to remove a sweet wrapper during a classical concert.

The curtains in ann rea's room were still open and the moonlight's rich beam highlighted the fact that ann rea's bed was still neat and tidy and, more importantly, had not been slept in.

She was not home!

It was 2.20am and she still wasn't home.

Get a grip, Kennedy thought. She's a big girl. Wasn't that what she kept telling him? 2.20am wasn't really late these days, was it?

'Catch yourself on, man,' he whispered to himself. So, behaving properly, he went to his room, undressed, had a shower, cleaned his teeth, went to bed and fell asleep.

Fell into a deep sleep.

His mother woke him at 8.15 the following morning. She was tapping on the door. She usually came in.

'It's time to get up, Christopher.'

'Okay, Mum. Is ann rea up yet?'

His door opened slowly.

'I thought she was in here with you. Her bedroom door is open and her bed hasn't been slept in,' Kennedy's mum said. He couldn't be sure but he thought he saw a relaxed smile of relief glowing all across her face.

Chapter Twenty-Eight

'SHE MENTIONED LAST evening that she thought she was seeing a black Morris Minor van around a bit,' Kennedy said twenty minutes later in the barracks. He was with McCusker and a few of the Portrush detective's officers. 'I ignored her but whoever was in this van was obviously following her. God, I've been stupid.'

'She was correct, Christy, she was being followed by a black Morris Minor van, but the passengers of that van were my men,' McCusker announced sheepishly. At which point two well-dressed young men, one black haired, one blond, started to blush. McCusker continued, raising his voice quite a bit. 'They were obviously too interested in their drink and the jukebox to notice ann rea leaving Kelly's yesterday evening.'

'Fair dues, sir,' the blond one began. 'We did see her leave Kelly's last night but she left with the detective here,' he nodded in the direction of Kennedy, 'so we thought she'd be okay.'

'You were tailing her?' Kennedy heard his voice say in disbelief.

'Well, I figured it was in her best interests, what with all the travelling she was doing, that someone was watching over her. I didn't want to compromise her relationship with you so I didn't tell you about the tail.'

Kennedy found himself feeling quite detached about ann rea's disappearance. In fact, truth be told, he found himself very detached about her current whereabouts. He found his mind racing along about whether ann rea's disappearance might in some way be connected to the death of Victor Dugdale.

"Okay, we know she was going to interview this Paul McCann. Let's get him in here immediately for questioning,' McCusker ordered the Morris Minor twins.

'That'll be easy, sir, he owns McCann Family Butchers over on the High Street in Coleraine. He's always in the shop,' one of the twins, the black-haired one replied, helpful and hopeful.

'Well, let's hope he's in today. Go on, get him over here.'

Thirty-five minutes later Kennedy, McCusker and McCann were sitting in the interview room in the basement of the barracks.

'Listen here, Inspector McCusker, I've got my rights. Hauling me in here like a petty criminal and right in front of some of my best customers,' McCann began.

McCusker's men had followed his orders to the letter. McCann was still dressed in his butcher's apron, complete with bloodstains, over a light-grey suit. He was in his mid-fifties, Kennedy guessed. He was on the plump side and had a full head of wavy, salt-and-pepper hair, all backcombed. His face was shined with a red flush; not from embarrassment, Kennedy guessed, but more from the demon alcohol. He wore a pair of brown Hush Puppies.

'Now I'm sure, being the respectable type that you are, Paulie, you're going to want to help us with our inquiries.'

'Aye, but it's a fine line, McCusker, a very fine line, I'll tell you.'

'Yeah, yeah. Look, let's get down to business here. We know that a London journalist was going to interview you yesterday evening.'

'Yes, a Miss Rea, a beautiful lady,' McCann replied.

'What time did you see her?' McCusker continued.

'Let's see now, we had drinks at Bates Hotel. She arrived about 9.30pm and she left me about ten o'clock. Yes, that was it, just after ten o'clock.'

'And then what happened?' Kennedy asked unemotionally.

'She left the hotel and I joined a couple of friends of mine for a nightcap in the bar.'

'What did you discuss?' Kennedy again.

'Well, fundamentally she seemed intrigued by the bridge club's recent visit to London. I'm a member, don't you see,' McCann replied, looking Kennedy straight in the eyes.

'And what information did you have for her?' this time McCusker asked the question, taking a long drag on the Player he'd just lit up.

'Well, I'd have to say that she knew most of the details already, that's from what I could gather, you understand.'

'It's just that she told us you'd promised her some new, important, maybe even vital, information.' Kennedy added the split second McCann had finished his sentence.

'Aye, don't you see, it's just that I discovered the secret of Colonel Saunders' secret recipe and I wanted to pass it on to the Masses,' McCann started up in a frivolous mood but Kennedy's stern look soon dissuaded him from continuing with his comic routine. 'Look, you know what journalists are like, every single assignment they're on is the scoop of a life-time to them.'

'And you don't know where she went afterwards?' McCusker added.

'Haven't a clue,' McCann replied with a great deal of finality.

McCusker made to continue the questioning but Kennedy rose.

'That's fine,' Kennedy said, 'for now, Mr McCann. If we need you we know where to find you.'

'Aye, good,' McCann replied also rising from his chair, relief written all over his face.

McCusker started pacing around the interview room after McCann had left.

'You don't think he knew more?' he asked Kennedy.

'No. I mean yes,' Kennedy replied quickly. 'I think he did know more but I don't think he was going to pass on any of his information to us. Did you notice that he never once asked if ann rea was missing or had anything happen to her? And the other main point was the way he'd set himself up with an alibi from the moment ann rea left Bates Hotel yesterday evening.'

'Sorry. You've lost me now,' McCusker said, sitting back at the interview table and drumming away on it with his fingers.

'Well, I think we're dealing with a bit of a set-up here. McCann and his supposed information was the bait, but because he was in an exposed position acting as the bait, he'd set it up so that a couple of mates were available to swear that as ann rea was leaving the hotel, McCann was settling down to a serious night of drinking with them. I'm willing to bet that they were loud enough and caused a big enough racket so the hotel staff will have remembered exactly what time they left the hotel bar.'

Kennedy paused and sat down at the table opposite McCusker. 'So, either ann rea was on to something or we're on to something and her kidnapping is either trying to scare me off, or to preoccupy me in the hope this will take my mind off this case.'

'We're on to something? Really?' McCusker said in genuine surprise. 'News to me.'

'Yes, me too,' Kennedy grunted. 'I think someone has played their hand too early. But somewhere in the midst of all this information we have something that is obviously important.'

'Yeah but why kidnap ann rea though?'

'Well, as I said, to get at me. They clearly know that ann rea and myself are in a relationship. So they figure I'll spend all my time searching for her and forget all about the Dugdale case until I find her,' Kennedy replied.

'Quite sound thinking to me. You'd have to agree,' McCusker replied, the intensity of his drumming increasing by the second.

'Not true!' Kennedy replied, deadpan.

'Sorry?'

'Not true. Here's what I'd like to do. I'd like you and your chaps to pull out all the stops to find ann rea. I know you'll have your snitches who'll have heard or seen something. Let's face it, you're going to have a much better chance of finding her on your patch than I am anyway. I'd like to put all my energy into the Dugdale murder. I also think solving that case is ultimately going to be the best way to find ann rea. In the meantime, I'd just like to take out a little insurance policy in the form of you and your boys.'

'Okay, that also makes sense to me. Everyone is talking so much sense this morning,' McCusker began, stopping his drumming. 'But you know, finding a needle in a haystack is 99 percent perspiration and 1 percent inspiration. Not that I'm ever inspired or anything like that but the point I'm trying to make is that I've got men better than me at finding people. Of course I'll oversee it, but I believe I can be much better use to you on your investigation.'

Kennedy found himself agreeing with McCusker.

All in all, he found himself to be quite calm and collected. He was surprised at this. He knew ann rea's life must be in danger and he would have thought he'd have been a complete mess by this point. Perhaps this was just the calm before the storm. He remembered an interview John Lennon had given where he said that when all the craziness was going on around The Beatles in the Beatlemania days, he still managed to feel completely sane. He said he felt this because the eye of the storm was the safest and calmest place to be.

Kennedy was shocked at how detached he could be. Working on the logic that the locals should track ann rea and he should stay on his case was not the most obvious thing he could have thought of. He couldn't help feeling that ann rea's disappearance must somewhere be tied in with the Dugdale murder. So, by continuing to work on that, he'd hopefully find her sooner than if he rode off into the distance, all guns blazing, trying to track her down. He wasn't so sure that ann rea would be happy to find out how dispassionate he was being about it all.

But then again, perhaps she would.

Chapter Twenty-Nine

HIS FIRST BREAK came pretty soon thereafter. With hindsight, he wasn't quite sure how big a break it actually was.

Anita McCann – God bless her – had not only placed the photograph in the early edition but she'd also managed to get it on the front page. No doubt another favour she called in from somewhere.

At 11.48am, as members of Portrush RUC were pounding the streets of the Port with a photograph of ann rea and checking out her movements on the previous evening, Anita was on the phone to Kennedy.

'We've had three calls so far,' she began between drags of her ciggy.

'Excellent!' Kennedy enthused.

'Yes, three possible sightings,' she continued. 'Two were from people who recognised our friend, Derek Shaw.'

'Oh!' Kennedy replied, unable, or unwilling to hide his disappointment.

'However, the third call was more promising. It was from an old lady up in Maghera who recognised Colin McCann,' Anita said mid-puff.

'Another McCann, any relation?' Kennedy found himself joking.

'Ah no. He's the chap second from the left in the photograph.'

'Did they know anything else about him?' Kennedy asked and he could hear her flicking pages. Anita was obviously checking her notes.

'No, sadly not, not really. She said the only reason she recognised the lad was because he used to come and play with her son. And she said he looked pretty much then as he did in the photograph. And before you ask, I did try and check out her son. Sadly, however, he died of cancer six years ago.'

Anita took another drag of her ciggy and Kennedy imagined she was expecting him to speak. He was thinking; thinking about whether or not he should tell her about ann rea. He knew if he did, she'd have to use it. He decided against it, for now; he wanted to avoid that whole circus for as long as possible. Eventually she filled the silence.

'I imagine there'll be more as the day progresses.'

'Hopefully,' Kennedy said.

'Okey dokey then. Look, are you okay today?'

Kennedy didn't answer.

'It's about ann rea, isn't it? Look, it'll be okay.'

Kennedy wondered how she'd found out so quickly.

'Well...' he started.

'It's okay. You've no need to explain, it's none of my business. She'll get over it... if she knows what's good for her. It happens all the time, she's probably just under a wee bit of a strain working away from home. She a great girl though, Inspector, and I can tell she's really into you. Don't give up on her.'

'Ah...' Kennedy breathed a sign of relief.

'Sorry, Inspector, my other light's flashing. It could be another call on the photograph. I'll speak to you later. Tudaloo.'

Before he could utter another word she was gone.

Two minutes later he had Detective Sergeant James Irvine on the phone.

'We've been going through all of Dudgale's paperwork, sir,' Irvine started after a quick introduction.

This could be good, Kennedy thought, Irvine was never a man to waste either time or money – particularly when the money, as in phone bill – was his own.

'As I mentioned to you yesterday, sir, he has about three hundred grand, give or take.'

'Yes?'

'Well, he left all of it to his daughter, Doris.'

'Kind of figures,' Kennedy said.

'Two further developments, though, which you might find interesting. One, the daughter doesn't want it and two, the will has been contested.'

"Now that is interesting, James, very interesting. Do you

know who's contested it?'

'Yes, just a name though. It's a Dauphine Stevens.'

'Do you have an address?'

'Yes, it's care of a firm of solicitors in Islington,' Irvine replied.

'Interesting. Tell me, do you know if Doris was aware that the will was contested when she gave up her claim to it?'

'No, she definitely didn't. She just wrote a polite reply to the solicitor saying that she'd no need, or rights, to the money.'

'What happens next?' Kennedy asked.

'Well, the solicitor says they have to check out the validity of the people who are contesting the will,' Irvine replied.

'Did he say on what grounds they were contesting the will?'

'No, he said he had a letter from the Islington solicitors saying that their client, Dauphine Stevens, contested the will and wanted to reserve all her rights.'

Kennedy thought for a few seconds then continued: 'Okay, could you check with the solicitor and find out if the contents of the will have been published. I'm eager to find out how Stevens knew about the will.'

'I was too, and the solicitor told me that the only person who knew about the will was Doris Dugdale. He received her letter of refusal and the letter from Stevens' solicitors claiming rights on the same day,' Irvine replied, a hint of pride in his voice.

'Interesting, very interesting. Okay James, excellent. Anything else?'

'No, but myself and Coles are going to check out this Stevens woman and then we were thinking about going back down to the Black Cat Building this morning to see if we can find anything else. There's nothing from forensic, but there must be something else that we're missing over here and that is the only place I could think to start looking.'

'Good luck, we could all do with it,' Kennedy replied as upbeat as he could.

'Not going so well over there, sir?'

'Well, we're getting somewhere it seems because we've been frightening someone.'

'Sorry?' Irvine said. 'I didn't quite get that; you've been fighting someone? Are you okay?'

'No, not fighting, I'm okay. Frightening, I said we've been frightening someone.'

'Oh, how so?'

'Well, someone,' Kennedy started. He suddenly realised how awkward the words were going to sound, 'someone has kidnapped ann rea.'

'Sorry?' Irvine replied in obvious disbelief. 'This is a terrible line,' he laughed. 'For a moment there I thought you said that someone had kidnapped ann rea.' He laughed at his own misunderstanding.'

'They have, James. She's missing. She didn't come back last night.'

'Unbelievable. Un-be-liev-able,' Irvine said. 'What are you going to do? Stupid question, I know what you're going to do, and here I am rabbiting on, wasting your time!'

'No, you see I figure whoever kidnapped ann rea wanted me off their trail and onto ann rea's, which is not going to happen. I need to stick to this case like glue to have a hope in hell's chance of finding her. In the meantime, McCusker's team will kick up a mighty cloud of dust that will be seen for miles around and hopefully that'll make whoever is behind this become a little complacent and, who knows, there's a great chance that McCusker's men will come up with something in the meantime.'

Kennedy felt he'd made his statement to Irvine as much to convince himself he was doing the correct thing as to give the information to his DS.

Chapter Thirty

KENNEDY'S NEXT PORT of call was a return visit to Doris Dugdale. He grabbed McCusker, who was halfway through a bacon sandwich, and they headed off, McCusker munching away and Kennedy lost in his thoughts. Once they were in the car and on the road, McCusker got on the radio to see how his chaps were doing in trying to track down ann rea.

Kennedy could hear, through the radio static, the Morris Minor twins give the following update:

'We've checked Kelly's and a few of the staff remember her. One actually gave a fair description of Detective Inspector Kennedy as being the man she left with. I've checked the car-park video around that time and we could see the young lady and Inspector Kennedy in conversation, ann rea runs off and Inspector Kennedy follows, but at a different speed. He obviously wasn't trying to catch her up.'

Kennedy nodded agreement.

'We visited Bates Hotel, some of the bar staff recognised ann rea. They confirmed she left the hotel around ten o'clock and that McCann stayed behind with mates. He left just before midnight. Nobody remembers seeing anybody suspicious following ann rea. Again we were able to check the hotel security cameras and ann rea definitely leaves the hotel of her own free will. It's marked as ten-oh-three on the hotel lobby camera. One little thing though,' the twin giving the report paused and Kennedy leaned closer to the dashboard to hear what was next.

'The external camera shows ann rea walking away from the hotel and taking a left at the entrance, which would have taken her back into the Port. It could be nothing, you understand, sir, but a beat-up Honda pulls out of the car park shortly thereafter and also takes a left.'

'Did you get their number?' Kennedy asked hopefully, thinking this was just a wee bit too easy so far.

'No, just the first two letters: 'DL'. We've sent the video off to the lab to see if they can enhance the numberplate for us, sir,' the Morris Minor twin replied.

'Okay. Anything else?' McCusker asks.

'No. We're just in the middle of checking all the late-night shops between Bates Hotel and the Inspector's parents' house to see did she make any calls. I've a question for DI Kennedy. Did ann rea smoke?'

'No, she doesn't,' Kennedy replied, not liking the inference drawn by the "did" but choosing to say nothing about it. 'But she does have a sweet tooth though.'

'Okay, maybe she stopped for sweets. We're doing a door to door as well, concentrating on all the hotels first. We want to try and get people who might have been around last evening before they checked out of their hotel. We'll get back to you when there's more, sir.'

The static was cut dead and the two drove in silence for a while.

'Donegal vehicle, interesting, very interesting,' McCusker said as they continued their journey.

'What? Donegal? How do you know that?'

'Well, in the Free State the number plates all start off with the first letter and the last letter of the county the car is registered in. So our Honda is from Donegal. We're a wee bit far in for the Southerners to be down here in Portrush. They usually only go as far as Buncranna or Bundoran. May be something, may be nothing.'

'What would any of this have to do with Southern Ireland?'

'Guns for hire?' McCusker said as he drummed on the steering wheel of the car.

Kennedy had sussed that whenever McCusker wanted to have a smoke and denied himself he drummed his fingers aggressively on whatever was closest to him to distract himself.

'Pardon?'

'Well it fits your theory of her being kidnapped. If this is the case whoever did it didn't want to use local cowboys because he knew we'd track them down too quickly.'

'So they went across the border to get their cowboys?' Kennedy replied picking up the thread.

'Only a theory, mind you,' McCusker said as he turned the car into Doris Dugdale's drive.

'Yes, but it's all we've got so far,' Kennedy replied as he unbuckled his seat belt.

'Aye, let's see what the boys in the lab turn up for us on that number plate. They're real boffins you know, they love all this and the more impossible a task we give them the more they love it,' McCusker replied as he exited the car.

'Ah now, would you just smell that wonderful bit of home cooking,' he said as he rang the doorbell.

The dog barked like last time. And, like last time, Doris bent over double as she held the dog's collar and opened the door at the same time. Unlike last time, however, Doris was dressed in her about-town clothes, as opposed to her about-the-house clothes. She looked genuinely pleased to see them, particularly Kennedy.

'Oh, hello youse two, and what can I do for you today?'

'Ah, another wee chat, if you don't mind,' McCusker replied, a very pleasant smile on his face as his nostrils were doing a bit of detective work of their own.

'You're both welcome. Come on in before Blackie gets out.'

'Thanks,' Kennedy said simply as they entered her house. She seemed to be in better humour today.

'I enjoyed our bit of Acker Bilk,' Doris said directly to Kennedy, a wee bit shyly.

'Acker Bilk?' Kennedy replied genuinely puzzled.

'You know, Strangers on the Shore?'

'Oh yes, of course, sorry. So did I,' Kennedy smiled again.

'Bit too oblique for me,' McCusker replied, sitting down and starting to drum on the kitchen table.

'We understand you told your father's solicitor that you didn't want you dues from the will.'

'Yes,' was the only word she used in reply.

'A wee bit of cutting off your nose to spite your face,' McCusker replied.

'Some may see it as that,' Doris replied as she moved a kettle over the heat of the stove and then looked directly at Kennedy, 'but after what I felt and said about him it would have been hypocritical of me to accept any of his money.'

'I can see that,' Kennedy replied. 'Tell me, did you know you were going to be in his will?'

'I suppose if I'm honest I'd have to say that it crossed my mind, you know, he didn't have anyone else. No one I was aware of anyway, and I had wondered what he would do with it.'

'Did you know the extent of his wealth?' Kennedy continued.

'Well, let's just say I wasn't shocked. My mother always said what a miser he was, a hoarder, so I didn't know exactly, no, but neither was I shocked.'

'If it had been more, would you have turned it down?' McCusker asked what Kennedy figured was a strange question.

'Why certainly, of course,' Doris replied, slightly taken aback.

'What I meant was,' McCusker began unsteadily, 'if, say, it had been a million quid, could you not have taken it and given it to a worthwhile charity?'

'No disrespect to your charities, but I didn't want to dirty my hands with his money. I just don't want him to be able to affect my life, even from beyond the grave, especially from beyond the grave,' she added as an afterthought. And then a much more pleasant afterthought altogether, especially for McCusker: 'Would youse like a wee cup of tea in your hands? Nothing fancy mind you, maybe a couple of my freshly baked scones?'

'That would be absolutely delightful,' McCusker said as he stopped drumming for the first time since he'd sat down.

Kennedy thought that her "wee cup of tea in your hands" was a funny turn of phrase and one that his mother often used when he was growing up. It meant that she wasn't going to set the table or anything fancy like that. But Kennedy always wondered what visitors would have done if she had done just that, literally poured the tea directly into their cupped hands. McCusker broke his mind game.

'Tell me, Doris, do you know a Dauphine Stevens?'

'No, never heard of her, why?'

'It's just that she's contesting your father's will?'

'Hmmm. Is she an illegitimate daughter or something?'

'We don't know,' McCusker replied.

Kennedy felt that McCusker obviously thought there was something behind the will.

'Well, good luck to her if she thinks she's got a claim. I hope she gets what she wants.'

'Aren't you interested in meeting her or anything? I mean, she might be your half-sister?'

'No, not at all,' Doris replied immediately and then thought for a while. 'I've really got no interest in anything to do with him. My mother, who really was a great woman and would never hurt as much as a fly, often used to say that she'd have swung for him if she'd gotten a chance. He was the only person I'd ever heard her speak ill of. At the same time, though, I'd hate for you to think that she bad-mouthed him in front of me all the time, because she never did. Just now and again in an unguarded moment she'd let something slip out and then excuse herself and move on.'

'Have you any idea what he'd done to your mother for her to hate him so much?' Kennedy asked.

'No, sorry, I really haven't a clue. And that's the truth.'

'Did you ever ask her? You know, what your father had done?' Kennedy continued. He felt this was a much better path than McCusker's line about the will.

'I did once. I was back here. I'd been out with my mates to a party and I'd had a few. When I came in my mother was waiting up for me, like she'd done when I was younger, and she was lost in her thoughts staring into the flames in the fireplace in the front room; she'd do that a lot, late at night. And I asked her. I asked her was she thinking about Victor. And she said that she was. And I asked her had she ever loved him and she said of course she had. And I asked her had he cheated on her? And she laughed and said: "No, of course not. Whatever he was he was never unfaithful to me." And I asked her what had he done that was so bad, so bad that she felt about him in this way; in a way that had all but destroyed her life. She stood up from her seat in front of the fire and came over to me. She took me by my two hands and looked deep into my eyes. I then saw for the first that she'd been crying. Her eyes were very red, like she'd been crying a lot. She gripped me firmly and said that not only would she never,

ever tell me but that she never ever wanted me to find out. I told her that I loved her and that had always been enough, and I certainly had not lost out on my life by not having a father around. I also told her, I promised her, that if it meant so much to her I'd never even try to find out. She hugged me like her life depended on it and said, through her sobbing: 'Please don't, Doris. Please don't.'

Now it was Doris' turn to sob.

McCusker said: 'Here, take a good drink of the tea, it's hot, it'll do you good.'

Doris looked at McCusker, her tears turning to laughter at McCusker's attempt to comfort her.

'Of course you're right, the hot tea will mend everything.'

A few minutes, a cup of tea, a few hot scones and a chat about the tourists later, Kennedy very tentatively said:

'Look, it's okay if your answer is no but we've got a photograph of your father with a troop of soldiers and I was wondering… well…'

'You were wondering would I take a look at it for you to see did I recognise anybody in it?'

'Well yes, actually.' Kennedy said gently.

'Of course, let's see your photograph.'

Kennedy did as bid and Doris stared at it for a few minutes.

'Victor looks so young. They all look so young. They really do look like children, don't they? There's Derek, Derek Shaw, I'd recognise him anywhere with those lovely eyes. And there's Miles. Aye, Miles, sure he's the splitten image av his bror.'

Kennedy took the photograph back and looked at the photograph and there it was, the thing that had been troubling him about the person in the photograph he thought he'd seen before. No doubt about it, despite the obvious difference in years, Miles shared the same bushy eyebrows as his brother, Terence Best. Yes, the Reverend Steven Houston's everdependable caretaker. The same caretaker who worked at the church where the wood for the Black Cat Building had been taken from and who was also a member of the bridge club that had travelled to London around the time that Victor Dugdale was murdered.

Chapter Thirty-One

WHAT NOW?

What now indeed, wondered Kennedy?

The more he looked at it, the more the connection grew between the bridge club and Dugdale's wartime group.

Be fair, he cautioned himself, two out of nine still could be a coincidence. Mind you, as Shaw had a habit of saying, the reason 'coincidence', as a word, is in the dictionary in the first place is because examples of such incidents happening are definitely possible, if somewhat infrequent, occurrences.

But two out of nine, wouldn't that be outside the realms of the laws of coincidence? What would be the chance of one in five members of an 1943 wartime troop caught together in a photograph either being in, or directly related to, the members of a 1999 bridge club.

Kennedy supposed that in a local community the possibility of such an outcome would stand a fairly high chance of success. People tend to put down roots in these rural areas and the roots take hold, and several generations later the same families are intertwined.

He was sitting in his makeshift office in the RUC Barracks in Portrush with his little notebook, comparing notes, and then he suddenly saw the word 'McCann' and remembered making fun of Anita when she told him that a wee woman from Maghera had rung up to say she recognised one of the members of the photograph as being a Colin McCann. Of course Colin McCann wasn't a relation of Anita, but could he possibly be a relation of the bridge club member, Paul McCann?

That would make it an astounding one out of three in the photograph being connected to the bridge club. Surely we're stretching even Shaw's liberal definition of the word coincidence with this one, thought Kennedy. He now resolved to try to find a connection between everyone in Dugdale's wartime photograph and the members of the bridge club.

He was breaking his golden rule of never making the evidence fit the lead. Going down that path you could weave absolutely anything you might find into your theory. Normally, he would insist on collecting all the evidence possible and then seeing what it naturally suggested rather than jumping to conclusions. At the same time he figured, with all this overwhelming evidence around, there wasn't much point in hiding his head in the sand.

He dug out his two lists and printed them neatly on two different pages.

1999 Ballyneagh Bridge Club
Derek Shaw
Terence Best
Paul McCann
Robin Kane
Eamon McKay
Malachy McIvor
Audrey Greer
Margaret Derby

1943 war troop
Victor Dugdale
Derek Shaw
Terence Best
Paul McCann
Alan Savage
Alex McCelland
David Kennedy
Unknown 1
Unknown 2

Next he wrote out the two lists side by side, with Victor Dugdale in the centre.

1999		1943
	Victor Dugdale.	
Derek Shaw	=	Derek Shaw
Paul McCann	=	Colin McCann
Terence Best	=	Miles Best
Robin Kane	?	Alan Savage
Eamon McKay	?	Alex McCelland
Malachy McIvor	?	David Kennedy
Audrey Greer	?	Unknown 1
Margaret Derby	?	Unknown 2

Put that way, it didn't look quite so convincing. Yes, with the first three the names did match up. But there was no connection whatsoever between the other ten people, two of whom he didn't even know in the first place.

He was tempted to drop this approach altogether; about eight people being involved in one crime.

A little far-fetched; more Ruth Rendell than Colin Dexter, Kennedy thought. On top of which, it was going to take a lot of man-hours to chase all this down and it would be an incredible waste of time if it came to nothing.

He decided he was going to go back to his golden rule and chase more evidence before he started to draw such conclusions. He went to see McCusker and asked him if he could put some people on chasing the family members, particularly past, of Maggie Derby, Audrey Greer, Malachy McIvor, Eamon McKay and Robin Kane. He was tempted to go for speed over efficiency and just have them chase down the relatives on two of the names on the list, but common sense prevailed and he gave McCusker the full list.

McCusker reckoned it shouldn't take *that* long. Kennedy guessed that was a wish rather than a reality and computers might not be as much help as McCusker hoped.

In the meantime Kennedy felt that another little trip to Derek Shaw, who'd always been the top of both lists, just might be pertinent.

McCusker checked his watch, smacked his lips and offered total agreement with Kennedy's timely suggestion.

The Beatles were on the radio, Here, There and Everywhere –
one of Kennedy's favourite tracks in fact – and Kennedy was
slightly annoyed to hear the static and crackle of McCusker's
two-way as it sprang into life. It was the Morris Minor twins,
this time the blonde one. McCusker turned the radio down.

'Right, what do ye have for us?' McCusker grunted, no-
nonsense style.

'Might be something, might be nothing.'

'Spit it out, lad, you sound like you couldn't bite your
thumb,' McCusker thundered.

'It's fine,' Kennedy said in a quieter, more reasonable voice.
'We'll take anything you've got to give us at this stage.'

'Well, you remember you said ann rea had a sweet tooth?'

'Yes?' Kennedy coaxed as McCusker rolled his eyes.

'Well, we've been checking all the late-night shops that sell
sweets along the route and there's one just by the edge of
town, just by the tourist centre.'

'I know it,' McCusker said, joining Kennedy in the more
friendly approach.

'Well, a girl answering ann rea's description was in there
yesterday evening.'

'And?' McCusker said, shaking his head for Kennedy's
benefit.

'She bought a large tub of Ben and Jerry's Chunky Monkey
ice cream.'

'And?' Kennedy and McCusker said in unison.

'That's it.'

'That's it?' Kennedy repeated, allowing a little of
McCusker's frustration to creep into his voice for the first time.

'And when did this happen?' McCusker asked.

'Around 10.40pm, well, as near as she could guess it was
10.40. They close at 11pm and the wee girl and her father,
who were behind the counter at the time, said they thought it
was about twenty minutes before closing.'

'Mmmm,' McCusker said.

'Okay?' the voice asked through the static.

'Yes,' McCusker replied. 'Well done, keep on it, eh?'

'Sure thing, we'll come back to you with more as soon as
we can. Over and out.'

'Yeah, 'McCusker replied, never a stickler for procedure. 'Over and goodbye.'

Kennedy turned the FM radio back up again only to hear the dying chords of one of The Beatles' finest tunes. He sat for a few minutes collecting his thoughts. He was going to say something to McCusker then decided against it, and then changed his mind one final time.

'It was a peace offering, you know.'

'Sorry?' McCusker replied, a look on his face implying that he either hadn't heard him or had been so lost in his own thoughts he didn't understand him.

'The Ben and Jerry's ice cream was a peace offering,' Kennedy repeated and expanded. 'When we had our little... whatever you call them.'

'Tiffs,' McCusker started with a smile. 'Tiffs, that's what we call them. Now let me tell you something. Tiffs are vitally important to a relationship. And it's not just because of 'the best part of breaking up is when you're making up' crap like they sing about in the songs. No, it's so that a man can get some peace and quiet. I positively orchestrate them in our house just to get a bit of peace and quiet. It's like when the missus and me row and she's off like a peacock, lots of show but no vocals so I can tune her out altogether. Or I can even use it as an excuse to 'go out for a wee walk to clear my head' and then end up down the pub. A wee tiff, it's brilliant I can tell you.'

Kennedy smiled.

'Well, anyway, after our tiffs one of us would return with a tub of ice cream as a peace offering.' Kennedy replied.

'So you'd been rowing,' McCusker continued, turning the radio back down slightly.

Kennedy figured McCusker either had his head in the sand up at Kelly's Barn – and there certainly was enough sand for such an exercise in the neighbourhood – or he was encouraging Kennedy to talk about it.

'Yes,' Kennedy replied. He was shocked at how self-conscious he was. It was as though he was betraying a trust to ann rea. At the same Time, though, by talking about it he might remember something or just talking may, in the old-fashioned way, make him feel better. Then again, he was

surprised how little effect ann rea's disappearance was having
on him.

'What were you rowing about?' McCusker continued as
professionally as Michael Parkinson.

'I wanted to go with her on her late-night interview. In
short, I wanted to protect her but her reality was that I was
crowding her.'

'Yeah, but she went off by herself and look what
happened,' McCusker replied, trying to be helpful Kennedy
assumed.

'That's the moral high ground,' Kennedy started.
'However, if I could just take her side for a moment; if this is a
kidnapping, these people are clever as it would appear they
didn't just tumble her into a van and head off into the night,
screeching tyres and all. No, they followed her around town
for about thirty-five minutes. After her interview with
McCann, if it was as fruitless as he says it was, she probably
walked around town to clear her head. The kidnappers
mustn't have wanted to touch her when she was in a built-up
area. So they must have tracked her around town. So I'd have
to say if I'd been with her, they would just have waited until
some other time for their chance.'

McCusker nodded as if to say he was agreeing with
Kennedy, who continued after two beats:

'Towards the end of her walk, she must have come across
the shop, considered the peace-offering treat and known I'd
be waiting up for her. She'd appear with the Ben and Jerry's
and we'd forget about the fight and…'

'I've got to try some of this Ben and Jerry's.'

'I'm surprised you haven't, Inspector McCusker. I mean
you seem to have eaten everything else around Portrush,'
Kennedy said, lightening things up a bit.

'Aye,' McCusker grinned, a Player to one side of his
mouth. His wrinkled face looked like a real dog's breakfast
with one side trying to smile and the other trying to puff on a
ciggy, with his eyes half-squinting to keep the smoke out of
them. 'But anyway, back to the Ben and Jerry's, it seems like a
miracle cure to me or is it more what you do for afters? I mean
after the afters.'

Kennedy remembered all the sexy adverts from a few years

ago with these young sexy couples in various states of undress, spooning each other an apparently magically potent, smooth ice cream, suggesting: eat some ice cream (Haagen-Dazs) and get laid. He and ann rea had tried it but as ann rea so succinctly put it, the last thing you want to do with a tummy full of ice cream is rumble around. Now the more wholesome Ben and Jerry's *after* the rumble, well that was a different matter entirely and had become one of their rituals.

Back to the case, Kennedy thought.

'So let's assume they followed her to the shop,' he replied, choosing to ignore McCusker's question. 'It's on the outskirts of the town; maybe she walked across the links in the direction of the seashore to come home that way. This took her out of the peopled area and gave the kidnappers the golden opportunity they'd patiently been waiting for.'

'What does that tell us?' McCusker asked, stubbing his Player out in a rather full ashtray.

'That tells us, I suppose, that they weren't amateurs, they were professionals.'

'And what does that tell us?' McCusker continued as he lit up another ciggy.

'That tells us that they were probably hired in.'

'Yes, indeed it does,' McCusker said, picking up the handset to his radio. 'BD7 to control.'

He repeated the call sign three times.

'Agh, for Pete's sake,' he said on the fifth occasion, raising his voice. 'Tom, are you there? It's McCusker.'

A lone, thin voice broke the static.

'Yes, Inspector, what can I do for you on this beautiful, wonderful day?'

'Cut the crap for a start, and stop sitting out on the steps of the barracks,' McCusker continued, and as the radio signal broke up he said to Kennedy: 'I'll tell you that man won't be happy until he can get his desk and radio out into the street and in the sunshine.'

'What can I do for you?' the voice repeated.

'Could you get in touch with our mates in the Gardai up in Donegal.'

'Ah, you mean Inspector Starrett?'

'I mean the very same man, Tom. Listen, could you ask him

on the QT who in Donegal would be up for a bit of kidnapping?'

'Enough said,' the voice replied. 'I'll get on it immediately. Bye.' And he was gone, leaving only electronic static in his wake.

A few seconds later they had arrived at the gate of Derek Shaw's house.

'God, we forgot to stop at the grocers,' McCusker said as he unclipped his safety belt.

Chapter Thirty-Two

DEREK SHAW OPENED the door looking exactly the same as he had when he'd closed the door behind the two detectives yesterday. That was from his brilliantly polished shoes right up to his grey-checked cloth cap.

'I could set my watch by youse two,' he began as he opened the door to his picture-postcard cottage wider, thereby inviting them in. 'Go through to the kitchen, you know your way well enough by now, and I'll put on the kettle.'

'I was wondering, sir,' Kennedy began stepping into the hallway but remaining there, 'if we could maybe use the front room for today's chat. We'd only a quick visit there the other night and it seemed to be a fascinating room.'

McCusker looked on in amazement and disappointment.

'Why, aye, of course,' Shaw replied, beaming from ear to ear. You go on through there and young McCusker here can help me with the tea. I'm sure we can rustle up a sandwich or two.'

The smile, which wasn't exactly a stranger, returned to McCusker's face.

Kennedy could hear the running water, kettle lids being removed and replaced, cups set out, cutlery clinking, and a few 'Ayes' and a few grunts and groans as he entered the good room. The good room – also referred to in Ulster as the parlour, the front room (even when it was at the back), the courting room and the quiet room – enjoyed a calm and peaceful atmosphere. It was a bit like a hallowed space; a place kept in memory of the war. Kennedy felt, though, that the whole point of Shaw's room, more like museum, was not one of glorifying or sensationalising war but more as a memorial to what Rifleman Derek Shaw and his mates had gone through while protecting their country.

Above the fireplace, directly on top of his pride-of-place medals case, was a blow-up of the Binyon lines: 'We Will

Remember Them':

> They shall not grow old,
> As we that are left grow old.
> Age shall not weary them,
> Nor the years condemn.
> At the going down of the sun
> And in the morning,
> We will remember them.

'We will remember them,' Kennedy said aloud as he wandered around the room looking at the artifacts.

'Aye, we will remember them,' Shaw said, as he walked through the door, full tray in his hands bearing cups, saucers, thick sandwiches, milk and sugar. McCusker brought up the rear with a teapot under a very flowery tea cosy.

'There's a lot to remember. Out of just under 6 million people serving, over 300,000 were killed in action out of the Allied Forces – that's excluding the Russians and the Americans. The US force had just over 16 million serving and over 400,000 of those lost their lives while serving their country. We'll never know an accurate figure for the Russians; they keep revising it all the time. And then there was the enemy; the Germans had nearly 18 million troops and 3.75 million sons and daughters didn't return to their mothers and fathers.'

Both the volume of the figures and the fact that Shaw had committed them to memory shocked Kennedy. Kennedy knew that a lot of people had lost their lives during the Second World War but he'd never dreamt the carnage and the loss of human life was on such a vast scale. He imagined that when you added in the Russian, Italian and Japanese losses the total was probably in excess of 8 million. That was similar to the entire population of Ireland!

Shaw seemed to know what was preoccupying Kennedy and said quietly:

'Aye, the problem as I see it is, who's going to remember them when my generation is all dead and gone?'

'Oh, I think people will remember the great wars forever,' McCusker said confidently as he poured the tea.

'Aye, maybe they'll remember the generals and the prime

ministers and presidents and all that,' Shaw started. Although he was mid-sentence he stopped to take a chunk of his sandwich.

Kennedy refused offers of a sandwich of his own. They were made with thick slices of plain white bread with slabs of either cold ham or cheese inserted between. Kennedy couldn't abide cold food, he really couldn't. Even the thought of it made his stomach churn. He always thought that perhaps this was the reason he always ate his food so fast; ie before it had a chance to cool down.

'But the troops, the foot soldiers, the ones who made all the real sacrifices, how long are they going to be remembered, answer me that? I think wars would be a lot simpler if the people who started them had to fight it out face to face. Can you imagine Churchill and Hitler in the ring together, bruising and bloodying each other? Don't you see if they both had to make personal sacrifices, like a broken nose, a cracked rib, a knee in the goolies, then perhaps they would have viewed things differently.'

Kennedy smiled.

'Oh, go one with you, smile away,' Shaw reproached him. 'I know that perhaps I'm over-simplifying things. But ships sinking are so much easier to stomach if they are little wooden models on a map in the war room in Downing Street. Churchill then could say, "Yes, yes" between puffs of his cigar as he toppled over and removed a little ship with his cane, and then in the same breath say, "We'll obviously lose this little frigate, but that will draw out the fire of their submarines and then our two destroyers can steam in on them, which will let the fleet get through safely."'

McCusker and Kennedy were impressed by Shaw's impersonation of Churchill; they both said nothing, waiting for him to continue.

'But if Mr Churchill had to have been on that little frigate himself, or he personally knew of the mothers waiting at home and how they'd feel when the man from the War Department knocked on the door and their lives, the lives of the mother and the rest of their family, ceased to be, maybe he'd have acted differently. And you multiply that by the number of people on the frigate and then multiply that by the number of wives or girlfriends the dead men had, and then multiply that by the number of children the dead men had.

'Now I never knew the man, and some say he did a good job leading us to war, but I can't help feeling he would have done a much better job leading us through peace.'

'But then Hitler would have walked all over us,' McCusker stated quietly.

'You see, right there, young lad,' Shaw started. Kennedy thought it very funny the way this war veteran continuously referred to McCusker, a man who was planning his imminent retirement, as 'young' and 'lad'. More surprising still was the fact that McCusker did not bat an eyelid any time it happened. Shaw repeated himself: 'You see right there, young lad, that's how a war starts.

'Hitler could only walk all over us because he had armies to follow him. Churchill could only take Hitler to task if he'd us, his foot soldiers, to back him up. But my point is, we should never be asked to back them up. These guys are the professional politicians. We pay our taxes and their wages so that they sort out all this stuff. People like me, we just want to work on the farm, with wood, in shops, in factories, in the clergy, in Barry's, in the pol-ice for heaven's sake. That's what we want to do. We're not soldiers, we don't want to be conscripted against our will. We certainly don't want to kill people, we're not murderers; we're simple folk. Now that's true McCusker, isn't it? You have to admit that, don't you?'

'Yes, well, I suppose you have a point.'

'Yes, of course I have a point, young lad. And that's the thing, don't you see if Churchill couldn't sort it out we should have gotten someone else who could sort it out. If, say, you're a carpenter, right, and you take on an apprentice and you tell him what he has to do, what you're paying him to do and all of that. Right? Aye. Well if he hasn't got a feel for working with wood and just can't get on with it, then you're going to have to let him go and get someone else better suited to the job. Equally important, he's going to find a job he's more suited to. And from the Germans' point of view, if Hitler couldn't do his job properly then they needed to get someone else to do it. Simple as that.'

'Ah, come on, Derek,' McCusker groaned, polishing off

the last sandwich. Kennedy put it down to four-two: four sandwiches to McCusker and two to Shaw.

'"Come on, Derek" what? Away out of here with you. You mean to tell me that the Germans are any different from us? Of course the boys we were fighting in the war were just simple boys like us. They had mothers and fathers and girls or wives and children and dreams and fears. And when a bullet went into them they bled. And if there were too many bullets then they were blown to bits, literally, the same way that we were blown to bits. Their pants stank the same way ours did during a battle. You don't mean to tell me that they really wanted be on a strange muddy field, fighting for their lives? No! Of course not. All they wanted to do was be at home getting on with their lives and with their loved ones. You don't think they actually loved, no scrap loved, you don't think they even liked Hitler, do you? Look how many times people tried to top Hitler. That wasn't out of respect, you know, or cowardice. Aye, if you ask me, I'd say Hitler and Churchill were two of the biggest skitters of the last millennium.'

Shaw paused. No one spoke. Kennedy was, as he felt McCusker was, thinking about what Shaw had been saying. He was considering it from two different perspectives though.

'And you know what? I'll tell you both something. The only good that came out of the last war was the fact that there will never, ever be another world war. Mothers in this country will never again lose their children to someone else's cause. Aye, but the sad thing is though, it's too late for me and my boys and my troop. I'll remember them, aye, and when I'm dead we'll all be forgotten.'

'Do you mind me asking you, sir, if you ever saw Victor Dugdale kill anyone?' Kennedy asked looking about the room.

'I don't mind you asking, son, and I don't mind telling you I did. I saw him and he had to,' Shaw stated firmly.

'Would you mind telling me what the circumstances were?' Kennedy continued. He'd finished his tea and was leaning on the table with his arms folded.

Shaw rubbed his forehead a few times with his cloth cap.

'Aye,' he began expansively. 'It was either Gerry or Victor; it was as simple as that. I mean, I'm talking now about one I know about. Like I said, when you're in a battle and you're pinned down under heavy fire then you just shoot indiscriminately into the distance, hoping to either pin them down until something can be done or to take one of them out before they do any damage to any of your lads.

'I, ah, we were out in, ah, we were going from France to, I think it was Belgium and we came upon this canal that we had to cross. We were pinned down on one side of this canal and we couldn't get across and the Germans had used the water to work against us. The canal was about maybe ten yards across – I'm sorry, son, I wouldn't have a clue what that is in metres,' Shaw said, his Paul Newman eyes sparkling at his own humour. 'So Gerry set up these watch-points every fifty yards or so and using the minimum of men they were pretty much able to immobilise us. The rest of their men they split into two groups and they were resting up in camps about a mile apart. Then we came up with this great plan. Actually it was Victor's plan. Aye, that's right, it was Victor's plan. On the first night there was a new moon so there was nothing at all we could do. On the second night it was pouring down and we were in pitch black. There was this little bend in the canal and Victor figured if we could build a little boat maybe three of us could get in and cross the canal and take out three of the watch posts in the middle, and then our entire troop could wade across under the safety of darkness.

'How do you make a boat out of nothing in the middle of nowhere?' asked McCusker.

'Victor and I came up with a plan for that. We used an idea we'd often used at the Port when we were young. We got a few branches and, using rope, we fixed them into a framework that loosely resembled a wee boat. We then fixed the canvas of one of our tents to it and three of us got in, lay down real low and right under their noses we crossed the canal. Alan Savage, aye Alan, I showed him to you the other day, he's in the photograph. Alan crept to the first post, me to the far one and Victor to the middle one and the plan was, at an exact moment, a time we set in advance…'

Here Shaw broke back into his Churchill voice: "Okay, synchronise watches!" He broke back into his normal raspy voice to continue: 'At that pre-agreed moment we would all hopefully take out our separate sentries. I was worried about Victor, I have to tell you. But when he was needed, son, he was right there with us. Aye, he was right there with us and we all took our men out and then stood guard on the opposite bank as our troops came across.

'Now don't you see?' Shaw continued, in full flow and lost in his memories. 'We'd split their platoon in half and we were just too powerful for either half. When we attacked one we destroyed them, actually most of them ran off. Then we hid in waiting around their camp for the other half to come up and when they did, we tore into them as well. It was a great victory for us, I can tell you. It was mentioned in the dispatches and it only worked because Victor was able to take out his man.'

'And you too,' Kennedy offered, affected by the man's modesty.

'Augh aye,' Shaw continued, a smile still on his face. 'I can remember it well now. Boys-a-dear, I'd nearly forgotten. There was this one boy… we'd fought off the first half of their platoon and we were fighting the second half after we'd ambushed them and there was this one boy, and I'd my Bren gun and I shot at him as they were running away, firing over their head like, and I clipped him on the ear. God, you should have heard the screaming. I went running over to him and there was blood everywhere and he was lying in the bottom of a ditch he'd fallen into. I think he thought his head had been blown off with all the blood and all of that but I could see it was just his ear so I kept my gun on him and shouted at him. I forget what I shouted, just some words very loud but it created the right effect because he jumped up and headed away over the fields.

'I often wonder what happened to him. Did he get home? What has he done with the rest of his life? Of course, I remember him as a young lad. He's probably well wrinkled now like the rest of us.'

Kennedy and McCusker were smiling.

'So was this before Victor got married?' Kennedy asked.

'Augh aye, well before,' was Shaw's simple reply.

'Do you remember the photograph we showed you yesterday?' Kennedy continued, preparing his own little bombshell.

'Aye I do that,' Shaw replied his voice going a little quieter.

'We've brought you a copy,' Kennedy again. McCusker was now looking at Shaw intently.

'Great. I appreciate that.'

Kennedy handed it over. 'Tell me, do you recognise anyone extra in the photograph today?'

Shaw went over to the dresser by the door and there, after hoaking around amongst several open letters and catalogues, he found his glasses case. He returned to the table, put on his glasses and stared at the photograph in silence for a few minutes. It seemed to be having exactly the same effect on him as yesterday.

He shook his head from side to side. 'Nope, just Dugdale, Alan, Alex and David.'

'Don't you think this lad here,' Kennedy said pointing to the photograph, 'looks a bit like Portrush butcher, and your fellow bridge club member, Paul McCann?'

Shaw laughed. 'I know they were taking us young but not that young. Paul would have been in his nappies in '43.'

'True, very true, Derek,' McCusker smiled, setting Kennedy up.

'But what about his father, what would his father have been called?'

'Now there's a question,' Shaw began lifting the photograph closer to his eyes, so close in fact that neither McCusker nor Kennedy could see his eyes any more. 'I'd have to give you that, there's a bit of a resemblance. But only a bit, mind you. I mean, that's only a slip of a lad like the rest of us, and Paul, well we all know he's a big fan of his own product. I don't think you could positively…'

'You see, it's just that we've a positive ID that the Rifleman we are studying is none other than Colin McCann, father of your very own favourite butcher.' Kennedy tried choosing that exact moment to bluff the 'father' bit.

'God!' Shaw lifted the photo close to his eyes, hiding them again, 'You know, you just might be right. I couldn't in a million years have remembered that but you just might be right.' He stopped and started to laugh. 'And I've known Paul all these years and never made the connection. Brave man was Colin McCann, aye, very brave.'

Kennedy felt a little sorry for Shaw to be drawing him in

this way, but there was no other way to do it. He was still working on the connection theory and he was still so far away from establishing anything concrete that he had to be very careful with his steps. He was figuring out how to proceed with the questioning when Shaw replaced the photograph between them and said,

'That was a great bit of detecting, truly wonderful. Managed to trace any of the others, yet?'

'Just one other,' Kennedy said.

Rifleman Derek Shaw was physically upset now, he couldn't hide it, and he shook his head, appearing to try to regain his consciousness.

'One other you say, and who'd that be?'

'Again, another relation of someone you know today and, surprisingly enough, the relation we're talking about is also a member of the bridge club,' Kennedy announced.

Shaw quickly lifted the photograph from the table and had another concentrated stare at it.

'That's a good clue, detective, now let me see…'

'You must re…' McCusker cut in, also appearing to take pity on Shaw and offering a little prompt.

'Of course,' Shaw shouted, 'of course, I should have known the eyebrows. Mind you, if you'd not mentioned a member of the bridge club I'd never have put two and two together. Terry's brother, Rifleman Miles Best.'

'The very same,' McCusker agreed. 'Still not remembered any of the others?'

'Nagh. I'm nearly pooped anyway. Mind you, it's not like you need me anyway, youse are doing perfectly well by yourselves. That's a great wee bit of detecting, I'll tell you. Youse two should be on the telly.'

'Don't you find it strange, though, that yourself and the son of Colin McCann and the brother of Miles Best should be in London at the time Victor Dugdale was killed? Particularly when you, Victor, Colin and Miles are all in this same photograph?' Kennedy asked.

'Coincidence,' was Shaw's one-word reply.

'Tell me what happened to Colin and Miles?' Kennedy asked.

'They were buried in a field far away in France,' Shaw said, his ice-blue eyes locking into Kennedy's green stare. Neither flinched. 'They both died on the battlefield.'

Chapter Thirty-Three

'YOU HAD HIM,' McCusker gasped in exasperation. It was ten minutes later and they were back in the car heading towards Portrush. 'You had him right there,' McCusker continued holding out his hand, 'and you let him go. Why?'

Kennedy smiled and sank back into his chair. 'We didn't have him at all. So what if he's in the same photograph as someone one who has been murdered? So what that there is someone else in the same photograph that Shaw knows? So what that he knows the relatives of two further people in the photograph? It doesn't mean a thing until we have more evidence.'

'But...'

'But look at him, McCusker, he's in his mid-seventies, for heaven's sake, what could he do?'

'But he had accomplices.'

'We think. We have yet to prove it,' Kennedy said and sank into his seat in thought, turning up the radio.

Five minutes later.

'I've just been thinking that you were pretty upbeat in there, I mean more upbeat than usual,' McCusker said, voicing something that he'd obviously been considering.

'Well, if Shaw is involved in this in some way, and if ann rea's disappearance is also connected to it, I wanted a message to go back that her disappearance wasn't affecting me.'

'Makes sense, I suppose.'

Just then, right on cue, the radio crackled into action. It was McCusker's office.

'The lab boys have made some progress on the number plates,' the voice announced over the airwaves.

'Excellent,' McCusker replied as Kennedy sat up in his seat.

'Yes, as far as they can make out, the full number is...' there was a pause and Kennedy got out his notebook and had his pencil at the ready when the number was read out. 'DL 89 5529 BUI. They say the car is a Honda Prelude.'

'Could you get on to our mates in the Gardai again and see if they can put a trace on it for us.'

'I already have,' the voice replied.

'Oh, good,' McCusker replied. 'Have they got any information for us yet on potential Donegal kidnappers?'

'Not yet. They said they were still working on it.'

'What's all that noise in the background?' McCusker asked.

'Oh, it's like a zoo in here, sir, 'the voice replied. 'Everyone is working on the births, marriages and deaths to see if we can get a trace on the people on your list.'

'Good,' McCusker replied. 'We should be back in about fifteen minutes.'

'Oh, just one more thing. Anita McCann rang in for Inspector Kennedy about ten minutes ago. She said she had some more news for him.'

'Thanks,' McCusker replied. 'Over and over.'

'No sir,' the voice replied, 'it's over and out.'

'Whatever,' McCusker replied.

Kennedy got through to Anita fairly quickly and he was happy to find out that she had managed to get the two names of the other people in the photograph for him.

Wesley McIvor and Norman Kane.

Kennedy wrote down the two names and then went to the page he'd been working on earlier where he was trying to draw the connections between the two sets of names.

Kennedy made a few amendments to his original list:

1999		1943
	Victor Dugdale.	
Derek Shaw	=	Derek Shaw
Paul McCann	=	Colin McCann
Terence Best	=	Miles Best
Robin Kane	=	Norman Kane
Eamon McKay	?	Alex McCelland
Malachy McIvor	=	Wesley McIvor
Audrey Greer	?	Alan Savage
Margaret Derby	?	David Kennedy

He studied the list for a few minutes then announced to McCusker:

'Two more names match up. Robin Kane and Norman Kane, and Malachy McIvor and Wesley McIvor.'

'Mmmm,' McCusker breathed more than spoke.

Kennedy studied his lists for a few more minutes before adding:

'Something else here, it could be nothing, it could be a coincidence or, equally, it could be something.'

'You got my attention.'

'Well, do you remember when we first took the photograph to Shaw and we asked him for the names of the soldiers?'

'Yes?'

'Well, don't you find it strange that the three names he gave us – Riflemen Savage, McCelland and Kennedy – were the only three names on the list that did not share the family name of anyone on the bridge club list?'

'Thereby hiding the connection between one list and the other,' McCusker announced proudly.

'Exactly,' Kennedy replied, undoing his safety belt as the car pulled up in the heavily protected barracks car park. He could hardly wait to get back into the police station and see what other possible connections McCusker's team's finger-work had turned up.

Ten minutes later he'd rewritten his two lists onto a foolscap sheet of paper, which he pinned to the notice board in his makeshift office, and he and McCusker took a few minutes to stare at the sum total of the investigation so far.

1999		1943
	Victor Dugdale	
Derek Shaw	=	Derek Shaw
Paul McCann	56-year-old son of	Colin McCann
Terence Best	65-year-old brother of	Miles Best
Robin Kane	19-year-old grandson of	Norman Kane
Eamon McKay	54-year-old stepson of	Alex McCelland
Malachy McIvor	22-year-old grandson of	Wesley McIvor
Audrey Greer	55-year-old daughter of	David Kennedy
Margaret Derby	20-year-old granddaughter of	Alan Savage

Either by pure coincidence or by luck, Kennedy already had McKay and McCelland matched up on the same line; he just hadn't known the connection between them. However, he thought, it did show that coincidences did occur and perhaps he'd be wise to keep stock of that as he continued the investigation.

But what was it all about? What had happened to the troop back in 1943 that could have cost Victor Dugdale his life? Why would someone want to murder a 74-year-old man towards the end of his natural life anyway? Why were a group of people, all relations of those in the original war photograph – apart that was, of course, from Derek Shaw who was there in person – why were they all members of the same bridge club in Ballyneagh and why were they all in London at the approximate time Victor Dugdale was being murdered?

Coincidence? Yes and pigs might fly, thought Kennedy.

'Obviously we need to know what happened to Riflemen McCann, Savage, Kane, McCelland, McIvor, Best and Kennedy,' McCusker said, rising from his chair, which was in fact an unopened cardboard box full of forms of one sort of other.

'We do indeed,' Kennedy agreed.

'I'll check with the Ministry of Defence, they should still have all the old wartime files.'

'That's the first thing we need to do. You get on to that and give me the number of your mate in the Gardai and I'll ring him to see how they're getting on with tracing the vehicle and their list of potential kidnappers. It must be a hell of a list to be taking so long.'

Just then the telephone rang.

It was the Reverend Steven Houston. McCusker left Kennedy alone to take the call.

'Yes, young man, I'm afraid I have some bad news for you,' Houston's voice declared bluntly over the telephone.

'Oh yes?'

'Yes, I got a call at the rectory about fifteen minutes ago,' Houston continued, very businesslike. 'It was from a man, I think he was a Southerner, he obviously had a handkerchief over the mouthpiece but I could hear the distinctive tones. Anyway, this man told me to tell you that they have your friend, Miss Rea.' Houston's voice distinctly accented a capital on Rea.

Kennedy was speechless. He couldn't work out whether it was because up until that point, even with the Honda Prelude and the number plates and the late-night walk and ice cream stop-off, he thought that ann rea could still have walked in from the street and said, "Sorry, I stayed in a hotel last evening because I was so annoyed with you." Or even that he might have received a telephone call saying, "I'm back in Camden, Kennedy, and I've had enough of this."

Up until that point either of those two options was a possibility as far as Kennedy was concerned. But now, with Houston's news, it was confirmed that she'd definitely been kidnapped. But why was Houston the bearer of the bad news?

Then, as if reading Kennedy's mind, Houston continued: 'Of course, it's quite a common occurrence over here, you know, for these types to ring the clergy with the bad news. Since the Troubles started I don't know how many doors I've had to knock on late at night with terrible news for those within. He sounded like a bit of a ruffian to me and he said to tell you that unless you give up immediately what you're working on and go back to England, then your friend will die, but not before they have some fun with her. He told me to make sure I told you that. Of course his conversation was interspersed with obscenities, which I've spared your from, but apart from that it's pretty much what he said, then he banged the phone down.'

'Did he not say anything else about the deal, like: "If he drops the case we'll release her on such a date"? Because obviously I'd need some kind of assurance.'

'Well I don't know about any of that but he sounded deadly serious to me. If I were you I'd heed him and then see what happens. I wouldn't go sticking my neck out looking for guarantees or any of that auld stuff.'

And then the funniest of things happened. The Reverend Steven Houston just disappeared; he disconnected. No words of comfort. No encouragement. He just vanished into the telephonic wilderness leaving Kennedy with the phone still stuck to his ear. He was now listening to a sea of hiss where once Houston's well-defined Ulster tones had broadcast.

Without missing a beat Kennedy replaced the phone, lifted it again immediately and, with a clear line, dialled the number McCusker had given him; the telephone number of the Gardai in Letterkenny.

Chapter Thirty-Four

KENNEDY GOT THROUGH to Detective Starrett immediately.

'Sure, weren't we just about to ring McCusker.' the soft Irish tones exclaimed, putting emphasis on the royal 'we'.

'How're ye doing? How's it going tracing that car for us?'

'Oh fine. Funny enough though, the same name was on the list of people likely to commit a crime such as the one McCusker described to us. The car is registered to the James brothers, Lennon and...' Starrett hesitated for a beat, just long enough for Kennedy to think he was going to say 'Jesse'. 'And Dylan,' Starrett continued, blowing Kennedy's theory. 'Their old man's a bit of a character himself. He was into John Lennon and Bob Dylan big-time. They're all from up in Ramelton. The old boy has had a few run-ins with us himself, never anything major mind you, but he's never done time. The other two, right pair of cowboys I can tell you. Mind you, I'd say they have hearts of gold; latter-day Robin Hoods, if you know what I mean.'

'You think they could have kidnapped the English journalist?' Kennedy asked hopefully and professionally.

'Highly likely, I'd say. I'd say there'd have been a right bit of change in it for them. They do love the old cash, you know.'

'Do you think they'd have brought her back there?'

'To Ramelton? I'd say so; they don't like to be away from the Bridge Bar for too long. That's their favourite watering hole, by the way.'

'So how should we proceed?'

'Officially, we should be going through the proper channels. Unofficially we don't have time to waste. We'll pick the lads up on something or other and see what we can, er... find out for you.'

'Good,' Kennedy replied. 'I... ahm... you know...'

'Listen to me, Inspector, for just a wee minute. Your girlfriend is going to be okay. Lennon and Dylan are not into harming people, that wouldn't be their style, no, not at all.'

'It's not them I'm worried about; it's the people behind the murder investigation we're working on. I'd be more worried about them,' Kennedy said then added as an afterthought: 'How would these people have contacted The James boys?' He was having trouble addressing them as Lennon and Dylan. Mind you, he thought, the James boys was pretty surreal as well.

'Oh, you know, talk around bars. Guinness is expensive, talk is cheap,' Starrett replied, not quite as profound as he'd hoped, Kennedy thought. 'Maybe they'd already done some job or other for your real suspect.'

'I don't think so,' Kennedy replied into his mouthpiece. 'I think this was a one-and-only crime.'

'Funny how quickly they adapt though, isn't it? First they murder someone and then they hire kidnappers when the heat gets too high,' Starrett said, apparently thinking out loud.

'Yeah, and that's a fact. I just worry about it, you know, they're not going to want to leave a trail and with kidnapping that usually means one thing…'

'Well not as far as Lennon and Dylan James are concerned. Their father brought them up well, you know. I know for a fact, Inspector, that he'd skin them alive if they were involved in any physical violence. They may not show a lot of fear or respect for the law but the auld man now, that's a different matter altogether, I can tell you.'

'So there is honour among thieves after all?' Kennedy said what he was thinking.

'You better believe it, especially with auld man James. He's battered their heads together before and he'll certainly do it again. Listen, I'm off down into Ramelton myself to see what's what. It's a great wee drive, down along the Swilly. Beautiful part of the world down here, Inspector, you should come and visit us.'

'I might be there sooner than you think,' Kennedy replied, thinking once again of ann rea and her predicament. 'Thanks for your help, detective.'

'You're very welcome. I'll give you or McCusker a shout as soon as I find out anything more.'

'Appreciate it,' Kennedy said to a dead line.

Kennedy then went to find McCusker who advised him that he'd just found out from the Ministry of Defence that all the people in the photograph, apart from Victor Dugdale and Derek Shaw, had been listed as killed in action. They'd all been listed as having died on the same day: Sept 20th 1943.

'Did they not have any more information than that for you?' Kennedy asked in disbelief.

'No, they said that was all that was recorded. They are going to go through their records and see if they can uncover anything else.'

Kennedy then advised McCusker of his two conversations, starting with Starrett's about the James boys and then the Reverend Houston's warning.

'Tell me everything exactly as he said it,' McCusker asked as they walked back towards Kennedy's office.

Kennedy repeated it word for word; everything he could remember that Houston had said.

'I don't believe that he had any such call,' McCusker stated as he pulled a packet of Tayto Crisps from his pocket and tore into them.

'I thought the same but why are you so sure?'

'Simple. No one north or south of the border has used handkerchiefs for the last twenty years. It's all down to Kleenex these days, isn't it? No one uses handkerchiefs any more. That is, of course, except the clergy. Particularly our Reverend Steven Houston and I bet he's even got a flowery 'SH' embroidered in blue in one of the corners. I think it's time we paid him another visit, don't you?' McCusker said as he rolled the empty crisp packet into a ball and expertly tossed it into a wastepaper bin at the far end of the office.

It was still rolling around the bottom of the empty bin as the two detectives exited the room.

Chapter Thirty-Five

MEANWHILE, BACK IN Camden Town, DS James Irvine was still scurrying around trying to pick up scraps of information for his boss on the Black Cat Building murder.

Irvine had trailed Coles back down to the Black Cat Building and they'd walked around the entrance hall and up the stairs to the boardroom, with its beautiful wood and ugly smell of death. They'd walked around the room for ages. Coles figured they'd covered every square inch of floor space, at least twice. She'd seen Kennedy do this several times. On some of the occasions she knew it wasn't as much what he was looking for on the floor as what he was searching for in his head.

And sometimes it worked.

Irvine, however, was not sharing any of that success. They were about to leave the boardroom when he began pacing out the distance from the front windows to the solid, wood-panelled wall on the opposite side of the room. Eleven paces exactly, which was probably a little less then eleven yards but a lot less than the total width of the building. Irvine left the conference room and instead of going to the front stairwell, opened a concealed door towards the rear of the lobby where he discovered a rear stairwell. He climbed down the five flights to the ground floor. He found nothing very interesting, just a fire exit door, which was probably locked on the night of the murder. The building wasn't at that point in time, nor since, occupied by the public, so the door wouldn't have had to be opened and would have been too difficult for police if it was. However, at the same time, it probably wouldn't have been too difficult for someone to come through the front of the building and open the fire exit from the inside. But Coles thought Kennedy had already sussed that. They climbed the stairs to the boardroom again. The rear stairwell was naturally lit by floor-to-ceiling windows. Irvine paused on the third landing and stared out through this window.

'It's a pity for the people who live in this crescent. When it was first built they would have faced a beautiful green and now all they see is the ugly back of this building.'

'Yes you're right. If they were at the front, or the building was the other way around at least, they would have an amazing view, architecturally speaking,' Coles replied, partly to humour him and partly to get a conversation started.

They were both staring out the window and looking along Mornington Crescent, right into someone's house. They could both see someone, a woman, a middle-aged woman, raising her fist and shaking it at them.

'Of course,' Irvine shouted, his tartan tones echoing up and down the entire stairwell. 'If we can see them, then they can also see into this building.'

'Yes?' Coles replied, not sure she should be encouraging him.

'Don't you see? There must be a chance that someone over there saw something going on in here,' Irvine said as he was scarpering down the stairs.

By the time they got to the first floor Coles reminded him that the doors were locked so they cut through the main building and ran out the front door. Irvine ran back in and used the telephone by the desk, requesting that the desk sergeant send down as many members of the Camden Town police force as possible to the building.

Flynn, along with Irvine and Castle, were the only members of Camden Town police force who Kennedy had advised of ann rea's disappearance. Kennedy felt the fewer people who knew about ann rea, the less chance the story had of getting in the papers and therefore, he hoped, the safer she would be. Flynn accompanied seven constables and three detective sergeants down to the Black Cat Building and within six minutes they had divided up Mornington Crescent and were knocking on doors and ringing bells.

Chapter Thirty-Six

'GENTLEMEN,' THE REVEREND Houston exclaimed insincerely, 'I have no control over what the general public do and choose to tell me. I am here merely as a vessel of God. He spreads his word to his flock through me. Sometimes people choose to use the vessel in another way, by asking for forgiveness, by giving me information. Now this chap who gave the warning about your young lady... tell me, Detective Inspector, are you and she married?'

'Actually we're not, but I don't see...'

'Be careful, my son, be careful for thy sins will find thee out,' Houston bellowed.

McCusker was fussing in his chair; they were all three sitting in the offending room in the rectory.

'Maybe this is a warning to you from on high,' Houston continued but was distracted once again by McCusker. 'For heaven's sake, McCusker, what's the matter with you, man? Can't you see I'm trying to...'

'It's just that I've got something in my eye and it's burning.'

'Oh, is that all,' Houston said, hoaking in his trouser pocket. 'Here.' And he threw a handkerchief across to McCusker. 'Get it out with this.'

The handkerchief was clean, still folded and pressed and there, in one of the corners, was a very ornate embroidery of the letters 'SH'. Neither McCusker nor Kennedy could help but laugh. Kennedy spoke first.

'Tell me, Reverend Houston, didn't you accompany the bridge club to London?'

Houston changed tack immediately. 'I did not travel on the minibus to London with the bridge club, no,' the Reverend replied very positively.

'Okay,' Kennedy started up again. 'It's agreed that you didn't travel to London...' Kennedy paused for a beat. He couldn't be sure but he thought he saw Houston visibly relax.

His jaw involuntarily eased into his dimples in a Jokerman grin, which revealed just how bad a condition his teeth were in. '...on the mini bus,' Kennedy added and Houston's jaw became rigid again. 'But how about on a flight? Did you fly to London that weekend?'

Houston squirmed around in his chair for a bit. If looks could kill, Kennedy thought.

'Well of course, I had to show them parish guidance and support, didn't I? I visited them in West Hampstead, said grace before dinner and then attended celestial duties.'

'And when did you return?' Kennedy asked.

'Oh, I think my last meeting was a lunch on Tuesday. I went straight to the airport afterwards and flew to Aldergrove on the next flight. I think I got back around teatime. Tell me, Detective Inspector, are you not worried about your Miss Rea?' Houston asked.

'We're very satisfied with our investigations in that area,' McCusker replied on Kennedy's behalf.

'Really?' Houston replied. 'It's just that the chap who rang me seemed fairly confident that he had the upper hand.'

'Interesting point, Reverend Houston, this is new information. You didn't tell me this on the phone earlier?' Kennedy said. He was trying to act as normal as possible.

He wanted to send out a signal that he wasn't at all concerned about ann rea. But was he trying too hard to achieve this and by trying too hard, was he in fact sending out the totally opposite signal?

'It was just the inflection of his voice, of course, just a little thing. But when you listen to as many people as I do, you know, in my line of duty as it were, well it's just that you pick up on these things,' Houston boasted.

'Very interesting,' McCusker replied as he blew his nose loudly into Houston's virgin handkerchief.

'I didn't mean for you to...' Houston interrupted. 'Oh, never mind.'

'No, as I said, it was interesting. It's just that my colleague here told me that you'd said that the person who phoned the threat had a muffled voice, as if speaking through a handkerchief. I was just wondering how the subtle inflections of his voice came through if he was using a handkerchief?'

'Oh!' Houston burst into fits of laughter. 'I suppose this is the point where you cuff me and take me away.' The Reverend, to emphasise his joke, brought both his wrists together and offered them out to the detectives.

'No, that won't be necessary,' McCusker replied.

Again Houston seemed to breathe a sigh of relief; maybe he was just mocking them, Kennedy thought.

'No, it won't be necessary, we won't need the handcuffs. We're sure being a man of the cloth you'll come peacefully.' Kennedy added quickly.

'Sorry?' Houston boomed, jumping up on to his feet. 'You've got to be kidding, what on earth for? I'm up for become a bishop. You can't do this to me.'

'We're not. For further questioning. Congratulations. We can. I think that answers all your points in the order they came,' McCusker replied. 'Now let's go.'

Houston threatened everything, including the wrath of hell's fire, but eventually he allowed himself to be escorted to the patrol car waiting outside. He wanted to exercise his rights to make a phone call. He was told he could make the call from the station if he still felt he needed to do so.

'You caught the Reverend a wee bit by surprise there, myself included,' McCusker said a few minutes later as they were driving back to Portrush.'

'Me too,' Kennedy admitted. 'I just wanted to make sure he wasn't in a position to make any phone calls. Talking about which, could we check with the telephone exchange about the telephone calls he's received in the last hour? From, say, about an hour before he rang me about the threat to ann rea, in fact.'

'Okay.'

'I think it's time to pick up all the members of the bridge club for questioning. I'm sure the bush telegraph is working overtime at this stage.'

McCusker radioed in Kennedy's instructions.

'Except for Shaw; let's leave him be. He's not going anywhere and I'd like to save him for last, preferably at his own cottage,' Kennedy said quietly.

'No complaints from me on that one,' McCusker replied, licking his lips.

Chapter Thirty-Seven

FOLLOWING SEVERAL HOURS of intense questioning, a uniform story began to emerge from all the members of the Ballyneagh Bridge Club. From a police procedural point of view, this was unusual; unusual in that all the stories were *not* identical. In fact, they all had some important piece of information missing; information that was always disclosed by at least a couple of the other club members. However, there were absolutely no contradictions in any of the statements. Should you have sat down and read the stories one after each other, you'd have had the complete story. Perhaps the gospel according to the Reverend Steven Houston, Kennedy guessed.

In the good old days, Kennedy recalled, you'd tend to be suspicious if more than two people had identical stories. Now here he was being sceptical because none of them were duplicating the facts. The other surprising thing that emerged from the interviews was that none of those currently 'helping the police with their inquiries' were either loud, cocky, quiet or overtly nervous.

This unlikely, extraordinary group of people, who were all linked by blood to those in the 1943 war photograph, had all travelled to London in the People Carrier. Dates, times and events were all as the police had already been advised. No visible discrepancies!

However, during the evening – the time when it would have been possible for (at least) two or more of them to have murdered Victor Dugdale – they were all alone in their own rooms with nothing but their own thoughts and not a hint of an alibi in sight.

For Kennedy, that was the first strange thing.

If this was a conspiracy, then shouldn't they all be tripping over each other in providing alibis? But no! At the crucial times – when they were outside the company of the West

Hampstead Bridge Club – it would appear that they were all holding none but their own counsel.

Now, was this someone being very clever or was playing bridge such a mental drain that they all needed to recharge their batteries and compose themselves for the following day's play? Probably not, Kennedy thought. Perhaps it was more a case of no alibis given, none to be broken; no personal resolve, which might be broken down with clever good guy/bad guy questioning.

Fortunately, the single thing that struck Kennedy during all the questioning was a little quote that had stuck in his mind from the earlier part of the investigation in Camden Town. When the North Bridge House team checked with a member of the local Masons (not in-house, Kennedy hoped) his reply had been: "You're looking for a butcher more than a Mason." This flashed into Kennedy's mind as he was questioning local butcher and bridge player, Paul McCann.

Kennedy also remembered that no traces of blood had been discovered in the Black Cat Building. So where had Victor Dugdale been murdered? Had McCann, because of his daily expertise, been the one chosen to carry out the grizzly deed as the others looked on?

Kennedy couldn't imagine Auntie Audrey Greer peering out through her large spectacles at such a scene. Nor Margaret Derby for that matter. She was barely out of her teens; surely she couldn't, or wouldn't, stomach such a macabre scene?

The interviewing team reported no obvious weak link in the Ballyneagh crowd. There was no one, potentially, who might spill the beans on the rest. No one down in the dumps or depressed about the whole sorry business. If anything, McCusker observed, his interviewee, Eamon McKay, appeared elated. When McCusker mentioned this fact to the rest of his team they all agreed, having observed similar responses from their own interviewees. Words like "high", "good-humoured" and "happy" were being bandied about. Again Kennedy noted no one said anything about observing even the faintest hint of cockiness. He felt that there wasn't much point pushing any of the Ballyneagh Bridge Club at this point; he knew it would be a fruitless exercise.

The one strange, even bizarre, thing that Kennedy kept coming back to was that all the Ballyneagh Bridge Club members were related to the members of Dugdale's wartime photograph. This was the one fact he was taking a little comfort from. But when confronted with this news the bridge club members appeared equally fascinated.

'I know, I've heard. Isn't that the strangest thing!' Audrey Greer had exclaimed.

McCann put it down to a 'coincidence'.

Robin Kane said it was 'un-effing-bel-iev-able!'

Eamon McKay thought it was 'Cosmic'.

Maggie Derby shrugged it off with: 'You must have your facts wrong, it's just not possible.'

Terence Best claimed it was due to the fact that they all came from a Small, tight-knit community. 'If you take any gathering from around these parts I bet you could make similar connections back to the photograph,' he advised one of McCusker's colleagues.

None admitted knowing much about their wartime relatives and, at best, gave some general family-background information.

Kennedy was granted his request to continue to hold them all, including Reverend Houston who'd yet to be questioned, in custody overnight. He needed more information before continuing the questioning. Most importantly he needed to know exactly what had happened in 1943 to Riflemen Shaw, McCann, Savage, Kane, McCelland, McIvor, Best and his own namesake, Kennedy (the father of cuddly Auntie Audrey Greer). He also wanted to know why he himself appeared so unconcerned about ann rea's disappearance. It was fast approaching a full twenty-four hours since she'd gone missing. She was about to spend her first full night in captivity.

Then he got the shivers.

That's when he started to wonder about her. Was she okay? Harmed? Tied up? In a locked room? In darkness? Raped?

RAPED?

He realised this was exactly why he'd forced himself not to think about her in her current predicament. He knew if he started to think about her, dark thoughts would automatically start to descend. Thoughts like she could be dead.

DEAD?

Well, it was a distinct possibility, wasn't it? Then he started to really freak himself out, wondering how she might have died. How might they kill her?

A knife? A knife was certainly a quiet, efficient method, especially in expert hands. But it could be messy and leave incriminating evidence.

A gun? Possibly not, it would be much too noisy and they'd risk discovery if they used this method. Unless of course they were away in some remote countryside spot or they had a silencer?

Strangled? Possibly, but knowing ann rea she would have fought tooth and nail for her life and she could possibly have marked or injured her attacker. Would they have risked that?

Poisoned? Certainly effective, maybe even a humane way for them to kill her without her knowing she was going to die. Probably too detectable afterwards in case they were caught. Also the purchase of said poison does tend to leave an obvious trail.

Hanged? Execution by hanging, this was a possibility and possibly even a link to the Dugdale murder. Could the same people have been involved in both murders? Indirectly yes, Kennedy thought, there must be the same brains behind both cases. But were they directly involved? No! Positively no, if he was to believe that Detective Starrett's likely suspects, Lennon and Dylan, carried out the murder. Murder was definitely outside of their league.

Every time Kennedy found a rock to shelter and take comfort from, things like the brothers being inept or a gun being too noisy, then along would come a fierce wave, like Dugdale's hanging, to pull him back into the stormy seas.

Talking about stormy seas, Kennedy thought, they could have drowned her. Now that would have been the perfect scenario for them, wouldn't it? Okay, just think it through properly, Kennedy prompted himself. They kidnap her. Kidnap: what a perfectly gentle and non-threatening word for such a cowardly and (usually) fatal act. Kidnap. Surely the word implied a child having a little snooze more than the devastating deed it usually turned out to be. What did a child taking a nap have to do, Kennedy wondered, with a person, or persons unknown, stealing the woman he loved? He forced himself back along his original thought pattern. They kidnap her, they use the kidnapping to warn him off the case and then when they achieve their goal, so that there is no incriminating evidence around - as in the case of a witness who could possibly identify something about them - they'd drown her. They'd merely hold her head underwater, sea water of course. Then, when she was dead, they'd dump her into the sea close to Portrush somewhere and she'd either be washed up later, or not. They wouldn't really have cared.

However, they probably hadn't killed her yet; ann rea hadn't fully served her purpose. Kennedy was still busy on the Dugdale case. Using this logic, he must still have a chance to save her. It all fitted together perfectly, didn't it? ann rea had rowed with her lover, in public, she'd wandered off into the night by herself. She'd had a few drinks by this stage; she went to another bar had a few more drinks with McCann, the butcher. She'd walked along the beach, felt like a midnight swim, gotten into difficulties and was washed out to sea. It was perfect really, wasn't it?

Then the horrors hit Kennedy.

If her captors were that clever they would have realised that if the Drowning-at-sea theory was to work, she'd have needed to drown on the previous evening, the evening she went missing, immediately after they'd abducted her. Otherwise the autopsy would show her time of death and should this time of death be a few days later then McCusker and his team would want to know what had happened to ann rea in those interim days.

This all made perfect sense to Kennedy. ann rea had to be dead already. People this clever weren't going to risk a wronged journalist, not to mention an irate lover-cum-policeman, on their trail.

SHE HAD TO BE DEAD.

It was all so logical now he thought about it. He kicked himself (literally) for not considering this option previously. If he'd reached the same conclusion earlier, would he have carried on throughout the day as he had?

Again he was shocked by how calm he still was about all of this.

Here he was thinking that his best friend in the world was dead. Yes, the woman he loved like no other, and the woman it had taken him the majority of his life to find, was dead. And he was being perfectly logical and totally calm about it all.

He didn't want to go out and get blind drunk. He didn't feel like pulling Lennon and Dylan in and beating them to within inch of their miserable lives.

He wasn't about to go off the rails. He didn't know how to, and besides what was the use, he thought?

He felt his eyes well up.

His phone rang.

Chapter Thirty-Eight

DS JAMES IRVINE was on the telephone line.

Kennedy immediately dumped all his recent thoughts and cleared his throat. He was happy to hear from Irvine. Truth be told, he was missing having Irvine with him on this case. In a way, he was pleased he was missing Irvine and his own team; it would remind him not to take them for granted.

McCusker and his people were great, absolutely brilliant. Kennedy had no complaints whatsoever. It was just that he felt something evolved, something very natural, when you worked with someone over a long period of time. Particularly someone (Irvine) whose work you respected. Maybe it was just the space with which you accommodated each other.

'James?' Kennedy said into the phone mouthpiece confidently, hoping that none of his recent dark thoughts were apparent in his voice.

Irvine, perhaps sensing Kennedy's mood, went straight into his report.

'It might be something and it might be nothing, sir,' the detective sergeant began.

'Okay, I'm listening.'

'Well, DC Coles and myself were down looking around the rear of the Black Cat Building and we noticed how close Mornington Crescent was to the back of the building.'

'Ye-es,' Kennedy said, encouraging Irvine by elongating the word into two syllables.

'Well, we thought some of the residents over there might possibly have seen something so we got the team down from North Bridge House and did a bit of door-to-door questioning. Well, sir, to cut a series of very long stories short, most of the tenants just complained to us. What with the main railway-line repair work on one side of them and the renovation work to the Black Cat Building on the other, they all said their

lives were currently miserable. If it wasn't noise it was dust;
apparently this dust gets everywhere, sir.'

'Really?'

'But none of the tenants really had anything particularly
useful for us, sir.'

'Except?' Kennedy interjected, anticipating, he hoped,
Irvine's next word.

'Except one old dear, sir. I mean she could have been
doting. She's as batty as a fruitcake.'

'We'll definitely find a place for her in this case then,'
Kennedy replied.

'She claims she saw a demonic procession on the night in
question. She saw 'devil worshippers', she called them. About
twenty of them, she claimed and they were carrying something; it could have been a body, it could have been a coffin
she said, and they were all being led by a priest who was reading from the Bible.'

'Oh yeah?'

'The old dear was so disturbed by what she witnessed that
she woke up her daughter who lives in the flat next door but
by the time the daughter looked out of her window the devil
worshippers had all disappeared from the Black Cat Building,
if in fact they'd been there in the first place.'

'Does the old lady often suffer from midnight sightings?'
Kennedy asked.

'No, not at all. That's why the daughter paid her some
attention.'

'But I suppose this could have happened any time in the
last year?' Kennedy asked, picking a lawyer's question in the
information.

'Well, no, that's the strange thing. Both the lady and her
daughter remembered it well because it was the evening of the
daughter's son's birthday party, which apparently the old dear
attended and the daughter thought the midnight illusions
might have something to do with all the sweets and deserts the
old dear consumed!'

'Interesting,' Kennedy surmised. 'What do you think?'

'Normally I'd side with the daughter, but there was something serene about the old lady as she recalled the story. It
seemed so vivid the way she told it, more an actual scene than

a dream. She seemed genuine and she also seemed genuinely scared by the experience.

'I wonder,' Kennedy began, 'could the priest possibly be the Reverend Houston?

'It would have to be a possibility, wouldn't it?' Irvine replied. 'I'm afraid I've a bit of a dead end though, on our other line of investigation, sir.'

'Oh?'

'Yes, the opulent Miss Dauphine Stevens is a compulsive coffin-chaser, sir. Apparently she contests a lot of widowers' wills. She claimed she and Dugdale were having an affair and he promised her he would include her in his will,' Irvine reported down the telephone line connecting Camden Town direct with Portrush.

'This could have been a lucky one for her, James. Dugdale's daughter, Doris, doesn't want any of the money and there are no other known dependents.'

'Yes, quite possibly. If only she didn't have a record as long as her le… I mean arm, as long as her arm of course, sir.'

'Yes of course, James. I was kind of hoping that she'd be related to one of the members of our bridge club; at least if that was the case we'd be heading in the direction of a motive of some kind,' Kennedy said resignedly.

'What's the news on ann rea, sir?'

'I think she's dead,' Kennedy said solemnly. The words were out of his mouth before he'd a chance to think about them. In a way he was happy to be able to share his nightmare with someone.

The telephone line was filled with silence. Not real silence; more like a sea gently rolling in the distance.

'I… you… it's…' Irvine grunted, struggling to find words. He sounded totally shattered.

Kennedy explained the logic he'd used to reach his conclusion.

'Ah, now come on, sir. You're always warning us never to make the evidence fit a certain theory. That's exactly what you're doing here.'

Kennedy just blew air through his lips.

'Come on now, sir. Look at it from their side of things. If they even just harm her in the slightest they know that you and McCusker's men, not to mention all of Camden Town CID and Scotland Yard and...'

'You've forgotten the Mounties, James,' Kennedy added, trying to lighten things up for his own sake as much as Irvine's. Now that he'd actually voiced his worst fears he was having trouble controlling his emotions.

Irvine ploughed on. 'But my point would have to be, sir, they'd never be that stupid, would they? I think you'll find out later that they're taking good care of her. She's probably been blindfolded all the time that she's been in captivity so that she won't be able to recognise her captors. I bet you anything you want that once they think they've gotten away with it, they'll release her on the outskirts of some little town and drive off into the distance and into obscurity.'

'Whoa!' Kennedy again blew a non-word through his tight lips. 'I do hope you're right. It's my fault that she's over here in the first place.'

'Oh, come on now, you know her much better than any of the rest of us. She found the first lead on this case. Not wild horses or yourself, sir, with the greatest of respect, would have kept her away from this One,' Irvine continued. He had the knack of making his words of encouragement sound real and factual and not just some hot air he was blowing in order to comfort someone, in this particular case his superior, Detective Inspector Christy Kennedy.

Kennedy disconnected from Irvine, not feeling much better but certainly not feeling any worse. It was time to get stuck into what he did best, which was methodically work his way through his case, making no rash judgements or jumping to any conclusions no matter how obvious they might appear at the time. This method had stood him in good stead in the past and he certainly hoped it would work to his, and ann rea's, advantage on this particular occasion. Perhaps that had been one of the problems with ann rea; dealing with personal, romantic relationships were not his finest moments. Detecting he was comfortable with and could get lost in, but when it came to dealing with the other personal stuff, well, tomorrow always was a magic number.

Anyway, it was time to clear his mind of all such thoughts. Time to get an update from Inspector Starrett. Following that, he and McCusker would question the Reverend Houston again and then they'd pay a visit to Derek Shaw.

Kennedy had the feeling that all the information was out there waiting, waiting for him to pick up on it. His mind was gradually working its way back up through its efficient gears.

Chapter Thirty-Nine

INSPECTOR STARRETT, JOVIAL as ever, seemed to be playing the whole thing down with Kennedy when they spoke on the phone.

'Ah, don't worry about it. She'll be okay.'

'Have you traced Dylan and Lennon yet?'

'Not quite,' Starrett replied, offering an embarrassed laugh.

'Not quite?'

'Well, they seem to have gone to ground. But they've got to surface soon.'

'Why have they got to?' Kennedy asked, thinking that the Inspector's elaborate investigation had furnished him with sufficient evidence to make such a prediction.

'Well, this is the longest period in living memory that they've not been seen around the Bridge Bar, so they've got to come up for air soon; aye, no doubt about it. And when they do, we'll pick them up immediately,' Starrett offered confidently.

'You sure about this?' Kennedy asked trying to be as friendly as he knew how; he certainly didn't want to annoy this man. Over the years he'd seen enough of: 'Oh yeah, your man from London, he thinks he knows everything; he'll solve it in his sleep.'

'Oh aye, positive. This is Donegal life; if you wanted to stay hidden there's no' a police force in the world with enough members to search you out. So there is no point in the world going out looking for the two boyos; that would just be a fancy fandango. No, eventually they've got to surface. They're going to need cash, food, clothes, a breath of fresh air, and to see their folks. These are family men; no matter what they're up to they're going to want to check in with their parents and their wives,' Starrett said, breaking into another laugh. This time it was a natural laugh, no embarrassment at all. 'I'll tell you what, these boys are more 'fraid of their wives than they are of us. Sometimes they'll even come running to us just to get a wee break from the ladies. They are married to two sisters, a farmer's daughters from up Inishowen. Now there are no flies on those two. Aye, I'd say they wouldn't mind the lads being up to a bit of petty crime here and there – a few extra bob for some clothes and all that – but sure, if they were doing absolutely anything to deprive another member of the community of something, or thinking of doing any harm to a person, the boys would live the rest of their lives in purgatory. You see, it's a very tight community up here, aye, very tight. Oh, don't you worry, sir, we'll have that young lady for you before you can say 'Dixon of Dock Green'.'

Kennedy's quick mental calculations worked out that he'd already had enough time to repeat 'Dixon of Dock Green' over forty thousand times since ann rea disappeared, but thought better of stating such a fact. He disconnected on a friendly tone.

'It's a different pace up there,' McCusker offered as they walked down to the interview room in the basement to talk to Houston. 'Old Starrett's good at his job; he knows his people. We'd be lost using his methods here, but in Donegal they work a treat. Of course there's crime and all of that up there but if someone's out of line the community will offer them up; it's like they don't want any bad apples amongst their own. It's like how it used to be here before the Troubles to some degree, although I'm not sure the Troubles has been responsible for it. Maybe just the passing of time, maybe even just the TV. You see the TV's not as sophisticated up in Donegal.'

'Right,' Kennedy replied as they opened the door to the largest room in the basement to find a constable guarding the Reverend Steven Houston.

All things considered, he was in quite a buoyant mood.

'I was just reminding this young lad here,' Houston started off in a friendly growl, 'that I married his parents and baptised himself.'

The lad looked suitably embarrassed.

McCusker and Kennedy pulled up a chair.

'This is a grim old business, isn't it?' McCusker said, obviously going for the friendly approach, Kennedy thought.

'And what business would that be?' Houston snarled back.

'Well, the death of Victor Dugdale and the disappearance of Miss ann rea,' McCusker replied.

Kennedy remembered how much ann rea hated to be addressed as 'Miss'.

'Well now, I'd have to say that in the battlefield a lot of great men, a lot of Ulster's sons, laid down their lives so that the rest of us, the rest of God's children, could live in peace,' Houston said full volume, obviously borrowing the trick from the Rev Ian Paisley. His delivery was impressive; perhaps something to do with the fact that if you spoke so loud and with so much conviction your words must be true.

'But Victor Dugdale didn't sacrifice his life, it was taken from him, and the second world war ended over fifty-five years ago,' Kennedy replied in disbelief.

'The war against God never ends. There's evil out there everywhere you turn. Tell me, sir, do you believe in God?' Houston directed his question to Kennedy. Kennedy wondered was this because he felt that McCusker was already a lost cause.

'Well, I believe that there's something out there,' Kennedy replied.

'We're not talking about the *X-Files* here, sir; we're talking about the House of God. We're talking about Jesus dying on the cross so that you may be saved, to bring you and me our freedom.'

'Well then, I'd have to say that I probably don't believe in the same God you believe in.' Kennedy replied honestly and continued: 'I'd like to get back to your bridge club and the trip to London.'

'I think I've told you all I know on both accounts, sir.'

'And your trip to London at the same time?'

'I believe I've also addressed that issue.'

'Look, Reverend,' Kennedy started moving up a gear but trying to keep aggression out of his voice. 'We have a very bizarre situation here, I'm sure you'll agree.'

Kennedy recalled chapter and verse of the mystery, from the time Victor Dugdale's body was found right up to ann rea's disappearance.

'And I'd like to be able to throw some light on it for you,

sir, but I don't believe that I have any additional information for you,' Houston replied at the end of Kennedy's summary.

'Reverend Houston, something evil has happened here, something very evil. Don't you think it's part of your responsibility as the leader of the church, as God's vehicle, to help us dig out this evil?' McCusker said, his voice unsteady as if he was accepting for the first time the enormity of the situation.

'Evil, Inspector McCusker,' Houston replied, his baritone voice ringing around every corner of the basement. 'Evil has been dug out!'

'Sorry?' Kennedy asked hopefully. 'What evil has been dug out and from where?'

'You know, The Evil,' Houston replied, quickly staring deep into Kennedy's eyes. They were so close that Kennedy could smell his bad breath, a bad breath that was rotting the Reverend's teeth. Kennedy wondered if all the bad teeth were rotting when Houston started back up again. 'The Evil that exists in this world causes aggression and this aggression causes men to do battle with each other. This in turn causes countries to go to war, sometimes with other countries and sometimes with themselves. The Evil that existed in the world caused our young men to defend our nation against the Germans: our young boys were plucked from the fields of their father's farms, from their jobs about Ballyneagh, from their families and from their lives and were set down in the middle of a battlefield with gunfire and shrapnel. And they had to defend themselves and their lives and their nation so they had to do vile acts, which you might consider evil, like killing Germans, killing the aggressor. Are they sinning? No, of course not, they had Jesus in their hearts. Jesus died to bring them and all of us freedom and some of our lads in turn died in the name of Jesus to bring us our continued freedom. They were continuing Jesus' work. Jesus brought them into a new personal relationship with God and so they were set free from the penalty of sin. Because sin, sir, is an eternal separation from God. And sin has a power over us and we can only break away from the power of sin if we have Jesus in our hearts.'

'I'm not exactly sure what you're telling us here,' Kennedy started to a loud sigh from Houston. 'Are you saying that

Victor Dugdale was killed in the name of God, and because he was killed in the name of God, the person or persons who killed him are free of sin?'

'God is ever-forgiving. He will take even the vilest of us into His flock,' Houston retorted.

Kennedy felt he was losing this interview fast. Houston was on his pulpit and, Kennedy thought, slipping certain tantalising bits of information into the conversation for sheer devilment. A reverend involved in 'sheer devilment': that thought brought a wry smile to Kennedy's tired face.

'But you can't tell me there are any circumstances where a man or a woman, or men and women, could murder another human, such as Victor Dugdale, and that you or God would condone it. That would just make a sham of God and His church.'

'You see, you haven't been listening to me, have you, sir? You have to listen. Men have ears to listen with and eyes to see with; why is it some choose neither to listen nor to look?' Houston asked smugly.

'Well, I get your point that in wartime there could be an argument for justification of a man killing other men. But this is not the war. Victor Dugdale was an old man, living out the rest of his life in peace and quiet. Who's to say that Mr Dugdale hadn't taken Jesus into his heart? Why could you even dream that there would be a situation where it would be okay for someone to murder him?' Kennedy pushed.

'There are instances,' Houston replied, his voice dropping a little for effect.

'There are instances where it is okay for a man to commit murder.' McCusker cut in: 'I never thought a man of the cloth would say those words.'

'You don't know what you're talking about; neither of you have been listening to me. During the war many, many soldiers made the ultimate sacrifice.

'Greater love has no-one than this, than to lay down his life for his friends.'

They made this sacrifice, the giving up of their lives so that we, all of us, might live in peace and freedom. We remember them and are obligated to them, indebted to them.

"Beneath the shadow of The Throne,

Thy saints have dwelt secure:
Sufficient in Thine arm alone,
And our defence is sure."
God tells us that if we serve Him, He will serve us,'
Houston added following his quote.

He didn't exactly break into song but he nearly did, he
wasn't far short. But you'd have to admit it was a great performance.

'But doesn't God also tell us to forgive? Doesn't he say that
if a man shall hit you, turn the other cheek?' Kennedy asked,
trying to take this conversation back to Dugdale.

'Turn the other cheek, Mr Kennedy, indeed, sir. What if I
was to tell you that your precious Miss ann rea is already dead
and bur...' Houston started smugly but before he had a
chance to finish both Kennedy and McCusker were on their
feet.

The constable looked on nervously. Houston wasn't quite
grinning at them but he looked like he was taunting them.

Kennedy's eyes flashed red, he wanted to fling the table out
of the way and go straight for this sicko, but something was
holding him back. He didn't know what. It certainly wasn't
McCusker. Kennedy feared that McCusker was going to dive
across the table first.

Before anything else happened Houston spoke again.

'You see there, in both of you, your eyes – anger, pure
naked anger – maybe even evil, gentlemen. If I hadn't baptised
this young constable and he was here to protect me in my
hour of need, goodness knows what would have happened.
You were both well capable of doing evil.'

Kennedy and McCusker sat down again. Kennedy was
thinking that Houston was totally accurate in his assessment.
He searched for words but none came, at least not before
Houston advised them:

'I apologise. Of course I have no notion about the young
lady's well being, I was merely trying to give you an example
where even you, the very same upholders of law and order,
would be tempted to take that law into your own hands. Then
where would we all be, gentlemen? Armageddon, I can tell
you. Armageddon for certain.'

Kennedy felt it was time to stop. They weren't getting

anywhere with Houston. Or maybe they were he thought.
Houston had kept saying: "You're not listening to me." Had
he been telling them something? And if so, what?
   What indeed?

Chapter Forty

'HOW FAR AWAY is Donegal?' Kennedy asked. It was thirty minutes later and he and McCusker were in an unmarked car on the way over to Shaw's cottage.

'Oh, about seventy-plus miles.'

'So we'd make it in an hour?'

'No, on these roads you'd need to figure more like two,' McCusker, replied slowing down his speech.

'Mmmm,' Kennedy began.

'Aye, I don't need to be a brain surgeon to know what you want. You want us to take a wee scoot up there, don't ye?'

'If you don't mind.' Kennedy was preoccupied with another telephone call he'd received from Starrett just before leaving Portrush Barracks. Lennon and Dylan had turned up at the Bridge Bar in Ramelton, just like Starrett had predicted. Starrett, obviously feeling he was on a bit of a roll, went even further on the phone and predicted the boys would be in the bar until turfing-out time. Starrett didn't want to pick the boys up; he wanted to leave them the night to their wives and follow them in the morning when they, hopefully, would lead the Gardai to ann rea.

Kennedy wasn't so convinced this would happen. He felt he should be up there doing something. Feck all this waiting around! Added to all of this playing on his mind, he felt he couldn't focus on talking to anyone coherently, let alone conduct a very important interview with Derek Shaw.

'Quite frankly, I'm surprised it took you this long,' McCusker laughed. 'I'd been counting down under my breath for the last five or ten minutes. They say the Bridge Bar does a wonderful pint of Guinness. What's the betting that'll knock at least twenty minutes off the journey for us.'

McCusker radioed in to the station to telephone Starrett and inform him that two private citizens would be visiting him later.

Both detectives sat quietly with their thoughts throughout the journey. In normal circumstances, Kennedy would have been totally in awe of the beauty of the countryside, particularly on the other side of Derry when they crossed into the Free State. The rugged, rolling hills were a contrast to the totally cultivated look of the Northern Irish countryside. However, they were nonetheless stunning. Particularly the view of the Swilly as you drove down from Letterkenny to Ramelton with the Swilly to the right, twisting and turning and pulling you further and further into Donegal.

They drove into Ramelton and were crossing the bridge that led to the Bridge Bar at exactly 10pm.

On entering the bar, McCusker made a beeline for a casually dressed man who looked like he'd just come from the golf course. Pink shirt, with a red jumper precariously hanging over his shoulders, blue slacks and white-and-brown brogues completed the loud ensemble. The L-shaped room was packed with people who obviously knew every other person in the bar. Consequently a few heads turned, ever so discreetly mind you, to clock McCusker and Kennedy. The fact that Starrett made a fuss of the two made everyone happy to ignore the visitors and get on with the job in hand; a jar and a wee bit of *craic*, all to the gentle sounds of Artie McGlynn playing in the corner. Rumour, not to mention a photo on the wall behind the bar, had it that legendary guitarist Jerry Garcia had visited this very bar a few years since while he was on a break from his regular marathon duties with the Grateful Dead. John Prine sightings there were also frequent.

The bar was jovial and friendly, very friendly, old and young conversed as they rarely did in other bars.

'A drink?' Starrett asked.

'Yew stannin?' McCusker replied, falling comfortably into Ulster-speak.

'Why God man, aye,' Starrett replied, pulling a brown leather wallet from his back pocket. Even this action did not dislodge his BMW jumper.

'In that case I wudden say no ta a chinnan tonick,' McCusker replied licking his lips.

'You'll have a double?'

'Howl on man or I'll go home stovin',' McCusker said,

resisting a wee bit of arm-twisting for possibly the first time in his life.

'And yerself?' Starrett smiled in Kennedy's direction.

'I'd love a milky coffee with two sugars,' Kennedy replied. He didn't feel like drinking and he was worried Starrett and McCusker were in for a session, on top of which he could feel his eyes grow heavy so he thought a coffee might give him the pick-me-up he needed.

'When we get these in,' Starrett replied, 'well go upstairs. I've booked us in for a wee bit of supper.'

'What about the two men?' Kennedy asked in a conspiratorial voice.

'Whisht, they'll hear you. They're right behind you,' Starrett replied, looking in the opposite direction and up at the ceiling. 'Come on though, they're not going to be going anywhere without me knowing about it. The fact that we're leaving will make them less suspicious.

'Oh aye, count me in for a bit of grub,' McCusker said, heading off in the direction of the stairs. Starrett and Kennedy following close behind.

Kennedy caught a glance of the two cowboys as he left the bar. He was shocked. They looked wholesome, all-Ireland boys. Dressed soberly, with clean-cut faces; one with short, curly, brown hair and the other with nearly jet-black and unkempt hair. These were the two who had ann rea in captivity? Unbelievable. Even more unbelievable was the fact that the police were going upstairs to have some food while the two boys drank the night away.

Patience. That's all he needed. He hadn't any stomach for food himself but McCusker made short work of his salmon. Starrett took longer with his steak but that was because he kept stopping eating to tell stories. Both raved about the food and Kennedy felt that McCusker would add the Bridge Bar to his unwritten, but well-used, good-food guide.

As they were about to start dessert a young punk made his way up the stairs and came over and whispered something in Starrett's ear. The boys were on the move!

'Probably going home but we better follow, just in case,' Starrett announced proudly as the punk whispered something else. 'Oh, perhaps not. Apparently they ordered *three* takeaways, a couple of bottles of wine and a six-pack of beer. Maybe they'll be going to leave some food off with their captive.'

'You're certain they've got ann rea?' Kennedy asked quietly.

'Oh, positive. The bush telegraph hasn't let me down yet,' Starrett began. Kennedy felt that he must have looked worried. Obviously Starrett did too because he continued: 'Aye, I can also tell you she'll be perfectly fine. They won't have touched a hair on her head. They'll be care-taking her like the perfect gentlemen they were brought up to be.'

Kennedy didn't take any comfort in the words; he knew that when push came to shove the boys would react to any chance of being caught by protecting their long-term well being with no witness, i.e. ann rea, to confirm to the police the details of the kidnapping. Such action would lessen the chance of their incarceration.

Starrett paid the bill with large notes and left a generous tip. Outside, as luck would have it, the moon was lighting up the proceedings. The boys had obviously decided to hoof it, leaving the Honda Prelude, which had already betrayed them, parked by the river side of the road.

The thing that struck Kennedy most about the streets of Ramelton was the silence; sheer bliss to someone like himself who had spent so much time in London. It was so quiet they could hear the river running underneath them as they crossed the bridge back into the village. Occasionally a door in the distance would open and shut as the cat or dog or husband was dumped into the cold night air. And the peace was broken twice in their journey as a car engine appeared to positively roar. They walked back up through the village, ignoring the main road out of town to their right, and continued up the steep hill of a potential picture-postcard street. At the top of this street, just as they were about to turn right, they came upon some youths whose catcalling fell to a whisper, then rose to a snigger and then full-scale laughter as the detectives left the corner boys behind them.

All the time, the punk from the bar was splitting the distance between the detectives and Dylan and his brother. They came to a fork in the road with a large church in the middle. As the moon fell behind the cloud, the silhouette of the church was quite spooky. Kennedy was thankful when the moonlight broke through the clouds again.

In the distance they could see the brothers take a left and then they heard a gate creak open and shut as Dylan and Lennon disappeared off the street.

'Oh, so they've got her in The Shack,' Starrett announced in a voice a little above a whisper.

'What's that?' Kennedy asked, also in a whisper.

Starrett looked about the houses to his left and right as he Announced: 'Oh, it's the place, a wee barn actually, where most folks around here were probably conceived.' He held his forefinger up to his lips as he looked at Kennedy and McCusker.

Kennedy wasn't scared but he definitely felt weird, weird like butterflies in the pit of his stomach. They were probably in for a fight of some kind and, assuming the brothers hadn't left her by herself, it could end up four on four. They had to be quick, Kennedy felt, to overpower her captives. Fighting was such a rare thing for Kennedy to be considering. The whole dance that human beings did of running into each other with arms and fists and heads and feet flying, trying hard to make a connection with the other human before they do so to you; well, Kennedy felt the whole thing was so dammed comical. He'd often thought that if aliens had landed on this planet and they saw two humans fighting it would probably be the most comical thing in their universe. But on earth it was a way of one human imposing his superiority on another. Arm-to-arm combat was one of the few fields where money or power or intelligence didn't come into it.

Yet here he was, preparing to do battle; to do battle for the one he loved. He didn't have any plan. He would just run into someone, one of the captors, with his arms, legs, fists and head flying about viciously in the hope that he would over-power one of them, and when he did so he would render them incapable. How would he do that? You see it all work so beautifully in movies, don't you? That's the thing, isn't it? You give someone a bop on the chin and they willingly oblige you and fall asleep until the fight is over, and then they all come round about the same time, usually when the cavalry arrive and they are all carted off to jail. But in real life, if you hit someone on the head the right way, which in fact could be the wrong way, then you certainly risk killing them. On the other hand, if you hit them the wrong way on the head they could go: "You bastard, that was sore," (or one of a number of crude variations on that theme) and bop you back again and hit you on your head in the right place, which could be the wrong place and kill you.

Kennedy had no wish to kill anyone, never had. He probably never would. However, and most importantly, he wouldn't want ann rea to be hurt or carried off somewhere else if the police attack was unsuccessful.

Kennedy's approach to fighting was pretty basic and pretty simple. He would try and find an iron bar or a piece of wood and as his attacker approached him, he would take careful aim and try and whack the assailant about the hands or ankles, thereby rendering the opposition incapable by causing the least possible damage. If someone had two broken wrists, don't you see, or even one, well, then they would hardly want to try and hit you, or stab you, or even shoot you for that matter, now would they? If they are limping from a broken ankle they are hardly likely to want to kick you, are they? No, of course not. Well, at least not according to Kennedy's theory.

Such thoughts filled Kennedy's head as they stopped outside the gate Dylan and Lennon had opened a couple of minutes earlier. The punk helped them all to scale the high wall so they didn't give any early-warning signals, such as a gate creaking. Kennedy noted the outline of The Shack in front of them. It was an old stone building, very old Kennedy guessed, as in maybe even a couple of hundred years. In a Charles Dickens kind of way it was quite quaint. There were no visible lights.

'They'll be in the loft,' Starrett whispered. 'There's nothing downstairs apart from cow shit.'

McCusker broke into a large grin. Kennedy thought he'd been thinking that Starrett must obviously have checked into this accommodation a few times himself.

Starrett signalled to the punk who immediately went off around to the other side of The Shack. The three policemen did a fair impersonation of the Keystone Cops as they, very animatedly, crept up the open stone steps at the centre of the building. First Starrett, he was the local; then Kennedy, his lover was being held captive inside (he hoped), and finally, McCusker, he'd no stomach for a fight after all the food he'd eaten in the Bridge Bar.

Starrett had his ear to the door and was visibly straining in the moonlight to hear what was going on inside. Bizarrely, a joke flashed into Kennedy mind.

The Gardai member turned to Kennedy and crunched up his face as if to Say: "I can't make anything out." He then proceeded to give a set of complicated instructions with hand signals, which lasted a good few seconds. Kennedy hadn't a clue what he was on about and he didn't feel like asking for a repeat performance so he turned to McCusker and using his forefinger gave the simple international sign that they were about to enter the building.

The communication was obviously more effective because McCusker nodded agreement. Kennedy hoped for that a bit of wood or iron bar just inside the barn. Without further warning, Starrett undid the latch on the door and burst into the barn, followed very quickly by Kennedy and even quicker still by McCusker, bringing up the rear.

There, in front of the three members of three different police forces, was one of the most peculiar scenes any of them had even seen.

In the middle of the loft, around a makeshift table of bales of hay, sat Dylan and Lennon James and ann rea. Dylan and Lennon were wearing Lone Ranger masks and ann rea whose feet were shackled to the floor was happily tackling some late night supper and a bottle of wine. Not the slightest sign of stress was visible on her face. Nor were there any signs that she had been hurt.

'Kennedy,' she announced, not missing a beat. 'What's kept you? Pull up a seat and have some dinner and a glass of wine, it's rather special.'

Chapter Forty-One

ONLY ANN REA could have landed on her feet with two of the most caring kidnappers on the island of Ireland. Apparently, as advised by the journalist, Dylan and Lennon were two perfect gentlemen, even apologetic for having to restrain her.

Initially she'd been nervous and had questioned them incessantly, telling them all about herself in a vain attempt, she hoped, that they would get to know her as a person and not feel able to kill her. Of course she'd omitted to mention to them that her boyfriend was a policeman. That might have made things different, she felt. The day had passed quickly and she'd heard children playing out on the street, she heard tractors and cows and sheep and workmen.

When they first dumped her in the back of the car, they'd been careful not to hurt her. At first, she claimed she thought it was a Kennedy trick, just to warn her what might happen to her. She'd treated it mostly as a joke to begin with and then they had put a black-cloth bag over her head and tied her hands in front of her and drove off. She kept waiting for them to pull into the side of the road and Kennedy to pop in the back seat with her and say: "There now, I told you it could be dangerous walking these streets late at night," and they'd live happily ever after. At first she was too embarrassed to scream and shout because she felt it wasn't a real kidnapping and everyone would laugh more at her when the joke was revealed.

After about thirty minutes, it dawned on her that it just might not be a joke. Then she thought it might have been Paul McCann who was behind it and he'd lured her out with a promise of a revealing interview in the middle of the night just so that he could abduct her.

She told Kennedy that she had been careful as she walked home. The only thing she'd been watching out for was the black Morris Minor van and the two smartly dressed boys; one black haired, one blonde. The late-night people she met were all friendly and when she nipped into the shop for Ben and Jerry's ice cream as a peace offering she felt great and couldn't wait to get home to Kennedy. It wasn't that she'd forgiven him for playing the role of mother hen. No, he was usually very particular about giving her her space. Thereby, she claimed, maybe creating some additional space for himself.

But in Portrush it was different. Kennedy was working on a case; a murder inquiry that had cost Victor Dugdale his life. So, she thought, why would the people who'd killed Dugdale shy away from an interfering London journalist? She'd made it personal and she realised she shouldn't have. Kennedy was behaving in a professional manner, exactly the same way he would have behaved had it been DC Anne Coles who'd been over on duty in Portrush with him.

'Well, not exactly the same,' she explained to Kennedy in the early hours of the following morning, in Kennedy parents' house. 'I mean, Coles wouldn't have stayed here, would she? And you wouldn't have chased the butterfly with her on the beach, would you? Would you, Kennedy?' she said as she nudged him in the ribs, not quite as playfully as he'd have liked.

On the drive back to Portrush with McCusker and Kennedy, she told them that Dylan and Lennon didn't know who'd hired them to do the job; they'd received their instructions by telephone, a different voice every time; received their money in cash, in a bag left for them behind the bar at the Bridge Bar; they were paid three thousand euros in advance and would be paid a further three when the job was done; they were meant to get her drunk when they were about to release her (after four or five days, they were told) and deposit her back on the West Strand beach at Portrush; they asked ann rea would she mind pretending to be drunk when they dropped her off, they didn't want to force her to do anything; they had a makeshift toilet, one they'd taken from their father's caravan, rigged up in the corner along with a basin, fresh jugs of water and soap; they had also nicked some of their wives' clothes and left them in a pile in the corner just in case ann rea wanted to change clothing.

'Really,' ann rea claimed, 'they just couldn't have been better hosts.'

She liked Starrett, she claimed, a fun guy who didn't take it all too seriously and she asked him not to be too hard on the James boys.

'Augh now,' he'd replied with a large grin on his face and a larger drink in his hand. They'd been back in the Bridge Bar just before ann rea, Kennedy and McCusker left Ramelton. 'Sure they'll be alright, they're harmless enough. We just need to scare them a wee bit so they never try a stunt like this again. Maybe we'll just threaten to let their father know what they've been up to, that would definitely do the trick!'

Now it was four o'clock in the morning and Kennedy and ann rea were alone in his parents' living room.

'I wasn't scared, Christy. Really I wasn't.'

Kennedy grunted to signal he knew what she meant. He was trying to get into a comfortable position with her on the sofa. The only noises in the house were their whispers, water pipes groaning, vehicles infrequently passing the window a few feet from their heads, clocks ticking continuously and occasionally chiming, and wood creaking. Kennedy felt the ambient performance sounded rather like the Modern Jazz Quartet. Tonight, with ann rea safely in his arms, he was enjoying their concert like never before.

'I just knew with all my heart that you would find me, Christy, I really did.'

'It was Starrett.'

'What?'

'It was Starrett who found you. He knew what he was up to, knew his patch and pretty much sussed it out immediately.'

'Oh,' ann rea exclaimed as she jumped out of Kennedy's arms and up from the sofa.

'What's wrong?'

'You're sure it was Starrett who found me?'

'Yes,' Kennedy replied simply, wondering where this was going.

'God, I nearly made the biggest mistake of my life. I was about to sleep with you,' she said now hamming it up something rotten. 'Where does Starrett live?'

Kennedy caught her hand as she pretended to leave the room. He pulled her down on top of him on the couch and they started (quietly) to chase the butterfly!

Chapter Forty-Two

THEY WERE FOUND, respectably robed, four hours later by Kennedy's mother as she wandered into the living room in her dressing gown to check if they wanted breakfast. From the look on his mother's face, Kennedy reckoned his mother knew that they'd worked up quite an appetite; she wasn't wrong.

As planned, a freshly shaved McCusker joined them for breakfast. For once ann rea was happy to stay behind. She said she had enough to write about to fill the rest of the week, besides which she needed the two of them to solve the Dugdale murder so that she could complete that exclusive as well.

Derek Shaw was coughing and spluttering a lot when he opened his door for them half an hour later. Kennedy put that down to the early morning clearing of the throat. But he also had to admit that the old man looked... old; yes, old was exactly how he looked. Even his Paul Newman ice blue eyes were not sparkling as before.

'Aye, I've been expecting youse two,' he began, his hoarse voice sounding more painful than was characteristic. 'Come on through, I'll rustle youse up some breaky.'

'No, it's okay, we've...' Kennedy started.

'That'd be great,' McCusker said, shooting Kennedy a "let's not be inhospitable" look.

So, for the second time in less than an hour McCusker sat down to an Ulster Fry. Where did this man put it all? Kennedy mused. There wasn't an ounce of fat on him.

'Look, Derek, you probably know we made the connection between the members of the Ballyneagh Bridge Club and the wartime photograph. Pretty soon we're going to find out from the War Office what happened to the men in the photograph, but I'd prefer it if you told us yourself.'

Shaw rose from the breakfast table. He used the front of

his cloth cap to scratch the brow of his head. He had another good coughing fit and cleared his throat by spitting in the sink. The action turned Kennedy's stomach but didn't seem to dampen McCusker's appetite one little bit – he continued with his seconds.

Shaw was dressed pretty much as he had been the first time they'd met. Kennedy found it hard to believe that had only been four days ago. The old man waddled across the room to his favourite, well-worn leather chair, softened by several battered and bruised cushions. He gingerly lowered his frame into the seat, removed his cloth cap and, as he placed it on his brown corduroy-covered knee, he started to speak, shakily at first.

'Of course I knew all the men in the photograph. I was so shocked Victor had kept a copy of it. He had remembered them. Hell, there were only nine of us left by the time the photograph was taken. I could even tell you the original names of the twenty-four members of the troop if you wanted me to.'

Neither Kennedy nor McCusker signalled that they would require such information so Shaw continued:

'Know the men in the photograph? How could I ever forget them? Fine Riflemen, one and all. Colin McCann, Alan Savage, Norman Kane, Alex McCelland, Wesley McIvor, Miles Best and David Kennedy.

'I remember our first day in camp. It was up in Omagh. We were such a fresh-faced bunch of youths. All our hair had been severely shaven and we all queued – friends, neighbours and strangers – to collect what would become our wardrobe for the next few years. When we left the mess we were laden down with a pair of black leather boots; two pairs of khaki trousers; two matching khaki high-collar jackets; three shirts; half a dozen pairs of brown socks; a steel hat; two khaki caps; several badges (brass and canvas); three pairs of underwear; a leather belt for parade purposes only; a thick, strong, canvas belt with lots of hooks for attachments (we were all very curious about those); a water flask; and a backpack that was much too small to contain all of the above. We all had trouble carrying our spanking new kit back to our huts. I was wondering how on earth we'd ever take on a German or two without sinking up to our neck in mud under the weight of our new kit. I was about to say so to Victor when the Sgt Major started screaming at us in this obnoxiously high-pitched voice: "Put an inch to your step and get changed into your kit, im-med-iate-ly!" Suddenly, all thoughts of the weight of my kit disappeared.' Shaw recalled the scene so vividly Kennedy imagined he was right there with him in the camp.

'I've told you bits and pieces the last few times you've been here but I didn't tell you about our big battle, the battle that wiped most of us out,' Shaw continued. Kennedy was intrigued to hear what was going to follow. He was sure whatever it was still had major repercussions on certain people's lives fifty-six years later. 'So, on this particular day we got the word that we were to move on Caen.' Shaw started back up again, the emphasis on his words indicating that he was getting to the important bit. He rose from his easy chair and joined McCusker and Kennedy at the table.

'This,' he said hoarsely, taking the milk jug, 'is Hill Sixty and it overlooks Caen.'

He took an unused clean, white plate from beside McCusker's space and placed it towards Kennedy's side of the table. 'Just to this side of Caen is the river, which runs alongside the church.' Shaw then marked the church with a saltcellar and the river with a knife.

'Now,' Shaw said, folding his arms in front of himself and circumnavigating the scene with his eyes. 'From Hill Sixty we had a great vantage point over Caen. We were quite exposed in a way because of this but the Germans didn't have any artillery heavy enough to cover that range so we were safe enough up there! Our Commander told us that we had to take Caen. It was all down to positioning and gaining ground and joining up all the dots to ensure our front moved strategically into ground the Jerries had already claimed. It was vital that our front moved.

'Monty was the only one who'd tell the foot soldiers exactly what was happening. Every now and then, when he had a chance to visit, he'd give you a little pep talk about what was going on in the war and what he was trying to do and why what we did was so important. So we had a vague idea as to the overall objectives.

'Anyway they, the Germans, were well ensconced in Caen and weren't giving much away. Naugh, they weren't. A troop of us, including myself on the Bren gun took a night trip, a bit of a recce, down into Caen and we did a bit of damage, but not a lot really. It was like taking a peanut to smash a milk bottle. There were Germans everywhere, aye, I can tell you, everywhere.

'We retreated back up to Hill Sixty and the following morning the air force flew in and dropped millions, aye, millions of pieces of silver paper to mess up their radio signals, as I told you. Then they dropped the hardware, the fireworks you know, to soften it up for us.

'A troop of us, twenty-four, went down from Hill Sixty to Caen later that day. It seemed to have quietened down but they didn't want to send any more in until they'd a chance to assess how effective the air force had been. We got caught out badly, aye, they set us up something rotten.

'As we walked into Caen there was this eerie air of calm. I mean, Caen had been blown to bits. Make no mistake about this, the air force had done their job. Entire streets were nothing but rubble and there were fires of varying sizes all around us. The predominant smell was of wood burning and smouldering. We were beginning to think that the air force boys might have done the job completely for us, when just to our left, high up in a red-brick warehouse that was barely standing, the enemy opened fire on us. We could see the red tracer flames. Caught us totally by surprise they did and they took two of us out. Aye.

'Cairns and Laurel. They were the best of mates, both from Portstewart. One minute they were leading the troop and next a small burst of gunfire, literally, and they were lying lifeless, right in front of our eyes. It was all over so fast. They'd have felt no pain. There was hardly any bleeding. I'd say their hearts had stopped beating near enough immediately. If it hadn't been for their contorted shapes amongst the rubble it would have looked like they'd just decided to take a little nap.

'Then, just as the rest of us were about to retreat to safety,' Shaw said looking down at the table solemnly, moving the HP Sauce bottle across to McCusker's side of the table (Caen) and then pulling a pepper-cellar up to a position to the left of that, 'this bazooka, which had been hidden in the remains of a house, lands right in the middle of our retreat path. It didn't hit anybody directly but it took out a telegraph pole that fell on two of our boys. It killed one of them, Jones – he'd always been a bit of a loner – and broke Alan Savage's leg. And then, just then, to add further insult to injury, another sniper opened fire on us with a Bren gun from here, the only bushes left, I'm sure, in Caen at that point.' Shaw moved a spoon to a position just to the left of the church, which created a triangle with the red-brick warehouse (HP Sauce), the bazooka point (pepper-cellar) and the Bren gun sniper (the spoon).

'We were right in the middle of their triangle and we dug in as best we could but there was nothing but rubble and we couldn't really manoeuvre around to build ourselves some kind of protection. Every time one of us moved an inch they opened fire on us, just to let us know that they were still there.

'I swear to you they were just playing with us. It went quiet for about ten minutes and then there was another intense burst of fire, first from the warehouse, then the Bren gun sniper, and then another bazooka. Luckily enough the bazooka was way off the mark but another four of us had been killed by the sniper fire; Ousby, a skinhead before his time; Foye, a great cook; Delaney, built like a tank but gentle as a lamb; and Wallis, a great singer, aye, a lovely voice he had. I swear to you, if it hadn't been for the war he'd have been as big as Sinatra. Honestly, I'm not kidding.

'We radioed back to Hill Sixty,' Shaw continued and then stopped and, quick as a blink, broke into a smile. 'I've often said, you know, over the last five years or so, if we'd had these mobile phones back in the war, aye, the war would have been over in a quarter of the time. Anyway, we got back on the radio to our boys back up on Hill Sixty and gave them our position and predicament. The commander told us to stay put. Wesley McIvor – he was always fighting mad always loved a good scrap – and myself, well, we were the only ones with Bren guns and so we crept together and got ready for the next time they fired on us.

'Well, when the Bren guns from the house fired up on us again we opened up fire on the source; you know, we could see the thin flashes of white-hot fire and sourced the gun. We just aimed our bullets at the point theirs had been coming from. McIvor, well, didn't he get one of them with his second burst of fire and we both kept firing on the remaining Bren gun. This obviously drew fire from the other two positions.' Shaw stopped talking to take a deep breath and to point to the warehouse and the bushes, the remaining two apexes of the triangle.'

'The bazooka took another pot at us; this time it scored a direct hit, blew three of our boys to pieces. That was the worst. It got Drayton, aye now, he was a great carpenter; Guinness, one of the oldest of our troop, already married with two little kiddies; and Morris, never really a popular lad but he didn't deserve to die that way. Aye, it was horrible. There was blood and guts and brain tissue everywhere. I found myself subconsciously checking my own body for wounds just to make sure it wasn't my own blood. The post, which McIvor and myself were covering, obviously thought the bazooka had done the business and taken all of us out because didn't the eejit stand up to get a better look at his mates' handiwork. Well, you just don't give McIvor a gift like that, do you? Bang, bang and the Gerry was dead. McIvor had, single-handedly, taken out this all-important position.

'So now, by covering each other, we could zigzag a retreat to some shelter.

The Germans could see we were escaping from their trap and they opened up on us again. God, they hammered us solidly for about twenty minutes. We'd lost ten men already in a matter of ten minutes. Now they weren't all my best mates or anything like that but I knew each of them, we all knew each other, and we were all in this together; we were tight. Well, you couldn't go through what we'd been through together and not be close, could you?

'Following another round of zigzagging back to the German position we'd just taken, the house ruins, we found two more of our chaps lying still and silent in the rubble behind us. Sinclair, now he had two gorgeous sisters back in Coleraine; and Doherty from the south who was a bit of a loner, friendly enough but kept himself to himself. Both dead, aye, I can still picture them lying lifeless, face down in the rubble. I often wonder what their last thoughts were. I used to think about that a lot during the war, and sometimes since. I mean, did you just merrily go about your business, you know: "I'd better not let my mates down," or "What are we, Gerry and me, doing, strangers in a strange land? If he'd stop firing at me, I stop firing at him and we both could go home," or more basically, "Feck this for a game of soldiers, I'm going to get you before you get me," and other times, "This is so unreal, I wonder do the folks back home realise how bad this is?" Sometimes you were preoccupied with more basic things like about your uniform or the state and smell of your body or even about a girl, which could have been a very dangerous thought. But did people who were killed have these thoughts just before they were killed or did God give them time to bless themselves and ask for forgiveness?

'Now there's a thing, us asking for forgiveness from Him? Surely He should have been asking forgiveness for getting us into that mess? But, I mean, I know I'll never know the answer to the question but every time I saw a dead boy I'd find myself thinking: 'I wonder what you were thinking when you died?' Twelve people were dead. Just like that. People I'd been joking with on the way down from Hill Sixty less than thirty minutes before. I knew it was nothing but sheer luck that I'd survived, that I wasn't one of those lifeless boys lying there wearing the exact same uniform as me. Don't you see that just shows what a complete waste of lives it all was? It was so indiscriminate. We'd take out some of their boys and they'd take out some of ours and then we'd be equal again and ready to start killing all over again.

'You know that game, the war game, some of the corporations play?'

McCusker replied: 'Aye, they say it shows natural leaders from amongst their staff.'

'Aye, well you know what? That's not a bad way to have a war. You still have all your armies but instead of guns with real live ammo you have paint guns, and when the other side splat you with yellow paint you get to go home and the rest of them stay behind to continue the game.' Shaw's hoarse voice did not display the slightest hints of humour so neither of the detectives laughed. 'Better paint than blood I'd say, any time.

'Nothing happened for about eight hours. That's the

worst, you know. At least when you're fighting, your brain is active and time passes quickly. But when you are just lying there in the rubble and every part of your body aches you start to think, why me? Why have I been spared? And you think, if I'm just going to be blown to pieces in a couple of minutes, hours, days, weeks, months then what was the point of sparing me? Just so that I had to endure some more minutes, hours, weeks, months of misery?

'We were a bit spread out at this stage. Victor was at the opposite end of the troop to me. He was with another mate of ours from back home, Sticky Doyle. Sticky was very popular and was the company runner. Anyway, they were whispering away to each other; by now it was night-time although there was a full moon that was proving to be a bit of a party pooper, it was so bright you could see the hairs on the back of your hand.

'Ping!' Shaw said with such a start that it shocked both McCusker and Kennedy. 'A single shot rang out as suddenly as that, shattering the silence, and when we gathered our senses again we discovered that Sticky had been shot. He was screaming and hollering and Victor was fussin' around, trying in vain to help him. I crawled over to where they were and found that Sticky had been hit in the neck and the more he screamed the more the blood oozed out of him. He was screaming that he was burning, shouting that his neck was so hot. Victor was holding his fingers firmly down on Sticky's neck and the blood was flowing freely, mixing with the dirt on Victor's hands.

'Sticky's eyes were opened so wide I was half-expecting his eyeballs to pop out. Don't you see, with his eyes he was beseeching us to do something to help him. He kept shouting to get the hot bullet out of his neck. Little did he know but hadn't the bullet already come straight out the back of his neck. He was kicking and struggling and then, in a heartbeat, he just fell limp. The blood slowly stopped flowing through Victor's fingers. Sticky was dead,' Shaw said quietly and stopped talking for a time.

Neither Kennedy nor McCusker spoke. Shaw started to cough again. This time it seemed quite serious, even painful.

'That's all it had taken to end Sticky's life. One bullet. One little piece of lead, shot though a man-made gun at a hundred miles an hour. What use were the painkillers and lotion and bandages and disinfectant to Sticky? Why did they make us trudge through the war with all that useless stuff on our backs? Why didn't they just stick a gun in our hand and point us in the general direction of the enemy and say: "Good luck! You're going to need it. Luck is the only thing that's going to help you get through what you're going to face."

'Another two hours passed and the boys up on Hill Sixty sneaked down and came up behind the two German posts,' again Shaw paused to point to the spoon and the pepper-cellar, 'and took them out, aye, but not before the Germans got two more of us: O'Neil, a great footballer, I'd say he'd have given Bestie a run for his money; and Burke, he was another chippie and a good one at that. Both of them died so far from danger, they thought, but in reality we all were always so close to death.

'We lost fifteen men on that particular operation. Aye, that's a full football team, a manager and three reserves. All gone in one night and all people you knew. People you had known who just ceased to be! And just like that. It was all of those lives and their families, you know, how their mothers and fathers had fed and clothed, educated, nourished and cherished them. And every time they fell down they'd have kissed their children's knees to make it better and sent them off again. Just think that all of that love, care, attention and cost had been a total waste of time. And maybe you could argue that the world was a better place through the loss of all those lives, but that never makes up for the fact that to all who knew those who died it was certainly a lot worse a place after their death.

'Anyway, the company commander had decided we'd taken enough for one night so he ordered us into the church to take shelter and rest for what was left of the night,' Shaw grimaced. He took the pepper-cellar (church) from the table, stared at it closely for a few seconds and returned it to its position over by the river.

'We settled in for the night and Victor was left on the first watch. I volunteered as well but he said no. He said he didn't want to sleep. I think he actually said that he was desperate to avoid his dreams. We all looked like shit at that stage; unshaven, all black around our eyes from lack of sleep, thin as rakes from lack of good food, and then when you did get something worth eating you threw it up again when you remembered the scenes you'd just experienced. Anyway, we looked a right ragtag and bobtail lot, as that photo of yours shows.

'It's funny, you know, I was totally unaware of that photograph until you showed it to me the other day and then just in a flash I remembered, just like it was yesterday, somebody herding us all together and taking a photograph. There were a few people around with cameras and movie cameras and things. Aye, just because they had a camera around their neck didn't mean that the Jerries' bullets would give them a wide berth. No, they got what we got, which is why I think people co-operated with them. Same with the clergy. Just because you wore a dog collar didn't mean that either the Germans or God for that matter would spare you.

'So, we're in the church. I think we all found it difficult to find a comfortable position but eventually tiredness took over and one by one we all fell asleep, comfortable, at least, in the knowledge that Victor was guarding over us. That night in the church some of the boys thought they heard the sound of a banshee singing. She'd come for the dead. It was freaking a few of them out and so I said it was just the sound of the wind whistling around the rubble. In the middle of the night – I mean, it could have been minutes later, it could have been hours later – but there's this almighty racket going on. As I say, I'd been trying for ages to get to sleep, then I was off and then this noise, all these flashes of light. I thought I might be dreaming; sadly not. As I came to my senses I realised there were a troop of Germans in the church tower with us and I could actually see the whites of their eyes by the light of the moon. They'd taken us by surprise and were shooting us in our sleep, just like you shoot at ducks on one of those fairground things. I reached for my Bren gun and all I got for my troubles was a thud on the side of my face and the lights went out.

'I came around about an hour or so later and found I was being attended to by two orderlies. I clearly remember struggling and pushing them out of the way and going from one corpse to the next. Riflemen Colin McCann, Alan Savage, Norman Kane, Alex McCelland, Wesley McIvor, Miles Best and David Kennedy,' Shaw said, recalling the names like in a roll call and pausing after he'd said each name, maybe out of respect, maybe in some obscure way perhaps hoping that they'd say: 'Present'.

Kennedy thought about how easily all the names Rifleman Derek Shaw had recalled came to him, remembering them just like they were players on his favourite football team or the names of his classmates. Kennedy couldn't remember the names of any of his school friends, he'd struggle after one or two, but here was this old man in his seventy-fourth year recalling the full two-dozen names without a hint of a doubt. Kennedy wondered did this mean that he thought about them every day of his life, remembering them one and all as a form of respect?

'All of them dead,' Shaw continued, now obviously very distressed, Kennedy felt. 'All of them dead except Victor Dugdale and me. I kept wondering why I'd been spared, why I was still alive when all my mates were dead.' Shaw started another bout of coughing, only this time it was so severe Kennedy felt he had to say that he thought it unwise to continue the interview.

'I've more to tell,' Shaw whispered in a wheeze to McCusker and Kennedy, his eyes pleading with the detectives to listen to him.

But his coughing got so loud and sounded so painful that McCusker used his phone to call for an ambulance, which arrived in a matter of minutes. Kennedy and McCusker followed the ambulance to the hospital where the staff immediately set about making the old war veteran more comfortable.

Kennedy waited until the doctor had done his work and then checked if Shaw would be okay.

'Okay?' the Yorkshire doctor replied with a gentle shrug of his shoulders. 'No, I'm afraid not. Derek Shaw is dying of cancer. Has been now for the last six months. He won't permit us to give him any treatment.'

McCusker and Kennedy looked at each other, McCusker

tightened his lips and Kennedy shook his head from side to side slowly.

'I'd say he's only got a month at the most,' the doctor said solemnly.

Chapter Forty-Three

'IT NEVER RAINS but it pours,' Kennedy announced as he set McCusker's office phone down thirty-five minutes later. 'First off, we couldn't find out even the smallest of details, like what time the Ulster bus was leaving town so that we could get on it to avoid the shame of getting nowhere and now… and now it's all falling out of the heavens on top of us.'

Some of it was due to ann rea. She obviously wasn't going to allow a little thing like being kidnapped in a strange country to slow her down. No, when McCusker and Kennedy had been interviewing Shaw, she'd looked up her old friend, Anita "okey dokey" McCann, and it turned out that Anita's researcher had dug up a few bits of information relevant to the case. One was an article under the headline: 'Local Boys Massacred on Hill Sixty.' It outlined the story pretty much as Shaw had done. It listed the sole survivors as Rifleman Victor Dugdale and Rifleman Derek Shaw.

Then, ann rea visited the registry office and found out that it was none other than the Reverend Houston who had married Victor Dugdale. Not only that, but another of the related articles that Anita's researcher had dug up informed them that Houston was a student-cum-prodigy of Terence Best's father, Ernest, and was best friends with Terence's brother, Miles.

'Oh aye, I'll admit it,' Houston's baritone voice rang throughout the basement of the barracks. 'There's nothing there to be ashamed of. He was my very best friend. He and his brother and father all treated me like family. My father now, well, that's a different matter altogether; let's just say he was more interested in the auld bottle than he was in the Auld Testament.

'Sure we were all tight in the early days. All good mates. Sure didn't Derek Shaw and Victor Dugdale and Miles Best do all the work in the rectory in the first place?'

'What, you mean the infamous woodwork?' Kennedy asked.

'Of course I mean the wood,' Houston growled, 'especially the wood. Sure, didn't the work they did with the panelling show they were all set to become master craftsmen?'

'Did you know Derek Shaw is dying of cancer?' McCusker asked, his voice not as confident as usual.

Houston didn't actually break into a grin, but there was definitely a shrug of the minister's body that suggested: 'Oh, the penny is finally dropping.' He was betraying an ounce of smugness but his answer was a sober:

'Derek is a member of my flock and he is now ready to meet his Maker.'

'So this has all purely and simply been about revenge?' Kennedy said, eyes glaring.

Houston continued with his smug look.

'Doesn't the Bible say that when someone hits you, you should turn the other cheek?' Kennedy asked.

'The Bible also advises us,' Houston said, beaming from ear to ear as he rose up to his imaginary pulpit, 'to claim an eye for an eye and a tooth for a tooth.'

'But Victor Dugdale was a seventy-four year old man. He was harmless. He couldn't have had much longer to live naturally, man,' McCusker said in disbelief.

'I don't think old age should be considered mitigating circumstances,' Houston began. 'I feel... I mean, I feel that Derek believes those who gave up their lives for their country have to be remembered. We promised to remember them. That was a vow we all took: "We Will Remember Them!" Don't you remember the Binyon lines?

'They shall not grow old,
'As we are left grow old.
'Age shall not weary them,
'Nor the years condemn.
'At the going down of the sun
'And in the morning,
'We will remember them.

'It's the same as all that nonsense a few years ago in the English press about the spy, you know, harmless old granny, Miss Melita Norwood. "She couldn't hurt anyone," they said and then she's shown weeding her garden just to show how harmless and frail she really is. Balderdash!' Houston roared, showing off his teeth to their yellowest. 'Balderdash, I tell you. That vile woman is suspected of being a spy. If the suspicions are correct she sold information for personal gain and her betrayal could have got some of our boys killed. You have to wonder how much blood she has on her hands, the same hands she now uses to weed her garden?'

'But if Victor did let his colleagues down…' Kennedy began.

'There is no doubt about it, Inspector. The boy deserted his post and as a result of that desertion, seven boys, seven local boys paid for it with their lives,' Houston lectured the policemen, his forefinger wagging furiously.

'Hang on a minute here,' Kennedy started slightly unsure of his ground. 'Are you now admitting that you conspired with Shaw and the rest of the bridge club to murder Victor Dugdale?'

'Oh no, certainly not!' Houston bawled. 'Let's just back up here a lot. I suggest that you need to have another conversation with Derek Shaw before you make any more of those ludicrous allegations.'

'But you and all the other members of the club were in London at the same time. You can't possibly be claiming that was entirely by coincidence after all that we've just been told,' Kennedy replied, rather short with Houston. 'You can't for one minute be expecting us to believe that this frail old man single-handedly murdered and cut up another old man and strung him up.' Kennedy let out a false laugh before finishing: 'Heck, that would be an impossible feat even for a man in the prime of his life.'

'I'm not, on top of everything else,' Houston continued, seemingly choosing to ignore Kennedy, 'going to be accused of putting words in Rifleman Derek Shaw's mouth. I really do think you need to talk to him before you and I can have a fruitful conversation. And believe you me, Inspector, it is going to be a fruitful conversation.'

Chapter Forty-Four

KENNEDY HAD ALREADY built up a scenario around what he was expecting Shaw to say, but he was way off the mark. Way off.

Those present in the small hospital ward were a staff nurse, to care and attend to Shaw; ann rea (at Shaw's request); one of McCusker's constables, to take down the statement; and McCusker and Kennedy. Shaw was propped up in the bed and there were a sufficient number of machines, all hissing or churning out their trademark sounds and all with their individual signature red, blue and green lights combining to create a dark, but obscure, Hockney painting. Machines to signify Shaw had kept up his insurance payments.

'Okay, here's the thing, and this is very important: it was me and me alone who planned and executed the whole thing.'

'And pigs might fly,' McCusker chuckled. 'Derek, there's no need for you to take all of this on yourself.'

'But don't you see, I'm not. I don't need to. I'm going to be dead within 28 days. I've heard the banshee sing, aye, and the song of the banshee is such a sweet song. I know what's happening to me so I've no need to lie to you. You and all of yours,' Shaw paused to look around the room, 'can't touch me where I'm going.'

Kennedy thought it was interesting Shaw had referred to his time left as 28 days and not a month or even four weeks. Was he, by giving it a greater numerical prefix trying to extend his time? He said, as comfortingly as he could: 'But look, Derek, he was your friend. He was a youngster just like yourself and scared shitless, and we might all have had done the same as him in similar circumstances.'

'But that's the exact point, isn't it? It's fine to be scared. Hey, I'll admit it; I felt like sending for my brown trousers on more than one occasion. But it's not fine to turn yellow on your mates and have most of them killed in their sleep as a result,' Shaw croaked hoarsely.

'Yes, yes. But equally you'll have to admit there is now a medical condition to describe what he was going through. He wasn't really himself, he wasn't really thinking clearly, was he? Now come on,' Kennedy said. He felt that by taking the defensive line on Dugdale's behalf he was shifting the spotlight to some of the true culprits in this sad affair.

'But it's not the way it worked back then. We didn't have a bunch of quacks running around after us in white coats, sweeping all our problems under the carpet of life. There wasn't a bunch of fancy medical terms and symptoms to hide behind. You took care of your mates. No matter how bad it got. That was the golden rule. You always looked after your mates. He didn't. He was on watch. We were all asleep. He ran away scared. They all died, they all died except me.

Remember I told you that I wondered for ages, why me? Why had I been spared? I think that I was spared so that I could seek retribution for all of them. You were right in a way, all the people in the bridge club did have family who died that night in 1943 in the church. We had to remember them!'

'Did they or did they not, the members of the bridge club, know what really happened that night in London?' Kennedy asked.

'That's not the issue. The only issue here is that I remembered my mates. I had nothing to lose and I always swore that when I had nothing to lose I would make Victor pay for what he did to all of our friends.'

'For heaven's sake, man, he was barely out of short trousers,' McCusker protested. 'He hadn't long stopped playing Cowboys and Indians on the streets.'

'We were all in it together,' Shaw repeated himself. 'We were all going through exactly the same shite. No one else chickened out,' Shaw said then he started to cough again. Kennedy noticed the fear creep into his eyes.

'I need to make this statement,' Shaw continued. After the bout of coughing stopped he was as hoarse as ever. 'I need to make it now in front of this independent witness.' Shaw stopped again and this time he stared at ann rea who was sitting by the bedside, trying not to interfere with the police work.

McCusker nodded to his constable to start talking the statement down.

'I wish to admit that I, and I alone, did abduct and murder Victor Dugdale. I was not assisted in this crime by any member of the Ballyneagh Bridge Club.'

Kennedy, McCusker and ann rea all raised their eyebrows in exasperation but said nothing, allowing Shaw to continue.

'I was helped by two people. I employed these two people to help me with the physical side of the task. I do not wish to identify these people as their involvement was purely a business arrangement.'

'How did you get to meet these people?' Kennedy felt compelled to ask. McCusker shot Kennedy a "let him get on with it for heaven's sake" look. Kennedy braved the stare; he felt there might not be time to go back over this ground again.

'Simple. I went to a couple of the local pubs. All types travel through a pub and you can tell by the look on a man's face what he's up for.'

Aye, Kennedy thought, and I can tell by the look in your eyes that you are lying. Only this time he heeded McCusker's glare and held his tongue.

'I told them I didn't want to know their names or anything about them. The first one took the job immediately; the second didn't but the first knew a mate who would be interested. I had to let them see the colour of my money up front though.'

'How much did they charge?' Kennedy asked, again cutting into the flow of Shaw's narrative and McCusker's wrath.

Shaw smiled. 'Okay, we've ascertained that you're going to check me on every detail. You've got a terribly suspicious boyfriend,' he warmed his smile to a laugh for ann rea.

'Please go on,' McCusker pleaded.

Kennedy felt that McCusker was desperate, too desperate, to get the signed confession from the old man. Neither of them believed that Shaw had kill Victor Dugdale, at least not by himself. Yes, perhaps he had been involved, but Kennedy very much doubted that he was as powerful as he was making out, or was being made out to be.

'I paid them a grand each in cash up front and promised them another two each when the job was finished.'

'Why didn't they just bop you on the head and take off with all the money and save themselves the grief?' Kennedy persisted with his cross-examination.

'Oh, probably honour among thieves,' Shaw began in reply and when he saw that Kennedy wasn't buying that he continued: 'It also might have had something to do with the fact that I let them know I didn't have the money with me. I told them I would take them to it when we'd successfully completed the job. Actually I'd hidden the money in a package and placed it at the back of the Fountain of Sorrow; you know, the bronze washerwoman up by the bridge on the way into Regents Park from Parkway.

Kennedy smiled to himself. The more Shaw said, the more he was convinced that whoever was behind this had thought of every possible question and scenario and had anticipated the police's every probe.

Shaw wheezed and continued.

'Anyway, I knew... I knew where he lived. I had his address. Don't you see that he had to die? He'd left all of us there to die in the church, and guess what he was doing at the same time as he was meant to be guarding us? He went swimming. Can you believe that? He went swimming. Don't you see that the reason I was spared, the reason I was left when all the rest were murdered in their sleep, was so that I could seek vengeance for all of them?

'I decided that when I was diagnosed with the big C I owed it to my friends. I owed it to them to remember them. I should have done something sooner. We'd always meet and talk about it and we'd always agreed we'd do it when it wouldn't hurt anyone. There was no sense in giving up another life for his life, now was there?'

'You said: "we'd always meet to discuss it". Who were the "we"? The bridge club members?' Kennedy asked.

Shaw completely ignored Kennedy and proceeded with telling his story as if Kennedy hadn't said a word. 'We went to his flat. It was weird, you know, the way he looked at me. It was strange...' the old man hesitated deep in his thoughts. 'In a way I suppose it was like he'd been waiting for me, waiting for me to knock on his door all those years since I'd not shopped him over his late-night dip.'

'So you covered up for his desertion all those years ago?' McCusker, much to Kennedy's surprise, asked in apparent disbelief.

'Yes!' Shaw replied solemnly.

'What would have happened if you'd reported him?' ann rea asked her first question of the session.

'He'd probably have been court-marshalled then taken out in front of a firing squad and shot. I guess I hadn't been thinking properly. At that time perhaps I thought that there'd been too much killing already.'

'So you're the sole reason he's been alive all these years?' Kennedy asked, figuring this was the sad fact someone had held over Shaw all this time. Perhaps the reason they'd been able to involve him in the execution, perhaps the reason Shaw was taking the rap for the murder himself.

'Yes,' Shaw said simply and sadly.

'So you could have chosen to have him murdered all those years ago and saved yourself and all your friends all this grief?' Kennedy persisted. He was desperate to punch a hole so big in Shaw's confession that even the old soldier would be too embarrassed to continue with this sham.

'Yes. Don't you see that's why I had to be the one to take his life?'

'What, and butcher him as well?' Kennedy pushed, now finding little resistance from McCusker. ann rea continued to do what she'd been brought there to do; observe.

'Don't you see it was a way to make a spectacle of him; an example, if you will, to other would-be deserters.

'There was a symmetry in all of this, you know. We – Victor, Miles Best and myself – we did all the original carpentry in the rectory. It worked out great altogether. We'd never have been able to kidnap him and bring him back here to Ballyneagh. So we brought a bit of Ballyneagh to him. I mean, we couldn't have planned it better. You have to think that there's the hand of a higher being involved in this somewhere. Perhaps there was some guilt there for not protecting all the boys in '43, I don't know. But it makes you think, doesn't it? Don't you see, though, it was all meant to be. The wood thing happened of its own accord; the Ballyneagh rectory's wood ending up on Victor's doorstep in Camden Town. I mean, we'd been thinking about this for a long time and then all the elements come beautifully together for us.'

'Who are the 'we' you keep referring to, Derek?' Kennedy again voiced his earlier (unanswered) question.

Again he was confronted with nothing but a blank look. But then… perhaps a little crack.

'You know, it was the Reverend Houston who figured all of this out in the first place; about Victor deserting and all of that stuff. He felt there was something wrong between the two of us when we returned from the war. He let it go for a couple of years and then he started digging. Digging around and chipping away like a dog with a bone. Eventually Victor confessed all. To be very honest with you, I think he was very happy to get it off his conscience. But his peace of mind was short-lived. The Reverend Houston insisted Victor leave the community immediately. He also insisted that he leave Doris and her mother immediately. He left Victor with no other choice. He told him he would tell his wife and daughter exactly what had happened, what Victor had been responsible for; the blood of all those boys.

'Victor came to see me way back then, just before he left Ballyneagh, and he said he wished I had reported him. He claimed that not reporting him had been a bigger punishment. He claimed that forcing him to live with his nightmares was the worst punishment I could have inflicted on him. I think he'd been expecting forgiveness from Reverend Houston when he made his confession. He got anything but forgiveness, I can tell you.

'Years passed and some of the relatives started to find out what had happened. I think Victor's wife forced the information out of Reverend Houston and then she, we think, told one of her friends – I mean, what Victor did is not something you could keep to yourself – and the friend told the relations of one of the men who died. Then the relations started to tell each other and then they started calling for blood. The Reverend Houston and myself persuaded them that it would be wrong to take another life for Victor's life. Anyone who killed Victor would themselves be found out and sent to prison. We assured them that eventually something would happen.

'Me being diagnosed with cancer was, honestly, a blessing in disguise.'ann rea looked at him in sheer disbelief.

'Ah, come on,' he smiled, 'how many people do you know who get to plan the end of their life. You know, we are all always planning every detail of our lives and then death, perhaps the biggest event of all, comes knocking on your door without any warning whatsoever, and usually in the middle of the night. When the banshee starts to sing our song there's feck all we can do about it.

'I've had a good life – hell, I've had a great life. This hasn't been eating away at me forever, you know,' Shaw said quietly.

Kennedy couldn't work out if the war veteran meant the cancer or the war incident.

'There have been years and years when I forgot about it altogether. Aye, I've had a great time and that's a fact, but now that I've heard the banshee sing it's time to put my affairs in order. This way I get to make up to all the families for not doing my duty and reporting Victor all those years ago. They, the families, can enjoy their revenge without any of them having to spill any blood. It all works out perfectly, really.'

'Perhaps just a wee bit too perfectly,' Kennedy muttered not quite under his breath but then raised his voice: 'Okay, so you and your two henchmen arrive at his front door... he looks like he's expecting you... then what?'

'Then he came with us quietly.'

'Where did you take him? There was no blood found in the Black Cat Building,' Kennedy said, perhaps unconsciously tipping Shaw off to a potential trap.

'I'm sure you have also traced the van we hired for the bridge club and checked that for blood as well?' Shaw said, half laughing, half coughing.

The ever-efficient Detective Sergeant James Irvine had indeed confirmed this very fact.

'I... you have to realise that I wasn't laughing there about killing Victor. It was at the fact that I could rest assured that you'd leave no stone unturned,' Shaw offered sincerely by way of explanation of his apparent show of irreverence. He smiled a "we're all human" look. His Paul Newman eyes tended to make Kennedy want to find a way to prove it wasn't Shaw who'd committed the horrific slaying.

Shaw merely offered what appeared to be a forgiving smile and continued. 'We took Victor. As I have already said, he came peacefully. We took him over to a garage I'd taken a short-term lease out on, over in Kentish Town, up by the Town and Country Club. You can check those details out as well. I had a plastic sheet spread all over the place and it was all ready for Victor, but when I got him there I was apprehensive. Forget apprehensive, feck that, I was petrified. The two boys were solid as rocks, though. And then the moment came where I had to take Victor's life and he looked deep into my eyes like he was willing me to do it. He needed me to do it. He *needed* me to kill him. He wanted redemption; needed total redemption before he died.

'He might have been a yellow-belly in '43 but I can tell you that he greeted his death like a true, brave warrior. I stabbed him with a stainless-steel knife. It was as if I was someone else, someone else was controlling my moves. It was remarkable how easily the cold steel goes through skin. At first the skin resists the blade, then the skin breaks and gives way. It's a bit like sticking a pin into a walnut. You feel it's never going to go through. It feels solid to your pressure, do you know what I mean? But then the pin slides into the nut quite easily and you are surprised. I was surprised how this piece of man-made metal was going to destroy a man. When the skin was broken I started to wonder where the blood was. Why was he not bleeding? All the time he was just staring me in the eyes; like he was hoping I'd have the bottle to do it. He never flinched once, you know.

'He still wasn't bleeding and I think that made me take the pressure off the knife and then the blood started to seep out, and then the knife started its journey again like there was an internal magnet drawing it deeper into his body.

'I stabbed him first off straight into the heart. We'd taken his shirt off and it was sad in a way, you know, because there was hardly anything to him, he was so frail. I stabbed him eight times, once for each of us. A couple of the times I stabbed him I hit a bone. Once I'd say, from the noise I heard, I felt I'd cracked a bone.'

'Why did you want to make such a mess of him? Why not stab him once in the heart and leave it like that?' Kennedy asked, his the only other voice in the ward.

'What?' Shaw asked incredulously, sitting up in the bed. His nurse automatically puffed up the pillows behind him in a vain attempt to make him more comfortable. For the first time, Kennedy felt sorry for her having to go through all this in the line of her duty.

'What?' Shaw repeated. 'You mean just like Riflemen McCann, Savage, Kane, McCelland, McIvor, Kennedy and Best? You mean just like how neatly and tidily they were killed? Just like how considerate the Germans were in ending the lives of the entire squad because Victor had gone off swimming?'

This outburst from Shaw seemed to exhaust him because his next words were barely above a whisper.

'I wanted to make a point. Selfishly, I wanted to feel better. I thought I would feel better when I stabbed him and I didn't so I kept on stabbing him, once for all those he'd helped to kill. On top of that I wanted to make a point. We promised to remember them. To remember all of our boys who died on foreign shores. Our country promised to remember all our boys and what do they do? They only go and suck up to the German government like they are our new best friends. Remember over 350,000 of our boys and girls died in World War Two. Just think on that figure, Inspector Kennedy, as you think ill of me! Remember that figure for the rest of your life. It's the very least we owe our boys and girls; to remember them.'

Truth be told, Kennedy felt anything but ill of Shaw, but a need for information pushed him onwards. 'And why the Black Cat Building?'

'Again, with all the attention it was receiving locally and with its obvious connection to Ulster, I felt it was a fitting setting from which to display Victor Dugdale's sins to the world.

'And you know what, after it was over I didn't fell any better. I don't feel how I imagined I'd feel. I don't feel as though I brought about my salvation. And the other sad thing – again, it's a bit like it was back then in France in '43 – it didn't feel wrong when I was killing him. I didn't feel that it was anything other than a matter of honour; a soldier's honour.

'That counts for a lot, you know, that in the name of war we all let ourselves get away with even the most horrific crimes. We're all forgiven if they are done with God and your country on your side.' Shaw's voice was now barely above a whisper, a hoarse whisper that was competing with the sounds of the equipment necessary to keep him alive.

'In the end, I suppose, in order to feel something I just kept hacking away at him with the knife, trying for something, trying to destroy his soul and all that stuff, you know.

'Eventually the boys restrained me, and one took the knife from my hand. I think he might have been a bit worried that I'd lost it completely and would tear into both of them, too.

'We cleaned Victor off, washed him down, wrapped him in plastic and, using the van I hired from Hertz at King's Cross – again, you can check this – we took him over to the Black Cat Building in Camden Town. We took him up the rear stairwell to the boardroom; to the room they'd used the wood from the Ballyneagh rectory for, and we hung him up. I hung him up to remember all of those he was responsible for allowing to be butchered in Caen.'

Shaw stopped.

McCusker stood up. He took a copy of the statement from his constable and gave it to Kennedy to check and initial. He then offered it to Shaw. Shaw signed it immediately without reading it. He just seemed totally relieved to get his name down on the paper. He was also insistent that ann rea check it and sign it too. Was that his own thought or a request he had been ordered to make?

With this statement, this sacrifice, Kennedy thought, Shaw was covering up for the multitude of sins of others. The Reverend Steven Houston and all the members of the Ballyneagh Club: Paul McCann, Margaret Derby, Robin Kane, Eamon McKay, Malachy McIvor, Terence Best and Audrey Greer. And those who had inflicted war on their nation in the first place. Those who would never, ever have to pay for their sins.

Shaw peacefully slipped back into the comfort of his

pillows.

McCusker and ann rea and Kennedy sat with him in silence for about twenty minutes or so and then, still wordless, Shaw appeared to drift off into a deep, peaceful sleep. They all quietly rose from their seats and tiptoed out of the ward into the ever-present smell of disinfectant in the hospital corridor.

The three of them had taken about ten steps towards the front door without sharing a word when the alarm sounds of the machinery in Shaw's ward broke the tranquillity.

The machinery was now signalling to the world that the life of Rifleman Derek Shaw MM had just ended.

Chapter Forty-Five

'SO ALL OF the others are going to get away with it?' ann rea asked one of her rhetorical questions. It was later that same day and they were on their way back to Donegal.

'Well, I wouldn't bet money on that!' Kennedy replied, choosing to answer the question anyway. He then fell into silence. He seemed to be happy to leave it there. ann rea wasn't.

'But it is pretty obvious he was covering for all of them. I mean, he couldn't possibly have done it all by himself. You can't convince me that all the members of the Ballyneagh Bridge Club ritualistically murdered Victor Dugdale and chose Derek Shaw's illness to hide behind. Neither will you ever convince me that the Reverend Houston is without blame.'

Kennedy continued to do nothing but stare at the road ahead. He felt it was important, very important that at least one of them did so. The Donegal road was notoriously dangerous, particularly when the vehicle driver (a London journalist), friend and lover of the navigator (an exiled Ulster detective), was wringing every ounce of her anger at the whole affair out of her steering wheel and into her accelerator.

'You're just going to sit there and let them all get away with it?'

Again not a peep from Kennedy except: 'Ah, you're maybe just a wee bit close to the edge of the road.'

'Kennedy, for feck's sake, talk to me about this.'

'We're on holiday!' Kennedy exclaimed quietly.

'We're in the ditch unless you talk to me. You're too quiet. What exactly do you have up your sleeve?'

'My arm,' Kennedy replied as she took one of her hands from the steering wheel and playfully whacked him on the offending arm.

'Okay, here's what we've got,' he continued eventually. 'At

the minute we can work on a conspiracy charge against all of them.'

'Including Houston?' ann rea asked in clear desperation as she slowed down a little.

'Oh, especially Houston,' Kennedy replied beaming proudly. 'We've got a lot more on the Reverend Houston. All circumstantial at this point but it's all adding up. I just spoke to Inspector Starrett before we left and he told me their recent investigations had dug up a priest, a Father Edward Heath...'

'Oh please, Kennedy, Father Ted Heath! Please stop messing around on this,' ann rea pleaded, her voice hitting tones of disbelief Kennedy hadn't heard before.

'I kid you not. Honestly! According to Starrett that's really his name – Father Ted. Apparently this particular Father Ted recalls an interesting, but equally bizarre, conversation he had with our Reverend Houston at a conference where the Reverend Houston steered the chat towards local crime. Houston grilled Father Ted about specific criminals in Father Ted's parish and what the various characters did, and how they were found and brought to justice. Father Ted originally picked up Houston's intentions all wrong, thinking he was referring to the clergy and their responsibility for attending to the lost souls of their respective flocks. But when word of your release was in the public domain as it were, Father Ted suddenly had a different perspective on Houston's conversation.'

'Mmmm!' was all that ann rea could say as she now started to relax and concentrate on the tricky roads.

'Then there's the old dear whom Irvine turned up who swears she saw a procession going up the rear stairwell of the Black Cat Building. She swears that the procession was at least twenty people strong.'

'And not the three Shaw claimed?' ann rea said, visibly relaxing before Kennedy's eyes.

'And not the three Shaw claimed,' Kennedy agreed and added: 'She said she wasn't exactly sure about the numbers involved in the group but she is convinced that it was led by a clergyman carrying a Bible.'

'Very interesting.'

'Yes, that's what I thought,' Kennedy smiled. 'Then, of course, there is the clue Shaw himself left us.'

'Sorry?'

'Shaw left us a clue in his final statement,' Kennedy said plainly.

'I was there, Christy; I heard it all at the same time you did. I didn't hear any clues,' ann rea said, somewhat frustrated to have missed something obvious.

'Derek said… I believe his exact words were: "It was as if I was someone else, someone else was controlling my moves." Again, perhaps we could be accused of grasping at straws and he could have meant he was in a trance, or it could also mean someone was telling him what to do.'

'Verily interesting,' ann rea said in her mock Rowan and Martin Laugh-In voice.

'Yes, that's what I thought,' Kennedy nodded as he started to futter with the CD packs in the glove compartment of the car. 'Not enough to put Houston or any of the others away, but enough to justify an investigation and who knows what we'll dig up later. I do think that we'll be able to make the conspiracy charge stick and McCusker has promised to keep some of his team on it for us.'

'Good,' ann rea replied, seemingly satisfied. 'I'd go as far as to say that I doubt Derek Shaw ever lifted as much as a finger against Victor Dugdale. I'd say that's for sure and I'd even go as far as to put money on it. Now Houston, he's much too creepy for me to be a man of the cloth. I…'

'Ah, here we are!' Kennedy said, interrupting her. 'I was looking for something… something spiritual to carry us over the border and away from all of this.'

Kennedy meant the investigation and not the countryside. ann rea interrupted the interruption. 'And you're going to take a holiday with me?'

'Yes!' Kennedy replied trying to open the CD case.

'A total, complete break?'

'Yes!' Kennedy shouted. ann rea would never be sure if he was answering her last question or just expressing his joy at having gained access to the CD case.

'And it's not because you're feeling guilty, you know, about me being kidnapped and all of that?'

'No,' Kennedy replied, knowing how bad she'd feel if he admitted to that.

'A proper holiday in Donegal?' she persisted coyly.

'Yes.'

'How long for?'

'I don't know.'

'But definitely no work?'

'Yes. No, I mean. No work. I mean none, that is, apart from a wee chat with Father Ted if we meet up with him,' Kennedy said as he removed the CD from the awkward jewel case and placed the CD carefully in the car player. He was careful not to let ann rea see the perspex-enclosed artwork until the music filled the car.

He selected track five and soon Van Morrison's rich, warm sound filled the space between them. The album Kennedy had selected was just over thirty years old but still sounded as fresh and exciting as if Van had recorded his masterwork only yesterday.

'We were born before the wind,' Van Morrison sang; his amazing, powerful, soulful voice providing the perfect sound-track to this very soulful countryside. He delivered the opening line upon which a thousand dreams were launched and then sang on to the line that the song title had been taken from. ann rea murmured a sensual 'Mmmm' as she and Christy Kennedy sailed into the mystic.

Also published by THE DO-NOT PRESS

Double Take
by Mike Ripley

Double Take: The novel and the screenplay (the funniest caper movie never made) in a single added-value volume.

ISBN 1899344 81 0 paperback (£6.99)
ISBN 1899344 82 9 hardcover (£15.00)

Double Take tells how to rob Heathrow and get away with it (enlist the help of the police). An 'Italian Job' for the 21st century, with bad language – some of it translated – chillis as offensive weapons, but no Minis. It also deconstructs one of Agatha Christie's most audacious plots.

The first hilarious stand-alone novel from the creator of the best-selling Angel series.

'I never read Ripley on trains, planes or buses. He
makes me laugh and it annoys the other passengers'
Minette Walters

Middleman by Bill James

The brilliant new thriller from the creator of the bestselling Harpur & Iles series

ISBN 1899344 95 0 paperback (£6.99)
ISBN 1899344 96 9 hardcover (£15.00)

Times are tough for 'middleman' Julian Corbett.

He operates as a half-respectable, half-crooked businessman in what was once the rough dockside of the Welsh capital. But a multi-billion pound redevelopment is transforming the seafront into the stylish Cardiff Bay marina-style housing and shopping area, and Corbett is determined to grab a piece of that action.

At first, Corbett thinks the opportunity to help shady developer Sid Hyson dispose of his lakeside casino/hotel/nursing home complex is his road to riches, but he soon realises that all is not well. Hyson is suddenly worried the sea might come flooding in and before that happens wants to 'liquidate' his assets.

Corbett knows that if he doesn't find an acceptable buyer – and quick – he's as good as dead. The body of one failed 'middleman' has already washed up on a nearby beach. Then Corbett realises he's negotiating with people twice as ruthless as Sid Hyson.

"Bill James is British mystery fiction's finest prose stylist"

Peter Guttridge, *The Observer*

Also published by THE DO-NOT PRESS

Blitz
by Ken Bruen

The fast-moving follow-up to the 'White Trilogy'

ISBN 1899344 00 X   paperback (£6.99)
ISBN 1899344 01 8   hardcover (£15.00)

> 'Irish writer Ken Bruen is the finest purveyor of intelligent Brit-noir'
> *Tina Jackson, The Big Issue (London)*

The Southeast London police squad are suffering collective burn out:

- Detective Sergeant Brant is hitting the blues and physically assaulting the police shrink.
- Chief Inspector Roberts' wife has died in a horrific accident and he's drowning in gut-rot red wine.
- 'Black and beautiful' WPC Falls is lethally involved with a junior member of the National Front and simultaneously taking down Brixton drug dealers to feed her own habit.

The team never had it so bad and when a serial killer takes his show on the road, things get progressively worse. Nicknamed 'The Blitz', a vicious murderer is aiming for tabloid glory by killing cops.

From Absinthe to cheap lager, with the darkest blues as a chorus, The White Trilogy has just got bigger. 'Getting hammered' was never meant to be the deadly swing it is in this darkest chapter from London's most addictive police squad.

Pick Any Title
by Russell James

RUSSELL JAMES is Chairman of the CRIME WRITERS' ASSOCIATION 2001-2002

PICK ANY TITLE is a magnificent new crime caper involving sex, humour sudden death and double-cross.

ISBN 1899344 83 7 paperback (£6.99)
ISBN 1899344 84 5 hardcover (£15.00)

'Lord Clive' bought his lordship at a 'Lord of the Manor' sale where titles fetch anything from two to two hundred thousand pounds. Why not buy another cheap and sell it high? Why stop at only one customer? Clive leaves the beautiful Jane Strachey to handle his American buyers, each of whom imagines himself a lord.

But Clive was careless who he sold to, and among his victims are a shrewd businessman, a hell-fire preacher and a vicious New York gangster. When lawyers pounce and guns slide from their holsters Strachey finds she needs more than good looks and a silver tongue to save her life.

A brilliant page-turner from 'the best of Britain's darker crime writers'
The Times

The Do-Not Press
Fiercely Independent Publishing

Keep in touch with what's happening at the cutting edge of independent British publishing.

Simply send your name and address to:
The Do-Not Press (Dept. HBS)
16 The Woodlands, London SE13 6TY (UK)

or email us: **HBS@thedonotpress.co.uk**

There is no obligation to purchase
(although we'd certainly like you to!)
and no salesman will call.

Visit our regularly-updated web site:

http://www.thedonotpress.co.uk

Mail Order

All our titles are available from good bookshops, or (in case of difficulty) direct from The Do-Not Press at the address above. There is no charge for post and packing for orders to the UK and EU.

(NB: A post-person may call.)